THE
LEGEND
OF
BLACKWICK

Kathleen R. Cuyler

Mocha Wave
Publishing

ISBN: 979-8-9880238-2-1
Library of Congress Control Number: 2024920996

The story, all names, characters, and incidents portrayed in this publication are fictitious. No identification with actual persons (living or deceased), places, buildings, and products is intended or should be inferred.

Book Cover and Illustrations by Story-First Marketing, support@story-firstmarketing.com

Praise for The Legend of Blackwick

"This series is a must read for people who enjoy the classics, fantasy, magical characters, and book portals. I'm excited to find out what's going to happen next in book 3!"
- **Aislynn Walsh, Goodreads Review**

"One of the best platforms for a fantasy series ever imagined"
- **Tilmer Wright, Jr, Goodreads Review**

*"Oh my goodness. I didn't think book two could top the emotional draw I had to Forever is eternity but this was phenomenal." – **Kearstin Ellis, Goodreads Review***

*"For anyone who loves literature, adventure, and the magic of stories, this book is a must-read. The conclusion left me deeply moved, reflecting on the journey so far and anticipating what's to come." – **Vivyana, Goodreads Review***

*"Cuyler continues to effortlessly weave a tale between worlds with a complex cast of characters, building on past relationships while simultaneously introducing new friends and foes alike. You'll find yourself rooting for the most unlikely of characters as this story unfolds." – **Nicholas Gentry, Goodreads Review***

*"Who would think that one adventure Forever is Eternity, where we meet Betty and her friends, could turn into an even bigger adventure filled with revelations, unsuspecting comrades and even more worlds all in one?" – **Jolene Scheepers, Goodreads Review***

To Terry and Crystal

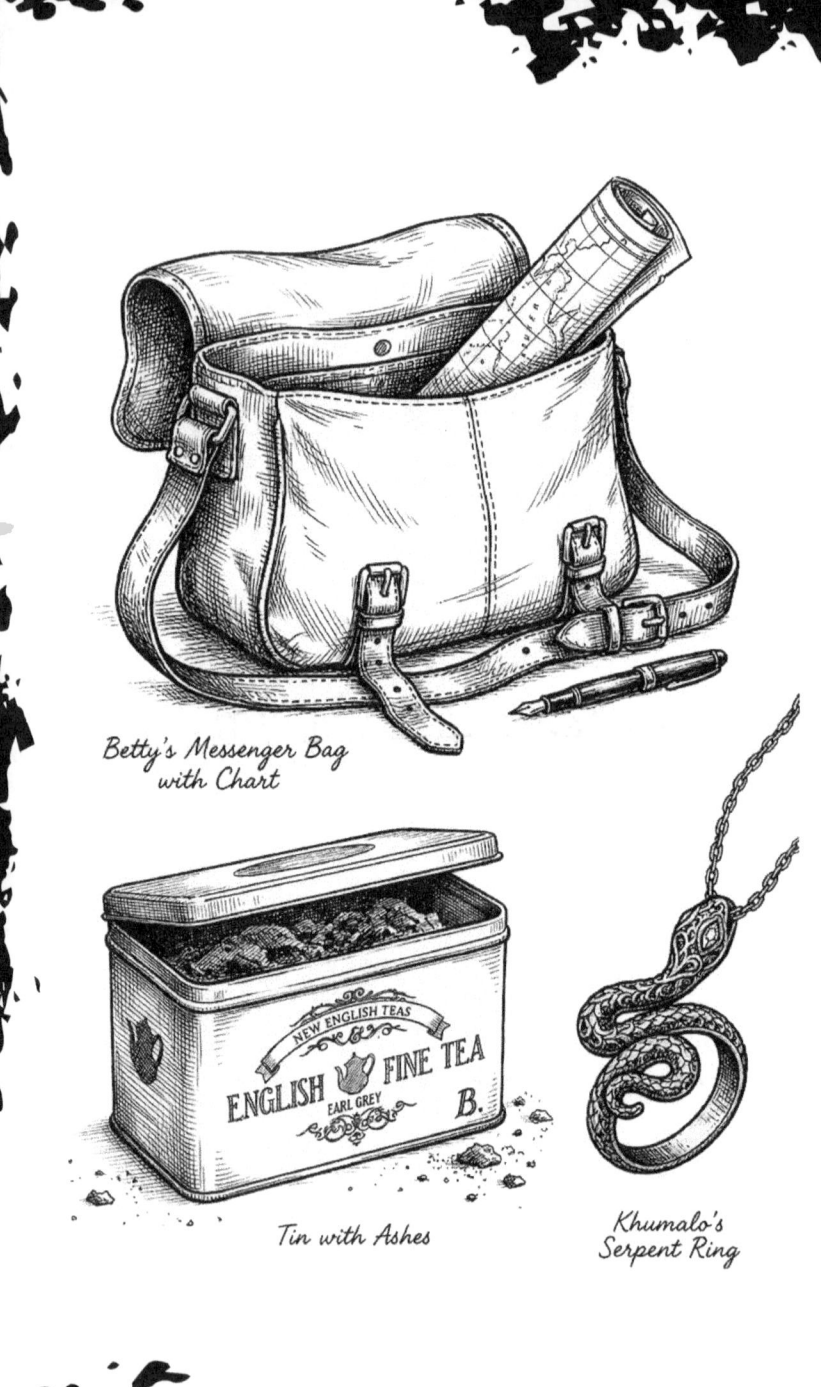

Betty's Messenger Bag
with Chart

Tin with Ashes

Khumalo's
Serpent Ring

Mer-shaman's
Conch of
Conscience

Foil to
Duel the
Count of
Monte
Cristo

Visit
Cairo!

Travel
Brochure

An Archivist's Record from the Golden Vigil

In the year 1936, Edmond Davidson, a young scholar of promise and ambition, journeyed into the Carpathian Mountains on a research scholarship. He sought answers in the library of Castle Dracula. Instead, he crossed a threshold from which there was no return.

For beneath the castle lay Alsó Világ, the Land of Shadow, ruled by Ordog, the Crimson Dragon. There, Edmond's soul was claimed and reshaped, bound into service as a werewolf.

Far away in Bedfordshire, England, Betty Talbin endured a quieter captivity. A housemaid by circumstance and a reader by nature, she found refuge in books, and through them, warnings of danger. When a mirror shattered, she glimpsed a living page beyond the world she knew and learned of Edmond's peril.

Thus, she discovered she was an Inter-Story Intercessor, one able to travel through portals into the worlds of the books she read. Guided by the secret order, she learned that stories are not inventions, but threads of a vast universe, watched over by the Golden Dragon, Vorever.

Yet not all dragons love the light.

Ordog, fallen and exiled, sought to reclaim his former power by gathering lost scales. With them, he aimed to raise an army and march against the story worlds, seeking to claim them as his own kingdom. The Inter-Story Intercessors were determined to stop him, and Betty, driven by devotion and fierce resolve to save her cousin, joined the quest. With the help of her friends from her own world and those from the book worlds, they confronted and defeated Ordog, rendering him helpless and caged.

The victory, however, came at a great cost. During the battle, Edmond gave his life to shield Betty from death.

Yet death was not the end.

With the help of Peter Pan's shadow, a magical lantern, and a drop of hope, Edmond's soul was reclaimed from Alsó Világ. He was reborn as Blackwick, a guardian sworn to seek out lost souls in the Story Worlds and to protect them wherever he could.

In the tower of Vandor, Vorever gave Betty a choice: to enter whichever book she wished and live out the life she would choose. She chose instead to remain on the Island of Vandor with Vorever as Keeper of the Golden Vigil, protector of the stories that bind existence together. When she speaks the words over the Candle of Vandor, she can summon Blackwick to her side.

But even as she guards the story worlds, evil stirs once more. Ordog escapes his confinement, and a mysterious green mist known as the Corruption begins to consume the books of Vandor. Forces older and more merciless than Ordog awaken beyond the margins of story.

One of the worlds most threatened is Charles Dickens' A Tale of Two Cities. Into this failing tale, Betty sends Blackwick, while she and her fellow Intercessors search for answers within the Inter-Story Intercessor Codebook.

Thus the record closes.

And thus, the next chapter begins.

PART ONE

THE CORRUPTION

Chapter 1
THE UNDERWORLD OF PARIS (1780S)

Beneath the cobbled streets of Saint-Antoine, Paris, a labyrinth of pipes clanged with the unsteady weight of hooves and carts above. The echoes drowned out the scuffle of the weird little lizard who scampered across the side of the pipe to avoid the muck.

Once the titanic dragon lord of Alsó-Világ, this pathetic creature, now no bigger than a rat, lit the dismal morass ahead with the conical red glow emanating from his one good eye. The other eye was seared shut, sealed by a ragged scar.

Ordog. Yes, yes, he had a name. He remembered now. Ordog. He had escaped his cage on Vandor. No sooner had he clumped from the cage to the floor, than a twisting smog had caught him and dragged him into this world of stench and steam. For a time, his memory had been hazy. But pieces were coming back to him. Yes, he was Ordog. And he remembered it was souls he needed to feed on . . . souls of the damned . . . to restore him to his former greatness and power. He remembered it was Beatrice Talbin, that interloping servant girl with her ever-present books, who had put him in the cage. But there was another. *Blackwick.* Yes, a strange new enemy, a formidable foe.

And other things were remembered, ancient things. Long ago he had been a golden scale upon the frame of the mighty dragon

Vorever. There were other scales like Ordog, scales who had not conformed to the will of the Golden Dragon, who listened to the voices in their dreams telling them they deserved to be immortals. But before they had a chance to ascend to their greatness, they had been ripped from their host and exiled into the abyss.

These, like Ordog, had transformed into mighty titans, but also like him, had been defeated. He did not mourn their deaths. They were weak. They had failed. But Ordog still lived. Ordog would continue to live and at last bring his own system of order to the universe. Vorever's universe of perpetual creation endangered Ordog's control. He would see to it there was only one story, and he alone would determine who would exist in that story and who would be erased from its pages.

He twisted his head to the side as he caught a tapping like a choir of leaking faucets. Rounding an elbow in the pipe loomed shadows with antennae waving, and Ordog saw what they were. A filthy trio of sewer roaches.

Ordog inhaled, stoking his internal flame to incinerate them with his fiery breath, but he suppressed his rage. *Not instinct, Ordog, but cunning. A lord must have slaves.* It was the way of things. There were those designed to rule and those designed to serve.

"Fallen creatures of the night," he called.

The lead roach stiffened and stared with glossy black orbs at this thing that blocked their passage. His antennae flicked, as one sensing the threat to power. He drew his prickly foreleg across his mouth in thought. "*Mes amis*, let us see who this foul creature be."

"Careful, Louis," hissed the bristly voice of the lighter brown roach with him. "He is not one of us."

"*Mais oui*, Thérèse," agreed the darker roach beside her. "He has the look of a spider to me. Or a rat."

"I am no vermin. I am Ordog, Lord of the Underworld. Serve me, or I will slay you."

The lead roach crawled forward, peering into the red glow. "I am Louis, leader of *Les Cafards*. In Paris, *I* am Lord of the Underworld."

Ordog rubbed his foreclaws together as curls of smoke rose from his nostrils. "Oh? That will never do."

Louis lowered his head, and the black orbs on either side glared as he charged Ordog. The gang of roaches sniggered behind the bends of their forelegs, ridiculing this foolish creature who dared defy their leader.

Ordog spread his jaws and let loose a blast of fire.

The charbroiled roach lay on his back in the sludge. His legs quivered. Then, he was still.

"Louis is no more," said the darker roach.

"*Oui*," agreed Thérèse. "Robert, what say you to joining with this Ordog?"

Robert bent his eyes upon the corpse of his former leader and grimaced with a gulp. "What do you wish us to do for you, *Monseigneur*?"

Ordog bestowed a patronizing nod upon the two roaches. "I can use two loyal slaves. Serve me, and I will make both of you rulers over a small portion of my world."

"That is not so bad," decided Robert with a shrug.

"We will follow you, my lord," agreed Thérèse, bowing her head low to the dragon.

CHAPTER 2
MONSEIGNEUR IN THE COUNTRY (1780S)

Outside the Fauberg District, a carriage flight away from Monsieur and Madame Defarge's shabby wine shop, was the grand country chateau of the Marquis St. Evrémonde. Along the path that spanned the moonlit lawn of the Marquis' residence, the silent marble gods with their silent archaic smiles boasted perfect symmetry and were pedestaled in precise alignment with one another. Two symmetric rows of shrubs shaped into flawless topiary spirals cast symmetrical shadows over the path leading to the portico. One shadow lifted itself from the clipped lawn, resurrecting into the shape of a man.

The man, though tall and athletically built, was not of flesh and blood, but of shadow and wax, with two flaming slits for eyes under the bent brim of his black cavalier hat. The shadow was Blackwick.

Blackwick slipped behind a Grecian column, one of six supporting the portico outside the Marquis' dining room. He leaned against the wall beside the casement windows to keep out of the light.

"You will use this book as your portal," Betty had told him before the sacred candle. The book she handed him was *A Tale of Two Cities*. "Many lives are at stake." Though she was now the Keeper of the Golden Vigil, guarding all the books in Vandor

Tower, to him she was still Betty, the one he had grown up with, the one who had saved his soul from Alsó-Világ. And, when the Golden Dragon Vorever had decreed he was to dedicate himself to being Betty's loyal protector, he took the charge to heart. He swore he would not fail her now.

He did not breathe as he flattened himself against the wall and watched and listened.

Marquis St. Evrémonde was a marble man, with a star-shaped beauty mark decorating his powder-white chin. He drew a lacy handkerchief from his silken vest and prodded open the twin casements with limp-wristed hands. He minced out upon the portico to taste the air and sneeze on snuff.

Another man, taller, younger, joined the Marquis under the arch of the portico. This man had the build of one who had labored to make his way rather than allowing himself to turn into an ornament of lace and lard like the Marquis.

"You're a fool, nephew, a fool. You are next in line to inherit these lands and this title." The Marquis' heavy eyelids barely fluttered, and his aquiline nose remained poised at a precise 45-degree angle. "You could have all this." He waggled his hand-kerchief at the extensive estate. Blackwick ducked further into the shadows to avoid the handkerchief.

"I would rather live my life as plain Charles Darnay, a simple schoolteacher, eking out a living by my wits, rather than inherit all this and the guilt of my fathers. Don't you see, uncle? With every injustice we commit against our fellow human beings, we add links to our own chains, and the masses will use these chains to pull us down."

"Human beings? Human beings? My dear nephew, you dare to call these beasts who wallow in the mire like pigs, you dare to call them human? Why, even today my coach ran over one of their spawn, and I offered a gold coin to compensate for the loss, and what do you think? They refused to take it, the ingrates."

The younger man's voice was heavy with regret. "Uncle, we need to change. All of us. Her majesty has spent a fortune so she can play at being a pretend peasant girl in a pretend peasant village built solely for her pleasure while real peasants are crammed into filthy alleys where they starve without even a crust of bread."

"It's not my fault these creatures were born to serve, while we were born to rule. *Someone* needs to pay the taxes."

"In some places they are saying humans, no matter whether they are rich or poor, are born with God-given rights."

"*Mon Dieu*! You speak sacrilege. Beware. You will condemn your own soul. If my forebears heard you . . ."

"My soul will be safe, for I have not sold it for wealth, as you have. I renounce the title of marquis. I renounce the name of St. Evrémonde. I will earn my own way in this world."

Blackwick warmed in solidarity with the defiant young man. He was the picture of himself when he was Edmond Davidson, ambitious and defying the hypocrisy of society. He wondered if this Charles Darnay was the one he had been sent into this world to rescue. A man of such mettle could be a strong asset to the Inter-Story Intercessors.

A third of Blackwick's nature was werewolf, and that third provided him with keen senses. At this moment, he could hear the rustle of a darning needle diving in and out of a woolen stocking in the servant's quarters at the far end of the chateau. He could smell the sweat on the neck of a guard who limped past his last round of cells in the Bastille. And he could sense the potential of another man's soul as it aligned with the coordinates of Vorever's compass. While Darnay possessed a soul with great potential for good, to Blackwick's surprise, he was not the one he had been sent into this story world to recruit. Perhaps later their paths would meet. For now, he let Charles Darnay storm past him down the garden path. Blackwick focused his senses once more on sizing up the Marquis. The forecast was not good for the Marquis.

St. Evrémonde sneezed on his snuff, patted the dints in his nose with a point of his handkerchief, and covered a yawn with the back of his hand. But the Marquis' previously dull eyes danced with a dangerous gleam.

Blackwick followed his line of vision across the lawn to a small, cloaked woman with a lantern, looking over her shoulder as she slipped to a low part of the garden wall. Blackwick tensed to alert as the Marquis chuckled, tucked his handkerchief into the lace at his sleeve, and slinked across the garden toward the young woman.

"Well, well, *mon Dieu*! It's the little seamstress from the village." He snatched the lantern from her and set it upon the stone slab of the wall.

The girl's eyes widened, and sweat frizzed the stray blond curls on her forehead. But she raised her chin. "Yes, Monseigneur. I delivered some dresses to Madame la Marchioness."

"At this hour, my wilting petal? My poor little fawn with no one to look after her." He grabbed the girl by the waist and pulled her to him. Her hood fell to her shoulders as she gaped at his leering face. He chuckled and pushed her body against the garden wall. "Such a pretty little fawn," he was murmuring, his eyes straying down her long, strained neck to her décolletage.

She revealed the blade of a knife from under the folds of her cloak.

The Marquis arched an amused eyebrow at the blade. "A threat, is it? That'll be the rope for you, pretty one. But your little dagger does not frighten me."

The cold, steel point of Blackwick's rapier tickled the Marquis' neck right above the folds of his silk cravat. "You should be frightened, Monsieur. Move aside, and let mademoiselle be on her way."

The Marquis stiffened. He moved his rigid hands from the seamstress' bodice, and she edged away from him, crossing to stand behind Blackwick.

The young woman peeked out from behind the tall frame of the shadow man. "Monsieur, you are brave to help, but the Marquis is a cruel man, and he will never forgive you."

"No." The Marquis narrowed his eyes at Blackwick. "I never forgive those who get in my way."

"It's you who are in need of forgiveness," returned Blackwick. "Though it will take a long penance to wash away *your* stench." He balanced himself in "ready" position and circled the point of his blade close to the Marquis' nose. Keeping his amber slits locked on the Marquis, Blackwick addressed the seamstress. "Do you have a way home?"

"Yes, my mare, La Petite Noire."

"Then, there is no need to wait."

The seamstress readjusted her hood, and, with one last anxious glance at her rescuer, darted toward the garden gate.

The Marquis exhaled his pent-up rage. "Who do you think you are?"

"Me?" The slits in Blackwick's black waxen face watched every twitch the Marquis made. "I am no one. Just a story that was told and forgotten. A candle flame that has burnt out. A wolf forsaken by the moon. But I am here, and you are here, Monsieur. You may return to your home and say your evening prayers, or you may stay and convince my sword that you deserve to live."

The Marquis trilled a tra-la of laughter and waved his handkerchief toward three burly men guarding the perimeters of the lawn. "You think a Marquis has no dogs to do his bidding?"

The burly men were upon Blackwick. The shadow man released an unamused sigh as the first brute wrapped muscular arms around his head and throat, while the second fellow wrenched his wrist to loosen his grasp on the sword. These idiots would offer little challenge. The third ruffian returned, hauling the seamstress and guffawing at her curses. Blackwick's shoulders stiffened, and the flames of his eyes simmered darkly.

The Marquis sniggered in triumph. "You three have earned your wine tonight. Pierre! Jean! Finish off this jackanape. I want to watch you tear off his ears and gouge out his eyes until he begs me to toss him to the sewage where he belongs. Marcel, take the girl to my special room. I have some delightful amusements awaiting her there."

When the Marquis' thin lips curled as he alluded to his sadistic plans for the seamstress, the beast inside Blackwick roared to be unleashed. The black wax encasing him cracked. It melted down the front of the oaf's shirt, into a black puddle on the ground. Blackwick reconstituted, rising into the silhouette of a wolf that snarled at those who had him surrounded.

The Marquis paled. He lifted the lantern from the garden wall and hurled it at Blackwick. It crashed at his feet and burst into a spiral of fire that encircled the shadow, and the shadow laughed as he absorbed the power from the lantern's flame.

The man who had filched his sword, dropped it as if the hilt had burnt him. In shock, he fell to the ground, eyes glazed, face singed. Blackwick whipped toward the man who had throttled him, and that man was hit by a barrage of blows landed so swiftly he never saw them coming.

The shadow dispersed into a cloud of ash and reappeared in front of the man who held the girl. The shadow wolf roared into the face of the brute, and the oaf's eyes went white and blank as his arms dropped lifelessly at his side. Blackwick, returning to the form of a man, caught the seamstress before she fell. Nestled in the strong arms of this black mask of a man, the young woman gazed up at his well-carved facial form. "Who are you, Monsieur?"

He did not answer her query. Instead, he set her on her feet and pivoted toward the Marquis.

"Jean! Pierre! Marcel!" stammered the Marquis, but his three men were stretched out cold and still on the neatly trimmed lawn. Paler than powder, the Marquis shook from the top of his wig to the toes of his delicate hose. A rattling emanated from his throat.

Blackwick remained in parry-ready stance, sword drawn, knees bent, his stare locked on the French aristocrat. In disgust, he watched as the Marquis' eyes enlarged and turned blood red. The aristocrat's tongue elongated and lolled out from his mouth. The fibers of his wig reared and writhed like a nest of colorless vipers. As if in shock at his own transformation, the Marquis clutched the sides of his now round, marble face and collapsed into a distorted huddle of fear against the garden wall.

"Stay back, agent of the hated one!" screeched the Marquis in a trio of female voices.

"What in the name of le bon Dieu!" exclaimed the seamstress.

Blackwick had no explanation to offer. The only shapeshifter he had met was the little dragon pet of the vampire Vlad Tepov, who could transform into an alluring woman or back into a falcon-sized dragon at will. Perhaps there was some diabolical connection. Blackwick kept a wary eye upon the creature before him while guiding the seamstress toward the garden wall. "Ma'mselle, leave this place. No one will stop you now."

The seamstress frowned her disappointment. She wanted to find out more about this enchantment that turned heroes into shadow wolves and villains into gorgons. She glanced up at the full moon with strong suspicions. But an enchanted shadow man was not one to argue with, so she scrambled over the garden wall, using the branches of the overhanging trees to help herself down on the street side. She heard a venomous chorus of hisses followed by a multitudinous scream. The next sound was a swift silver slice followed by two clunks slumping to the ground.

The seamstress was a plucky girl, but she shivered at the cold stillness that misted the air and the thought of the beheaded gorgon of a Marquis on the other side of the wall. She ducked into the shadows to where her mare was tethered. She rubbed the mare's muzzle and whispered, "Let us be off, La Petite Noire, before the madness overtakes us all."

As she urged her mare down the street, a raven with peculiar dints in its beak screamed over the wall from where the Marquis had fallen and flapped off southeast toward the point of a rooftop on the horizon.

CHAPTER 3
THE TUMBRILS (1780S)

Thérèse and Robert crouched in the mouth of the sewer drain, their exoskeletons reflecting glints of light from the iron-framed streetlamps of Paris. The filth, the stench, all comforting and familiar to the two roaches. But there was something not so familiar transpiring in the world of the human trespassers. The roaches flexed their antennae as the reverberations of a rumbling rolled under their padded claws.

"Shall we report this to Monseigneur le Dragon?"

"Wait, wait," Thérèse hissed. "He will ask questions. We must gather information."

They braved a peek at the street above the ditch. A mob of men wearing red stocking caps and brown breeches trudged beside the rolling tumbrils, brandishing torches and muskets and shouting for the death of "the aristos." The tumbrils, drawn by bony black horses with lowered manes and fierce red eyes, conveyed the pale, fainting aristocrats, bereft of powder, bereft of hope, to their fate with Madame la Guillotine. One mare planted her hooves and held back, snorting her protest. The citizen clutching her reins brought his club down upon her back until she relented, swung her head, and proceeded against her will.

Robert scampered up the iron post of a streetlamp. He framed his eyes with the bent front section of his foreleg and watched as the revolutionaries escorted the aristocrats toward their doom. A drunk across the street accepted a jug from the pale hands of a little man dressed in black. The little man pointed to key junctures of the square, and Robert looked in the directions to discover armed men lurking at the street corners and in upstairs windows, with all the tension of a trap about to be sprung.

"*Vive la révolution!*" cried Robert as he returned from his surveillance. "It looks like a meeting of the Tribunal has decided that tonight more perfume-wearers will die. What is more, I think this is the night the elusive Englishman who tries to rescue the perfume-wearers will fall into the net of the *citoyens*."

"Good," said Thérèse. "The perfume-wearers scream and faint when they see us. They chase us with their shoes. It is good for them to die."

"I am waiting!" echoed a deep voice.

The two roaches exchanged winces, and they scuttled back into the dark, hollow depths of the pipe.

Ordog's cockroach slaves had created a comfortable though temporary throne room for their new master. His throne was a deposit of limescale, and the carpet was a bed of dead leaves.

"Mighty dragon lord." Thérèse bent her front legs and dipped her chin in a bow.

"The dirty ones are winning, mighty Ordog," announced Robert. "They will chop the perfume-wearers and lop off their screams, and there will be much blood of humans in the gutters."

A satisfied sneer wreathed the muzzle of the miniature dragon, and he tapped his foreclaws together. "Hatred, yes, violence, yes. There will be many souls lost and much fear to feed on. I shall dine well before my long voyage across the sea."

A green-tinted moon hung over Paris. Blackwick scrambled across the loose shingles of the rooftops, evaporating into the smoke from the chimneys, whirling with a flurry of autumn leaves, and reconstituting on the neighboring rooftop, where he perched, cape billowing about him like the wings of a fallen angel. He bent forward over his knee and surveyed the street with narrowed eyes.

"*Down, Evrémonde! To the guillotine all aristocrats! Down, Evrémonde!*" came the hoarse cry from the rabble thronging the streets as the tumbrils carted those who displeased the Tribunal to the slaughter. Some of the victims stood like rigid, colorless scarecrows, in too much shock to react. Others swooned like discarded marionettes over the sides of the carts.

Blackwick cringed, for even far above the streets, he heard their choked breaths, smelled their bloodless fear, and felt their unheard pleas for mercy jar each vertebra down his spine.

The soft voice of one person alerted his internal compass.

"They say it is rapid."

That is the one. The one I have been sent here for. Blackwick zeroed in on the pale face of a young woman with large, blue eyes half hidden by the tousled strands of straw blonde hair. He recognized the seamstress he had helped near the Marquis' chateau.

"Yes, they will be rapid." The man who spoke stood in the cart facing the seamstress, her hands in his, his shoulders shielding her from the looming guillotine as the black mare dragged the cart forward. The man resembled Charles Darnay, the nephew of the Marquis, but instead of the well-groomed, sharp-eyed, tall-postured young man, this man was disheveled, weary, and bent. His soul bore the bittersweet aroma of regret.

Blackwick flattened himself into a shadow. He slipped off the side of the roof, spiraled down a drainpipe, and oozed to a halt, lying level with the cobbled road in the harsh light of the streetlamp. His black-gloved hand shot up from the street and clutched the drooped stocking on the ankle of a drunken revolutionary.

The drunk dropped his jug of wine and crust of bread and screamed. He looked down, and his vision swam as he took in a shadow lifting itself from the cobblestones. The drunk sank into a faint.

Later, Blackwick, dressed in the red stocking cap, cotton shirt, ragged breeches, drooping stockings, and buckled shoes of the drunk, followed along with the bloodthirsty crowd. He staggered and waved the sloshing jug of wine high above his head and shouted, "To the Guillotine with 'em! Death to the aristos!" louder than any other zealot in the procession. A dirty waif, pale and thin, stood on the sidelines gaping up at the parade of death. Blackwick paused, pondering the boy sadly. He tousled the boy's thinning hair, and the boy nearly fell over, so weak he was. Blackwick took the crust of bread from his pocket and folded it into the boy's hand.

The disguised shadow man followed the carts to the Place de Grève where the guillotine was mounted on a wooden platform and the Monsieur de Paris in his red hooded mask and cloak, stood, holding the release handle, ready to ply his trade.

The blade fell swiftly, slicing through the air with a chilling swish, ending in a heavy, sickening thunk.

In the back of the tumbril rolling up to the platform, the man who resembled Darnay stood between the seamstress and the blood-splotched blade as it was cranked back into position. "Keep your eyes on me." He pressed her hands to draw her focus.

Her eyes lifted to his. "What is your name, monsieur?"

He brought his lips close to her ear. "Sidney Carton. A simple lawyer."

"Do not let go of my hand, Monsieur Carton."

"I won't."

The two shared a steadfast gaze, ignoring the cackling of the wives and mothers of the revolution, who sat in their chairs, knitting near the platform, keeping track of the score of heads the baskets had collected that day.

Blackwick started as a man's hand clutched his wrist, and an Englishman's voice rasped in his ear. "Distract the rabble while we rescue Carton and the girl. Orders from the Scarlet Pimpernel." The Englishman was disguised as a guard, and

Blackwick realized he had been mistaken for a confederate of the man referred to in whispers as the Scarlet Pimpernel. According to rumor, the League of the Scarlet Pimpernel consisted of a small band of daring young English aristocrats who risked all to save the lives of those endangered by the wrath of revolution. The Scarlet Pimpernel's identity was unknown to most. He was a master of disguise, so he could be anyone right now, one of the old hags knitting, one of the blood-thirsty onlookers, or even the stalwart guard beside him. Whether the guard was *the* Scarlet Pimpernel or not, Blackwick sensed nothing but courage and heroic intentions in the young man, so he nodded his readiness to join forces with their worthy cause.

The revolutionaries were dragging the seamstress, Carton, and an elderly woman out of the tumbril and onto the platform. Carton surveyed the jeering mass with a sad smile, and he released a resigned but contented sigh.

Blackwick hurled his jug at one of the revolutionaries, and it smashed against his head. "Hey, Frenchie!" He leapt up onto the platform and shoved the executioner away from the elderly woman who trembled before the wooden pillory at the guillotine's base.

Blackwick drew his sword and inserted himself between the rabble and the woman. "A whole crew of you sots against one little lady? You think there's enough of you boyos?"

The citizens near the platform were at first too shocked to move. The guards recovered and brandished their muskets as they surged toward Blackwick. The executioner shoved Blackwick's head toward the wooden crescent built for the necks of intended victims. The executioner pressed Blackwick's neck into the groove. With a hearty roar, Blackwick thrust back his head and shoulders, throwing the executioner off balance.

"You can't take me *that* fast, my dear!" Blackwick flew into a cloud of ash, which gusted around the executioner like a blinding dust storm. The executioner's eyes crossed within the eyeholes of his mask as he tried to follow what had transpired.

With a whoosh, Blackwick reconstituted and used his sword to cut loose the ropes from the wrists of the seamstress and Carton and ushered them back into the tumbril. As Blackwick backed off the platform, a slew of guards had at him with their swords. Blackwick staved off the blades with dexterous parries and tapped down the wooden steps.

Carton was blinking like someone questioning how long one must be off the booze before hallucinations go away. The seamstress clutched Carton's arm in her excitement. "It's my brave shadow man!"

The citizens were in an uproar, and the guards were clamoring around Blackwick as he leapt into the tumbril. The Englishman disguised as a guard ushered the remaining victims away from the platform and out of the fray.

Blackwick drew his pistol from the holster at his thigh and pressed it into Carton's hand. "Use this!" He turned his attention to the citizen in front of the cart who clutched the reins of the horse to keep it from bolting. Blackwick pulled back his fist and landed it on the citizen's surprised upturned face.

The mare shook her mane and snorted as the citizen tumbled into the ditch. The horse rolled her eyes back as if searching for someone in the cart. "We are free, La Petite Noire," called the seamstress to the mare.

"Not yet." Blackwick indicated the guards converging upon the cart.

Carton studied the pistol to determine how it worked. The seamstress huffed and grabbed the pistol from him. "What did they teach you in England?"

"Latin and law, my dear," admitted Carton. His eyes sharpened, and he pointed. "That brute there!"

A ruffian was climbing into the cart. The seamstress fired the pistol point blank. "Take the reins, lawman," she ordered Carton as she cracked the butt of the pistol over a revolutionary's head.

Blackwick propelled Carton to the front of the cart. The swarm of revolutionaries was too thick. "I'll distract them," he told Carton. Blackwick whistled loud and sharp. The rabble turned on him. He whirled himself into a tornado of ash and shadow with a force that blew the hats off the citizens nearest the cart. They gasped and stared at the shadowy storm that whipped over their heads and resumed a human shape next to the execution platform. Summoning his wolfish strength, he rammed his shoulder into the planks of the platform, and the entire edifice cracked and toppled, the guillotine itself breaking asunder.

The heavy, long rectangle with its thick blade plummeted. The elderly woman in its path gaped up, too weak and stunned to move. Blackwick sprang to the lady and pulled her to safety with one hand while lifting his other hand to catch the sharp end of the blade. The blade cut into the waxen skin of his hand, but instead of blood, the red of burning embers pressed through the fissure. He threw down the blade in disgust.

Many shouts of amazed relief arose, but those who had erected the blade of death were not rejoicing.

"It's the Scarlet Pimpernel, you idiots!" came a shrill voice from a little man with fox-like eyes and a nervous air of authority. "I'm Citoyen Chauvelin! I represent the Tribunal! In the name of liberty, fraternity, and equality, arrest that man!"

A confused knot of guards encircled Blackwick. One of scaled the rubble and clamped a hand upon the shadow man's shoulder. "That's all for you, Pimpernel!" And in his ear the voice whispered, "Let me arrest you." It was the Englishman from the League of the Scarlet Pimpernel.

Blackwick threw himself into the role with zest. He swung his arm to punch the guard but let the guard get the better of him. The guard wrenched Blackwick's arms behind his back and bound them. "You'll stand before the Tribunal tonight, you devil!"

"Long live the King!" shouted Blackwick at the top of his lungs as he was escorted away. "Death to the oppressors! Rule, Brittania!" The guard shoved him away.

Meanwhile, the iron portcullis was rattling down to cut off any escapes. The seamstress leapt onto the back of La Petite

Noire, and Carton climbed up behind her. The seamstress dug her calves into the mare, and with a "*C'est le moment!*" she urged the mare to take off at a gallop just in time to clear the closing jaws of the gate.

CHAPTER 4
THE FISHERMAN'S REST (1780S)

La Petite Noire cleared the gate. Like a dream from a distant time, a woman's voice called to La Petite Noire. She sang the song of the bending grass and the guiding stars, the song the mother horse sings as she leads the unsaddled herd through the wild lands. La Petite Noire followed the voice and launched through a golden ring that opened onto the white sands of Dover. The mare whinnied, and her nostrils quivered at the salty waft of the channel, a welcome change from the stench and terror of the square.

The reins hauled back, and the mare's hooves skidded to a halt at the foot of a winding path. The path sloped upward with wooden slats leading to an inn. There to greet the new arrivals stood a little Englishman, nearly bald, wearing a frockcoat over woolen breeches. He almost waved, but, instead, he twitched nervously and wrung his hands. "Welcome, travelers! I'm Jeremy Spinderbeck."

Sydney Carton slid from horseback and helped the seamstress dismount. Both stared at the sudden change in scenery like ghosts new to the job. "It would seem," said Carton, "we haven't escaped after all. Although I imagined Saint Peter would be a trifle taller. That is, if I managed somehow to make it in the right direction."

A smile tugged on Spinderbeck's mouth as he blinked up at the disheveled lawyer. "Ah, a far, far better thing you did, my friend. Congratulations, indeed. But, dear me, no, I am not Saint Peter. I'm not even saint anything. I told you, I'm Jeremy Spinderbeck. That at the top of the slope is The Fisherman's Rest, a refuge in these dark times. Perhaps you've heard," here Spinderbeck stood as tall as he could and raised his eyebrows in a savoir-faire manner, "of the Scarlet Pimpernel?"

The seamstress was patting her mare's mane and soothing her with soft words. At mention of the Scarlet Pimpernel, she ducked out from behind the horse. "Mon Dieu! Are *you* the Scarlet Pimpernel, the hero of all France, the man of mystery with his league of brave Englishmen?"

"Uh. No." Spinderbeck coughed into his fist. "But he recommended The Fisherman's Rest as a safe place to do business."

Two stable boys arrived to tend to the mare. One took her reins and the other offered her hay. "We'll take good care of her, mum," they assured the seamstress. She thanked the boys and gave her mare a reassuring nod.

Spinderbeck gestured for the new arrivals to follow him. "This way, please." He headed up the wooden slats and glanced back to make sure the two were following.

From an open upstairs window of the inn, Betty Talbin was watching. The nineteen-year-old slipped the loose strand of her long, black hair behind her ear and held back the curtain to get a good view of Sydney Carton and the seamstress.

To Betty, these characters would ever be associated with unbidden tears as she half whispered the melodramatic ending of *A Tale of Two Cities* in the reading nook at Perlgate. She recalled the nerve-wracking servant bell clanging non-stop while she power-read through to Carton's "far, far better thing I do" as he went to the guillotine in place of Charles Darnay, the husband of the woman he loved.

"He looks better than Ronald Colman." Frieda Fernsby interrupted Betty's thoughts, referencing the film version Hollywood had produced a couple years earlier in their own world. Betty glanced back at her friend, still having trouble adjusting to her being thirteen rather than the middle-aged mentor she had first met at Hamberdeen's Used Book Shop in Bedfordshire in 1936. Frieda, now reminding Betty of an Alice in Wonderland with spectacles, joined her at the window.

Betty noted the bow of her friend's white pinafore was loose, and being a former housemaid, her natural reaction was to put things in order. "Perhaps." She retied the bow. "But his eyes are much sadder than I expected."

"Spoken like a true Inter-Story Intercessor." Frieda waved Betty's hand away. "Now, none of your fussing over *me. You're* the Keeper of the Golden Vigil. *You're* the one who summoned them, and *you're* the one they've come to see."

I'm the one? Betty checked her own appearance in an oval mirror propped on the dressing table, hoping she could somehow live up to her friends' expectations. Yes, it had been exciting to share the adventures of her favorite book characters, but now she felt a wave of misgiving, like a general on the eve of war realizing how little one knows of commanding real people to plunge into real danger.

Betty gave her reflection a critical scrunch of her nose. "It still feels strange being the Keeper of the Golden Vigil."

Frieda stepped back like a lady in waiting, bearing a rolled-up chart for a scepter and a golden candle for a sword. "It always feels strange when a leader recognizes the gravity of her responsibilities. It means you are taking the role seriously, and that is a good sign."

Betty smiled a little, but the heaviness returned as she regarded the 1900s edition of *A Tale of Two Cities* set upon the quilt covering the four-poster bed. She clenched her teeth and flicked open the cover of the book. The pages were wrinkled and ripped, and a greenish ooze was eating at the binding. Her finger accidentally poked the ooze, and it crawled up to her hand and stung her skin like nettles. Betty sucked in her breath and withdrew her hand, and the ooze sprang back to its source in the binding.

"It's getting worse," noted Frieda. "Are you all right?"

Betty hid her hand behind her back and nodded. "I'm all right. But Blackwick is still there." She squeezed her eyes to shut out the view of the corruption spreading across the pages of the world she had sent him to protect.

Frieda gave her friend a gentle, motherly smile. "He's part werewolf, part shadow, and part Edmond. Blackwick will be fine. And now we have a chance to try and stop this thing, whatever it is. Come, my lady." Frieda gave an exaggerated curtsy to lighten the mood. "The League of the Inter-Story Intercessors awaits your orders."

After tugging on her gloves, Betty closed the book and balanced it in the crook of her arm. She accepted the chart in one hand and the candle in the other and forced her face to relax. "But tell me." Betty's dark eyes twinkled, as she allayed her own fears with a touch of playfulness. "Do I descend the stairs with my nose tilted upward like a queen? Or with my head bowed like a priestess?" She practiced craning her neck in exaggerated disdain, then lowered her eyelids and bent her chin over her relics like one about to swing the incense and chant in Latin.

Frieda opened the door. "Just be yourself, my dear."

Betty wondered what being herself really meant. She opted for a middle ground expression, head held erect, eyes forward as she followed Frieda down the stairs. They curled around to the front area of the inn. There, Sydney Carton stood warming himself before the hearth, taking a moment to help the seamstress wipe a smudge of dirt from her face.

Frieda cleared her throat.

Carton turned, and his expression softened in surprise to see the little girl before him. "Why good day, young mistress . . .?"

"Fernsby. I'm Frieda Fernsby. It's been quite a day for both of you, I'm sure. Sally, could you fetch some ale and dinner for our guests?"

The flirtatious, buxom blonde daughter of the landlord giggled and disappeared into the kitchen.

"And may I present to you, Miss Beatrice Talbin, the one who summoned you both here." Frieda moved aside to reveal Betty, dressed in eighteenth-century redingote and travel boots and a full skirt fluffed by layers of petticoats.

"Ah, Mr. Carton. And?" Betty blinked at the seamstress.

"Constance," replied the seamstress.

"Ah." Betty gestured with her chart for Carton to sit in a chair on one side of the fireplace and with her candle for the seamstress to be seated on the other side.

Frieda sat on the stone hearth near Carton. "I'm awfully glad you survived *this* time."

"This time?" Carton leaned back in his chair. Sally was pouring the ale, making eyes at Carton and being coolly polite to the seamstress.

A clatter of dominoes collapsing startled the room, and they looked toward a darkened corner. A gentleman with salt and pepper hair and spectacles rose from the corner and cleared his throat. "Frieda, you're confusing our poor guests. You tend to start the wrong side up so often, but I suppose that comes with growing down. When you've been over a certain age and are now almost thirteen, it must make everything seem a little, well . . ."

"Higgledy-piggledy, that's what it is," inserted Spinderbeck, closing the door to the inn. "Just higgledy-piggledy ever since *you know who* escaped."

Betty bit her lip at the mention of Ordog. She caught Spinderbeck's nervous cringe. Her cheeks burned. *They won't say it – they're too kind for that – but they still remember Ordog's escape happened on my watch.* Betty, anxious, turned to Frieda, and her friend broke the tension by addressing the gentleman in the corner. "Well, then, *you* explain it, Mr. Hamberdeen."

"No, I think Betty ought to handle this." He gave Betty a humble, deferring nod.

Betty lowered her eyes and took a breath to resume an attitude of calm. She set her candle, chart, and book upon a little table to the side and sat with her back to the wall. She touched the wick of the candle, and a flame shot up from the wax. The seamstress started in surprise.

Betty was pleased with the effect she had produced and steepled her fingers at her chin. "I am so glad to see Blackwick made it in time."

"Blackwick?" asked Carton.

"You know," put in Spinderbeck, "tall man, dark form, a lot like . . ." He pointed to Hamberdeen's shadow cast upon the wall by the hearth flames.

"Oui, my brave shadow man!" exclaimed the seamstress. "If not for him, my head would say adieu to these shoulders for good." She touched her own shoulder the drooping sleeve had revealed.

Betty stiffened when the seamstress mentioned "my brave shadow man," but a glance back at the book reminded her this was no time for personal pettiness. "Yes, Blackwick is a loyal ally. He is a good friend to the Inter-Story Intercessors. I'm Betty Talbin, and my friends and I, well, we try to help people like you whenever we can. But there's an even greater purpose for your rescue." She opened the book to reveal the crumpling, disintegrating pages of the novel. "This is your world. Now it's happening in France, but this corruption soon will spread even here to England."

Next, she unrolled the chart. "But we think there is a solution." She pointed to a circled landmark that read "Paris 1780s," and beneath it in scarlet ink, *Find the heart double broken.*

Mr. Hamberdeen blinked over the rims of his spectacles at Carton. "That would be you. After all, you were a double of Charles Darnay, and your heart has been twice broken, has it not? Once by regret, and once by the woman you loved?"

Carton set down the tankard of ale and slouched over his knees, clasping his hands before him. "Supposing I still had a heart, pickled though it be in demon rum, what would the breaking of it be to you good people?"

Frieda frowned. "The evil one has escaped."

Betty lowered her eyes.

Frieda continued. "He was last seen on his way to your world. Now, something terrible is spreading its influence across its pages and across the pages of many books. And what we have to work with is a chart. The members of our society are of a mind that if we follow what the chart says, we may be able to establish a stop gate, something to hinder the corruption from spreading."

"Please, sir," said Betty, "if you would touch the book. Your sacrificial aura may be the solution we need." She moved the book toward Carton.

He pushed himself to his feet. "As a lawyer, I would say touching it would not be enough. We need to make this legal and binding." He took a quill and inkpot from the mantel, made sure the tip of the quill was sharp and well-inked, and set it to the page. The spreading ooze shrank back from the sharp point of the quill. He scratched his signature across the page and scribbled the shape of a heart next to his name, ending with a long stroke drawn through the middle of the heart. But the corruption was only temporarily stayed. Before Betty could thank Carton, the ooze was working its way toward his signature.

"Oh, dear me," exclaimed Mr. Spinderbeck.

"Now what?" asked Mr. Hamberdeen.

Betty paled. *And Master Yamada was so sure it would work!*

Carton puzzled. He met the seamstress' worried eyes, and an epiphany lightened his own expression. "Of course. What a jolterhead I am, what a dunce. To make anything legal, it takes the sign of two!" He bowed to the seamstress and offered her the quill with the graciousness of a courtier offering a grand heiress a turn on the dancefloor. "Will you do the honors?"

The seamstress pulled back in surprise, then smiled. "I never learned to read and write," she confessed. "But I know my initials." She scratched a C and a B next to Carton's signature and added another heart next to the one he had drawn, with another stroke drawn through both.

The corruption rolled back, and the ooze receded into the threading.

Carton smiled and patted the seamstress' hand. "There you have it, a heart double broken, that may now be on the mend."

Betty allowed herself to breathe at last. She dripped the candle above the signature and waved her hands over the golden wax to add the official signet of Vandor to the page. "I cannot thank you enough, Mr. Carton." She offered her hand to him, since that was what young ladies usually did in novels like *A Tale of Two Cities* or *The Scarlet Pimpernel*. He took her fingertips and bowed over them humbly. "And you too, Mademoiselle," she added to the seamstress.

"And *merci* to you too, and your brave shadow man." The seamstress curtsied low to Betty.

"And now," said Mr. Hamberdeen, "anchored not far from here is a sleek yacht with the words the *Day Dream* painted on its hull. The gentleman who owns that worthy craft will be more than happy to take you both and your horse wherever you wish to go."

Carton guided the seamstress by the elbow. "What do you say, my young friend? Perhaps a certain Charles Darnay would not mind a little legal advice from an old friend. Or perhaps a young seamstress would not mind helping a shattered wreck find the pieces of a broken life?"

"That will take some doing, monsieur," replied the seamstress, "but fortunately I am used to mending things."

They followed Thomas Hamberdeen and Jeremy Spinderbeck out the door.

Betty blew out the candle, rolled the chart, and held the book in the crook of her arm. "And now?"

Frieda used the poker to stir the fire in the hearth. "Peter's calling me back to Neverland. Such a silly boy. But," she added as a sad sort of wistfulness crossed her features, "he seemed awfully worried."

Betty did not want to see her friend leave so soon. It seemed ages since their last meeting, and she was sure Peter Pan could spare Frieda for another day or two. Frieda, however, set down the poker, wiped her hands on her apron, and drew on her cloak, and Betty knew there was no chance of detaining her friend.

Gazing into the reflective surface of the silver tankard before her, Betty could almost see the wild meadows of Neverland beckoning. She handed the tankard to Frieda. "You will be careful, though. With Ordog loose, and now this whatever it is spreading across the story worlds, I'm tempted to make you stay here with me."

"I would stay in a heartbeat," Frieda assured her. "But, try as we Intercessors may, we've not yet mastered the art of being in two places at once."

Frieda covered the side of the tankard with her hand as if not quite ready to say goodbye. Betty broke the awkward silence. "Remember, if you need me at all, please . . ."

Frieda nodded. "I know how to summon you, Betty. Remember, I was an Intercessor before you were even born."

Gazing into her friend's wise eyes, Betty did not even consider it strange the words came from a girl who looked at least six years her junior.

CHAPTER 5
NEVERLAND (THE NEVER YEARS)

The air channeling through the hollow was cooler than usual. Leaves scattered in its wake, wrinkled and brown. Dragonflies hummed in a frantic whir past Frieda as she emerged from a glistening silver of dew into the clearing in Neverland. There in the meadows on the other side of the ridge, she spied Peter Pan standing in the middle of the path, scratching his head under his Robin Hood cap.

Peter pressed his lips in a frown, and his back tensed. She thought how very grown up he looked. Indeed, his shoulders were a tad broader, his legs a tad longer, and his expression grimmer. His elven ears strained to listen past the buzz and breeze of the meadow.

"Something's bad." He peered into the wisps of clouds sailing across the dusking sky. "Something's very bad."

Twanging a twig on a tree, he bolted across the meadow, through waves of grass. Frieda hurried after him, the soft earth springing gently under her bare feet.

At the edge of the meadow was the jungle. She paused to catch her breath, but Peter pushed through the tangles, not heeding the flutter of the hummingbirds, the swaying of a sloth, nor the squawking of the parrots. The jungle was humid, and Frieda's spectacles slid down her moist nose, as she raised herself on tiptoe to see past the curtain of vines Peter drew aside.

An odd mist hovered over the lagoon, an odd greenish haze reminiscent of the ooze Frieda had seen spreading across *A Tale of Two Cities*. The jungle blossoms hung limp upon their browning vines, and the waterfalls were a mere trickle.

Frieda wiped the steam from her spectacles. "The corruption. It's happening in Neverland now."

"Something bad, whatever," Peter answered simply.

"Perhaps the Mer-shaman will know what to do."

Peter sat on a moss-shrouded log and threw one leg and then the other over it. As he did, he offered his arms to Frieda, and she leaned on his shoulders as she vaulted over the log.

Peter hung his cap upon a limb and loosed his belt, flinging it along with his dagger onto a nearby rock for safekeeping. Frieda untied her white pinafore and hung it next to his cap and set her spectacles next to his belt. She squinted into the blur.

Peter leapt onto a rock and from there dove into the center of the lagoon. Frieda balanced herself on the bank and hesitated. She was not much of a swimmer, and she wished Peter had waited for her. She took a deep breath. Peter bobbed to the surface, pushing back wet strands of hair that had plastered his eyes. "Remember, just think lovely, wonderful thoughts. It's like flying, but down instead of up."

"Oh, all right. Lovely thoughts." She thought of Mister Hamberdeen's used book shop, having tea with Betty in Bedfordshire, and she held her nose and plunged feet first into the lagoon.

Peter laughed, and his laugh became a gargle as he dove beneath the surface, caught hold of her hand, and dragged her past algae and a school of fish to the underwater cavern where the Mer-shaman ruled. The cavern was in a pocket of air, surrounded by shimmering walls of blue water. Framed by the pillars of the central archways, the mermaids suspended in the walls of water by gently sweeping their fins. Their hair billowed upward as they strummed sad chords on their lutes.

Peter sprang out of the inlet like a seal and slid onto the stone ledge. Frieda caught hold of the arm he offered and dragged herself up beside him, where she paused to cough and let the water drain from her ears. Once she had regained her equilibrium, she heard the mermaids sing their haunting farewell to Neverland.

Neverland mahana
Neverland mahai
Naga mia naga molo
Lama a'a eyai

Peter and Frieda exchanged worried glances. With heads bowed, they approached the dais where the Mer-shaman knelt, her bronzed face buried in weathered hands. Her grizzled hair hung like a shawl over her shoulders, and the shoulders shook as she sobbed a prayer in the ancient tongue of her people.

Aidi gamanga ama'a
Aido malaka ga'ema

"Oh, great Mer-shaman, mother of the sea, we come in answer to your call." Peter knelt on one knee and bowed his head. Frieda joined him on her knees and held her hands together near her heart.

The Mer-shaman dropped her arms and shook her head. Her dark cheeks were streaked with tears. "My children, my poor children. I called you here to say goodbye. A long, long, long goodbye."

"No! You can't go!" snapped Peter, but he checked himself and lowered his eyes contritely. "I mean, how can we get on without you?"

"With Ordog on the move again, we'll need all the help we can get," insisted Frieda.

"Ordog and his fallen dragons led the way for this evil to follow." The Mer-shaman tilted her head and heeded the chant of the mermaids. "Daughters of the sea. They foretell the coming of another, the one bound and chained in The Netherworld. Zed-Cyphrr."

Peter frowned and scratched his head. "Zed-Who-phrr?" He looked blankly at Frieda. Frieda shook her head and shrugged.

The Mer-shaman lifted her hand out of the water, and the sea-weed clinging to it shriveled and turned to ash. "All of Neverland will die. The destroyer's spirit is abroad and soon will corrupt this and other beautiful worlds."

Frieda stood and dared a step closer. "But there's a way to stop it. You are powerful. Use your magic. You gave Betty a chart, and it helped us hold back the corruption in Paris. We can use it to stay one step ahead."

Peter see-sawed his head in desperate confirmation.

The Mer-shaman's brow was vexed as she touched the side of the three-paneled mosaic behind her dais. The panels lit to display a story, like a motion picture from the cinema. One panel showed a stained-glass dragon with two heads challenging a stained-glass dragon of gold. "Long ago," the Mer-shaman proclaimed, "Zed-Cyphrr convinced themselves they were the greatest of the celestial dragons, greater even than Vorever.

"But Vorever defeated Zed-Cyphrr and imprisoned them in the deep." The second panel depicted a burst of painted flame issuing from the Golden Dragon's mouth, and the two-headed dragon was pulled into a book. In the third panel, the two-headed dragon was dragged by long chains out from the last page of the book and clamped into shackles within a dark, subterranean passage. "All the poisonous words of Zed-Cyphrr were bound inside the *Tome of the Netherdragons*. And this tome was entrusted to my ancestors, and we have faithfully guarded it here for thousands of years." The panels dimmed.

"Less than a season ago, a land dweller infiltrated our lagoon while I was away on my pilgrimage to the burial grounds of my ancestors. This land dweller, one of the wise sisters of old, put my daughters into a deep sleep and stole the book from its place within this altar." She pushed aside a stone slab, and it fell with a hollow thud, revealing an empty crevice within the altar. "The words in that book make promises to those who will use it to summon Zed-Cyphrr back into the story worlds."

Peter stood and clenched his fists. "I vow to stop Zed-Cyphrr! I forbid them to set one foot in Neverland."

"But the land dweller has opened the book, and Zed-Cyphrr's corruption is already here. Tiger Lily and her tribe have sensed it. They've taken their boats far from this island. We see it in the mist that settles on the surface, in the algae that chokes out the sunlight. My daughters cannot live with such contagion. I must protect my daughters. This day we migrate to the open sea, far away from this lagoon that has long been our home."

"What can we do?" asked Frieda.

"As Betty trains on Vandor, she will learn how to interpret the clues the chart provides. But you, Frieda Fernsby, child of light, for you I have a gift." From under a bed of seagrass on the lagoon's shifting floor, she drew a conch shell. "When all seems lost and the way unclear, call on this shell, and I will hear. And if that call is not enough, three more times will wake us up."

Frieda held the conch close to her heart.

The Mer-shaman sent up a cry that rippled through the walls of water surrounding them, and the mermaids gathered close. "I have sent word to Vandor. It is up to you, Peter Pan, and you, Frieda Fernsby, to hold back the corruption as long as you can. When things are right again, my daughters and I will return."

CHAPTER 6
THE TOME OF THE NETHERDRAGONS (1930S)

The hunting lodge, once the remodeled castle of Count Vlad Tepov, was in ruins. The heraldic banners of the Draculae were replaced by cobwebs swaying like moth-eaten curtains in the Carpathian wind.

Ilda, former servant to the late count, sprawled in the throne like a Viking warrior relishing the glory of victory. Her blouse and skirt hung loose upon her large-boned frame. Her blood-shot eyes roamed the emptiness. Her cracked lips spread into a gloat as she reflected on her recent infiltration of the mermaid lagoon and the spoils of that maneuver. Already she had dabbled into the mysteries of the forbidden tome, and the voices of the mist had promised her much.

Once impressive double doors of solid timber and hand-forged iron guarded the entrance, but now, upheaved from their hinges, they lay crossways, emitting a triangular stream of dying dusk through the crack between them.

A hulking shadow surged into that light. One of the doors scraped heavily upward, and a man's low grunt erupted into a yell. A tall, bearded man with an impressive expanse of shoulder lifted the door and heaved it out of the way. His long, graying hair was tied back with a scrap of leather. He wore a bandolier, stocked with ammo, crossways over his muscular chest.

He adjusted the rifle slung over his shoulder and stood at ease before Ilda's throne.

Ilda scowled at the man's relaxed attitude. "So. You've come."

"Yes, my lady." His rugged features crinkled into a gruff smile. "Lieutenant Tynan of the 10th Werewolf Platoon."

"We mustn't tarry. The sun is setting. The time of shifting will soon be upon us." She tested the weight of her mace in her calloused hand. "Report, Lieutenant. Do the werewolves of the mountains finally recognize Ilda as Conqueror?"

"I tell you what, my lady." The lieutenant leaned against the wall and rolled a cigarette. "There are them, a few, that are for throwing in with you. But Dmitri, Czerny, all them." He poked his cigarette toward her to emphasize his point. "They're convinced Ordog's coming back."

"Where are they now?"

He jerked his head northward to indicate the craggy peaks visible past the toppled stonework. "In the caves. Hiding from the sun. Hunting their prey by night." He placed the cigarette on his lower lip and patted the pockets of his olive trousers, searching for a match.

The urgent bay of a hound distracted him from his matches. He smirked. "That's Skender. Lots of rabbits in the brush. Skender! Get your tail in here."

A gaunt hound scrabbled over the rubble and bounded to his master. The hound had a short muzzle and alert, rounded ears. He was brownish gray with patches of white across his belly and around his muscular shoulders. Skender panted and leapt onto his hind legs, but the man pointed to the floor. The hound settled on his haunches, his eyes fixed upon his master.

Ilda frowned at the interruption. "Whoever heard of a werewolf with a dog?"

The lieutenant hunched next to Skender and rubbed him behind his neck. "Skender and me, we've been together a long time. He's good on the hunt, and he's loyal. I would rather have Skender by my side than an entire legion of Dmitris and Mikhails."

"Dmitri's crew, they will not swear allegiance?"

The lieutenant stretched back to his full height. "No." He snapped a match and struck it against the wall to light his cigarette. "Just me and my band. *We're* no fools. We saw the fall of Death-Guardian. We saw the lady of Vandor defeat Ordog. But them, they still call themselves Accusers and pray to the Crimson Dragon Lord."

Ilda rose. "Ordog is gone. The count is gone." She stretched her arms into a V, brandishing the mace on high. "Only I remain."

The man blew out a puff of smoke. "Permit me a word, my lady. Dmitri's bunch are skittish. When Ordog reigned, he could crush two of my kind in each claw while spitting out the bones of three others. You can't blame them for needing reassurances."

Ilda's visage grayed, and her neck veins bulged. "Reassurances, eh? Ha. We'll give that soulless, cringing dragon bait reassurances. Come." She trudged toward the room that once had been the library. The lieutenant stomped on his cigarette and put up a hand to the dog. Skender lowered himself to rest his chin on his paws. The lieutenant nodded and followed Ilda across the uneven floor into the dust-embalmed room. Here, the only light came from a smoldering flicker from behind the shattered window. Littered across the floor were half-burnt pages torn from the spines of ancient books and chess pieces from a never-finished game.

Ilda yanked a cord, and a curtain flew back, revealing a wooden podium engraved with the twisted figures of goblins, wolves, and owls. On the podium was a large book with a cover the color of dried blood. The silver lettering on the cover was in the ancient runes of the dragons. "Do you know what this is?"

"It's the forbidden book! Where did you find it?"

She lifted the cover, but he pressed her hand down. "You know what Tepov said about that book. To read it aloud means banishment and one's name struck from the ranks of the brave."

Ilda planted her fists on her hefty hips. "Count Tepov is gone. We who once served can now do what we please. Your pack wants reassurances. Then listen to Ilda. My mother was one of the wise sisters. And she taught me well. Already, I have tapped into the powers. Zed-Cyphrr is greater than Ordog, for the two-headed dragon rivaled the Golden Dragon as ruler of the ancient cosmos. The spirit of Zed-Cyphrr is strong. And with this book, I can cast the spell that will break the chains and call them forth from the deep. Their voice has spoken to me from the Netherworld, sometimes a shout and sometimes a whisper. The voice is inside me but also all around me." Her eyes glazed, and her mouth twitched into a grin. "They tell me I can defeat Ordog, I can defeat the Golden Dragon. To harness their great power, I simply must travel to the ancient lands and recite the words written on a specific page in this book."

"To defeat Ordog and Vorever? What a coup that would be!"

"Do you think Dmitri and his pitiful pack will come to me now?" Ilda lifted the cover of the book.

"Of course, my lady. With the help of . . . *that one* . . . you will be invincible." He crept closer to peek inside the book.

A shriek erupted from Ilda, startling the lieutenant into jumping backwards and grabbing for his rifle. "What is it? Where?"

"The page! Look!"

The lieutenant lowered his rifle and returned to Ilda's side. Where the page had been, only jagged edges remained creased in the gutter of the book.

"That is the one page we need to wield the power of Zed-Cyphrr! Who has it?" Ilda's fingers convulsed over the ripped edges. And loud enough to shake the souls trapped below in Alsó-Világ, she roared, "WHO HAS IT?"

CHAPTER 7
THE TOWER OF VANDOR (1930S)

Betty entered the training room dressed in the folded gi and long, skirted hajami of kendo practice.

The dojo, with its wooden floor, sidebars, and mirrored wall, looked like paintings of a ballet school she had seen in a book. As a little girl in charity school, she had never dreamed those books she loved to read would one day lead her here to the island of the Golden Dragon Vorever, celestial guardian of all story worlds.

She slipped off her sandals and left them outside the door. "Am I late?" she asked Portia, the gray kitten. The kitten rolled and purred in a patch of sunlight on the glossy wood floor and stretched a paw toward Akira Yamada.

Half in silhouette softened by the filtered streams of sun, Yamada commanded the center of the room. Betty was always impressed at how precisely her Sensei executed the series of komae, or stances, of kendo. He moved his bamboo sword expertly as he shifted from one stance to the next. When he was done, he lowered the sword and bowed toward the window in the wall opposite the mirrors. Only then did he let his attention stray to Betty, who now supported herself on the sidebar and practiced side-to-side leg swings.

"So." He wrapped his overlapping shirt around his chest and adjusted the cloth belt at his waist. "Are you ready for your training, young one?"

"Just warming up." She winced as she yanked her leg back just a bit too far. Determined not to let him see her expression, she faced forward and proceeded with her squat lunges. To fill the tense silence, she announced, "Your idea worked. We stopped the corruption from spreading in *A Tale of Two Cities." Down, stretch forward, stomach muscles taut.* Instead of responding, he faced away. Worried, she rose unsteadily from the lunge with a short "oof" and rubbed the thigh she had strained.

Yamada's features, though placid, conveyed his disappointment. "You are not focused, young one. You are not balanced in here." He pointed to his own heart. "Tell me, where does the balance come from?" He handed her his bamboo sword.

She bit her lip and hesitated, wondering if she dared accept the sword, or if he would pull it away and tell her she was not worthy.

"Go on. Take it."

The bamboo sword he handed her bore the weight of ages, and its top end tugged at her arms. As she gripped the hilt, the wood seemed to sag, as if it, too, longed for a rest.

"Once more," persisted her Sensei. "Where does the balance come from?"

"Peace of mind?" She sucked in her breath and forced her arms to lift the weight of the bamboo sword.

"Yes . . ."

"Faith in Vorever?"

"And?"

Betty frowned. "I always forget the last one."

"Release of self," he reminded her.

The strain on her muscles was too much. She dropped the sword and exhaled her pent-up air. "Oh, yes. That's the one." She looked at her bare feet.

Yamada shook his head and retrieved the bamboo sword. He gazed at Betty as one gauging whether she had enough of whatever it took to be whatever it was they expected her to be. Betty caught a glimpse of this gaze but quickly refocused on her feet.

"Here." He unfolded his hand from her to the mirror. "Look."

She forced her eyes to lift to her own reflection. She saw a girl with an untidy strand of hair falling across her pale, drawn face.

"Alone, you are nothing. *I* am nothing. But with Vorever, we are *everything*," said Yamada. "We are not meant to stand alone. We are meant to fly on the wings of dragons. You *are* the Keeper of the Golden Vigil. You have been granted the light of the greatest dragon of all."

"Will that light be enough to stop the corruption?" asked Betty. "Did I do the right thing back at the Fisherman's Rest?"

"You have put a small patch on a very large wound. Look." He pressed a square on the wall beside the mirror, and the mirror slid upward to reveal a bookshelf. Betty crept closer to the shelf and witnessed the books withering with decay, a powder of green dust shrouding their covers. The sight of the green dust made her hand sting like it had back at the inn, like a stubborn rash that refused to heal.

Yamada sighed deeply. "Young one, I am afraid the time is coming when you will face the greatest challenge of your life. It is not so hard to be a strong warrior when you sense Vorever near, but what will happen when he feels far away? What will happen when you cannot feel his wings bearing you to the sky or when the warmth of his light has turned cold? It is for this you must be ready. For one year, I have been training you here on Vandor, but you have much more to learn, and we have so little time." He rested his sad eyes upon her, his brows lifted as one who dared the tiniest bit of hope.

That touch of compassion, that unspoken reliance on her abilities filled Betty with renewed determination. Yes, she *was* the Keeper of the Golden Vigil. She *was* the friend of Vorever. She would not let her friends down.

Betty twisted her unkempt hair into a bun and slid in a decorative comb to hold it in place. Her eyes snapped to attention as she faced her Sensei and bowed. "Ah!" She did her best to imitate her master's vocal patterns. "But *what* is *time*?"

Yamada's eyes crinkled in delight. "Good. Good. Time is but an increment of eternity."

"Used to measure the length of our current tale," added Betty, from memory. "And now, shall we cross blades at last?" Her heart was beating quickly. This was her chance. She lifted the bamboo sword.

But her Sensei took the bamboo sword. From a shadowed corner, he gathered his baldric upon which hung his katana. He draped the baldric over his shoulder and drew the ancient blade. "This is a mighty sword," he declared, gazing into the shine of the layers of steel forged into the blade. "This sword defeated the monster centipede that once terrorized my homeland. This sword has struck fear in the realms of evil for many centuries." He held it out to her.

Shocked, she staggered back a step. "No, master. It's *your* sword."

"Try it," he urged.

Her hands trembled, but, with a blush, she bowed and accepted the weapon. Her fingers curled around the grip of the katana.

"First, you must learn to connect with the sword. Right now, you are trying to control the sword as if it were solid. Instead, move the sword as if it were liquid, just as the story worlds are liquid. The katana you hold comes from the legends of old, and all legends are in constant motion, in a dance of light and shadow guided by the author, the reader, and the characters."

Betty stopped exerting her own energy and let the sword guide her wrist, shoulder, waist, knees, and ankles in a fluid, gliding motion.

"And now the time has come for you to cross blades, young one. But not with me."

What was he talking about? Who else?

Yamada opened the window, and a large wasp buzzed in past the shutters. No, it was not a wasp. It jingled and sparkled as it whipped about and landed on his shoulder.

"Tondor!" With delight, Betty left the sword on a table and joined her Sensei and the pixie warrior. "What news from Neverland?"

Tondor fluttered her wings and lit from Yamada's shoulder to Betty's cupped hands. Tondor was two inches tall and had stunning blue eyes and two blue wings sparkling in the light. Part of her long, flowing red hair was tied back with a strip of leather into a braid. She was dressed as a warrior should dress. A leather vest covered her white linen shirt, and a baldric crossed over her chest, connected to the twin scabbards she bore on her back. She also wore two belts. The one worn around her waist held the sheath for her dagger. The one looped down over her right hip held the flintlock.

"Ah." Tondor shook her head, resting her hand on the butt of her flintlock. "I haven't been to Neverland in many tocks from the crocodile's clock. But drums tell me the tribes have sailed to the Forgotten Islands, and the mermaids are migrating to the sea. Peter Pan and Frieda are reinforcing a keep on Marooner's Rock to defend Neverland from invaders."

"And we're on our way to help. We *are* on our way, aren't we, Sensei?" Betty blinked at her master, anxious for him to give his blessing for her to travel with Tondor to back up Frieda and Peter.

"This spirit seeping into Neverland is far more dangerous than you can imagine," was his response. "Before you face this foe, you must first test if you can face an even greater challenge. Ready your sword, Tondor."

Betty stared at Tondor in disbelief. "I can't fight *her*. It wouldn't be fair. She's so . . ."

"Little?" finished Tondor, affronted. She swished one of her swords out of its scabbard and flourished it with finesse. "Well, if it's my size that's worrying you . . ." She leapt from Betty's hands, and as she did, she flapped her wings twice, and in a sparkle of light, she appeared before them as one of human size, albeit five foot two.

Betty could hardly believe her eyes. "How on earth!"

"No, only on Vandor," explained Tondor. "And now, Beatrice Talbin, you must test your mettle with *me*."

Betty bowed and lifted the katana. She held it as Yamada had taught her, samurai style, with the palm of her hand steadying the blade. She lashed forward. Tondor blocked the blow with a sideways tilt of her sword. The pixie barely moved. Her graceful wrist worked wonders as her sword twisted and spun to ward off Betty's series of forceful strikes.

Betty stopped and leaned on her upper legs to recover. "I don't see what fighting our friends is going to accomplish."

Tondor laughed. "You call *this* fighting? Come, little human! Do your worst!"

Betty glanced at Yamada. He gave her a meaningful look that reminded her it was not she who moved the sword, but the sword that moved her, for within the sword rested the memories of a thousand noble warriors who had fought before her in countless legends of old. Remembering this, Betty charged forward and bore down upon the pixie's sword.

Tondor broke free of the parry lock and leapt onto a table. She grabbed a second sword from the sheath on her back and formed an X with the two blades. She sprang toward Betty, and Betty arched backwards, swirling her katana forward to block the collision. Tondor jumped backwards, then brought the two swords together in a blow that could have cut off Betty's head had Betty not instinctively ducked. Tondor's two swords crossed again, lower, and Betty jumped into the air, her knees high. She landed on the flat of the two swords, breaking them out of Tondor's hands.

"Well done, champion!" Tondor bowed.

"You have learned much, young one," said Yamada. "But you still have much to learn."

Exhausted and a bit discouraged, Betty plopped down on the floor, one hand falling on her raised knee and the other propping up her chin.

Portia stretched herself on Betty's raised knee and mewed to be petted.

Tondor sat down with both legs crossed in front of her. "What Master Yamada means is we never stop learning. You may be the Keeper of the Golden Vigil, but, as such, you need all the more training."

"This is so," acknowledged Yamada.

Her thoughts upon the past, Betty absent-mindedly scratched Portia under her ears. "I should have watched Ordog more closely."

"Betty," came a serene, fatherly voice. A large, sea-blue eye surrounded by a golden-scaled lid peered in through the window.

Betty pushed to her feet and hurried to the window. She gazed at her own reflection in the shiny eye, her brows raised with uncertainty and eagerness to please. "I'm so sorry I failed you."

"No, you have not failed me. As long as you listen for my voice and trust in my desire to help you, you cannot ever fail me." Vorever drew back so Betty could see more of the dragon's gentle smile and the steady gaze of both his eyes.

"But so many story worlds are in danger."

Vorever's brow creased in thought. "Ordog thinks he is hidden, but he will soon be found. The chart will indeed show the way to ward off the corruption. But first there is something you must retrieve. A page. A page ripped from a book called *The Tome of the Netherdragons*. Finding that page will help your friends far more than any other thing you can do. Akira, consult the codebook to determine which book will take Betty to the one who stole that page."

"And I will go with her," said Tondor. "We shall fight side by side!"

Vorever smiled a kind laugh. "You have a stalwart heart, brave one, and it is good for Betty to have such a friend. But the one Betty will need on this quest is right there. Are you ready, Portia, guardian of Vandor?"

Portia's head popped up in surprise, and she blinked.

CHAPTER 8
APPLEDORE TOWERS (1890S)

Dark clouds scowled over the estate in Hampstead. Out of a pocket of low-hanging fog, emerged Betty, Portia in the crook of her arm. She followed the blear of the two lamps guarding the front porch and read the bronze plate fixed to the arch around the door. The plate proclaimed the fortress as Appledore Towers.

"Right on the button. The good old *Inter-Story Intercessor Codebook* never fails. See?" Betty lifted the kitten to show her the bronze plate. "That passage from Doyle's story was perfect." The kitten formed a lion-roar with her mouth and mrrowed with a rising inflection. Of all the dastardly villains that raised their ugly heads in the Sherlock Holmes stories, Charles Augustus Milverton was certainly one of the dastardliest, and as such, the most likely handler of something as dangerous and sought after as the stolen page from the *Tome of the Netherdragons*.

Betty adjusted the kitten in her arms and stepped back as she tipped her head to appraise the foreboding fortress. She gnawed her lip and nodded as if the movement of her head would induce more confidence. "Now, Portia, we just ring the bell and order him to hand over the page. Yes. That's what we'll do. If he asks, 'What page?' we'll say, 'You know jolly well which page, Mr. Evil Blackmailer.'" She leaned in toward the front porch, but her feet refused to budge. She looked down at her shoes to reproach them and caught a glimpse of the new attire the portal had provided. "I can't believe this."

She had hoped for 1890s finery, the gown of a wealthy duchess. Instead, she wore a white mob cap and matching apron over a plain black dress. Embroidered on the side of her apron in black thread were the initials C.A.M. The portal had given her the attire of a maid.

"A maid? I thought I was past that." Though books had been a refuge for her, she could not rub out the past as an orphaned charity ward put to work dusting, mopping, and sorting at Perlgate, the stately home of her wealthy aunt and uncle. And she knew being a maid in 1890s Hampstead would not be any better than being a housemaid in 1930s Bedfordshire.

The only part of her costume she liked was the brown messenger bag, a satchel with a long strap that hung over the opposite shoulder from the hip the bag balanced upon. The accessory made her feel like Greta Garbo in a spy thriller, and that was some consolation.

Portia mrrowed a warning, eyes fixed on the driveway. The wind was picking up, but Betty could make out a horse-drawn carriage rolling and clopping toward the front. As the coachman steered the brougham and pair around the circular driveway, Betty ducked among the shrubbery framing the veranda.

She peeked past the branches. The coachman dismounted and threw open the passenger door. A spry, slender man leapt down, cloaked in an ulster, his hat pulled over his eyes. He lingered to speak to a fellow passenger who remained in the carriage. Then, he bounded up the stone steps to the front door where he pushed the bell with the jeweled top of his cane.

"I can't see his face," whispered Betty to her kitten. "Who is he?"

Portia simply meowed and watched in suspense.

The door opened, and an elderly butler ushered the guest inside. Fortunately, the floor-length casement windows of the study had been left ajar, so Betty, from her hiding place in the shrubs outside, could see the occupants silhouetted in the blaze from the hearth and could hear most of what they were saying.

The gentleman waved the butler away. He removed his top hat and balanced it on the end of the cane. A heavy-set man rose from a high-backed chair at a desk, his back to Betty, and greeted the gentleman near the mantelpiece.

"Do you have it?" The gentleman spoke with a refined European accent.

"The rumored page from a certain book? Soon. I should have it soon," came the low response.

"You said to be here by nine o'clock precisely." The gentleman flicked open his gold pocket watch and consulted it. "It is not yet two minutes past." He snapped it shut.

The occupant of the house chuckled. "Dear me, no need to fret, sir. She'll bring it, never fear."

The gentleman turned his back on the heavy-set man with a definite edge. He placed his free hand on the mantelpiece, his bejeweled fingers glimmering, and lowered his eyes to brood upon the fire. "You appreciate, I am sure, a man of my position has precious little time to spare."

"Well, well, it cannot be helped." The occupant poured himself some wine. "I'll have it by tomorrow."

Portia ffft-ed at the portly man inside. Betty shushed the kitten and continued to listen.

The gentleman turned, and Betty could make out the shape of his profile, a wavy slant of hair that fell across his forehead, neat sideburns, an aristocratic nose, protruding upper lip, and sharp chin. "Tomorrow will be too late. My ship sails for Cairo tonight."

"Ah, me. That is a pity. And with all that lovely treasure too. But I assure you, Count . . ."

The gentleman shirked off the over familiar hand set upon his shoulder.

Betty whispered to Portia, "A count? Not Tepov, surely!" Portia meowed. "You're right. It couldn't be Tepov." Even so,

Betty crossed her fingers behind her back. With vampires, one could never be too careful.

"I'll be at my hotel." The gentleman was striding from the room. "Send your man when the page arrives."

He stalked out the front door and to his brougham. The coachman whipped up the pair, and the brougham rattled away.

Betty peered through the window to catch a glimpse of the occupant, her breath forming a fog over the glass. She used her hand to squeak the fog away so she could see better, but the man in the study was bent over his desk once more, adjusting the rim of his spectacles. "Charles Augustus Milverton," whispered Betty. "And we want that page too. It looks like we are going to have to wait a little longer."

Portia prrowed a question.

"I suppose he *could* be lying, and the page *could* be stashed in his safe right now. Perhaps we should wait until he leaves the study and sneak in."

Milverton's head rose as if his ears had detected her voice. He pushed away from the desk and was rounding it to approach the casement windows.

Betty's heart jumped, and her breath froze. She backed away and scurried across the lawn. She tripped over her own feet and sprawled forward, dropping Portia. Portia landed on her paws and returned to nudge Betty's hand that had sunk into the mulch. Betty scrambled to her feet and raced to the cover of an arbor near the spiked wall. She who had faced dragons now crouched like a scared little girl running from the bogeyman. She hid behind a laurel tree, clutching the trunk of the tree to keep her hands from trembling.

"Oi, there!" A working-class man called from the other side of the barred gate. Betty jumped.

"Aggie? Aggie me love." The speaker was a tall, ruddy man with the tuft of a goatee. He wore a jaunty cloth cap and chewed the stem of a clay pipe.

Betty set her finger over her lips to hide her smile as she exchanged knowing looks with Portia.

Meow Rah? asked Portia.

Betty nodded. It was indeed *Meow Rah* — or Sherlock Holmes, to be precise, disguised as a plumber. The touch of reddish makeup on his earlobes and the chestnut wig gave him a youthful glow that defied his true age, which, Betty suppose, must be his mid to late thirties.

She remained angled behind the tree trunk, not sure she wanted Holmes to see her all mud splattered. Anyway, in the story, it was the maid, not Betty, with whom he had his rendezvous. She peeked past the low branches at him.

"Shy are we for once?" The disguised Holmes held to the bars of the gate like a jailbird.

Betty coughed and sought to disguise her own voice, but her theatrical Cockney accent came out forced and squeaky. "The plumber, is it?"

The "plumber" angled his pipe to the side and showed his teeth in a bright smile. "Aye, now, Aggie lass, you know we are past all that. Escott to me mates and Johnny Boy to me love. That devil of a watchdog, all chained up, is he?"

Portia's ears flattened. Betty certainly *hoped* the watchdog was not loose. She glanced over the lawn and did not see any watchdog, but she held Portia closer to be safe.

She returned her gaze to Holmes' smile. He had a nice smile, just as Paget had depicted in *The Strand* illustrations. She was tempted to yank the false beard and eyebrows away and say "Surprise!" She remembered, however, Holmes had come to pave the way for breaking into the blackmailer's fortress, bent on saving Lady Eva's honor. Agatha the maid, poor girl, was just another tool in his burglary kit to gain access to the incriminating letters locked up inside. And for now, it seemed, he assumed Betty was Agatha.

The reminder added a bite to her tone. "So, it's Johnny Boy now, eh?"

"None of your pranks, lass, none of your pranks. A storm's rollin' in, but we still have time for a bit of a stroll. Unlock the gate and let me in." He rattled the bars.

Betty remained at a distance. "Tell me, *Johnny Boy*, what are your true feelings for me?"

His eyebrows raised in a hurt expression. "The strongest feelings a man can have, so help me! How can any man resist your soft, auburn hair and your fairy-blue eyes?" He leaned his cheek against the gate and heaved a lovelorn sigh.

Hmph! Betty glared, pulling the frill of her mob cap more closely to conceal her *black* hair and her *black* eyes. She had always admired the famed detective of fiction and had fancied he might return at least a little of her affection. But once Ordog and his dragons had been defeated, Holmes had vanished back to Baker Street. And to hear these words spoken as a lie intended for another woman irritated her. She decided to get even her own way. She blinked and made her lips tiny, like a stereotypical ingénue. "But did ye bring me a bunch of blue ribbons, Johnny Boy?"

"Ah, leave the cheap stuff to yer Jimmy Vane. It hain't worthy of a princess like you. And once he's back from his voyage, I expect he'll have a trunk full of them. But they can't outshine this." And here Holmes drew something shiny from his coat pocket. He grinned past his pipe and thrust the object through the bars. "A bit of all right, what?"

It was a gold ring with the smallest speck of a diamond. "Blimey! How'd you nick *that?*"

"You take me for a thief, Aggie?"

"Aye, you have the looks of a thimble-twister to me. Or even a safecracker, I fancy." Betty looked sideways, wondering if he would catch the implication.

"Have I? Have I really? The only thimble I wants to twist is the passion in your heart."

Laughing inside, Betty glanced at Portia, who wavered her paw up and down to say his performance was so-so.

He continued outpouring his heart. "It's the truth, God help me. And if you lets me in, I'll prove it by asking you to trade that ring of Jim's for the one I have here in me hand."

"Ah, Johnny Boy, I don't have the key. But if you promise to marry me, I'll pinch the key tonight."

His eyes brightened. "Will you, ah, will you, my sugarplum princess?"

Both Portia and Betty's expressions agreed "sugar plum princess" was definitely overdoing it.

Betty stepped toward the gate. "But, first, promise. We're engaged to be married now?"

"If that's what you'd like to call it, my little scone with treacle on it." The plumber accent was faltering, and Holmes held his pipe with a more elegant bend of his wrist.

Betty held the bars and scrunched her nose in a laugh. "Oh, really? *Scone*? With *treacle*? That's the worst one yet."

He lowered his eyelids, smiled complacently, and put a match to the bowl of his pipe to relight it. "Begging your pardon, miss, to be sure. Such a nomenclature fails to do justice to the Keeper of the Golden Vigil herself. Beatrice Talbin." He shot a glance at her from under his eyelids.

Betty started at hearing the clipped stentorian tones. "Well, I had you fooled for a little while."

"Not for long," he replied. "How could I mistake your eyes for Agatha's? And that amateur vocal imitation."

"Well, I knew it was you the moment I saw that ridiculous beard," she flung back.

A poorly suppressed smile played on his lips. "Besides," he said through a wreath of smoke. "You read the book."

"Yes, and since I did read the book, I know the letters you're after are in the safe. But what I'm after hasn't arrived yet. I'll hide out here a bit longer and watch for it. At least that will give you the time you need to go back to Baker Street and fetch your burglary kit."

Holmes' eyebrow twitched. "How did you . . ." He stopped. "You're as good as a palm reader, you know." His face grew serious. "But promise me you won't face him alone." He put his hand through the bars and rested it on her shoulder. "I know you are a powerful and capable young lady. But Milverton is a low, cold-blooded snake, and we're both going to need help taking him on." He licked his lips as he calculated his plan. "Remain here, if you insist, but for heaven's sake, stay out of sight. I'll be back at midnight when Agatha swears the whole house is in bed. And I'll bring Watson. And my burglary kit."

"At midnight then."

"Midnight." He gave her hand a squeeze of reassurance. He drew away, but Betty held his hand a second longer.

"And Sherlock?"

He glanced back.

"Don't forget to tell Watson, you and I, we're engaged."

"Oh, heavens!"

CHAPTER 9
CHARLES AUGUSTUS MILVERTON (1890S)

66 **T**his waiting is madness." Betty crouched with Portia in the flowerbed where they had a clear view of the front gate to Milverton's estate.

Agatha, Milverton's maid, whistled shrilly from the porch. A hefty Saint Bernard waddled up to her from where he had been drowsing and raised his resigned eyes. The maid jabbed her pointer finger toward the kennel, and the dog grumbled himself through the kennel gate. She locked it and clinked through the rest of the keys on the ring, muttering words she had learned in Frying Pan Alley. Her pudgy, freckled face grinned as she held up one key. She hoisted her skirt and galloped to the front gate to unlock it.

As she did, she tore into a tune from the music hall.

Me Johnny was a right one,
But he'll need to fight for me.
Me Johnny was a toff a 'right
And 'andsome as can be!

She turned, tucking the key away in the bosom of her apron. Her black, buttoned boots barely missed Betty's hand as she clomped back to the house.

65

The storm clouds writhed with thunder. Betty ducked under the shelter of a stone bird bath to avoid the splatters of rain. Scummy green mud puddles formed in splotches amid the grass. *Ugh. We couldn't find a nastier spot to hunker down, could we?* Betty's nose itched, so she rubbed it vigorously with her knuckle. The mud from her knuckle felt cold and prickly on her nose. Making a "blech" face, she used the corner of her apron to brush the mud away.

The night blazed with lightning. Portia's fur stood on end. Betty held Portia closer and blinked past the curtain of rain to the clouds. Breaking through the clouds was an ominous winged creature, with a diamond-shaped head pointing toward the estate as it skimmed down in a circular pattern toward Milverton's house. The creature skidded to a landing. The lightning flashed again, and Betty recognized the falcon-sized dragon, Avian.

Avian flapped her ruby-red wings and hopped onto the stone banister and down to the tiles of the veranda. She sidestepped on her back claws toward the casement windows and rapped on the pane. Her brow lowered, and she darted mischievous eyes to the right and to the left.

The window opened a crack, and a gloved hand shot out.

Avian presented the rolled-up document. "The page from the *Tome of the Netherdragons*," she hissed. "And I'm taking a great risk, so you best keep your side of the bargain."

"Of course, of course," replied the occupant. "Blood is thicker than water, they say. I will remember you when the great one comes into his kingdom."

"But before I hand this page over, what reassurances, my love, what reassurances? We're playing each hand against the other, and I need to know who's my friend and who's my foe."

"You have my word!" insisted the occupant.

"Not enough."

"Then what?"

"His signet ring. Give it to me."

"But the count gave that to *me* as *his* reassurance he would pay handsomely for the page. I couldn't part with it. Not until he keeps *his* part of the bargain."

"The signet ring or nothing," demanded Avian.

"Very well. Wait here."

Avian waited, tapping one talon impatiently.

At last, the gloved hand was thrust out once more, presenting a gold and iron ring.

"Yes. The crest. Perfect, my love!"

The gloved hand dropped the ring into a small case and placed it into Avian's outstretched claw.

She tossed the case once with satisfaction. "Now he can't give *us* away without us revealing *his* secrets as well."

Avian relinquished the page to Milverton and pushed herself back into flight, orbiting the house twice. A long, distant howl of a wolf erupted, echoed by a chorus of brother howls, sounding even closer. Heavy paws galloped through the mud, veering, and departing, growing fainter, as Avian disappeared into the storm. Betty held her breath and crouched as low as she could in the grass.

"A fine night, wouldn't you say?"

The voice startled Betty, and she bopped her head on the bowl of the bird bath. "Oof!" She rubbed her head, moved out from under the bath, and joined Holmes and Watson in the rain.

Holmes' collar was pulled up, and the top part of his face was masked in black silk with eyeholes cut out.

Watson took off his coat and draped it over Betty's shoulders. "Shall I congratulate you on your recent engagement?" His eyes twinkled.

Holmes exhaled with impatience. "Not now, Watson. We've got work to do."

Betty allowed herself the luxury of one pout, and Watson drew two more masks from his pockets, one for Betty and a smaller one for Portia. "Came prepared," he bragged. "Portia the cat thief." Watson chuckled at his own pun as he tied the scarf behind the kitten's ears.

"And all the tools of the trade." Holmes gave his bag a shake to clink the metallic objects inside.

"But Milverton's still awake." Betty tied the ends of her own mask behind her head and pulled the collar of Watson's coat more closely around her chin.

Holmes frowned. "And Agatha promised."

"Well, she did cage the dog and unlock the gate," Betty pointed out in the servant girl's defense.

"If only women could be more precise." Holmes stepped away with his hand curled around his chin, recalculating his strategy as Betty frowned at his remark.

"Holmes. Look." Watson pointed toward the house.

The light in the study had darkened. A moment later, the room next to it lit, revealing the portly form of Milverton bending over a billiard table.

"Here's our chance." Holmes nudged Betty to hurry her toward the house. Portia and Watson exchanged glances that agreed this was rather foolhardy, but they fell in behind the other two.

Betty led them to the casement windows. She pressed in the middle where it had been open before, but the latch was now firmly locked in place. She looked to Holmes for a solution. Holmes rummaged in his bag, withdrew a sharp tool, and soon had cut a hole in the glass large enough for him to reach in and lift the latch. He pushed the window open enough for them to crawl in one at a time.

Betty, bedraggled by the rain, moved close to the fire to warm. Along with the scent of crackling wood, Betty detected the overtone of a rich cigar and Milverton's musky cologne.

Holmes surveyed the study, the sumptuous desk with the red-leather, high-backed chair. Across from it was the hearth, and, next to that was the bookshelf with the safe beside it.

Betty tiptoed to the door leading to the billiard room and slanted her head to listen for any footsteps or voices. All she heard was a low murmur and the click of cue sticks followed by a scattering roll of billiard balls.

Holmes whispered in her ear. "If you hear anyone coming, close the door and bolt it."

Betty nodded.

He slipped up to Watson. "Make sure that door is locked." He pointed to the door to the hallway. Watson touched his brim in a salute and stationed himself by the door. Portia climbed onto the desk and curled into a circle of fur to lick away the rain from her coat.

Holmes pulled a stool up to the safe so he could sit and study the mechanisms. "What do you say, Betty? L. Duvilers and Sons?"

Betty peered over Holmes' shoulder at the safe. "I suppose so." To herself, she added, *Doyle didn't actually say.*

"But you did read my monograph?" Holmes glanced up at her with a surely-you-of-all-people-would-have-at-least-read-the-monograph look.

Betty shrugged to say I am terribly sorry, but the last thing I wanted to read was a monograph on antique safes. "There's no combination lock."

"No. This is an older safe, but a good one. The key is hidden in a secret drawer that only opens when the dials are turned in the right sequence. We could work it out with simple mathematics, but the other way is much faster."

Holmes removed his coat and flung it over the desk. He spread out his instruments, flicking his fingers eagerly as they hovered over the tools. Next, he rolled up his sleeves like a surgeon and selected a diamond drill and a sectional jimmy. He hummed to himself as he went to work on the safe.

Betty was impressed when the safe opened as if by magic. She had been so engrossed in watching Holmes at work, she was unaware someone was wheezing on the other side of the door of the study. That someone pushed the door open, knocking her halfway across the room. Charles Augustus Milverton filled the doorway, dressed in a rich black smoking jacket and gold-rimmed glasses. He snapped on the electric light, and Betty gasped, for Milverton was not human but a human-sized rat standing upright and smoking a thick cigar. His long black nose twitched, and his two front incisors snicked over his lip, as his keen eyes whisked from one masked face to the other. His claws were wrapped around a pistol, which he held on the intruders.

Betty shivered and looked at Holmes. His face was granite as he studied Milverton like a strange specimen under a microscope.

"Breaking and entering?" tsked the man-rat. "Ransacking my private belongings? Rifling my safe? I've caught the lot of you! My man is already on his way to summon the bobbies."

With due respect to the threat of the gun, the three intruders raised their hands before them.

"Bad idea to point that." Holmes nodded to the gun. "You little know with whom you are dealing."

The rat bared his sharp teeth and snickered. "We've dealt with you before, *Sherlock Holmes*."

"Oh, I don't mean me. I meant . . ." And here Holmes waved his raised fingers in Betty's direction.

The rat's eyes darted to Betty. "Is it . . .?"

Betty was grateful for Holmes' acknowledgement but wondered what he expected her to do against a readied gun.

"The pawn of Vorever. Good." Milverton sneered as he veered the gun toward Betty. "I have wanted to meet this one. And now . . ."

Portia sprang at the man-rat with a bristling war cry, and Milverton screeched, "A cat!" He spread his claws.

Portia's back arched as she growled Milverton into a corner. Milverton gulped and readjusted his grip on the gun. Portia kept her narrowed eyes fixed on the rat.

Watson moved forward. Milverton waved his gun back around to ensure all knew he still had them covered. Watson stopped. "May I ask a rather silly question?"

Milverton's whiskers twitched as he darted a nervous glance down at Portia and back at Watson. "You may ask one."

"Why do you look like a rat?"

Milverton puffed himself up and was about to fling back a repartee when a shot was fired. It was not Milverton's gun. Milverton dropped his gun, and his jacket seeped with blood as he gaped in shock toward the casement windows.

Betty followed his stare. A veiled woman stood in the opening, the lightning revealing her tall, well-shaped silhouette and a ribbon of smoke drifting up from her gun. Betty expected her to fire at Milverton again, but instead she jerked her weapon toward the three of them. "I want the page. And the signet ring."

"*I* haven't got them," answered Holmes.

The woman looked from the rat-man she had shot to Holmes to Watson, and her eyes landed on Betty and strayed to the messenger bag. "You. You have them."

Betty tried to peer through the woman's veil without success. Past the awful smell of dissipating gunpowder, she caught a perfume – the sweet scent of jasmine. "What do you want with the page?"

"You don't know me," said the woman, "but I know who you are, Beatrice Talbin." Betty touched her own home-made mask to reassure herself it was still in place. It was.

The woman continued speaking in an accent Betty thought could be Greek. "You Intercessors serve Vorever and think it is up to you to protect the universe. The Accusers think they can overthrow the Intercessors and put Ordog in charge. But some of us have a higher purpose. We of the Epilogues choose to serve no one, and our aim is greater than anything the Intercessors or the Accusers can imagine. Now. Give me the page. And the ring."

Another faction? The Epilogues? What could this mean? Betty glanced at Holmes for help.

"Don't look to them," the woman told her. "People will fail you. But your heart will tell you what I say is –" The woman stopped, distracted by Milverton groaning. He was reaching into his vest for something that glinted in the firelight.

The woman shot him full in the chest once more. He fell limp, moaning, "You've done me." His whiskers twitched, and his head twisted and dropped to the side. From his pocket rolled something shiny. Portia pounced at it and swatted it into the corner. It was the signet ring. Betty was confused. She had seen Milverton give the ring to Avian.

The woman swung her gun back at Betty. "Tell your cat to move away from the ring."

Betty glanced at Holmes. Holmes frowned and nodded. Betty sighed. "Portia, come here." The kitten's tail flicked as she guarded the ring between her front paws. Betty reached for the ring, but Portia whirred a growl.

"Give me the ring," insisted the veiled woman.

"Portia, I-I-" Betty sneezed. The sneeze startled Portia, who screamed a *mrrrrrooowwww* and sprang toward the woman with a karate chop motion of her front paws. The woman spun toward the movement. Watson and Holmes took the chance to close in on her and pry the gun out of her hand.

"Haydee! Here!" called a man's voice from the open window.

The woman kept a cautious eye on those in the room as she backed toward the corner, plucked up the ring, and faced the window with desperate eyes. "Let me past."

Betty edged away from the window. The gentleman who had called earlier helped the woman climb out to him. Past the rain and rolling thunder, there was the scuffling of footsteps, followed by galloping hooves swallowed by the night storm.

"Milverton's man will be back any minute with the boys in blue," said Holmes. "Quick! The safe! Get your page and help me throw everything else in the fire. Watson, hold the door until we're done."

Betty took the page from the safe and slipped it into her bag.

Holmes gathered armful after armful of letter packets and papers. "We've had enough of blackmailers and their schemes," he said as he threw the incriminating information into the fire.

Someone was banging on the door from the other side. Watson stood firm, hand grasping the door handle and shoulder pressed into the door.

"Out the window and over the wall, let's go." Holmes grabbed Betty's wrist and pulled her along.

"Wait." Betty yanked herself free. Holmes glanced back with a question. Betty headed to the bookshelf. She set a thoughtful finger over her lips as she searched the shelves. "Doyle mentioned Pickwick. I wonder."

"I can't hold them much longer," called Watson.

Betty breathed more rapidly as she hurried to find what she was looking for. Portia jumped onto the second shelf and patted the spine of one of the books. Betty grabbed Charles Dickens' *The Pickwick Papers*.

"Perhaps we'll meet again?" She gave Holmes a sad smile. She turned to a specific page, grabbed up Portia, and read: "*Happy, happy Christmas . . . that can . . . transport the . . . traveller, thousands of miles away, back to his own fireside and his quiet home!*"

With that, the bookshelf slid away, opening a hidden hallway glowing with light. Betty stepped into the light. She glanced back. A green mist remained where the study had been. Holmes, Watson, and Appledore Towers vanished, although she caught a glimpse of a raven flapping up from the floor and disappearing with the others into the mist before she turned and followed the light back to Vandor.

Chapter 10
A CUP OF TEA (1930S)

The hallway of light led Betty from Milverton's study to a door brambled by white and yellow sea mayweed. The familiar crash of the ocean and the cry of the gull assured her she was back on Vandor. She pushed her hand through the overgrowth and grasped the iron door pull ring. The door opened with the familiar rush of herbs and spices welcoming her into the medieval front room where Vorever awaited her return.

Her servant garb had transformed into a fur-lined cuirass with clasps at the shoulders for her long, flowing cape. Over her shoulder, she still wore her messenger bag, in which was stashed the page she had pinched from Milverton's safe.

The Golden Dragon's wings were folded, and his large body hunched before the fireplace, his head ducked, his neck rounded against the vaulted ceiling. It never ceased to amaze Betty that no matter how big or small the room, Vorever always managed to fit inside.

He smiled his greeting as he levitated a teapot from the hob and motioned for it to pour a stream of steaming water into a mug. "Sit." He spread his talons toward the rocking chair. "You've had a long day, and you need a rest. What will be your brew today?"

Betty pondered the shelves with tea-tins. One tin was light pink, labelled "Rose Tea." Another was beige with the words "Chamomile." One was black with the outline of the London skyline etched on it, the words "Earl Grey" in dun-colored letters in place of the fog.

Vorever noted her gaze fixed on the last one, and, conducted by a golden-lit loop of his talon, the scoop measured out the tea and poured it in the infuser. The infuser followed the glow to dunk into the mug. The tangy, spiced aroma wafted as the dragon sprinkled in some vanilla and sugar and slopped in a splash of milk. He guided the motion of a spoon in crescent shapes through the brew, and the teacup floated into Betty's hand.

She blew on the concoction to cool it and took a long sip. It soothed her scratchy throat. "Thank you. It's perfect." She sat in the rocking chair. Portia yawned, stretched, and hopped into her lap, and Betty steadied the mug to keep it from spilling.

Vorever folded his front legs over one another and settled his chin on his talons like a grandfather happy to spend time with the young folks for a change. "How was Sherlock?"

Betty blushed and focused on scratching Portia behind the ears. "Same as always, I guess." She glanced at the dragon out of the corners of her eyes, and she caught him frowning at the back of her hand.

"Hmm," he groaned. "You're in pain."

Betty lowered her hand. "Just a little."

Vorever's shoulders sagged. He exhaled a plume of smoke through his nostrils and turned to watch the hearth flames.

Betty hesitated, not sure if this was a time for talking or a time for silence. "Who are the Epilogues?"

"Those who serve Zed-Cyphrr." Vorever's brow rumpled sadly as his gaze trailed off into memory. "Zed and Cyphrr were two of the great celestial dragons who communed with me long ago. But, while most celestial dragons found joy in sharing visions of knowledge and beauty, Zed only brought his desire for chaos and Cyphrr her words of temptation. And when both he and she joined forces, uniting into one colossal foe, they targeted my own scales, luring them to turn against me. It was the universe you know as your own that I dreamed to fill the empty place near my heart where the corrupted scales had once been. But, when Zed-Cyphrr crept into your world to spread the contagion of their lies, I intervened. I and the other celestial dragons imprisoned Zed-Cyphrr in the netherworld, and a great stone edifice was placed over the gate to ensure they never escaped. The bits of corrupted stories that remained were gathered into a single tome, and a law was spoken, prohibiting anyone from opening the book. But now someone has opened the book, and the corruption is once more spreading, like the contagion that has marked your hand."

Betty glanced at the rash on the back of her hand and lifted her gaze to the dragon's eyes with a plea for help.

"Fear not," he reassured her. "You have enough of my energy within you to stave off the worst effects of the corruption. My energy will fight off the infection in time. Others have been touched by the corruption and have not been so fortunate. Zed-Cyphrr promises what people in their darkest moments crave: riches, power, revenge. And these others do not have the will to resist."

A stern voice came from the side doorway. "That is why they must never lay their hands on that one page."

Betty looked to Yamada in the doorway. His dark hair hung half on his shoulders and half pulled back into a topknot. He wore a wide-sleeved silk robe with a thick cloth belt wrapped around the middle. His face was like flint. "That one page is the key to unlock the chains that bind Zed-Cyphrr, put there in the event they prove themselves worthy of a second chance. The words on that page would serve as the leash to hinder Zed-Cyphrr from harming others and guide them into a more perfect path. But the Epilogues would use that page to harness the power of the two-headed dragon and bring about the destruction of all story worlds, for that is what Zed-Cyphrr desires." Yamada extended his hand toward her. "Did you bring the page?"

Betty felt in her bag for the page but could not find it. Her heart skipped in panic. "I had it. Where is it?" She glanced around and found the rolled-up page under the rocker where it had dropped. Blushing, she retrieved it and handed it to Yamada with a humble incline of her chin.

"She has proven herself an excellent Keeper of the Golden Vigil." Vorever's chest expanded with pride as he smiled upon Betty.

Yamada unrolled the page and scanned it with a scowl. "She still has much to learn."

Betty looked down.

Yamada shook his head. "No one can be trusted with this. No one except . . ." He held the page up to Vorever.

The ridges in the dragon's forehead furrowed, and his head lowered. He reluctantly took the page in his talon. He breathed fire upon the page, and it crumbled into ash. He scooped up the ashes and put them into the empty Earl Grey tin and fitted on the lid. This tin he held out to Betty.

Alarmed, Betty drew back, but Vorever's expression firmed. Puzzled, she sought his eyes to read his purpose. The mysterious depths of that sea blue reached out to her, drawing her into his very soul.

"She is too young. Evil forces will seek it and try to reconstruct the page. Her life will be in danger." It pleased Betty to catch concern in her Sensei's voice.

"But she is the only one, Akira, the only one." Vorever's deep voice put an end to any debate. "She has been touched by the corruption, and she has survived. She will be immune to its more deadly effects. When she is able, she must take the ashes far from this place, far from me. I would want to be merciful to Zed-Cyphrr, and that would endanger the world all the more."

Betty, though pale at the thought of the "more deadly effects," bowed and humbly accepted the tin from Vorever. She pushed it deep into her bag and whispered, "I promise to keep it safe."

"Even so," put in Yamada, "beware. Both the Accusers and the Epilogues will try to take that tin, and you may be tempted to give in. Remember, you must not give in."

"But," Vorever's voice soothed the tension, "for now, you must renew your strength here on Vandor." He waved his talon, and Betty's empty teacup floated through the air, and a scrub brush met it halfway to squeak it clean.

Betty was about to question him further, but she interrupted herself with a cough that racked her ribs.

Vorever with sympathy raised an insistent talon. "You must rest and recover."

The coughing had left a nauseating pain in her skull. She tried to stand up. "But we don't have time." She collapsed back in the chair.

"Time is but an increment of eternity," said Vorever. "I am eternity by my very nature. So let me worry about time, and you focus on getting stronger. Summon Blackwick, hear his report, tell him what we have discovered, and then you must rest, my child."

PART TWO

THE QUEST

CHAPTER 11
SUMMON BLACKWICK (1930S

Summon Blackwick. Then rest. Betty's throat burned, and her head ached. She looked forward to curling up in the cocoon of the warm featherbed in her room. But first Blackwick. She entered the cupola atop the tower and paused, leaning against the doorframe. In the middle of the chamber was the Golden Candle of Vandor, about the size of a small altar or a large cauldron. The flame dancing on the candle called to her, as it always did, but she hesitated, scratching her hand.

Portia plopped on her haunches, annoyed at the delay. Betty's scarf brushed over the kitten's perturbed ears as she moved to the nook in the far corner where she had arranged her own personalized space. Here was a large, comfy cushion beside a gramophone and a stack of records in their cardboard covers.

When Betty was not feeling up to par, she would lose herself in a book, and she liked listening to music while she read, to immerse herself in whatever mood best matched her reading of the day. For an enticing pirate yarn, a bolero was perfect, and for a bit of Jane Austen, a dash of Pleyel. But now, the weariness in her limbs and the heaviness in her heart took her back three years to 1934 at a specific debutante ball.

She selected Jerome Kern's "Smoke Gets in Your Eyes" per-formed by Lew Stone and his band. She placed the record on the player and fixed the needle on the first groove of the black circle. She watched as the circle spun around and the arm with the needle dipped in and out of the grooves. She could almost see her reflection in the shiny black shellac. She could almost see *Blackwick*.

The voice crooning recalled to her the dance she had had with Edmond when he had returned to Perlgate from university, back when he was the toast of society and she the housemaid. She imagined herself once more sixteen and him guiding her across the floor. She momentarily forgot how awful she felt as she lifted herself on her toes and let her outstretched arm rotate her body like a slow-moving hour-hand. Then, she had been like a little sister to him, and he had been engaged to the wealthy debutante Daphne Graham.

The needle shrieked as Betty yanked it across the shellac. *Daphne Graham.* She was overtaken by a strenuous fit of coughing. As she recovered her breath, she glared at the scratch on the shellac. *Why is it that I've always had to be the one in the background? The one scrubbing in the corner, the one training in a tower — while the Daphne Grahams of the world have their pretty little parties and their slews of handsome suitors.*

But the look in Portia's venerating eyes reminded Betty that, while other girls may have their normal lives, she was the Keeper of the Golden Vigil. She was the friend of Vorever. She had faced down vampires and subdued dragons. The fate of the story worlds depended on her keeping the ashes safe and ensuring Blackwick carried out his mission. Under the weight of this responsibility, she sank to her knees before the candle altar. Portia hopped up on a stool near Betty, pawing the smaller white candle. Betty took the candle and used a wand to flick the burnt wick of the white candle into the melted gold wax of the larger candle. Her mouth formed the words as a matter of routine. "Seven drips, from the wick, and from the thick, will come Blackwick."

She waited and watched the flame. She breathed unevenly through her mouth as she gazed into the smoke and melting wax.

A warm gust of air flurried in through the window, shuddering the open panes. The flicks of black from the candle's wick gathered themselves together to form words. *Ordog in Paris.*

CHAPTER 12
ORDOG IN PARIS (1780S)

The two roaches pushed their heads through a small hole in the wood panel of the garret apartment. Their feelers detected the after-burn of gunpowder, contention, and blood. The only motion they sensed was a spider spinning its web in a corner of the window and the dust particles filtering down through the moon haze.

"It is safe, my lord," announced Thérèse. The two roaches scurried onto the floor and crouched on either side of the panel in the wall, attendants waiting upon their king.

The panel cracked as Ordog shoved his way through. He shook the splinters from his crest and shoulders and stood still, his nostrils ingesting the aromas of the place.

"Ahhhh." A stream of smoke wafted off his tongue. "A dark soul. Its essence calls to me."

He moved into the room, the two roaches falling in behind him. The door of the apartment was ajar, and slumped in front of the door, blocking the exit, was a woman, a dead woman, her head thrown back and twisted to the side as if still in shock. Madame Defarge, the fanatical leader of the revolution who had borne an unremitting grudge against the lineage of St. Evrémonde. This grudge had led Madame Defarge to seek the death of Charles Darnay and, not content with that, the death of his wife and child as well. Now, her glazed eyes stared at some unseen terror, her mouth hung in a wide frown, mimicking the theatrical mask of tragedy. A pistol remained where it had dropped in the struggle, in the folds of the dead woman's skirt.

The aura of the room told Ordog what had transpired here. He could visualize Madame Defarge invading this room, vowing to drag young Mrs. Darnay and her child to the guillotine. However, it seems she had not counted on a will more powerful than hers. Another woman, an Englishwoman, the former nurse of Darnay's young wife. Impressive for the old woman to defy the fury of one so powerful as Madame Defarge to buy time for Darnay's wife and child to escape. The two women had wrestled for the gun – Ordog smelled the struggle. The gun had fired with a terrible explosion. The English nurse had lost her hearing. The French zealot had lost her life. Such hatred, such contention would make the soul all the more delicious.

Indeed, Madame Defarge's soul was tangy and bitter, like burgundy with wormwood. As Ordog infused the green mist that issued from her mouth into his nostrils, his size increased.

The two roaches bowed low and peered up at their dragon lord, now the size of a fox. "You are magnificent," blurted out Robert.

A fragment of broken mirror slanted across the floor, and Ordog's lips curled at his reflection. "Yes," he murmured. "Yes, I am. I must return to the old land. The voyage will be long, and I may yet need your service." A glistening strand of webbing swung down from the shutters beside Ordog, and dropping to the floor from the webbing was a fat black spider. Its eight eyes bulged at the sight of the two cockroaches, and its fangs dripped with venom. Robert eeked, and Thérèse ducked behind the leg of a table. Ordog wrapped his orange tufted fingers around the abdomen of the spider and crushed its body in his talons. It crick-cracked and oozed from between his fingers. *Invigorating! My power returns.*

Robert and Thérèse trembled toward the dragon in awe.

"Do my bidding, little bugs, or be destroyed." Ordog clawed up the side of the wall and pushed open the shutter. He whipped his fiery eye back upon his two slaves. "Meet me at the docks of Marseille." He breathed in the air of the night, his chest expanded, his wings spread. He leapt from the ledge, and his wings impelled him forward over the gray, lopsided roofs of Paris.

Unseen by Ordog, upon the roof, Blackwick sat with his back against the chimney, watching the dragon wing toward the harbor. Ordog would not be difficult to track now.

Blackwick bent his chin against his chest, his face hidden by the broad brim of his hat. He fixed his eyes on a book in his lap. It looked like a prayer book. The image on the front cover was the golden outline of a candle with a flame. On the page open before him were scratched out the black words, *Ordog in Paris.*

He waited, watching the facing page. When Betty summoned him, he would see the words form on the page in golden calligraphy.

The clouds drifted past the moon, and a stream of light fell against the gray shingles, exaggerating the length of the shadow. Most of the time, he found himself adapting well to his new incarnation. When the thrill of desperation seized his heart, when the shadow remembered its readiness with the blade, and when the wolf exerted the full extent of his power, Blackwick relished this new existence. But when the job was done and the light of the moon caught him in her grip . . . then it was he felt the war within.

Why doesn't she summon me?

Blackwick glanced into a garret window at an empty room. He imagined the room aglow with electric light, a roomful of children giggling and romping about, a large dog herding the children into their beds for the night, and the gentle voice of a mother singing them to sleep. He remembered it as if it had been his own memory, but he suspected it was a leftover recollection from when the shadow had belonged to Peter Pan. For, like Peter Pan, Blackwick felt like he was stuck on the outside, unable to open the latched window. Perhaps that's what he really was. A disconnected shadow, a ghost, one lost in the darkness of the past.

A cold gust of wind shuddered Blackwick.

She should summon me! His eyes burned like a wolf in pursuit of his quarry. *I saved her life. She's mine*!

Silence, you! That voice was much more familiar, more like the voice of Edmond Davidson, the man he once had been. *Something is wrong, can't you tell? She's in pain*. He lowered his eyes and clenched his fist, frustrated that he was here and not there to take the pain away.

The werewolf within him was about to snarl back something disparaging when Blackwick's eyes caught movement on the facing page of his book. The golden calligraphy appeared. *I'm glad you found Ordog. It looks like we stopped the corruption in the story world where you are. Does it seem any better*?

With a sigh, he waved his hand over the opposite page, and black lettering appeared as his response to Betty. *Odd things are happening. The Marquis turned into a gorgon.*

The golden calligraphy once more wrote on the page. *Perhaps an effect of the corruption? It might have twisted the words in the stories to transform villains into monsters. Doyle mentioned a rat. Dickens mentioned a gorgon.*

The black writing responded. *What now*?

Again, the gold calligraphy: *Follow Ordog. Learn what he plans. Then, return to Vandor.*

Blackwick slipped the book into his vest and darted down the center ridge of the roof to catch the last glimpse of Ordog before the night swallowed him. At the edge of the gable, he poised like the figurehead on the bow of a ship. He could still hear the flap of the dragon's wings and feel the current of the air veering in the direction of Marseilles and the sea. He shook his head as he prepared himself to whisk into the clouds and follow the dragon. *I just hope whatever authors wrote about Marseilles did not mention anything worse than gorgons or rats.*

CHAPTER 13
THE CLIFFS OF VANDOR (1930S)

After three days of bed rest, Betty's fever broke, and her lungs no longer ached when she breathed. There was a slight prickly sensation on the back of her hand when she thought about the corruption, but, other than that, she was feeling comparatively better. The soft sunlight settled in a lancet window shape across the quilt. She pushed her pillow up further so she could sit back and let the sun embrace her still sore body with its healing warmth. Running a hand through her hair, she felt how straggly and tangled it had become during her illness. She yanked a comb through her long, knotted hair and winced at the tugging. She weaved the strands into a braid. Her weaving was interrupted by a soft pat at her bedroom door.

She tightened the tie on her silk wrap, cleared her throat, and used her trying-to-be-dignified voice. "Come in."

The door pushed open, and Portia pranced in. On the other side of the door was a book left by Master Yamada. Her Sensei was determined to use this time of bed rest to enhance her knowledge of all things required for the mission ahead. The day before, it had been a book called *The Origins of Myths and Fairytales*. Today's book had the prepossessing title of *Runes, Hieroglyphs, and Pictographs*.

"I'm glad Master Yamada is able to find some books that are untouched by the corruption," noted Betty as she settled back into bed and soon became absorbed in what these ancient forms of writing meant and how to distinguish the different symbols. The book even discussed the ancient dragon runes, which, apparently, dragons all over the universe could read. Egyptian hieroglyphs, it seemed, were related to dragon runes. The book was interesting but not overly exciting. But she knew she could not get away with skimming even the boring parts. Her Sensei would expect detailed notes, handwritten in cursive, and then typed, with the typed copy stapled to the originals, all placed into his drawer where he kept her progress under lock and key until the leaders of the Intercessors could assess it.

That afternoon, Betty felt well enough to get out of bed, get dressed, drape her messenger bag over her shoulder, and take a walk across the island. She listened to the roll of the ocean as she gathered a bouquet of blue marsh orchids and yellow kingcups for the front room. The salt in the air invigorated her lungs. But the steep hills quickly tired her muscles, so she threw herself into the swaying grass on the bluff and gazed into the blossom she twisted in her hand. The flower, though lovely, made her feel sad. "I wish . . ." She had startled herself by saying the words aloud.

She wished a lot of things. She wished her mother had never died. She wished she could visit Frieda Fernsby again, to know she was safe. She wished Blackwick would return, and that all this nightmare about the spreading corruption would soon be over.

A hummingbird darted close to her nose. It beat its wings into a blur as it zigzagged up and across as if in a battle against time. Betty gently extended her index finger toward it and said, "Don't fret. Vorever has all the time in the world."

The tiny bird chirped and turned one bright eye toward Betty. Betty tilted her head, wondering what the tiny creature was trying to tell her. The bird twittered and gestured its wing toward the ledge overlooking the ocean. Then, the hummingbird whizzed away to sip the wildflowers across the island.

Betty moved in the direction indicated by the little bird. The clouds rolled in, and the wind tugged at her clothes and hair. A colossal wave broke against the white cliff and recoiled into the sea.

Betty walked onto the jutting ledge of the cliff. Her hair billowed backward. She stopped at the tip of the ledge, gazing into the teal peaks of ocean.

An expanse of shadow spread beneath the surface. With a crash, an enormous golden dragon erupted from the sea, his gentle blue eyes focused on Betty.

She blinked past the splinters of the ocean that precipitated from the dragon and smiled. It was nice when he joined her for tea in the front room, curled up by the fire, but now Betty's breath was stolen away at the sight of his sheer majesty. His wings unfurled to their full expanse, no longer confined by four walls and a ceiling. She spread her arms up to him, like a child reaching for her parent to hold her.

Vorever cupped his talon on the cliff and allowed Betty to crawl into the warm crevices of his palm. He lifted her to be on a level with his eyes.

A stream of his warm breath comforted her, like the softness of an eiderdown bedspread.

"I am here, my child." A tear rolled from the corner of one eye, streaming down to his sturdy muzzle.

Betty peered into the drooping eyes of Vorever with an unexpected realization. "You're . . . sad."

"I am the words, and the words are me," he sighed. "When *they* harm the story worlds, they are doing the same to me. When they touch my child, they stab me through the heart."

Betty lowered her eyes and rubbed the back of her hand. "But you are huge. You can make them stop."

A smile softened his muzzle. "When I called forth the first spark of inspiration, I set in motion a series of spontaneous creations. Every author has a choice. If I forced every story to follow my own plan, I would be no better than Ordog, no better than Zed-Cyphrr. That is why I included that page in the *Tome of the Netherdragons* in the first place."

Betty's heart ached as she shared a fraction of the heaviness within him. She pressed her cheek into the crease of his thumb. "I wish I could make all the bad things just go away."

"Thank you, Betty, for your sweet compassion. But you will need to be very brave. Of all humans, only you can bear the ashes for the length of time needed. And soon you will embark on your journey, taking the ashes far from Vandor, drawing the corruption away from this place."

"Where will I go?"

"Simply follow your chart. Meanwhile, I, too, must leave Vandor. I must travel to the farthest reaches of the universe to seek the help we will need."

"When will you return?"

"Before the last page of the last chapter, I promise you will see me once more. Now close your eyes," he whispered.

She hesitated, but his steady gaze reassured her, and she complied.

"Do you feel my energy within you now?"

She concentrated. But all she could sense was her own weakness, confusion, and loneliness. "No. My hands are cold. My head is numb."

"But," he said as he gently lowered Betty to the cliff's ledge, "I am here all the same. Even when you do not see me. Even when you do not sense my presence. Even when it seems like everything is going wrong. I am with you."

She opened her eyes and blinked a smile past her tears up into the dragon's eyes. With a farewell nod, he resubmerged into the water. She saw his golden scales undulate up and down, swashed by the foam of the wild waves, as Vorever plowed into the rays of sun breaking through the clouds.

Chapter 14
THE PHARAON (1840S)

The Black Sea appeared a wide expanse of churning tar. Now and then, a fleck of light glinted from the moon as that wandering orb avoided the tangles of cloud. Among these clouds winged Ordog, now the size of a pterodactyl. He had feasted well on souls in revolution-ridden France, but now, invading this new story world of the 1840s, he still hungered for souls.

The strata of cloud beneath him shifted to open a sphere of vision through which he sighted a three-masted merchant ship braving the waves.

With a malevolent glint in his one good eye, Ordog cast his shadow across the deck as he hovered down and roosted on the spar. There he hurled a roar into the night, his crimson scales assailed by the cold spray of the sea. He gave his wings a shake and surveyed the deck. The merchant seaman on watch raised the alarm as the dragon's weight threatened to off balance the vessel.

Men scrambled on deck.

A giant of a man, a tattoo stretched across his broad chest, led the charge, armed with a harpoon. He drew back his muscles to hurl the harpoon at the beast, but Ordog rolled his eye and spewed out flames. The harpoon crashed to the deck in a pile of human ash.

The wooden planks of the ship burned. Some men fired pistols, others fought to suppress the flames, and others crossed themselves and dove overboard, screaming. The first mate, a tall, bearded man wearing a dark stocking cap, pushed himself forward past the smoking rigging, dropped his pistol, and raised his hands on either side in surrender. "Whatever you are, have pity."

The dragon pulled back his head. "Pity is not a word known by Ordog."

The weary first mate dropped on his knees. "Quarter, then. The ship, the men, they are yours to command."

Ordog burst forward at the sailor, staring him straight in the eye. "Is this the *Pharaon*?"

The first mate could not meet the intense eye of Ordog. "Aye, the *Pharaon*. Her owner's Monsieur French. She carries chests full of treasure. She sails for Egypt."

Ordog smacked his lips. "Yes, the treasure calls to me. Tell me of this treasure."

"Emeralds, diamonds, sapphires, and onyx.'"

Ordog touched his back, and onto his talon crawled the two roaches. "Robert, Thérèse, scour the ship. Find where they keep this treasure." He set them onto the railing, and they scuttled toward the hatch of the cargo hold. "Meanwhile, *slave*," he condescended to the first mate, "change the course of this vessel and follow me. We sail for the Baltic Sea."

"As you wish."

Chapter 15
THE TREASURE (1840S)

Blackwick swung over the rail and crept onto the deck of the *Pharaon*. He slipped behind a bulkhead to avoid being spotted by a crewmember. Ordog flew before the ship's figurehead, leading the vessel into the blast, fixed on his destination.

Blackwick slid through the crack of the hatchway and spiraled down a rope into the cargo hold. The lantern that swung to the rocking of the vessel was unlit. Blackwick focused his attention on the wick, and it combusted into a flickering flame.

By its light, he discovered treasure chests stacked to the ceiling, marked with labels reading "Thomson French, Esq., Cairo, Egypt." In the center of each chest was a coat of arms, a gold mountain in a field of azure with a crimson cross.

Blackwick wrapped his gloved hand around the lock of one of the chests, and heat emanating from his palms melted the metal. With one yank, he pulled the lock away. He swung open the lid and was propelled backward by a piercing sound wave. He caught himself against the sandbags propped along the opposite wall. He crept forward and concentrated on the contents of the chest – a sparkling mound of gems, green, white, blue, and black. He heard voices coming from within the heart of the gems.

"We must not let Beatrice Talbin live! She'll kill us all!"

"Fool! We can feed on her soul as we've fed on the others!"

"*Sssilenssss! She shall be mine!*"

"I am the watcher, the door that is locked. She will never get past *me*."

Blackwick drew as close as he dared and focused on the gems. His sight zoomed in upon the gems, and within each he detected tiny figures trapped within, like flies swimming in a pool of crystalizing amber. The figures were grotesquely dragon-like.

He slipped the book from within his shirt and opened it to a blank page, where his thoughts formed in black cursive. "Ordog taking fragments of the scales to Alsó-Világ. Instructions?"

He waited, watching the page. A tiny twitch in a darkened corner startled his attention, the flick of an insect antenna protruding from the shadows. Blackwick pounced and snatched up Robert.

Thérèse zipped around a sandbag and scampered through a crack to the deck.

Blackwick frowned at the cockroach in his hand. "What is this?"

The cockroach shrugged. "Eh bien, today, a miserable roach. But my master will make me great one day, you will see. You better not harm me, or he will breathe the fire and burn you to ashes."

Blackwick sighed at the empty threat, for as a man of shadow, cinders, and wax, he was not afraid of fire. "You are a fool to trust Ordog. He will use you and then destroy you."

A discordant clanging rattled the night as Thérèse clung to the clapper of the alarm bell and let herself swing back and forth to alert the crew.

"Allons! Here! In the hold!" cried the little voice of Robert. Blackwick glared at him, his fist squeezing tighter around the thorax of the roach. The stomp of the first mate rattled the planks of the deck. While Blackwick was distracted, Robert wriggled himself free, clomped to the ground, and swished out of sight.

The first mate clambered down the hatch. His pale eyes scanned the hold from one side to the next.

"But he was here, he was here!" insisted Therése, roosted on his shoulder.

The first mate squatted and lifted the melted lock from the floor. "The chest has been forced open. But how could he get out? There are no doors nor windows except for the hatch, and no one could have gotten out that way."

He scowled, scratching his beard. He stood, snatched the lantern, and swung its light across the area. To the right. Nothing but sandbags and ballast and cargo. To the left. Nothing but treasure chests and . . . Wait. Was that a shadow? No, it was gone.

Blackwick had sunk into the shadows in the deepest corner and hid himself there until the first mate gave up, hung the lantern back on the hook, and returned to the deck.

He felt the flame inside the lantern drawing him in as if he would become one with the flame, the wick, and the smoke. At last. She was calling him back to Vandor.

CHAPTER 16
THE LIBRARY OF VANDOR (1930S)

Blackwick funneled up from the wick, a smoky whirl. Resuming his human form, he leapt to the floor in a sweeping bow before Betty. As he rose from his bow, the brim of his hat lifted to reveal his eyes of flame. They connected with the golden swirls in her onyx eyes.

She smiled at him past a stray strand of hair, which she swept behind her ear. "You're back."

His molten core flared inside his chest at the sight of her, and the werewolf part of his nature was for snatching her up and cradling her slender form in his arms, but he reined in his instincts. Instead, he leaned stiffly against the wall and folded his arms across his chest. "You summoned me, my lady?"

"Oh, none of that summon nonsense." She pouted, and that was all he needed to remind himself he would dare a fire-breathing dragon and a never-ending hell if it would bring that smile back to her lips and the sparkle back to her eyes. He tilted his head in concern as he noticed the faded circles around her eyes and paleness in her cheeks. "You've been ill. And . . . you've been in . . . pain."

"But I'm all right now," she reassured him.

He stepped toward her. "You do not need to bear the burden alone, my lady. When you call, I will always hear you. Always. No matter how far apart we are." He took her hands in his.

Yamada entered.

Betty blushed. Blackwick released her hands, lowered his face, and brushed the brim of his hat as he veered to the side.

Yamada assumed a stance of meditation before the sacred candle. "Blackwick," he acknowledged, not looking at him.

"I followed Ordog," reported Blackwick. "He's found the fragments of the dragon titans. They are stored in chests labeled 'Thomson French.' Ordog was taking them to Alsó-Világ, no doubt to revive his army."

"And while Ordog prepares for war, Zed-Cyphrr continues spreading their dark influence upon the world." From his sleeve, Yamada withdrew a copy of *Peter Pan* by James Barrie and set it upon a raised podium before the candle. "Listen. What do you hear?"

From the book echoed roars of battle and cries of pain. From the binding issued clouds of green dust, like the after-haze on a battlefield. Betty clutched Blackwick's arm with tense fingers, the back of her hand burning with empathy for those caught in the grip of the corruption. "Frieda! Peter!"

Yamada solemnly lifted the corner of the cover. Whisking out from between the pages came the pixie warrior, Tondor Char, her face smudged, her clothes tattered, her swords drawn. "Hurry! Close the book!"

Yamada slammed the book shut behind her. With her last ounce of strength, Tondor fluttered to the window ledge and collapsed upon her knees, heaving to catch her breath.

Betty stepped to the window. "Tondor, what happened?"

Tondor sheathed her swords, and, from her belt, she untied a velvet-swathed bundle. She pulled herself to stand at attention, the bundle held like a helmet against her chest. "Neverland is falling. Werewolves have been sighted in the woods and near the cove. And there's something wicked haunting Crocodile Creek. Casualties are high. Every hour another firefly's light goes out and another flower dies. And worse. Peter and Frieda have been captured. I barely got away with this." She presented the bundle to Betty. "When we are ready to go to war with Zed-Cyphrr, this will call the Mer-shaman and her daughters to our aid."

Betty's lips parted in fear as she took the bundle in her hands. Her fingers warmed around the bundle, and it expanded to its original size, and the velvet wrapping slipped away to reveal the Mer-shaman's conch. Betty ran her hand over the splinted ends of the spikes and the cracked whorls of the shell. Her voice was choked. "Will the conch slow the corruption?"

She hesitated and set the conch on top of the book. An ooze spread from the book and crawled toward the shell. Tondor leapt from the ledge and swished out her swords. With a series of strikes, she held back the ooze. "Take the shell away!"

Betty snatched the shell and cloaked it once more in the velvet covering.

The ooze shrank back into the book.

Betty looked from Blackwick to Yamada. "If the conch doesn't work, how can we get in to save them?"

"One thing is certain," said Yamada, "no one can release the full power of Zed-Cyphrr as long as you guard that tin of ashes." He pointed at her messenger bag. "The remnants of the page Vorever left in your keeping."

"The chart," said Betty, recalling Vorever's instructions. "We must consult the chart."

Yamada unfolded his hand, gesturing for her to proceed.

Betty closed her eyes and focused on Vorever. Her hands tingled as the Golden Dragon's power relaxed her shoulders, her neck, and her wrists. Drawn by the candle flame, her body moved closer to the candle. There, she waved her hand to borrow the light and released a stream of gold from her palm. The golden light swirled about the room, gathering the chart from the shelf and unfurling it across the floor. The landmarks *Switzerland 1890s*, *Neverland*, and *Bedfordshire 1930s* were circled. An X, like one found on a pirate treasure map, was scratched across the word *Neverland*. An arrow from *Neverland* spread across the chart toward the ragged outline of *Bedfordshire, 1930s*. Near Bedfordshire, was the clue, "Consult the hidden panel in the book that's drawn."

"Hidden panel?" Tondor landed upon the chart where she marched straight to the word "Neverland." She tilted her pixie ears in confusion. "What tosh and nonsense is that? Book that's drawn? What could it be?"

All eyes fixed on Betty, waiting for what she would say.

"Let's check the library. If there's a book that's drawn, I'm sure we'll find it there." Betty opened the door. The others followed Betty down the stairs to the endless circle of shelves within the vast inner walls of the tower. The winding red carpet guarded by bannisters of gold sparkled with magical possibilities.

Since her arrival, Betty had become more familiar with the way the books on Vandor were organized. The lowest level held the original tales from the earliest times, tales spoken and carved in stone. The next level were the epics and legends committed to papyrus, then those inscribed on parchment. The third and fourth floors were stories from Victorian and Edwardian England. The highest levels were the language of song: chants and ballads; sonnets and symphonies.

The shelves were arranged so that offshoots of other stories were in a Cartesian plane from one another, depending on how they intersected with other tales. Portia jumped onto the shelf most at eye-level with Betty, and paced, rubbing her sides against the spines of the books.

"A book that's drawn. Drawn from the shelf, perhaps?" Betty selected *Tales of Neverland*. She flipped to a page and read aloud. Nothing happened.

"Try again. A different part." Tondor Char flew to the book and kicked the pages forward with the toe of her boot. "This one!" It was a part where Peter appealed to the lost children to clap their hands to show they believed in fairies. Betty read it aloud. Nothing happened.

Betty released a frustrated sigh. "It usually works. When I focus on where I want to go and read the right passage, the portals take me *somewhere.*"

Yamada's eyebrows knitted in concentration. "Some portals are locked more tightly than others. With the corruption overtaking Neverland, it will not be easy to find an open door. I will retrieve the Codebook."

"Wait," said Betty, hoping to solve this on her own. "I remember, Milverton locked his front door, but we were still able to get in. We broke our way in thanks to a side window and a bag of burglar tools. So perhaps the chart is telling us to find a hidden side door, and that side door is in Bedfordshire." Betty pressed her hands to her head. But then, she had an idea. "Portia."

The kitten turned her attention to Betty.

"Vorever has gifted you with a connection to these books. Which one will take us to Bedfordshire, 1930s?"

The kitten sauntered up to Betty with the deliberation of one saying, "You might have asked me in the first place" and rubbed her whiskers across Betty's leg. Portia closed her eyes complacently and moved to the shelves. She leapt up to the first shelf, then, the second shelf.

"Lively now," urged Tondor.

Portia leapt up to the third shelf. There, she pushed a ragged, thick paperback down from the shelf. Blackwick, with lightning reflexes, caught the book as it fell. "1937 Edition of Bradshaw's Railway Guide?"

"Look. This page is about to tear out." Betty flipped to the page sticking out and found, circled in pencil, "Bedford Station 3:51 aft." She smiled. "Well, Cousin Leslie did say traveling by train is what any *normal* person would do."

CHAPTER 17
GATEWAY TO ALSÓ-VILÁG (1930S)

Ordog's weight rattled the bridge as the elephant-sized dragon thumped across the extension spanning the icy chasm to the courtyard of the Carpathian lodge. He was followed by the remnants of the merchant ship's crew. The sailors were bent, red streaks from a whip across their backs as they dragged the treasure chests along. Dmitri and the werewolves loyal to the Accusers drove the sailors with snaps of the lash and devilish snarls. Thérèse and Robert rode on top of a treasure chest, like tiny sultans borne in a litter.

Avian, in dragon form, perched on the centermost spike of the iron gate guarding the lodge. She crooked her neck down at the approach of Ordog. "My lord, my lord!" She flapped down and bowed low. "Your enemies are scheming. You return just in time."

Dust flew around Ordog as he settled before the gate. "And how is it with Alsó-Világ?"

"It hungers for your presence, my lord."

His muzzle curled with a self-satisfied sneer. "Yes, no doubt." He raised the brow that arched his one good eye, as he examined his front talons. "Fear not, small one. Soon I will resume feeding on the souls within. Soon I shall revive my army. Soon my enemies will be vanquished."

Ordog ruffled his wings and pushed forward to enter the gate, but a shield of woven green light pulsed across his path. Wherever he tried to move past the bridge, a web of green light sprang in and out.

Dmitri's whip poised in mid-motion as he stared in awe at the phenomenon. "It is powerful, my lord."

Fury rippled down the scales on Ordog's back as he grimaced at this new obstacle. "What is this thing that dares come between me and my lair?"

The sailors exchanged fearful glances and viewed their new master with a tinge of doubt. The two roaches flicked their antennae as if unable to grasp what was happening.

"WHAT IS IT!" Ordog's roar blared across the mountain peaks.

Thérèse and Robert crouched low on the treasure chest and sought a crevice to hide in until the "all clear."

Avian pointed toward the towers with her talon. "There, my lord, there! The one who has betrayed us all!"

"Betray me?" Ordog reared his neck, throwing his crimson muzzle across the dusk in fury.

Up on the battlements, between the turrets, sparked the glints of ready rifles, aimed by the wolfish marksmen who had Ordog and his followers in their sights.

A woman's cackle echoed from the highest tower where stood Ilda, her arms spread wide and her eyes ablaze. In one hand, she waved the silver mace as if she alone could conduct the symphony of the skies. In the other hand, she brandished the *Tome of the Netherdragons*.

"Stop, Ordog! You don't frighten me anymore. I reclaimed the *Tome of the Netherdragons*! Its power protects me now. Leave this place! You are no longer welcome here!" The spiked metal ball at the top of the mace caught the rays of the dying sun, and it deflected a shaft of blinding light in the direction of Ordog's werewolves. Dmitri howled in pain, and his fellow wolven taskmasters threw their arms over their eyes, whimpered, and slung backward.

Lieutenant Tynan and his fellow wolf guards exchanged snickers at the plight of the former alpha of their pack.

The sailors released their hold on the treasure chests. Avian's eyes darted from Ilda to Ordog, as if wondering who would dominate the day.

Ordog snuffed out a puff of disdain and sneered. He scraped his talons across the ground before him as a beast gearing up for the charge. He lowered his neck and pointed the horned top of his head like a battering ram. He heaved forward, crashing through the force field. A green pane of light splintered and cracked, and, with a zip, it disappeared.

Ilda lowered her arms, dumbfounded.

The sailors cringed and bowed before the chests to once more surrender to their burdens.

"The forbidden one has no power," screeched Avian with a look blending dismay and amazement. She flapped out of hiding and strutted back and forth before the gate. "The page! The page! I tore out the page! To save you, my great lord, I tore it out!"

"Hmmm." Ordog shrugged. He cast his challenging leer back up at Ilda. "And you? Will you serve me, slave?"

The guards on the tower looked to their pack leader. The lieutenant firmed his mouth and raised his eyes to Ilda.

Ilda cursed under her breath and forced her back to bow and her knees to bend.

The lieutenant's head dropped to his chest and his shoulders slumped. With a tug of his mouth to the side of his muzzle, he gave the signal for his men to lay down their weapons and yield to the might of Ordog. Skender, crouching low behind his master, flattened his ears back, and rumpled his nose upon his paws, glancing with worried brows from his master to the rest of the disheartened guards.

Ordog's laughter shook the mountain tops and echoed across the valleys. "Ordog has indeed returned. Alsó-Világ awaits. Come, Dmitri! Come, Mikhail! Sons of the moon, souls of the damned! Follow Ordog, and we shall raise the titans once more. We will be more powerful than Vorever."

"Aye! Aye!" cried Dmitri with renewed zeal. "We follow Ordog! Hail Ordog!"

"Hail Ordog!" echoed the sailors.

"Hail Ordog, hail Ordog!" squawked Avian.

"Hail Ordog," said the lieutenant in a low growl.

Ilda spat through the gaps in her teeth. "We will need an ally."

The lieutenant stood a step behind her and to her right. "Fear not, my lady." He kept his eyes on the horizon and his voice low. "I know of such an ally."

CHAPTER 18
BEDFORDSHIRE (1930S)

The train braked with a grind and a whoosh at Bedford Station, Bedfordshire, where January snow was powdering the platform. The middle-aged men in their black coats and black umbrellas, and the middle-aged women in their beige coats and green and red scarves pressed out of the train doors. The conductor waved them on, telling them to "mind yer step now" and "have a care there."

Betty stepped off the train and looked around the platform with the sort of unease one feels after a long stretch of being shut away from the public. She wondered if she would remember how to behave like a working-class girl from Bedfordshire. She fixed the beige beret the portal gave her at a slant and tightened the belt on her mauve coat. Hung over her shoulder was the messenger bag with the tin of ashes.

Blackwick followed her off the train, carrying a frayed-edged black umbrella with a handle shaped like a wolf's claw. He angled the panels of the umbrella in a way to disguise his shadowy appearance, and what with the snowfall and the clatter of the station, he blurred with the other gentlemen with their black coats and black umbrellas.

Tondor balanced herself on the metal stretchers inside Blackwick's umbrella, as if sitting on a twig of a tree back in

Neverland. "*Ayai*, it's cold!" Her teeth chattered as she drew her hood up around her red-tinged pixie ears.

Blackwick growled. Betty looked at him in surprise but saw that a splat of snow had struck his arm, causing his skin to steam as if scalded by acid. Alarmed, Betty touched his sleeve. It felt like cinders sifting through melting wax.

"A chemical reaction," he explained, gritting his teeth. "When water meets burning wax, combustion is imminent. So says Professor Walsheim."

"What does that mean in plain pixie?" asked Tondor.

"It means," interpreted Betty, "we need to get out of this snow. This way." She clutched his hand in hers and led him to the newsstand. His hand felt firm and warm.

The newsstand with its round metal roof and protruding eaves afforded protection from the flurries. A young man stood near the front waving the latest edition of the *Bedfordshire Times* and proclaiming the latest talks of Germany with Italy and the local news of a fire in Kingsley Road.

Betty skimmed the headlines while Blackwick leaned against the brick wall of the newsstand and spread the wax of his sleeve over the area the snow had scalded. "Where to first, my lady? Shall we stop by Perlgate and give Aunt Amelia a bit of a fright?" He drew his cape mischievously across the lower part of his face and chuckled like a villain. "I am the ghost of Edmond past!"

Betty could not resist a laugh and gave him a playful push. "Don't you dare."

"No time for detours." Tondor sounded cross. "We need to find our way to Neverland. We need the hidden panel in the book that is drawn, like the chart says. Peter and Frieda are counting on us."

"There's only one place in Bedfordshire to rival Vandor for books," put in Betty. "And that's Hamberdeen's shop."

The thought of Mr. Hamberdeen surrounded by his stacks of books that no one came to visit anymore but that he continued to arrange and rearrange with the diligence of a guardian of the realm made the wintry afternoon seem warmer and the clouds less gray.

"Look! The snow is letting up a bit, and the shops are only a ten-minute walk from the station." Betty led the way. "Just keep to the eaves and mind the slush."

It had stopped snowing by the time they arrived at the shopping district of Bedford. The pedestrians had left boot prints in the snow on the pavement, and the occasional vehicles had left tire tracks in the slush on the street. The old Barley and Rye commanded the corner. The pub was a gabled brick building. Through the bay windows, the passers-by saw a warm glow surrounding the silhouettes of the working-class patrons. Across the street on the corner opposite the pub, Blackwick stopped Betty.

"You might warn me when we're approaching the points." Tondor caught hold of the umbrella's frame to keep from tumbling.

Betty followed Blackwick's eyes to the side door of the pub where a red-scarved woman in a trench coat and high heels slipped out and cast furtive glances down both sides of the street.

"Avian." Blackwick guided Betty into the shelter of a shop door's overhang.

"What is she after now?" Betty stretched her neck to catch a glimpse of Avian over Blackwick's shoulder. His clothing was softer than she expected, with the warm scent of burnt cedar wood.

His chest tensed against Betty's coat. "From now on," he bent his chin to look Betty in the eyes, "we assume everyone is after that tin in your bag. Everyone." He angled his head as if to catch the faintest sounds. "She's gone." His chest relaxed a bit.

But Betty could not relax. The once familiar street was cloaked in fear. The wind felt colder, and the shadows stretched longer and darker. The rosy-cheeked proprietress in the doorway of Aunt Fanny's Antiques gave them a nod, but her smile looked forced, and her eyes glared suspicion.

"What do we do?"

"Mr. Hamberdeen will know." Blackwick prodded Betty to continue along the pavement. She held his arm as they passed the antique shop and approached the bookshop. Every voice, every passerby startled her. Mr. Pennington, on the other side of Hamberdeen's Used Books, popped out of his confectionary shop to turn over the wooden sign hanging from the doorknob to show "out to tea" instead of "welcome." Betty had often visited Mr. Pennington to order holiday sweets for Aunt Amelia, but today he acted like an ill-tempered stranger.

The sign declaring "Hamberdeen's Used Books" was a comforting sight. Betty's foot was nearly on the doorstep when Blackwick once more stopped her. Tondor, jolted by the abrupt standstill, cursed in Pixie.

Reflected in the glass of the bookshop window was Avian directly across the street. Her face was half concealed by the newspaper she held, but her piercing ruby eyes peeped over the top and zeroed in on Betty.

Betty clutched the strap of her messenger bag and backed away from Hamberdeen's door. Perhaps Avian could sense the ashes. Betty feared her visiting the shop may make Hamberdeen a target for their pursuers. She moved her lips, barely making a sound. "We need to find out what she knows."

The shadows in Blackwick's face worked as he pondered their options. At last, he gripped Betty's shoulder. "You stay here and watch the bookshop. I'll slip around back and take her off guard."

"But I want to –" began Betty.

Blackwick held up one finger. "Stay here with Tondor." Before she could protest, he handed her his umbrella and whisked away into the alley.

Tondor slid down the pole to the crook of the umbrella handle and formed a shield over her eyes to focus on the woman. "I could make short work of her. Just give me the word."

Avian dropped the paper from her face, and a predatory grin curled on her crimson lips. She crushed the paper, flung it away, and charged toward Betty.

Betty pressed against the wall of the bookshop, keeping a steady eye on the approaching woman. Tondor drew her dagger and breathed on the blade for luck.

A lorry vroomed around the corner and shook the street between Betty and Avian. Once the lorry had passed, the woman had vanished, but flapping wings and a grating squawk resounded above the street, and Betty blinked up to see Avian in dragon form soaring in and out of the clouds.

Betty looked around for Blackwick but in vain.

"There she is!" Tondor leapt from the umbrella into flight. Betty jerked to her right where dragon wings were disappearing into Aunt Fanny's antique shop.

Setting aside the umbrella, Betty dashed into the shop.

The bell on the door clattered, and the heavyset proprietress raised her weary attention from polishing a brass vase. Tondor ducked behind a cluster of vases.

"What'dye want? Oh." The proprietress tilted her head. "Ain't you the parlor maid what used to work up at Perlgate?"

Betty's attention darted across the shop, a clutter of dinted armor, chipped wood, cracked porcelain, and molding bronzes. Tondor lit on a display table, edging behind the knick-knacks, dagger ready.

"Yes, ma'am," Betty said. "Did someone come in here?"

"No one as I saw," replied the proprietress. "And mind you don't drop nothing. The items in this shop are priceless, and I doubt even Sir Eric would cover the cost."

Betty nodded and crept past a shelf of staring porcelain dolls, scraped up model ships, rolled up canvases, and empty picture frames. She slipped to the back where unsteady stacks of unopened crates marked "fragile" lined both sides of the aisle. She caught movement to her left, and she turned to look. It was her own reflection in a tarnished mirror propped against a crate next to a steel jemmy. Betty closed her eyes in relief, but when she opened them, Avian's dragon jaws were swooping at her face. Betty gasped a startled scream, and, in an instinctive action, she snatched up the jemmy and used it like a sword to block the dragon's lunge. The clang of the collision propelled the dragon backward against the bric-a-brac.

Avian shook herself in a flurry of ceramic fragments. She hissed and glared at Betty. "You stole the page from Milverton. Where is it?"

"I don't have it." Betty forced herself not to look down at her messenger bag. She held the jemmy Kendo style, the goose neck end pointing inward, and the chisel point aimed outward toward her opponent.

Avian ruffled her wings. "You killed Milverton."

"No." Betty stepped in an arc to gain a good angle of attack. "That was someone else."

A knowing glint flashed in Avian's eyes, and her maw gaped in an eager grin. "Thomas Hamberdeen. Ahhhh. You were taking the page to him!"

"No," retorted Betty, her heart pounding in fear for Mr. Hamberdeen. She firmed her grip on the jemmy.

Avian lowered her head and raised her dancing eyes. "Perhaps I need to pay him a visit, eh?"

A shadow of a wolf loomed across the dull glimmer of the antiques. A congealing pillar of cinder, wax, and shadow reconstituted into human form on the other side of Avian, and an arm crooked around her neck from behind.

Blackwick growled into Avian's ear. "Tell Ordog it's no good sending the *little* dragons."

Between gasping for air past the chokehold, Avian smirked. "Ordog, my love?"

"So." Tondor leapt out from behind a cracked basin, her tiny dagger aimed at Avian's pupil. "You work for Zed-Cyphrr!"

"Me?" Avian snorted a laugh. "I work for myself, for whichever side pleases me most." She rolled her eyes back toward Blackwick and wriggled her scaly body in his arms. "Like you once pleased me, *Professor* Davidson."

In disgust, Blackwick backed away from her. The dragon sent out a shrill screech of exultation and shot straight up. Tondor leaned on her dominant leg and let her dagger fly after Avian, but the subdragon ducked. Blackwick lunged after her, his fingers stiff and curled. He swiped at the dragon's tail, but she whisked out the backdoor.

The proprietress peered down the passage between crates and jumble. "What's going on here?"

Blackwick, chin sunk on his chest, blended with the dusky debris. Betty looked anxiously from him to the backdoor to the shop owner.

"I cut myself." Betty bit her lip at the lie but thought it preferable to saying the dragon had gotten away.

"Oh, come here and I'll fetch you some sticky plaster," grumbled the proprietress.

"I'm all right. I'm leaving," Betty told her. Blackwick met Betty's disappointed gaze and winced his apology. She simply shook her head.

The proprietress muttered back to her work.

"We can't go to see Mr. Hamberdeen now," whispered Betty. "We can't let Avian know he has anything to do with our mission. Anyway, just because he owns a bookshop does not guarantee he has the book we need."

Blackwick tore off his hat and rumpled it with frustrated fingers. "Why else would we be sent here?"

"'Consult the hidden panel in the book that is drawn,'" Betty recited once more from the chart. "'Panel, drawn.'" Betty pressed her palms together and rested her mouth against the index fingers as her mind reached for all associations related to the chart's clue. "What is a book that is drawn?"

"A picture book?" suggested Blackwick, with a doubtful side flip of his hand.

"Or a drawn book with panels," Betty continued. She paced a few steps forward and turned back to face them. "I've got it. Comic books. The little sectioned off illustrations are called panels."

"But hidden?"

Here, Betty could not resist a triumphant smile. "Who do we both know who hides their comic books?"

Blackwick's eyes glinted with amused realization. "Not Sir Wheeze-a-lot himself."

"Yes, I mean, no, not 'Sir Wheeze-a-lot.'" She gave Blackwick a scolding shake of her head. "Our cousin Leslie. Aunt Amelia thought they were a waste of time, so I was always finding them under his pillow or stashed in his underpants drawer."

Tondor folded her arms across her chest with a cynical scowl. "I don't know. What kind of comic book would have anything to do with Neverland?"

"Wasn't he barmy about that Inspector Farnesworth chap?" Blackwick asked. "'Inspector Farnesworth Down the Nile.' 'Inspector Farnesworth in the Klondike.'"

Betty nodded and clapped her hands. "I wouldn't be half surprised if there's an 'Inspector Farnesworth Climbs the Matterhorn' or 'Inspector Farnesworth versus Captain Hook.'"

Blackwick's tension eased. "So, it's off to visit Perlgate after all, is it?"

"No. Not Perlgate. Instead, I think I'll give Leslie a ring. It's almost teatime, but we may yet catch him at police HQ." She strode down the aisle and peered around a clanky suit of armor at the proprietress. "Ma'am? Might I use your telephone?"

"My telephone?" The woman looked as if she were about to spit up a piece of bad meat. "There's a phone box round the corner. My telephone indeed!"

"Right." Betty felt in her messenger bag, hoping the portal had given her enough change for the call.

CHAPTER 19
LESLIE'S COMIC BOOKS (1930S)

Leslie felt silly sitting in the tea shop. Most of the patrons were older ladies in decorative hats with matching pocketbooks, sipping tea and gabbing about the weather, which had been dreadful, and about their husbands, who had been equally dreadful, and about their diets, which they were going to forget just this once since the other ladies insisted they try the cakes and scones.

Leslie ducked his head to hide between the tiered serving trays, one with puffs and the other with petit fours. Why had Betty asked him to meet her *here*? Why couldn't she have oozed her way through the shaving mirror in the office water closet or emerged through the precinct maps past the thumbtacks and masking tape? Why did those Intercessor chaps always have to make things so dashed complicated?

"Aren't you Mr. Mallowan?" A young lady's voice startled him.

Leslie turned to drop a curt greeting to whichever friend of mother's it was. He did a double take of the mousy blonde and her fidgeting hands and bolted to his feet. "Miss Graham. I didn't see you. Please, do sit down. And *Inspector* Mallowan." He pulled out a chair for Daphne Graham, daughter to one of Bedford's leading families and the former fiancée of his cousin Edmond Davidson.

She sat, clutching her gloves and her purse on her lap. She squinted her blue eyes. "Now, I must know. Is what they say true?"

Leslie's mouth paused half open. There was a lot for someone to wonder if it could possibly be true or not. Had he met Sherlock Holmes? He had. Had he used a magical book to defeat a dragon? He had. Had he escaped death from a blood-thirsty vampire and had breakfast with Peter Pan? Of course. Why not?

But before he could ask her to clarify, she continued. "If Edmond's going to throw me over for some snip of a servant girl, at least he should have the decency to tell me himself." She fumbled with the snap of her purse as she sniffed and her eyes grew red.

Leslie reached for the handkerchief in his breast pocket but paused to reflect on whether he had used it or not. Satisfied it must be clean, he offered it to Daphne. "I don't think it's like that at all. Betty thinks the world of Ed, but it's not anything –"

"How would *you* know?" She snatched the handkerchief and frowned even more. "Anyway, you're an inspector now. The least you could do is tell me where Edmond has gotten to."

Leslie leaned back in his chair. He had become accustomed to playing it cool since his run in with the vampire. Sometimes a chap had to make it up as he went along. "Yes, Edmond. He's a bounder. Always was. All that knight in shining armor rot was his way of getting around people."

"How dare you. He is the most wonderful man in the world. You're just jealous of him." And Daphne sobbed loudly into the handkerchief.

Leslie glanced around, hoping no one thought he was the one who had made her cry. "What? Me? Jealous of ol' Smarty Pants?" He was about to tell her about how "ol' Smarty Pants" had gotten himself turned into a werewolf but then had died but then had come back again thanks to Peter Pan's shadow, a lantern, and a drop of bottled hope. But before the words came blurting out, a restraining hand landed on his shoulder.

"Leslie. Daphne." It was his cousin Betty who stood behind him.

"Ah! There you are, Betty ol' girl." Leslie was relieved to finally have someone to help him manage Daphne.

Daphne averted her eyes to the corner of the ceiling like a little girl who would throw a tantrum if her favorite scones were not served.

Leslie glanced from Daphne to Betty and noticed Betty had assumed the simmering aloofness of her servant days. Not wanting to appear rude, he helped Betty with her chair and reseated himself. "There now. Here we are."

"I'm sorry, but I have an appointment." Daphne rose, so Leslie had to return to his feet and help her with her chair in reverse.

"Oh, must you toddle off so quickly?" Leslie was doing a bad job of masking his relief at her decision.

"Do stay, Daphne," said Betty curtly.

Leslie scowled at Betty as if to say why on earth would you ask her to stay.

"No, I really must be off," insisted Daphne. "But you will look into the matter for me, won't you, *Inspector*?"

Leslie made a little bow to say he would, and Daphne left with her friends. She reached for the door, but the door swung open on its own. She blinked at the door and at the shadow hovering against the wall, a shadow that bowed toward her. An odd expression clouded her features. But she recovered and followed her friends out the door.

"Thank God Daphne's gone," Leslie declared once the door had swung shut behind her. "Now, don't we have . . ." he leaned across the table and lowered his voice to Betty ". . . Intercessor business to discuss? By the way, how did you get here? In a puff of smoke?"

"No, I took the train, like any *normal* person," Betty retorted with a smirk. "I asked you to meet me because we need your help."

"Well, you've called in the right man. Daphne's looking for Edmond. No doubt you want me to find him too. Inspector Mallowan, at your service."

"No, Leslie."

"No what?"

"I know where Edmond is."

Leslie watched her with foreboding. "Do *I* want to know where Edmond is?"

A cold tap on his shoulder and a shimmer of a shadow out of the corner of Leslie's eye told him they were not alone.

"Don't tell me it's you, Ed."

"Actually, it's Blackwick now," corrected Betty.

Tondor Char stepped out from behind a small stack of bite-sized cakes on the table and leaned against the milk pitcher.

"Well," Leslie smiled, "I had forgotten about the . . ." He stopped himself, looked around warily, leaned forward, and whispered, "pixies."

Tondor frowned and pushed her auburn hair back from her shoulder. "I have not forgotten you, Crossbow-archer and Dragon-slayer. And right now, we of Neverland can use a brave man like you."

"I knew it." Leslie whipped out a little notebook and pencil. "Point me to the scene of the crime, and I'll have it solved for you in no time."

Betty crossed her arms and rested her index finger upon her lower lip. "In short, we need to stop the corruption from spreading into every book everywhere before the Accusers and Epilogues discover I have the page they are looking for. Only now there is no page, nothing but ashes in a tin."

The outline of a hand pressed on Betty's shoulder. She looked up at the vague impression of Blackwick. He shook his head sternly and directed her attention toward a table across the room.

Betty gasped at seeing Avian in her human form seated at the table, sipping tea and focusing on a folded newspaper.

Leslie blinked and shook his head to clear it. "Eh, what? Page? Ashes? Tin?"

"Sh!" Betty lowered her voice even more. "What we actually need are your comic books. Did you bring them like I asked?"

"Yes, but you can't be serious." He put away his notebook and pencil.

"Deadly serious," Blackwick's voice whispered in Leslie's ear.

Leslie scratched his ear with annoyance. "Stop breathing in my ear. You sound like a dying smokestack. And, yes, as a matter of fact, I do have my collector editions right here." He drew the comic books from the pocket of his overcoat draping the back of his chair. He slapped them onto the table.

"Softly," warned Blackwick. "Accusers are everywhere."

Leslie moved his chair a few scoots away from the shadow.

Betty moved to the chair closer to Leslie and picked up the comic book on the top of the stack. "Hmm." She looked at the title. "*Inspector Farnesworth Never Says Die*, eh?"

"Right." He grinned and rubbed his hands together eagerly. "There are at least four juicy murders in that one. Wait." His hands slowed. "Don't tell me we're traveling through a comic book to a place where *we* might be the juicy murders?"

Betty nodded. "Mhm."

Leslie groaned and buried his face in his hands. "I should have thrown those comic books out like mum said."

Tondor prodded Leslie's sleeve. "Come, brave warrior. Neverland awaits."

Betty looked toward the table where Avian had been, but the chair was empty. Betty kept the comic book, excused herself, and navigated past poised cups and rattling caddies to the deserted table. She checked behind the curtain and under the tablecloth to make sure Avian had really left.

Blackwick slipped up beside her. "She must have overheard us."

Betty lifted the discarded serviette from the plate and found a notebook with the top page ripped away. She held it under the lamplight to read the indentations. "Thank goodness she has a strong hand. If we examine it carefully, we may yet make out what she wrote on the page she took with her. They're dragon runes." She turned the notebook under the glare to inspect it. "It's a list. 'Two Cities,' 'Crocodile Creek,' and 'Mountain Pass.'"

"The first two are crossed out," discerned Blackwick, looking over her shoulder. "There's an arrow next to the last one."

Betty traced the direction of the arrow with her finger. Her heart clenched. "They're settings from the stories in the order of their planned invasion. Paris, Neverland, and . . . what is the other place?"

"Do you have the chart?" He lifted the flap of her messenger bag and withdrew the chart, which he unfolded across the table so he could study it. "Oh, yes. *Neverland* is marked with the words 'Find a foe that is a friend,' and next to *Switzerland, 1890s*, it says 'Find the words never spoken.' What book do you know that's about Switzerland?"

"*Heidi*, of course." Her eyes widened at the thought of the danger targeting the little orphan girl staying with her grumpy grandfather in the Swiss Alps.

"These Epilogues are moving faster than we can keep up, it seems," said Blackwick, refolding the chart. "We'll need to split up. Tondor and I will go with Leslie." He slipped the chart back in her bag and, raising his hand, he adjusted his vest.

"Right," said Betty. "Meanwhile, I'll visit Mr. Hamberdeen to find a way to Switzerland."

Returning with Blackwick to Leslie and Tondor, Betty handed the comic book to Leslie and asked him to leaf slowly through the pages. One panel caught her attention. "Stop," she said. "That's it." It was a purple panel where Inspector Farnesworth, his eye a straight black line over a dot, stared out a window. A word bubble floated over his head, and Betty read the Badaboom font. "'Egad! Have they up and flown like a fat lot of pixies?!!'" At that, Leslie, Blackwick, and Tondor were swept away in a portal of light, and Betty remained in the tea shop. She worried the other patrons may have seen the unusual departure of her friends, but Maggie, the lady at the counter, only shook her head and tsked that her companions would be so rude as to leave her to pay the bill.

CHAPTER 20
AVIAN'S BARGAIN (THE NEVER YEARS)

Avian, in human form, ripped the red scarf from her head and shook her hair loose as she did a model-runway walk into the Napoleonic study. Punctuating her walk was the steady tick and tock of a clock on a mahogany desk. The timepiece was an iron circle of Roman numerals, its gears worked by the tipping back and forth of weighted scales, like the scales of justice.

The lamplight cast her shadow upon the majestic map of the world spread across the wall. Her shadow collapsed upon itself and grew jagged wings, and once more Avian was the falcon-sized dragon. She flapped up onto the desk, framed by quills in inkwells.

"Ahhh," the subdragon croaked. "Monsieur French. I know what you seek. You did not find it at Milverton's, eh? And what of your treasures, my love, your treasures? I know where they are. I can bring them, yes, I can bring you everything you seek."

At the desk sat the gentleman who had called on Milverton. A fur-lined, gold-braided coat was fastened over one shoulder of his close-fitting uniform. Haydee stood on his right, her perfect hands folded serenely before her as the clock continued to tick and tock.

French bent his chin upon his steepled fingers. "So, the favored one of Count Tepov. Whose side are you on today?" He pushed back his chair as he stood. He lifted a letter opener from the desk and studied its hilt. "The rat, Milverton, he was supposed to deliver the page. Whatever became of that page, I wonder."

"The hated one. She has it."

"The hated one?" He stabbed the letter opener into the corner of the desk. The clock ticked. The clock tocked. "Ah, she who haunted the old well. I remember."

"Yes, yes, she is on her way here, aye, to Neverland."

He wrenched the blade out of the wood and used it to point at Avian. "Are you sure?"

"Of course. I overheard their plans."

"And I am supposed to trust you?" French held the blade of the letter opener under the subdragon's chin.

Haydee placed her delicate fingers on his arm to calm him.

"It takes much risk." Avian tapped back from the point of the tool. "But I will deliver to you the page and the treasure. For a price."

French flung the letter opener onto the desk with a disgusted oath. "What is your price, you miserable spy?"

"Spy, my love? Perhaps you would be more reasonable if I told you I know who you are." She fluttered her wings and reassumed the form of a woman in a red wrap and matching heels.

French's eyes narrowed, and he tilted his head back a bit. "What do you know?"

"The ring. Yes, I have the signet ring." She lounged across the desk toward him.

Haydee clutched French's shoulder and drew him closer to herself. "*You* do not have the ring."

Avian laughed. "Don't I? Milverton gave it to me. The ring with the same crest I saw on your treasure chests. The same you have engraved on your letter-opener." She flourished her prize, the small case Milverton had given her, but when she opened it, it was not a ring at all, but a gold-colored cigar band. "Curse that blackmailer! He palmed it after all." She flicked the cigar band aside.

A knowing smile hovered over French's lips as he drew the signet ring from his pocket and slipped it onto his finger. "Did you mean *this* ring?"

"No matter." Avian crossed her arms in a tantrum. "The point is, I know your true identity. Perhaps Ordog, too, would want to know. You are a man with a treasure, the title of count, and you seek to balance the scales of justice. In all the pages written, one name stands out. Edmond Dantes, the Count of Monte Cristo!"

"Hush!"

Avian's eyes lit, and she uncrossed her arms. "There is a price for my hush."

"What is your price?"

"Ah, my love, not gold, no, nor rubies, nor diamonds, nor any of your vast treasure. I only ask that I may be there when Beatrice Talbin hands you the page and you unleash the full power of Zed-Cyphrr."

Haydee glared suspicion. "We have heard your loyalty lies with Ordog. Why have you so suddenly changed your mind?"

"Ordog is my father and the father of my brothers, but he cursed and exiled my brothers, fearing they, as the male heirs, would rival him for his power. Me, he thought he could control. But he did not know I am to be feared far more than my brothers ever were. When I call, my brothers will work for *me*."

"Very well. Help me recover that page . . ." Here French jutted his sinister glare close to the face of Avian. ". . . and I will give you whatever you ask."

"Beatrice Talbin will do anything to save the ones she loves. It is her weakness. That's how you will control her."

French raised a cynical eyebrow and turned to the woman beside him to read her view on the suggestion. "Haydee my dearest?"

Haydee's mouth curled a fraction. "We will see what our new recruit has to say about this one."

French tilted his head with a slight smile. "Yes, a good plan. Lieutenant!"

A side door pushed open, and Lieutenant Tynan, in human form, barged in, chewing the meat off the leg of a well-braised fowl. He paused, wiped his beard, and looked from one occupant to the other. When he recognized Avian, he glowered and tossed the meaty bone to the hound following at his heels. "It's Ordog's little toady!" The lieutenant readied his rifle and raised its barrel toward Avian.

She sniffed and looked away from him into her compact mirror, tracing the rouge on her lips with the nail of her little finger. "What about you, old man?" She turned to the lieutenant, letting a streak of red smear across her chin. "Leaving old Ilda for greener pastures?"

The lieutenant's finger tightened on the trigger. "We've been tracking you, little harlot. When you fell in with Ordog, I called out for an ally through the werewolf dispatch, and we located our former brother." He indicated French.

Avian darted French an interested sidelong glance.

Haydee rested a calming hand on the lieutenant's shoulder. "And you have shown yourself to be a warrior with honor. I value your word. Tell us, can we trust this Avian to help us find the page and reclaim our treasure?"

The lieutenant leaned forward across the desk and studied Avian like a hunter studying a false lead left by his quarry. He wrinkled his nose in distaste.

Avian raised a weary expression. "That evil smell is your own."

The lieutenant snarled, and his fingers closed in on her throat. She laughed and snapped her compact shut in his face.

"Avian! Lieutenant!" ordered French. "At ease."

The lieutenant grumbled and forced himself to relax. He looked to his dog, Skender, who returned his gaze with comradery.

"Our main objective is Ordog," explained Haydee. "We may not be able to trust this *subdragon*, but we can use her help, if she can do what she promises."

"I do not make promises I cannot keep," said Avian.

Haydee kept an impassive expression. French looked at her for an answer. She gave a slight nod in response.

French hinged back toward Avian. "Very well. Bring me the rest of my treasure, and we will deal with Beatrice Talbin."

PART THREE

FRIENDS AND FOES

Chapter 21
HAMBERDEEN'S BOOKSHOP (1930S)

M r. Hamberdeen sighed as the snowflakes speckled the front display window of his used book shop. Outside, the shoppers with their wraps and trench coats merged with the snow, like colors on an impressionist's canvas. A tap on the window startled him out of his reverie. He adjusted his spectacles and stepped closer to the window. Past his own salt-and-pepper-haired reflection in the glass, he saw a young lady with bright black eyes and a beige beret. She gave him a smile and a wave, and her lips formed the words, "Let me in."

Hamberdeen could not help but return the smile. "Why, it's Betty." He smoothed his rumpled cardigan and hustled to the door.

As she worked her way out of her coat, Betty ran her eyes over the dusty shelves tumbling with old books. She hung her coat and messenger bag on the coat tree near the entrance and headed back into the familiar nooks of the old shop.

"So many memories." She slid her hand over the back of the settee. "Sherlock sat here I remember. And Daniel Khumalo was in that chair. And Miss Fernsby . . ." She glanced back at the rare books section where she had first met her friend.

"Yes," sighed Hamberdeen. "Still in Neverland, I hear."

"Yes, poor Frieda." Betty sat on the edge of the settee. "I'm afraid we're up against something awful now. The corruption . . ." She scratched the back of her hand.

"Yes," he replied grimly. "I've moved several books to my storage room in the back, hoping to keep it from spreading. What does Vorever say we are to do?"

She bent over the table. "All we can do now is follow the chart. Leslie's comic books have taken the others to Neverland, and now I need your help to get to Switzerland and 'find the words never spoken.' Here, I'll show you what the chart says." She stepped back to the coat tree and reached in past the open flap of her messenger bag. She found the chart, but gasped when she realized the tin was no longer there. *Where's the tin? Her mind raced. It was there when I made the call from the telephone box. Who took it? Avian? No. Who was close to me?*

"Edmond. Blackwick. He took it. That's right. He was worried about Avian." And a flashback of that moment replayed in her mind in slow motion. As he had returned the chart to her bag, she had caught out of the corner of her eye the shadowy outline of Blackwick pocketing the tea tin in the front of his vest.

"But *he* can't take it," exclaimed Betty, her anxiety mounting. "Vorever says *I'm* the only one immune to its dangers. If Blackwick has it . . ." Her breath sped up as her mind whirled.

"It's all right, Betty. It's all right." Hamberdeen's calm certainty helped her to relax, but her eyebrows remained uplifted in concern. "Remember," he explained, "Blackwick is not like you and me. He's been to the Land of Shadow and back. A candle made from the golden wax of Vandor burns at the core of his being."

Betty squeezed her eyes shut and told herself that what Mr. Hamberdeen said made sense.

"Now, what were you going to do with the chart?" he asked. "Something about Switzerland?"

Betty unrolled the chart. "I think it might be a copy of *Heidi* we need, probably an early edition."

"Ahhh." He raised his index finger. "It couldn't be *Heidi.* Johanna Spyri published *her* book in 1880. The chart indicates we need a book set in the 1890s. And you and I both know of a book from the 1890s where Switzerland is a key setting." He smiled with a twinkle in his eyes. "I think you can guess what it is."

Betty puzzled. "No, I . . ."

"Oh, come now." He stood and looked over the bookshop, peeking under papers, lifting cushions, and putting misplaced halves of pencils into his pocket, removing them, and putting them back onto the shelves. He recited, "'It was on the third of May that we reached the little village of Meiringen, where we put up at the Englischer Hof . . .'"

Betty tapped the side of her head. "Of course! Why didn't I think of that! Sherlock Holmes. 'The Final Problem.'"

"Exactly. And it so happens I have the 1894 edition of *The Memoirs of Sherlock Holmes* published by George Newnes Limited. It's somewhere back here." Hamberdeen led Betty down the familiar, creaking slant to the rare books section. She breathed in the familiar musty smell of faded covers and cracked leather spines.

"Ah! Here it is." Hamberdeen set his hands on a book with a faded blue cover and a gray spine. On the top of the spine was a horizontal gold bar, under which were engraved dark gold letters over a gilt square spelling the title *THE MEMOIRS OF SHERLOCK HOLMES*, and below it, in slightly smaller letters, by A. CONAN DOYLE.

Betty took the book and opened the pages with delicate care, for several of them were already loosening from the binding. As she leafed through the pages, a dusting of green particles puffed from the pages, but the particles seemed to be avoiding her hand. She coughed and examined the table of contents. They were still intact, so she turned to "The Final Problem."

She met Hamberdeen's eyes, and they both seemed to be thinking the same thing. "He dies at the end of the story," she said.

"Yes, I remember," replied Hamberdeen.

"But he comes back in 'The Empty House,'" she added, mostly to reassure herself.

"True." He nodded and adjusted his spectacles.

She looked away from the book into the darker recesses of her mind. "But Watson didn't know he was still alive when he wrote it. What if . . ."

"The story worlds work in strange ways, and now we have this corruption mess on top of it," acknowledged the bookshop owner, straightening the ends of his cardigan. "But we're Intercessors, are we not?"

"We are."

"Then, are you with me?" he asked.

"You know I am."

"Very well. Next stop, Reichenbach."

CHAPTER 22
ILDA'S LOT (1930S)

Ilda raked the bramble and leaves into hapless piles in the wild wastes of the garden. Muttering curses, she scraped and clawed at the dead things the way she wished she could be scraping and clawing at Ordog. The drone of insects and the caw of scavengers competed with the scuffle of Dmitri and his werewolves prowling the perimeter of the ruined lodge. They watched to keep Ilda in her place and her werewolf followers in exile.

Before he had withdrawn deep within the mountain, Ordog had surveyed the ruins of the lodge. He grimaced in distaste at the gardens. "The hated one. Her energy lingers here." To diminish Beatrice Talbin's hold on the lodge, Ordog had commanded Ilda to clear the old garden and dismantle the well while he ingested the essence of the souls bound in Alsó-Világ. "It will take time to savor the souls of these sailors," he had murmured. "Men who have been broken have the tenderest souls of all." That was the fate those loyal to Ordog could anticipate.

He had left his two roaches in charge of guarding the treasure chests in his inner sanctum. They were to sound the alarm the second any thief set foot in the treasure room. When he was ready, Ordog would call on Ilda to perform the ritual to

134

summon the trapped titans out of the gems and back to their former greatness. And she would have no choice but to obey.

Ilda's rake froze as a woman's voice interrupted the dusky din with an eerie lullaby.

Shadow children, hear my tale
Born of woe, born too frail
Bones are brittle, blood's too dear
But shadow children need not fear

Ilda lifted her head and parted the straggles of hair that had fallen over her eyes. *Not that Beatrice Talbin again.* Ilda raised the prongs of her rake to strike.

But the woman seated upon the well's ledge was not Betty. Avian in her human form took in Ilda's expression and trilled a triumphant laugh. "No fears, my love, it is Avian."

"Traitor." Ilda shook her rake and flung a haggish "Bahhh!" at the subdragon. "You stole the page."

"And where is the book now? In Ordog's keeping, yes?" Avian leaned back on the base of the well. In each hand, she held one of the ropes connected to the well's bucket and swayed back and forth, like the girl who monopolized the best swing on the playground. Her glint of superiority was fixed on Ilda. "So would the page to harness the power of Zed-Cyphrr be if I had not taken it. I traded it to Milverton, and Milverton was to trade it to another, one destined to awaken the two-headed dragon at last."

Ilda yanked the bucket from Avian's hold, and Avian had to catch herself to prevent tumbling into the murky depths of the well. "Thanks to you," raged Ilda, "all my plans, everything I've worked for is wasted! Now, I have no page, no book, and no werewolf army. Nothing."

"Only as long as Ordog remains." Avian rose to her feet. "We serve him because it is wise . . . for a time. But your mother taught you many spells, not so?"

"Of course, it's true," she huffed as she retrieved her rake, "as my husband learned too late. I can concoct a poison that will still even a vampire's lips. I can turn a fly into a falcon, and a subdragon into a worm." She shook the handle of the rake at Avian as if the rake were a magic wand about to work its curse.

"Wait. Hear me."

"Talk." Ilda's frown deepened, and her eyes throbbed as if ready to explode.

"The spirit of Zed-Cyphrr is strong. With the aid of that spirit, I believe you can work the spell for transporting the treasure into another story world."

Ilda released a fraction of her tension, and a leer spread across her wrinkles. "Yes. Yes. Perhaps I could. But where would we send it?"

"Another seeks revenge. An ally. He will help us get the page that will channel the might of Zed-Cyphrr, if we can deliver his treasure."

"It will not be easy," muttered Ilda. "First, the roaches. You will need to trap them before they can sound the alarm and awaken Ordog."

"Easy enough. They will think I am bringing a message to our great dragon lord. They will never suspect me."

"Yes, good! But to transport the treasure will require the use of the *Tome of the Netherdragons*. Ordog has hidden it."

Avian laughed. "But the irony of it is, the great one put me in charge of keeping it hidden. Mark my word, you will have your book."

"And the man you mentioned. Will he work with us or against us?"

"He is someone you know from years past. He hates Ordog as much as we do."

"Who?"

Avian flipped her hair as her eyes sauntered across the garden. "He calls himself Monsieur French, but he is really the Count of Monte Cristo. You and I know him as . . . Miroslav."

"Miroslav is alive?"

Avian nodded.

"He is determined, indeed." Ilda scraped her hands together as her eyes gleamed with eager anticipation. "Then, it is as good as done."

CHAPTER 23
HAUNTED NEVERLAND (THE NEVER YEARS)

Neverland was never a land like this. A green mist hung over the hills. The toadstools and tree stumps that usually danced with the merriment of pixies, were now dark, decayed, and silent. The grass, dry as hay, bent haplessly in the breeze. The trees were moss-shrouded and gnarly with gaping hollows like silent, ghostly screams. A yellowing pollen dropped in steady streams from the boughs.

The ground was sloshy, which Leslie discovered as he took his first step in leather slippers, and the cuffs of his striped pajamas felt damp on his ankles. *Not quite fair ol' Shadow-Togs gets to be the lone musketeer, while I'm left in my beddy-bye best.*

Blackwick balanced on a hollow log, scrutinizing the ground for traces. He stopped and stooped to pluck a drooping daisy half-submerged in mud. He twisted it in a forlorn pirouette between his thumb and index finger, his eyes cringing in compassion.

Tondor hovered near Leslie, staring in dismay at the decay all around. "The corruption is spreading faster than I thought."

Blackwick handed the faded daisy to Tondor and jumped from the log to a mossy boulder to fix his eyes on the horizon. "Find the foe that is a friend." The words escaped under his breath.

Leslie noticed the weight of the daisy made Tondor sink, and he took it from her hands. He was about to toss it away, but she stopped him.

"Don't. It once danced happily on the meadow and gazed into the light of heaven."

Leslie shifted, discomfited by so much to-do about a dead flower, but when she crossed her hands over her heart and heaved a sad sigh, he nodded in condolence and hunched down to lay the daisy to rest in the shade of a tree stump.

Glancing up from the burial, he blinked, for he could have sworn the stump had a window and a door. He bent closer and peered in. The interior of the stump was like a doll's house, with little furniture made of leaves, twigs, and discarded bits of bric-a-brac. On a little table made of a used thread spool were a tiny seed cake and a berry pie. A shapely pixie with dark bobbed hair, wearing a close-fitting, forest-green kirtle over a beige chemise, spun about upon her toes as she gazed at her reflection in a shard of glass. As she spun, she noticed she was being watched, and her face turned bright red.

Leslie was about to stammer his apology when the pixie burst out the window in a fluster of wings and high-pitched curses and buzzed about him like an angry wasp.

"Beg your pardon," said Leslie.

The pixie planted herself on a toadstool and gave Leslie a scolding sidelong gaze. "There *is* a door knocker. It may surprise you to know door knockers are used to knock on doors." She drew back with an exaggerated gasp as if the news had startled her. "Anyway, how dare you romp about in nothing but your night things, Mr. L. M. Whoever."

Leslie looked down at his smoking jacket, noticing the initials L. M. embroidered on the chest pocket with silver thread. He patted the initials with approval but felt something inside the pocket. It was a pocket notebook and a pencil. "I did say I was sorry." He seated himself on the above-ground root of a tree. "But we'll need to take a statement. Procedure, you see." He prepared the pencil. "Name, occupation, and whom do you suspect?"

The pixie's face brightened as if seeing him for the first time. She fluttered her eyelashes and darted close to him. "I'm afraid the mist was in my eyes. But now that I see you . . . My, aren't you a lovely human. We don't have gobs of them here, you know."

"Humans?" Leslie wrinkled his brow.

"No. Lovelies. And you *are* a lovely, I must say. My name's Katrinka, what's yours? Don't tell me. 'L. M.' stands for 'Lovely Man.'"

"No. It's Leslie. Leslie Mallowan."

"Oh, gosh! Not *the* Leslie Mallowan. Leslie Mallowan the destroyer of Death-Guardian and friend to Peter Pan?"

"Ah." Leslie, pleased with the recognition, smiled and tossed his head to the side to encourage his hair to wave back across his forehead. "I mean, I did have *something* to do with it. I could tell you stories that would . . ."

"Not now," said Blackwick from his look-out. "I see something. Just over those hills."

"Oh, yes." Katrinka snapped her fingers. "Where's Tondor? I must tell her. Something terrible has happened. Something awful."

Tondor had been surveying the area to check for signs of danger. At hearing her name, she pushed the tufts of grass aside and charged past them to her fellow pixie. "What is it, Katrinka? Speak up."

Katrinka plopped down on the toadstool, her thigh-hugging skirt creeping above her knees, and she sobbed. "It's awful. It's terrible. What are we going to do?"

"You mean the fiend that haunts the creek?" Tondor shook Katrinka by the arms.

"Yes. I mean, no. I mean, there's something even worse." Katrinka's eyes widened. "The pixies are all in hiding. They've burrowed themselves in to hibernate until this dark season ends. All except me. I'm too curious to sleep. There's a handsome

140

gentleman who's seized the keep, and they've got Peter and Frieda under lock and key."

Tondor reached for her swords. "Yes. The werewolves almost caught me as well, but I managed to elude them just as their great galoot of a hound was about to pounce. The last thing Peter cried out before they were dragged away was, 'Find Betty! Find Blackwick! Call for backup!'" Tondor flashed her twin swords before her battle-ready face. "The backup is here. Let's go."

"Wait. Listen," commanded Blackwick.

A distant gravelly voice bellowed a tune more than a little off key.

Blackwick whisked himself away in a wisp of smoke and materialized at the crest of the hill before Leslie had even started up the slant. Tondor buzzed into flight with Katrinka fluttering after her. Leslie had to hurry to keep up with them.

Out of breath upon reaching the top, Leslie drew the comic book from his side pocket and rolled it to form a sort of spyglass. Through this, he had a view of Crocodile Creek below. Despite its name, he saw no crocodiles. In fact, he saw no life at all, except for an overspread of algae half hidden by a low-lying fog.

Tondor landed on the outstretched limb of a leafless tree and pointed eastward with her sword. "There."

Leslie and Blackwick looked in the direction from which the discordant voice was coming.

Fifteen fiends in a Deadman's Swamp
Ten to scratch and five to chomp
Fifteen fiends in a skewered plot
Yo-ho-ho and a bottle of rot

A raft loomed up from the east and glided down the creek. The singer was a piratey sort. That is, he wore a black tricorn hat and an eyepatch and was dandified in the finery of the seventeenth century rogues of old, but he was not a human pirate. Oh, he stood upright like a human, leered like a human, and even sang like a human, but he was, in fact, a crocodile, with a wide grin, one trouser leg tucked into a handsome silver-buck-led boot while the opposite leg was a stump finishing up as a peg leg of silver. He leaned his weight on a wooden crutch tucked under his left arm, and, with his free hand, he waved a broad blade and poked the tip of it at the lad who worked the long oar. The lad simply stared and obeyed, as one under a spell.

Tondor returned her blades to their scabbards and drew her flintlock from her thigh holster. She checked its barrel for ammunition, steadied the aim, and fixed her best eye on the target. "So, Silver Boot is back. Ready for a round of pixie pepper, eh?"

Leslie lowered the barrel of the flintlock with his index finger. "Wait. First, we need a statement. We'll nail him on charges of kidnapping, trespassing, and disturbing the peace." He scribbled some notes.

"This isn't Scotland Yard," Blackwick reminded his cousin. "What we need to do is find the foe that is a friend. Solve that riddle, and we can stave off this fiend's grip on Neverland."

"Ugh. Riddles give me migraines, I . . ." Katrinka was flitting past the tree with a woebegone face when she stopped and stared at Blackwick, stunned. "Oh my! Aren't you a vision of shadowy bliss."

Blackwick was taken aback. "Um, thank you. But." He cleared his throat. "Who is this Silver Boot? I sense something familiar about him."

"I bet *you* can guess, my darling." Katrinka swayed with her pudgy arms held coyly behind her back. "I bet *you* know everything."

"Katrinka!" scolded Tondor. "I'm sorry. I've tried to teach her manners, but there's no help for it. She's a shameless flirt." Tondor shook her head and re-aimed her flintlock at the croc-odile pirate.

Katrinka giggled and sang, "When life provides a lovely view / I can't help shouting view halloo!" And she expressed her exuberance with a series of somersaults in the air.

Blackwick waved his black gloved hand to brush away the momentary interruption and focused on the raft and its crew. "The boy. He's under a spell. Could he be one of the lost boys?"

Tondor perched on Blackwick's shoulder. "Not any lost boy I remember."

Katrinka rounded her hands and formed an imaginary spyglass with them in front of one eye while she winked the other. "Whoever he is, he's certainly cute."

"You stay far away from that raft," warned Tondor.

The raft was rounding the bend.

Fifteen men on a dead man's raft
The angels cried, and the devils laughed
Fifteen hounds from the pit of gloom
Yo-ho-ho and a bottle of doom

Katrinka held her hands behind her back with a look of exaggerated naïveté. "If you ask me, great big shadow man, that pirate is nothing like Captain Hook. Nor Starkey. Nor Mullins. Nor Jukes. Not that I had any dealings with the crew, mind you."

Leslie scratched his head as if invigorating his scalp with thinking power. "So, if he's not one of the local pirates, he must be from *somewhere else.*"

"Brilliant, Mr. Bad-Marks-in-Geography." Blackwick doffed his hat and slapped it against his thigh to free it from the stream of pollen. "But there are lots of places that are *somewhere else.*"

"But lots of somewhere elses with crocodile pirates?" challenged Leslie. "Ha! Let that sink in, Mr. Wolf-in-Wax-Clothing. Half a mo." A new brainstorm hit him. "Wasn't there a book where some dreary lot kept singing about 'fifteen men,' 'a dead man's chest,' and a 'yo-ho-ho, and a bottle of rum'?" He hopped on one foot to empty his right slipper of pebbles. "Of course. The song, the peg leg, and all. It's Long John Silver!"

Blackwick blinked, impressed. "*You* read *Treasure Island*?"

Leslie checked his slipper and replaced it on his foot. "Well, ahem, there *was* a comic book, you know."

"Very well, Mr. Silver." Blackwick returned his hat to his head and set the brim low. "It's between you and me now. We'll see who is a foe and who is a friend." He skidded down the slope of the ridge, keeping his balance as easily as if the dirt were the ocean waves and he was a dolphin. At the base of the slope, he catapulted forward but caught himself at the rim of the swamp.

Tondor and Katrinka soared close behind, and Leslie scrambled after him.

The raft was close.

Blackwick sprang from the bank and landed upon a rock in the midst of the creek. One more leap and he would board the raft and confront Silver Boot. But the crocodile pirate chortled from the depths of his scaly throat and called across the expanse of the creek. "Don't try it, me bucko. Ye can't fight the Misty Bane. Touch one foot on that swamp water, and it'll suck the soul right out of you."

Blackwick stretched out both arms to regain his balance on the narrow rock, recalling what a little melting snow had done to his arm at the station. "The Misty Bane, is it?"

"Aye, yer power to dematerialize and wisp about will do ye no good *here*. And if that is not enough to deter ye, let's see how you fare against me pretty pollywogs."

The crocodile pirate waved his saber, and with a glug, gurgle, glomp, something nasty rose out of the swamp. It looked like a blob of muck rising a rounded head with two stubby tentacles on the topmost peak.

Leslie scrunched his face in disgust. "What is *that*?"

"The swamp slugs," cried Tondor. "If they catch hold of you, they'll drag you down to Deadman's Mere."

With a discordant chorus of pops and gurgles, the swamp teemed with hungry slugs rising out of the mire like glops of eyeless goo with tentacles twitching and wreaths of razor teeth grinding. Katrinka ducked behind Blackwick to avoid those teeth.

The first swamp slug creeped with rhythmic waves up the side of the rock where Blackwick stood. The shadow man recoiled to jump backwards, but a swarm of slimy tendrils were bobbing up on all sides, hemming him in.

Blackwick drew his sword, guarding the rock, ready to ward off the overgrown slugs. Katrinka huddled behind the fold in his brim and covered her face with her hands. The slugs spat slime at Blackwick. Blackwick winced in pain. Tondor fired her pistol at the largest slug's head. The bullet tore off its head with a splat of slime but did not deter its wobble-bobble up toward Blackwick with the rest of the swarm.

The raft was moving past now, and the pirate laughed. "The Misty Bane, I tell ye!"

Blackwick glared after the disappearing raft.

Tondor tossed away her empty flintlock and tugged on Leslie's sleeve. "Don't just stand there. We need a plan."

"Salt. Slugs hate salt." Leslie's eyes moved to the side to consult his memory. "I think."

"Yonder cove is brimming with the salty waves of the sea." Tondor pointed south-west. "Fetch back as much as you can carry. I'll help Blackwick ward them off." Tondor sliced her two swords together like a chef ready to make quick work of the vegetables.

Leslie's slippers slapped the marshy banks as he vaulted over fallen tree trunks and dodged mud mounds, his mind also racing. *Salt. Sea salt. Yonder cove. Yes. Tondor knows what she's talking about. She knows her Neverland. Anyone can see that. First class, that pixie, a real brick.*

Leslie wiped back the matted hair at his forehead and pushed onward. The mouth of the cove was in sight, partly masked by overgrown reeds. Slugs. They'll finish off ol' Smarty Pants for sure. Either that or the boggy creek will do him in. Salt. That's the thing. But how? No buckets. Not even a whiskey flask. How the deuce am I supposed to . . .?

He stopped. A refreshing wind blew in from the sea, cool and clean enough to allow a little air into the muggy swamp.

He could smell the salt wafting in on the breeze. He could taste it. But he still had nothing to carry the water back except his two cupped hands, one of which still clutched the comic book. *What was it you used, Leslie ol' chap, to bring down the infamous dragon hitherto known as Death-Guardian? A book, it was. A blinking, miniature book.*

He remembered how, in the last-ditch effort of the Intercessors to defeat the Accusers, a magic book had turned into a lasso, which he had wielded to noose the titanic dragon and yank the hulking lout down. Why couldn't his comic book turn into something handy like, say, a water pitcher or even a giant salt cellar?

Delighted with his own insight, he flicked open the pages and ran his eyes down the panels for a mention of something useful. In a gulp and choke, he felt a sickening rush and a throbbing in his head, and the world spun up, around, and upside down. His ankle was trussed up in a knotted rope and his body was dangling from the treetop. It was a trap.

He wished his pencil had not dropped out of his pocket when he was snagged because he might have used the sharp point to pick away at the rope scraping his ankle. He strained his arm for the pencil but caught sight of a circle of movement creeping forward. Congregating beneath the pendulum of his body were six large, wolfish men.

Capital. Werewolves. Now they're in Neverland.

The largest one was a gray-matted werewolf with a bandolier of ammo draped across his chest. He wore a bandana wrapped around his forehead and ragged olive trousers with a canteen strapped to his belt. He waved his fellow werewolves forward. A hound crouched at his side and sniffed the air with caution.

"Aye, Skender." The werewolf tossed the stub of a cigarette to the ground and mashed it underfoot. "We caught another one of them Intercessors."

"Interferers, you mean," snarled a scrawny werewolf with a weaselly muzzle and a sardonic grin.

The werewolves continued to circle Leslie. It occurred to him it was daytime, and he hoped there was enough light to disorient or shift the wolf men, but the grungy mist made the afternoon no different from twilight. The muscular one wearing the bandolier readied his rifle and smirked. "Monsieur French will be pleased. Sergeant, cut him loose."

"Yes, sir, Lieutenant," replied another bulky werewolf. He whisked a dagger out of a thigh holster and whacked the sharp edge across the ropes. Leslie collided with the ground. He rubbed his sore arm and sat up, spitting out dried leaves and moss.

"Take him," ordered the lieutenant.

The rest of the werewolves yanked Leslie to his feet, bound his wrists, and forced him to stumble along with them back into the rotting tangles of the woods. The hound bounded along beside the lieutenant, keeping ears alert for his voice.

Leslie glanced back where his comic book lay on the ground, and he hoped Blackwick and Tondor were meeting with better success. Then, an even worse thought crossed his mind. *If I die here in Neverland, what becomes of Inspector Mallowan in Bedfordshire?*

Chapter 24
CHATEAU D'IF (THE NEVER YEARS)

Tondor swished her blade, and the slug sent out a wail. Blackwick and Tondor exchanged encouraging nods. The slugs could be defeated after all. Tondor clenched her teeth in a determined grin. "Come, vile filth! Come taste a warrior's blade!"

Another slug crept up and wound itself around Blackwick's ankle. Blackwick swung his sword and slashed away the vermin. However, more were on their way, rising and stretching toward him like vines, tangling around him, dragging him closer to the swamp.

Tondor twirled her sword adroitly and went to work on the slugs, freeing Blackwick with a swoosh of her blade.

"We could use some help," Tondor called to Katrinka. "Where is Leslie with that salt?"

Katrinka was buzzing about in panic. Unable to use her pixie dust so close to the "Misty Bane," she felt helpless. The pirate raft was about to be swallowed up in a bank of fog. *Trying to get away, you ol' pirate?* Katrinka squared her shoulders. *Not so fast. I'll captivate you with my beauty and make you call off these ugly slugs.* And before the others noticed, Katrinka skimmed after the disappearing raft.

To Leslie, with his eyes masked by a bandana, the world was a chill mist slipping past his face, a steady scrape, creak, and slosh of oars. He slumped in the rowboat, squished between two burly werewolves who reeked of wet fur and mud. He heard panting and felt something sleek and lean circle about and plant itself nearby.

Where are they taking me?

He tried the old Inspector Farnesworth technique of measuring the distance by the number of oar dips and assessing the temperature by the amount of condensation that gathered on his forehead, but he soon lost track.

He was grasped up by both his arms and heaved over the side of the boat as if he were a sack of coal. He braced himself for a cold crash into the sea, but instead he rolled onto a slick, rocky surface. The werewolves yanked him to his feet, and he tripped forward, panicked he would topple, unable to catch himself with his hands bound behind his back. Someone caught him by the shoulder and ripped the bandana away.

He blinked and looked up.

A gray, stone tower frowned upon him, turrets exalted into the writhing clouds like the horns of some wide-bellied beast rearing its head. Over the front double doors rattled a wooden sign with the words *Chateau d'If* whittled in jagged cuts.

The lieutenant's hound sprang from the boat onto the rock. He shook himself vigorously, and, after growling at Leslie, the hound nuzzled under the outstretched hand of the lieutenant.

The lieutenant hammered on the door. A square peephole pushed open. "Who goes there?" came a squeaky voice. "Ye nabbed him, eh? Well done, Lieutenant." The peephole clapped shut, and the heavy doors scraped open.

On the other side was a hunched over werewolf with patches of white in his dark mane.

"Bruner, tell Monsieur French we're here," ordered the lieutenant.

"Oh, aye, right away, right away." Bruner hobbled toward a dark passageway.

"Never mind, Bruner." The voice was soft but authoritative, with a sharp Eastern European accent. It came from the shadowed opening at the top of the stone stairs. The speaker stepped into the wavering lantern light. Monsieur French wore a fur-lined cloak, a military style top, and black form-fitting trousers with matching boots. He clasped his hands behind his back and descended the steps with a steady clip.

In his presence, the werewolves bowed on their knees in awe. "Your greatness."

"No need to grovel before me." French tipped his head upward a notch. "I am not Ordog. Nor am I Count Tepov. I do not subject my followers to shame and torment."

The werewolves exchanged uncertain looks and faltered to their feet. "We brought the captive, like you asked." The lieutenant pushed Leslie forward.

"Well done, Lieutenant." French stopped before Leslie and raised one eyebrow. "You are Leslie Mallowan, son of Sir Eric and Lady Mallowan of Perlgate in Bedfordshire. You have two cousins: Edmond Davidson and Beatrice Talbin."

Leslie, after being trussed up like a chicken and dragged here like a goat, was not in a congenial mood. "Full marks." His voice was edged with sarcasm. "You must have read that in a book. And *please*, sir, may I *please* call you your greatness?"

The gentleman's fierce green eyes narrowed, unamused. "Yes. I am. But, if you prefer, you may call me Monsieur French."

French strode past Leslie, then pivoted to face him. "And where is Davidson now?"

"I left Ed in a standoff with your crocodile friend and his pet slugs."

"Slugs?" French knitted his eyebrows.

"Big. Ugly. Mean."

French spun to cast full fury upon the werewolves. "I told you. No harm must come to Davidson."

The lieutenant cringed. "I just did what ye said. It's that Silver Boot. He summoned the swamp slugs."

"Bungler! Fool! I . . ." French fell silent as something past Leslie caught his attention, and the storm brewing in his face made way for a heavenly glow of admiration.

Leslie looked over his shoulder. Framed by a stone archway posed a regal woman with olive complexion and deep, dark eyes. Her smooth profile resembled a Grecian cameo. The back of her hair was pinned up, and waves of loose curls framed either side of her cheeks. Her gown was a tasteful merging of early Victorian finery and Middle Eastern elegance. Her full eyebrows lifted as she draped the sheer shawl over the arm held out toward French.

"My darling." Her expression remained impassive.

"Haydee."

Haydee drifted past the werewolves without a glance and resumed her stance before French. "Has Silver Boot overstepped his bounds again?"

"My dearest." French bent over the woman's lace-gloved hand and brushed it with his lips. The corners of her perfect mouth spread a fraction to acknowledge his attention. He raised his eyes to hers. "Subdragons like Silver Boot are useful for guarding the perimeter, but we do not want Blackwick dead."

"Do not worry, my darling. Let me handle this."

"But there will be danger."

The lieutenant, keeping his head bowed, moved forward. "Let me go, my lady."

Haydee waved him away. "I do not fear danger. Fear is for those who serve others. Thanks to my husband, I am a free woman, and I know how to deal with troublemakers." Her raised chin defied any who would challenge her resolve.

The lieutenant bowed more deeply in his deference and drew back.

French hesitated and relinquished her hand. "I will be all anxiety until you return safe to me."

After she withdrew, French cleared his throat and looked back at Leslie, a tinge of a blush still coloring his cheeks. He wrinkled his brow at Leslie's arms. "Oh. Forgive me." He drew

151

a dagger from a sheath hidden under his cloak. Leslie flinched to avoid the blade, but French set it to the ropes and soon had Leslie's wrists free. Leslie rubbed his wrists to encourage circulation.

"And do not worry." French returned his dagger to its sheath. "My wife will see to Silver Boot. Meanwhile, come, Mr. Mallowan."

"That's *Inspector* Mallowan," Leslie corrected, following him up the steps. As he followed, he examined the stone walls, the tapestries, the lanterns, looking for a clue as to where in Neverland they were.

French faced Leslie, walking backwards up the stairs. "But tell me, how does Lord Mallowan sound? Or King Leslie the Magnificent?"

Leslie's eyebrows formed a squiggle as he questioned if Bedlam were not this man's next stop. "Sounds a bit dodgy to me. Lord Mallowan, maybe. But king? There's only one king in England, and I'm not in line for the job." He gave a shrug to show there was no help for it.

"Ah!" French touched a panel on the wall, and the grand hall at the top of the stairs lit up with brilliant light blazing from a series of diamond chandeliers. "But we're not in England *now*."

He gestured Leslie's attention toward a buffet against the wall, a buffet filled with the most delectable things to eat, all the food Leslie liked best: a plump, juicy roast with ladles of brown gravy, a glass tureen filled with syrupy stewed peaches, a long platter decked with chocolate bars, a wooden cutlery board with slices of fresh bread accented by grapes and walnuts and wheels of orange, beige, and white cheeses. Warm foods sat atop tiny burners. Chilled foods were kept on majestic ice sculptures of cresting waves.

Leslie had not eaten since teatime, and the pang in his stomach drove his hands to grab a plate.

"And," French swerved to the other side of the hall, "while you enjoy your snack . . ." He pulled aside the luxurious velvet drape to reveal an antechamber off the great hall. Inside were several large treasure chests. He hovered his signet ring over the lock of one of the chests. The mechanism sprang with a click, and the lid popped open. He threw back the lid to reveal mounds of diamonds, onyx, sapphires, and emeralds.

Leslie's chin dropped, and his hand, clutching a fork with a fatty bite of roast, froze midway to his mouth. "Is that real? Did you ransack Solomon's Mines?"

"This treasure is my own. And we Epilogues are generous with our friends."

"Epilogues?"

French gestured Leslie toward a settee. Leslie sank into the comfort of the velvet cushions, balancing his plate on his knee. The shimmer from the treasure reflected across his face as he gazed toward the man silhouetted in front of his vast wealth.

"Ordog sought to rob me," continued French, "but it found its way back to me, thanks to an old friend of mine." An ominous cloud shrouded his expression. "Soon Ordog and all the Accusers will suffer as I have suffered. They will be crushed, humiliated, tortured, and destroyed."

"Oh. So, you're one of us, then." Leslie smiled, relieved at the realization. He popped a grape into his mouth and took a pinch of sliced bread. "Betty says Vorever will . . ."

French slammed down the heavy lid of the chest. "No. Not Vorever. Never Vorever. He is not strong enough to stop them. He hides in his fancy tower, ignoring the cries of the oppressed."

Leslie sagged and glanced at his food like one who was told Father Christmas would not be coming that year. When he glanced back up, French was bending over him, studying his face as if he could tell a man's worth by his physiognomy.

"Don't feel too bad, my young friend. The Epilogues are greater than Ordog, greater than Vorever. The one feared by all, Zed-Cyphrr, will soon set everything right."

At the mention of the name, the chandeliers dimmed and relit.

French stepped away from Leslie to contemplate a wall-length painting framed in silver on the wall. The painting depicted a sad wolf with glowing green eyes. French shook his head as if to banish a painful memory. He rested the bridge of his nose between his finger and thumb. "What is one thing greater than duty, greater than wealth, and even greater than love?"

Leslie shrugged and resorted to unwrapping the gold foil from a chocolate bar.

French looked green daggers into Leslie's eyes. "Vengeance. Ordog has taken much. Vorever has failed to mete out the fair measure of wrath. But soon, we Epilogues will have the final word." His mouth curled in a grin, relishing the future he envisioned.

From behind one of the drapes stepped Ilda, cloaked in velvet and fur, her wrinkled arms and neck adorned with priceless jewels. From behind the drape on the other side, emerged Avian, slinking in her black cocktail dress, her wrists and neck clasped in diamonds and rubies. The two women framed Monsieur French, and the formidable triumvirate faced Leslie.

Leslie's mouthful of chocolate paused for a moment as he stared from one to the other of the women. These two women had once aided his enemies. But the chocolate was the richest, creamiest, sweetest chocolate he had ever tasted, and he dismissed his forebodings about Ilda and Avian as he focused on an intense hope Monsieur French and his Epi-whatevers had more chocolate bars stashed somewhere.

"Convince Beatrice to give us the missing page," said Ilda, "and you will not just be *Mr.* Mallowan or *Inspector* Mallowan, but a king over any story you wish to rule."

The idea was tempting. The more Leslie thought about it, the more tempting it became. Yes, his father was well-to-do, but Leslie had often felt like no one appreciated him for all his real talent. He blushed a bit, though, when he admitted to himself he could have done more to prove himself. But why should he have to? After all, Sir Eric Mallowan was a rich, ambitious man, and Leslie feared he must have been a disappointment to him. Every childhood illness someone could survive Leslie seemed to have contracted. He was not exceptionally strong, smart, or ambitious. He liked comic books and letting the servants do all the rough work.

Being king would be nice. Yes, being king would suit him quite well. King in a world full of roast beef, chocolate, and lovely cream puffs, where doing clever things and taking bows for them was simply the order of the day. And if he ever was too tired to think of clever things, he could hire a room full of wise, bearded philosophers to advise him. And they would shake their long, white beards and say, "Oh, but you inspired us, oh wise King Leslie." His dream shattered when a realization hit him. "But there isn't any page."

Horror struck the faces of Ilda and French. They both turned on Avian.

"No!" she protested. "The page from the *Tome of the Netherdragons*. Nothing can destroy that."

Leslie shrugged. "Oh, well, no page per se. Just a fat lot of ashes in a silly little tin. That's what Betty said."

"Ashes! Ah, but where are those ashes?" demanded Ilda.

"Betty. She has them. And she's not here. I left her in Bedfordshire."

"Ah." French collapsed into the couch, lost in concentration. "But Edmond Davidson is here. Lieutenant," he called. "I will need your assistance once more."

CHAPTER 25
NEVER THE TWAIN (THE NEVER YEARS)

Every direction she turned, Katrinka ran into a wall of fog. But her little ears picked up the garbled echo of the baritone voice, singing like a foghorn.

> *Fifteen men on Marooner's Rock*
> *Heads to lop and planks to walk*
> *Fifteen men in Chateau d'If*
> *Yo-ho-ho and a bottle of grief*

The raft came gliding out of the fog patch. And the boy with eyes as blank as ghost-lights dug the oar in and pulled it along, steering the raft across the mire.

"Avast ye! Keep at it, lad. We've got to show 'em landlubbers we're in town." A grin spread across the crocodile pirate's long, green snout. He stood aft, his one booted leg with silver buckle gleaming and his green-scaled wrists aflutter with frills at the cuffs. He adjusted his black and red baldric and clanked his sword at his hip. "Aye, we'll show these Neverlanders a thing or two, by the Jib o' the lady and the Spar o' the lord."

"Aye, Captain," the boy said in a toneless voice. His face was fixed with a lost sort of look, the sad look dreamers get when watching their dreams fade away. He was about fourteen, tall and lean, with a wiry frame. His clothes were old cast offs, his baggy trousers hanging on by one suspender, while the other suspender had fallen across the crook of his arm. The legs of his trousers were folded up halfway to his knee to keep them from dragging in the sludge.

"Lively, my lad. 'Less you want to taste me cat o' nine tails."

"Oh, no, sir," said the lad. "I reckon that's one feline whose company I could do without."

The crocodile chortled. "Ye've got a turn for a phrase, lad. Like a poet. But being a poet won't save yer skin, so mind the oar and pull us through. And keep a weather eye out for any blasted pixies or tribesfolks or any other creature we can send to Davy Jones."

"Davy Jones. Yep. I ain't fixin' to socialize with that one neither. There's them's you can socialize and them's you can't socialize. And them's you can't, you shouldn't."

"Wait. Ahoy, matey! I see a sparkle-sparkle. By all that wheezes and wallops. Steer me close so I can get a better lookee-see."

The lad steered the raft closer toward the glow of light bobbing amid the fog. Katrinka yanked her dress down over her thighs more firmly. She smoothed her wispy bangs to the side while fluttering her lashes. *Now for operation beguile.* But before she could manage a coy wink or make eyes with a sidelong glance, the crocodile scooped her into his tricorn. "Why blast me bones! If it isn't a wee bit of pixie. Say how d'ye do to the little lady, Huck, me lad."

"Hello, little lady," said the lad.

"Well." The crocodile spread his greedy jaws wide. "It appears I've caught me own sparkle-sparkle. I've always wanted a sparkle-sparkle."

"But," protested Katrinka, using her most ingenue-like voice, "I only came to be friendly."

The crocodile chortled. "And a naughty sparkle-sparkle at that. Ye best be watching yourself, me bonnie lass. Yer mother never tell you what happens to bad little pixies who flaunt themselves before hungry pirates?"

Katrinka's cheeks burned, and her eyes widened as a drop of saliva slid down the crocodile's sharp incisor and splatted close beside her. "You'll never get away with this."

"That's the oldest line in the history of books, me lass. Hmm." He licked a tongue across his lips. "I feel a hankering, Huck, me lad. I rather like me a bit of quail or a nice wriggling fishy. Folks do say pixies taste a bit like quail. Especially when you spit them and broil them just so."

"I don't think I'd like the taste of pixie. Them's gentle critters, like wildflowers on the fields and robins in their nest. Seems their sole purpose is to bring a bit of joy to those who need it, and it don't seem right to set a slingshot on 'em, nor buckshot, for they ain't got it in 'em to shoot back."

"Ahhh, yer gonna make me cry, Huck me boyo. I'll have me tender meaties just as I please."

"Oh, no you won't." Katrinka flushed bright red as she struggled to pull free. "I'll put a pixie curse on you!"

"Slap yer trap, me hussy. It's better'n you deserve, flauntin' yerself like that. If ye hadn't dared close to ol' Silver Boot, ye wouldn't be in this pickle." He clapped her into a bamboo cage and hung her up like a lantern. He wriggled his claws as he contemplated the morsel soon to embellish his platter. But his mouth stopped watering when his head tilted toward a steady lapping sound drawing closer.

"Another craft to starboard," announced Huck.

"Ye think I be deaf?" snarled Silver Boot. "It'll be the skiff of the lady."

At the mention of a lady, Katrinka held onto the bamboo bars of her cage and peered out, hoping a friend had arrived to rescue her. An ancient Egyptian-style skiff glided close, pulled by the paddling crocodiles who had once made the creek their haunt. At the front of the skiff stood the alert and graceful form of Haydee.

"Captain Silver Boot." She enunciated each syllable.

He swept into a low bow, doffing his tricorn. "My lady."

"Word reaches us the one known as Blackwick is here in Neverland."

"Aye, but never fear, my lady. The deadly swamp slugs will make short work of him, no mistake!"

"No."

"No? What say ye now?" Silver Boot waddled against his crutch closer to the skiff. "Did me ears hear aright?"

The woman whipped out her fan and positioned its accordion folds like a veil over her nose and mouth. Her luminous eyes commanded his attention. "Beatrice Talbin has the page we seek, and Blackwick is devoted to her. The key to anyone's heart is the person they love the most. We must have Blackwick alive."

If a crocodile could sweat, Silver Boot would have been drenched in it, but, as he could not sweat, he merely let his maw gape as he panted in panic. "There may yet be time. The pollywogs may not have eaten every bite of him yet."

"Hurry, then. Call off your vermin. Zed-Cyphrr will not be pleased to learn a mere subdragon thwarted his plan." She snapped her fan closed.

"Aye, my lady. Fear not. I'll handle this, and before ye know it, he'll be safe and sound at Chateau d'If with his friends. Heave ho, me lad! And if yer too slow about it, I'll have you for the main course and the pretty pixie for dessert."

CHAPTER 26
SILVER BOOT (THE NEVER YEARS)

Each new wave of slugs was bigger, tougher, and meaner. As soon as Tondor cut one down, four others took its place. Blackwick, too, had put up a gallant defense, but the slugs shot out from the swamp waters like the tentacles of some monstrous kraken snatching its prey from every angle. With a concerted effort, the longest slugs coiled their eelish bodies in an unyielding grip around Blackwick's legs, waist, chest, and neck. The brackish spillage from the slugs burned into his waxen skin. He strained to suppress moans of pain. Tondor spun to his rescue, but a slug caught her by the narrow tip of its tail and waved her body in the air like a prize.

The raft hove from the mist.

"Ahoy there!" hailed Silver Boot.

Blackwick growled and fixed Silver Boot with a glare. His arms flexed, struggling to free himself and finish off the gloating pirate. But the tendrils were tightening around his body, and the wax of his jacket was cracking, and black wax with molten orange bled through the fissures.

The pirate's teeth gleamed. "Don't try to be brave, me bucko. No good can come from that. The more ye struggle, the nastier me pollywogs will be." He drew his saber. "But I did not come back to vanquish ye."

He waved his saber in an arc across the sky, and a snow-storm of salt shook down from the tangled overhanging tree branches. The salt spread across the slugs, and they sizzled, shrank, and dried up into flakes of ash and slime that merged with the swampy sludge.

Blackwick shook off the dried coils and caught Tondor as the slug holding her exploded into powder.

The shadow man's eyes were on fire, and the wolfish instinct within him was all for pouncing upon the raft and tearing the crocodile apart.

"Hold there. I come with a truce," cried the pirate.

Tondor shook the slug ash out of her hair. "A truce?" She tossed an indignant glare at him. "Look what you've done to my Neverland. And you think there's room for a truce?"

"Ahhh. But you have a bit of something I be hankering for, and I have a something you'll be wanting back . . . *unharmed*." Clutched in his claws, bound and gagged with a patch and some twine, was poor little Katrinka. She uttered muffled cries of protest and fought against the bonds.

"Katrinka!" Tondor drew her dagger and aimed it to propel at the crocodile's eye. But a dip net whooshed down and scooped her in its mesh. She twisted to free herself, but a large werewolf shook the net and bared his teeth in a snarl.

"Well done, Lieutenant!" The pirate chuckled in triumph.

Without looking behind him, Blackwick knew more were-wolves were closing in. "What do you want, Silver Boot?"

"I want you and your friends to give yourselves up without too much fuss or hassle. Ye see, I heared a rumor a certain lady friend of yers has a certain piece of paper. I want that piece of paper, and I think ye'll convince her to hand it over. Just look me in the eye."

"Don't look!" Tondor pressed her face against the netting. "He bewitched the lad, and he'll bewitch you too!"

"Quiet," snapped the lieutenant, shaking the net once more. Tondor fell backward into the net. The lieutenant's hound snapped at her, and she clutched at the side of the netting to keep away from his teeth.

Silver Boot snickered. "Just a wee keek in my eye, me bucko, and you will soon find where your friends may be." His voice had a gruff, musical quality that could convince even the sharpest chap he meant no harm. "What were their names? Ahhh, the boy who lost his shadow." Here he shot an accusing stare at Blackwick. "And the little lass who may never grow up again. Frieda Fernsby. Ah, yes, that were her name. I be remembering now." He leaned forward on his crutch, the eye not covered with a patch pulsing toward Blackwick. "And what of poor Mistress Talbin? The lass what thought the world of ye, and who ye left with no one to protect her."

Blackwick winced with guilt. Betty. He raised his eyes, and, before he knew it, he was met by the eye of the crocodile pirate. It was throbbing in a rhythmic pattern, like a clock ticking and tocking.

Blackwick entered a dream state, a limbo land with nothing but white light all around him. And within the glare of that light, his shadowy form nearly faded.

"You best give in," came a young voice that hailed from the Mississippi River.

Blackwick lowered his arm to look. A fourteen-year-old boy sauntered up to him through the light, tall and lanky, with ragged cast offs for clothes and a battered straw hat set back on his head.

"Huckleberry Finn? I remember you. Before I met Peter Pan." Blackwick was often caught off guard by memories he had no recollection of, except that they must have belonged to Peter Pan's shadow once upon a time.

The lad started, surprised. "You must be my shadow friend that'd go in and out with me when my drunk of a father had no time for me."

"Don't listen to him, Huck lad," came the voice of the crocodile pirate. "Bring the shadow man to *me.*"

The lad scratched his ear. "Someone keeps a-tellin' me I ain't better listen to ya."

"But you're *Huckleberry Finn*," protested Blackwick. "You want to do what's right. I know you do. That's what I taught you many years ago, so long ago I almost forgot. It's the way Mr. Twain wrote you."

"Don't reckon I heared the name Twain before." The lad plunged his hands in his pockets with a shrug.

Blackwick waved the detail aside. "That doesn't matter. What matters is you were once a lost boy, just as I was. But we both wanted to stand up for what is right."

"Put yer fingers in yer ears, laddie! Make him call the lass! She has what we need."

The lad looked back over his shoulder. "A voice keeps a-sayin' I oughta do what they say. But I don't wanna do nothin' *really* bad. 'Twould be a shame if the pretty little pixie was cooked up and et up."

Blackwick squatted before Huck and set his hands earnestly upon the lad's shoulders. "Listen to me. I had a drunk for a father too. I know what it's like. And I remember boys like you at school. We had people telling us what to do day and night. But you know what I did? I defied them. The more they yelled at me, the more defiant I became. They tossed me into the cellar, and that's the one thing I feared most of all. To be alone in the dark. Now look at me. I *am* the dark."

"You know," Huck planted his hat more firmly on his head and frowned with concentration, "you're right. I don't have to listen to that voice. And a bad voice it is, too." Huck drew his hand from his pocket, holding his Barlow pocketknife. He unfolded it and looked back toward the raft with a determined glint in his eyes.

The bright light melted away as the raft hove to shore. "Yer time is up, Blackwick." Silver Boot leapt onto the shore, holding up the captive Katrinka. "Come with me quietly, or the pixie dies." The werewolves raised their hunting rifles and levelled them at Blackwick.

Blackwick drew his sword. Huck tested the sharpness of his knife. Back-to-back, Blackwick and Huck readied themselves for a fight.

The werewolf lieutenant gave his rifle a pat. "We don't want to hurt you, mate. You once were one of us. Come quietly, and I won't need to use this."

"It was because of Ordog I was one of you," retorted Blackwick. "I am not that creature any longer."

A private clanked his rifle's cartridge forward, and the lieutenant grabbed its barrel to lower it. "It wouldn't be fair, guns against swords. Never has a Tynan stooped to an unfair fight."

"Then drop your rifles." Blackwick circled the point of his sword toward the gun. "Let's see how you get on sword to sword and hand to hand."

The lieutenant sized up the shadow man and nodded with the hint of a smile. "We shall see." He motioned for his squad to set aside their guns and drew his own saber from its scabbard. With his free claw, he beckoned for Blackwick to bring on the fight.

The shadow man and the river lad sprang toward the werewolves, Blackwick with his sword and Huck with his knife. The river lad had experience dodging bullets from angry homesteaders and ducking blows from his drunk old man. Despite his lankiness, he outmaneuvered the slashing of the sabers and the catching of the claws.

His eye red with rage, Silver Boot slammed Katrinka on the planks of the raft and raised the tip of his crutch to pinion her to the wood. She squirmed out of its path, and the tip crashed down within a hair's breadth of her head. She let out a muffled scream and rolled, but the tip came barreling down again. Her eyes widened in terror. But he roared and dropped his crutch, tumbling back to the mast, grasping his claw in pain. It had been pierced by a miniature arrow.

Tondor rearmed her crossbow and zeroed in on the fiend who had dared to threaten her home and her friends. While Silver Boot was occupied with the splinter in his paw, she swept down to rip away the gag and cut through the strands that bound Katrinka.

"Thank the Neverbird," sighed Katrinka, pale and wobbly. "I guess that shows me for thinking I could be a hero."

"No." Tondor glared sharply at Silver Boot. "That shows *him*. He'll pay for what he's done to you."

CHAPTER 27
REICHENBACH FALLS (1890S)

"It is, indeed, a fearful place." Even as Betty quoted Dr. Watson's description of Reichenbach Falls, she felt the crackle of the paper and smelled the sharp, bitter printer's ink. The words from the page swirled around her in a green haze. Hamberdeen extended a fascinated finger to touch the stem of an S and the stroke of an A as the serif fonts whipped about them like ghosts. *Smoke. Chasm. Half-human shout. Abyss.*

The words cleared like clouds after the rain. Betty caught her balance on the Swiss mountain ledge and steadied Hamberdeen before he tumbled over the lip. Her senses were assailed by pines, earth, and gravel. The spray from the falls pelted them with a shower of icy spears. Betty was glad she had thought to gather her coat and messenger bag before she had read the passage. The portal had allowed her to retain her 1930s wardrobe, and the coat afforded a little protection. She shielded her eyes and looked further up the path as she wound her way forward.

"What are we looking for again?" Hamberdeen had to shout to be heard above the deafening roar of the falls. He watched his step as he followed Betty around the bend. The thunderous torrents drowned out most of her response, but Hamberdeen caught "Sherlock Holmes" and "words not spoken" and "chart."

A strident curse pierced the turmoil.

Betty stopped and sucked in her breath.

Before them two men grappled on the ledge. One was Holmes, his jaw set, his footwork adroit, and his black-gloved hands sure of their grip.

But the other was something not human. He was a tall and powerfully built lizard man. His wild yellow eyes were deeply sunk, and his leathery skin was grayish green. Atop his high-domed head, covering the straggling strands of gray hair, was a Victorian top hat. The tails of his black frock coat flew out over his violently whipping reptilian tail as his claws lashed at Holmes.

Professor Moriarty. Betty recalled Doyle mentioning something reptilian about the way Professor Moriarty, Holmes' arch nemesis, moved his head from side to side. That one detail had now consumed the entire character. Betty edged her way closer, hoping the corruption that had transformed Moriarty would not also take liberties with the fate of Sherlock Holmes.

Holmes pushed with his full strength against the stronghold of the lizard man's arms. Moriarty swung Holmes' body about and leered over the detective's shoulder. Moriarty's brow arched, and an evil gleam leered as he locked eyes with Betty's. She jolted at the sight of those eyes, but the next second, Holmes had thrown Moriarty back around, and she saw the detective's eyes fixed on his opponent.

Moriarty hissed past a jutting forked tongue and thrust Holmes to the ground. The detective's head hung over the abyss, and the villain's claws clutched at his throat.

Hamberdeen spoke in Betty's ear. "He'll be all right."

Betty was not convinced. She had read the entire collection of Sherlock Holmes stories several times and knew that another story, "The Empty House," later revealed that Holmes survived the contest, but how could they predict what twisted slant the spreading corruption would have on the lives of the characters?

She clambered further up, her boot toes digging into the wet ground. Though she was still weak from the illness and her arms ached, the sight of Holmes in danger filled her with an indignant surge.

"Moriarty!" she screamed, her arm outstretched, her palm open toward the antagonist. "Let him go!"

Holmes turned to her. "Betty, stay back!"

Betty pushed her palm forward to propel the power of Vorever against Moriarty, but only a tense tingling sensation stretched through her palm, no magic, no powerful ray. She stared at her hands in disbelief.

Moriarty threw his head back and laughed. Holmes took advantage of the moment to ram his own body full force against that of Moriarty. Holmes spun about, exchanging positions with the villain. Moriarty clung to Holmes' neck as the detective threw his weight against the lizard man. Moriarty's eyes widened and his forked tongue flailed in fear as he slipped off the edge. But cruelty distorted his lizard features once more as he grabbed hold of Holmes' throat at the last second and pulled the detective over the edge with him.

Betty flew to the ledge and caught Holmes' hands in her own. Her arms strained as if they would pull out of their sockets. She gritted her teeth and pulled with all her might, but the sharp stones dug into her elbows and her chest as the weight of the two men dragged her over the edge. Hamberdeen caught her waist to anchor her.

Holmes tried to off balance the weight by propping his foot against the face of the cliff. His worried eyes lifted toward Betty's.

"You must let go. Tell Watson . . . the letter . . ." He pulled his hands out of Betty's, and he hurtled down, Moriarty still clinging to him, down into the haze of the abyss.

Betty's face drained. She stared down into the roiling mist of the falls, hoping she could catch a glimpse of Holmes clinging to a tree branch or climbing up the side of the mountain. They had succeeded in saving Sydney Carton from the guillotine. Surely, they could save Holmes from his fate as well. But he was gone.

Hamberdeen scratched the back of his head and looked up the sheer wall of the mountain side above them as if he expected to find Holmes clambering up to safety.

Betty's arms ached. She tried to stand. Her body went limp, and Hamberdeen caught her before she dropped to the ground. *We were too late.* She forced her weak, shaking knees to move, and, with Hamberdeen's support, she felt her way down the path. They came upon an alpine stick leaning against a large boulder. A cigarette case glinted on a flat part of the rock. Holmes had said, "Tell Watson . . . the letter." Betty lifted the case, and the note she sought beneath it fluttered down. She picked up the note and focused on the words in Holmes' own handwriting. "I am pleased to think I shall be able to free society from any further effects of Moriarty's presence, though I fear that it is at a cost which will give pain to my friends, and especially, my dear Watson, to you."

And to me too. Betty crumpled the note, and hot tears streamed down her cheeks. "I thought I could save him. He was supposed to survive."

Hamberdeen clutched one side of the letter. "These are his last words. The words never spoken. This is it."

"Holmes! Holmes!" Watson's desperation reverberated in a rolling echo from the cliffs around them. Betty was about to fold the letter in her messenger bag, but she hesitated.

Instead, she unrolled the chart against the bolder and held the letter so Holmes' signature touched the Swiss landmark. The signature burnt a copy into the map, and the green haze around Betty and Hamberdeen dissipated as if washed away by the torrential falls.

Betty was tempted to keep the letter, but she shook her head. "Holmes wanted Dr. Watson to have this." She smoothed the note, and, with unsteady hands, replaced it under the cigarette case for Watson to find.

She squeezed her eyes shut and pictured the words she knew would take them away from this place, and the falls dissolved into a splatter of running colors.

Betty and Hamberdeen were huddled once more on the front porch of his used book shop. The squealing tires of a passing car shot up a spray of slush, and in the melted snow was reflected the glimmer of traffic lights and streetlamps. A long shadow entered the reflection, and Betty looked up to see a statuesque, middle-aged woman, sheltered by a black umbrella, a no-non-sense expression in her pinched eyes.

"Aunt Amelia?"

Chapter 28
MAROONER'S ROCK (THE NEVER YEARS)

The werewolf platoon had surrendered. They were on their knees on the creek bank, their arms bound behind their backs. Huck gathered the rifles and sabers in a pile.

The victory had been too easy. Blackwick knew from experience the intense power werewolves were capable of, and in the battle on the creek bank, the lieutenant and his soldiers had not even displayed a tenth of their potential. As Blackwick reviewed their captives, he caught the lieutenant giving his sergeant a knowing nod.

"Let us in on it, Lieutenant," demanded Blackwick.

"There's nothing to say." The lieutenant heaved a disgruntled breath. "You won this time, shadow man." Blackwick remained skeptical.

Huck relieved the pixies of their charge over Silver Boot. He moved behind the bound pirate and held the blade of his Barlow knife at the softer folds of the crocodile's throat. "Well, Captain? I think you owe these fine folks an apology."

Silver Boot kept his jaws tightly locked.

Tondor wiped down her sword against a blade of grass. "Tell your troops to take us to the keep and past the guards."

"And if I don't?" Silver Boot forced a charming grin to crease the side of his trembling muzzle. "Why, ye haven't got it in ye to kill a creature in cold blood."

Blackwick circled the point of his rapier close to the werewolf sergeant's nose. "I don't know. The sun sets, and the rising moon is full. I've not killed a fiend since Paris." The magenta dusk reflected ominously upon the shadow man's grim countenance.

"Be that as it might," put in Huck, "'taint necessary. You see, I'm recollectin' I been to that shadow deef place. I can get ye in."

"Gentlemen, ladies," announced the pirate, a glint in his eye and a sparkle on his teeth, "allow me to be your guide. Your ticket into the keep is a simple promise to send for your lady friend, and we'll all let bygones be bygones, eh?" He twiddled his claws in front of himself.

Huck pressed the blade against the crocodile's throat. "Best be puttin' a clamp on that trap of yers, Mr. Silver Boot. Or I'm thinkin' my old Barlow knife and your old insides'll be real good friends."

Blackwick scuffed the lieutenant with the side of his boot. "Get up."

Skender growled.

Blackwick turned from the hound and faced the captured platoon. "The plan is for you to row us out to the keep and get us past the watch. Once we're there, Huck will get us in and lead us to Frieda and Peter."

Under the watchful eyes of their captors, Silver Boot and the werewolves rowed the victors down the creek toward the outlet to the sea. Against the moonlit horizon was a rugged rock island, and looming above the island was the grim tower of Chateau d'If.

Blackwick tensed. "There are more guards than I anticipated. All lined up and ready to meet us. We're heading into a trap."

"A trap?" echoed the crocodile pirate. "Would I do anything so low as that? You lot won fair and square, and that's how Silver Boot will deal with ye, too."

Tondor signaled Katrinka to lie low in the bottom boards of the rowboat. Katrinka hiccupped on her fear. Tondor put a stern finger to her lips. Katrinka clapped her hands over her mouth and nodded.

Blackwick shoved a gun into the lieutenant's ribs. "Hail them. Let them know all is well. Then row to the other side of the island." He ducked behind the lieutenant, blending with the dark corners of the boat. He stroked Skender to keep him calm, but the hound only growled.

"Ahoy!" The lieutenant hailed the armed werewolves assembled before the gate. "All's well."

The scrawny werewolf on shore craned his neck to survey the approaching vessel. "What! Didn't ye bring back the shadow man like the commander said?"

"Naw. Got away."

"Oh, no, he didn't! He's here!" Silver Boot sprang to his feet, rocking the vessel, and heaved Huck over the side. Huck's startled cry was cut short by a crash and gargle.

"Huck!" Katrinka flitted to the rail to search the waters for any sign of the lad.

The boat pitched back and forth, and the two pixies flew up from the boat to avoid toppling into the bottom.

Blackwick fired the gun at the crocodile's head. Silver Boot's throat hissed and rattled. His tail flopped. His head flung back with his jaw snapping shut, and green slime oozed out from between his teeth as he slumped lifeless over the gunwale.

The two pixies hurried to lift Huck's face out of the water and guide him back to the boat.

A boom from the shore, and a cannon ball broke through the hull. The sea poured into the boat. Blackwick twisted back to avoid the onslaught of waves and wisped into a cloud of ash. The cloud flurried with the gun smoke on the breeze toward the lantern of an approaching boat.

Huck held onto the side of the sinking boat. A raven with a patch on one eye screamed up from the boards where the crocodile pirate had expired. The raven gripped the lad by his hair with the claws of its only leg. The lad fell backwards, but the lieutenant caught him.

Tondor drew her swords to ward off the raven. The raven assailed the pixies with violent wings and razor claws. Tondor fell upon the railing, propped by her left elbow as she whipped at the raven with the sword and slid backward on her hip. The raven pressed his advantage. Katrinka sought the wreckage for something to wield against the fowl. She spied the discarded peg leg sinking as the slosh filled the boat. She zipped to the silver leg and tried with all her might to lift it, but it was too heavy. The lieutenant surfaced from the water near the pixies. He gave the raven a fierce growl through sharp incisors. The raven shrieked and scattered away toward the keep.

Tondor eyed the werewolf lieutenant with suspicion. "Why are you helping us?"

He lent his finger to help the pixie to her feet. "That Silver Boot was out of line. Monsieur French says to bring you to him unharmed."

The boat tipped, and the werewolf plunged back into the deep. Skender paddled toward him and used his head to prod his master's face above water. "Thanks, pal." The lieutenant saw the semi-conscious Huck sinking beneath the waves, and he scooped the water with powerful strokes to reach him. He flung the boy's arms over his broad shoulders and swam toward a rowboat approaching from shore. Tondor and Katrinka flew along beside them.

On the prow of the approaching boat swayed a lantern. The panes of the lantern smashed and, out from the lantern, emerged Blackwick, in a wave of smoke and ash, forming the ghostly shape of a man. The werewolves rowing the boat yiped and scrambled overboard. Blackwick claimed the deserted oars and steered the boat toward his friends.

The lieutenant flung his arms over the railing, heaving Huck into the boat before himself. Blackwick aimed his gun at the lieutenant. The werewolf shrugged with a rueful smile. "Truce?"

"He helped us," put in Katrinka. Skender scrambled into the boat and shook his fur dry.

Blackwick measured where the werewolf's loyalties aligned. He sensed a long and honorable ancestry, a noble family line blemished only by one man's curse. Tynan. That was his family's name. And he sought to atone for his ancestor's sin, to uphold the family honor once more, so their souls could finally rest in peace. All of this reeled through Blackwick's mind's eye in a matter of seconds.

Blackwick holstered the gun and extended a hand to help Lieutenant Tynan aboard.

CHAPTER 29
THE KEEP (THE NEVER YEARS)

Skender's cold nose in Huck's face snapped the lad out of his groggy haze. He coughed, pushed back the hound's slobbery jowls, and took a moment to reorient himself with where he was and what was going on.

"Skender. That's enough, boy." The lieutenant had been slouched against the transom in the stern of the boat. He gave the dog a nudge to allow the youngster some space. As Skender circled back to his master, the lad slid forward on the boards to the front of the boat. He leveled his chin with the railing, like someone lying in the brush waiting for a clear shot as he surveyed the rugged rock of an island. "There's a secret dock to leeward," Huck told Blackwick. "You can't see it from here. Atween them ledges knowed by the name Devil's Claw. Leastwise, that's what Silver Boot called it."

Tondor poised on the prow, her hand shielding her eyes as she peered through the darkness. "And Peter and Frieda?"

"They're safe." The lieutenant settled back against the gunwale, scratching his hound behind the ears. "Brave little warriors they were. A gallant defense. It went against my grain to lock them in the dungeons."

A heavy splash made Huck whip his attention back at Blackwick plying the oars as if cutting into the heart of the waves. "Even a werewolf should know better," muttered Blackwick. "A dungeon? They're children!"

The lieutenant held up a hand of reassurance. "Uninjured, I promise. Regular rations, spirits undaunted. They're fine."

Blackwick was silent, lost in a dark memory.

The dock was tucked in an inlet half-encircled by a horseshoe of craggy rock, the Devil's Claw. The lieutenant and Huck moored the boat, and the lad led them up the ridge toward a lonely, unguarded wall over-sprawled with brown vines and dry twigs.

Blackwick closed his eyes, assessing their surroundings: the cold tang of mud, the mineral bite of stonework, the salty sift of the sea . . . and the click of rifles not too far away. His eyes flicked open. "We must be quick."

"See there?" The lad pointed straight up. "There's a window with a shutter that won't stay put. They latch it up at night, but it won't stick. That's where they store their artillery and such like. And look." He pushed aside a large rock and unraveled a rope ladder stashed there. "We can use this to scale the wall."

"*You* can, kid," said the lieutenant. "But we werewolves prefer the easy way. Come, Skender!" The dog sprang into the lieutenant's extended arm, and, lugging the hound along with him, the werewolf scrabbled up the wall with the dexterity of a lizard. Blackwick funneled into a cloud of ash and whisked through the ajar window.

Huck's shoulders sagged. He turned to the pixies and offered them the rope with an apologetic shrug and half smile.

Katrinka fluttered her wings and batted her eyelashes. "Well, I think it was very clever of you to hide the ladder there." She tilted her head and gave him an aren't-you-cute wink. "Would you like to climb up that way, or would you prefer to fly?"

"Katrinka," Tondor scolded. "You know mortals are sensitive about doing things themselves. If he wants to use the ladder, we mustn't disappoint him. Here, we'll fly the ladder up and let it down for him."

Katrinka scrunched her nose at Huck. "Very well, but it would have been fun to pixie dust you."

Tondor scowled and yanked Katrinka away from the mortal and toward the window, rope ladder in tow. The pixies anchored the ladder on the window ledge and tossed the length of it down.

Midway up, Huck paused, arm hooked over the rung, as he leaned out to double check the area. He caught sight of wolven shadows scouring the island. "No time to waste, Huck," he whispered as he skittered up the rungs. He gave the shutter a push and swung into the armory. Skender sniffed at the half-opened crates piled against the wall. Tondor lit on one stamped Cairo, Egypt. "These Epilogues mean business."

"An odd assortment of weapons," agreed Blackwick.

In the crates packed among the wood shavings were weapons that hailed from the mid-1800s, flintlocks, gunpowder, and derringers. Piled in the corner were cutlasses, blunderbusses, and sabers that might have been pilfered from the *Jolly Roger*. The lieutenant plucked a grenade from a pile as if it were a choice piece of fruit. "We smuggled these babies in from the Balkans." He waved his hand over the pile of grenades, clips of ammo, and machine guns, like the ones toted by American movie gangsters. He tossed the grenade, and Blackwick caught it with lightning reflexes. The lieutenant nodded, impressed.

Blackwick held the grenade close, sensing a cold kind of anger crystalizing within. "Who is this Thomson French?" he wondered aloud.

"That's not for me to tell." The lieutenant reclaimed the grenade and returned it to its pile. "I'm taking you to your friends, but I won't betray the ones I've sworn to serve."

"I'm thinking," said Huck, perusing the choice of weapons, "we could've done that well enough on our own." Like a connoisseur, he selected a rifle, nodded his approval, and shouldered it.

The cave-like corridor with its low arched ceiling plinked and plunked in a hollow echo. Huck stopped where a crevice in the rock-cobbled floor surrounded a square detached from the others. He kicked a latch, and a trap door sprang open. He held the door and indicated narrow, winding steps leading downward like a tornado made of stone. "This way to the dungeons. And mind the spider webs."

"The spider webs better mind *me.*" The lieutenant shoved his way past the others and down into the passage, his broad shoulders scraping the dust off the cramped walls. Skender ginger-stepped down the narrow footholds, and the others followed.

They made it to the dungeon level undetected. Huck warned them to pull back into the shadows. Before them in a courtyard, three werewolf guards lounged against a well in the middle. The courtyard was the center where the mouths of three corridors converged.

"Now what?" asked Tondor.

"The cells are down that corridor." Huck pointed.

"Let me handle this," offered the lieutenant. "Skender, stay with these folks. Help them find their friends." The dog remained planted at the side of Blackwick as the lieutenant sauntered out of the shadows and into the courtyard. He patted his pockets. "Anyone got a smoke?"

A weaselly werewolf with sneaky eyes and a suspicious smirk drew a cigarette from his shirt pocket. "Right, Lieutenant. Here you go."

The lieutenant set the cigarette on his lower lip and gestured toward it. Another guard held a lighter to the cigarette. "What's the word, Lieutenant? Blackwick caught yet?"

"Well, I'll tell you what, men." The lieutenant leaned his weight against the well. "It isn't easy trapping a thing of smoke and shadow. He can burn through rope and slip through cages."

The weaselly werewolf snorted a cynical laugh. "Everything's got some kind of weakness."

"Aye." The lieutenant blew a stream of smoke as his gaze wandered to the inside of the well, to the scummy circles in the water. "Everything does."

Skender's ears lifted as he noticed something gleaming on a stool against the wall to his right. It was a ring of keys. Tondor drew the others' attention to Skender as he used his nose to nudge the ring of keys off the stool. The keys clanked, and Skender hopped away.

The weaselly werewolf sprang forward at the sound and tickled the trigger of his rifle. "Did you hear that?"

The lieutenant clamped his paw over his fellow werewolf's shoulder and laughed. "You're on edge, sergeant. That's just the gate clanging shut outside."

"Aye," said the other guard. "That means the patrol's come back to report. Hope they caught them."

Once the werewolves were huddled back around the well, smoking and mumbling, Blackwick nodded to the hound to precede them quickly past the courtyard and into the shadow-laden corridor.

Skender snuffled at the doors as he passed, intent on the scent. Blackwick snapped his fingers and ignited a flame between them, lending light as they peered past the rusting metal bars that gated the cells. Most of them were empty.

Skender stopped in the middle of the corridor and lifted his paw. Katrinka hauled the ring of keys in the direction the hound indicated, and in her enthusiasm, she clattered the keys against the wall. Tondor glared. Katrinka blushed and mouthed a "sorry."

Blackwick tensed. He turned to Huck and jerked his chin toward the end of the corridor. Huck nodded and backed from the cells, his rifle ready, alert for any unwelcome visitors the noise may have drawn.

"Psst!" Peter Pan's face peered out from the bars of the cell where Skender waited. He gave Blackwick the scolding look one gives a runaway little brother. "Shadow. Seems you loosed yourself from my shoe again. Will you never learn to stick?"

Blackwick shrugged an apology.

Tondor and Katrinka framed the cell, overjoyed to find Peter Pan safe and sound. His face was smudged, and his Robin Hood hat and hose were mottled with straw, but his smile was as bright as ever.

"Tondor, Katrinka!" Frieda joined Peter at the cell door. "Is Betty with you?"

"Betty's with Mr. Hamberdeen." Blackwick inserted the key and pulled back the latch.

"Well," said Peter as he sprang to his feet, "it looks like it's war, chaps. These Epilogues won't stop until Ordog and Vorever are done for, and you know what that means. No more story worlds. No more world at all. So, we'll need every able-bodied boy we can muster to stop this dastardly crew."

"Yes, sir." Huck drew his knife and cut through the ropes that bound Peter and Frieda's wrists. "And every able-bodied pixie and lady, and dog, too."

"Say," Peter said, looking Huck in the eye, "I know you. You're one of the lost boys, aren't you?"

"We'll all be lost, I reckon, if we don't skedaddle on out of here in a hurry," replied Huck.

A shout rang out from the mouth of the corridor. "There they are!" It was Leslie. He had exchanged his dressing gown for Napoleonic splendor, close-fitting white trousers and a gold-braided, blue Hussar jacket. He stood half in the corridor, half in the courtyard, his concerned eyebrows lifted toward his friends but his hand waving the werewolves forward.

The guards surged in and surrounded the group. They plucked the pixies out of the air and scooped them into a bird-cage before Tondor could unsheathe her swords. Huck aimed his rifle, but the guards behind him yanked the weapon out of his hands. Peter hit the ground and was caterpillaring between the legs of the guards, but they caught him by the scruff of his neck and heaved him up in the air. Peter shouted protests and flung his fists to clobber them, but they held him away and chortled at his vain attempts. Frieda rammed her shoulder into the guard's chest. "How dare you! Two grown werewolves against one boy!" She hit them with both fists. "Let him go!"

The werewolves laughed even harder, and Skender growled, not at the children, but at the guards. Another guard leveled the muzzle of a pistol at Frieda's temple. Skender leapt for the wrist of the werewolf, snarling and worrying at the werewolf's joints. The guard howled in pain and dropped the pistol.

"Skender, no!" The lieutenant grabbed the hound by the scruff of the neck and shook him until he let go of the guard's wrist.

Blackwick dipped to his knees to grab the gun, but as he rose, he found himself hedged in by cutlass points and gun barrels, including the lieutenant's rifle. Blackwick glared resentment at the lieutenant. Skender crouched, his tail between his legs.

The werewolf guards shoved their captives into the courtyard. Blackwick released a short, bitter laugh as he passed Leslie. "This tower is teeming with traitors, it seems."

Leslie scowled. "Just let me explain."

Katrinka sat cross-legged in the bird cage, staring through the bars at Leslie with the lost look of one whose idol had fallen. "There's nothing to explain."

Tondor leaned her back against the bars and folded her arms, her furious glare fixed on the locked door of the cage. "Mortals. You can't trust them."

French stood at the foot of the stairs, flanked by Ilda and Avian. Two ravens perched on Avian's shoulders. Another clung to her arm, and one with an eyepatch roosted on her head.

Blackwick drew back in surprise at the sight of French. The werewolves pushed Blackwick forward, and he brushed the brim of his hat as he approached the gentleman warily.

French lowered his eyes and rubbed his forearm.

"Miroslav?" Blackwick, when he had been Edmond Davidson, had witnessed Miroslav, then the servant to Count Vlad Tepov, dragged down into the pit of Alsó-Világ. It didn't seem possible he could still be alive.

French half lifted his heavy expression. "Not Miroslav anymore. Miroslav died a pitiful wretch. I had given up hope. But

Haydee found me." He extended his hand toward the stately woman who descended the steps to join him. "She brought me back to the world I thought I had lost when I was betrayed by the Accusers. Just as you once were Edmond Davidson, I once was Edmond Dantes, and now, I have returned to the land of the living as the Count of Monte Cristo, or, as I prefer my alias, Monsieur Thomson French."

"Whatever name you go by now, I am glad you found your way back."

"Yes, not many of us find our way back from the Land of Shadow." He met Blackwick's gaze with a sad smile, acknowledging a brother who has walked the same path of suffering and survived.

"But if . . . why . . ." Blackwick threw a confused gesture toward Ilda, Avian, and the guards.

"They're villains, that's why!" snapped Peter, straining to free himself from the grip of the guards.

French shrugged and gestured to the guards holding Blackwick. "I must have the tin with the ashes. And Leslie tells me your friend Beatrice has it."

The lieutenant gripped Blackwick's arm and growled.

Blackwick ran a cautious hand down the baldric across his chest. "What tin? What are you talking about?"

Leslie shouldered his way past the werewolves and stood beside Blackwick. "It's no good, Ed. They know everything."

Blackwick glared reproach at Leslie. "And you handed it all to them without a thought for your friends." He seethed out disappointment. "I bet you took an awful beating." He ran a cynical eye over his cousin's gaudy uniform.

Leslie's eyebrows raised as if the reaction had stung him deep. "It's not like that at all. They're on *our* side. They hate Ordog as much as we do."

Frieda pulled against the grip of her captors. "You poor, stupid boy! Look what they've done to Neverland! Do you seriously think the Intercessors would agree to something like that?"

French stepped forward, his hands folded behind his back. "The Intercessors are fools. They are doddering old men and absent-minded women. Call Beatrice Talbin. Summon her here. We must have that page if we are to destroy Ordog once and for all." He snapped his fingers in Blackwick's face. "Come."

Blackwick raised his chin and remained silent. Two torches hung in wrought iron sconces on the wall. Blackwick reached toward the flickering flames to draw the power of the fire. The werewolves stared in dumb amazement as the flames on the torches bent toward Blackwick like the arrow on a compass drawn magnetically to the north. The flames whipped toward him, and the werewolves guarding him leapt back.

"Stop him!" shouted French, but the flames formed protective rings around the shadow man.

The lieutenant barreled forward, bearing two buckets of water from the well. "This will stop him." The werewolf flung one bucket's contents over the flames and sloshed the other at Blackwick. The shadow man screamed as the black wax smoked and sizzled, and the embers of red tore in zigzags across his entire frame. He dropped to his knees, arms strained backward, rigid with endurance. He tried to lift his sword, tried to draw once more from the torches, but he no longer had command of his own limbs.

Peter screeched as he felt his former shadow's pain.

"Stop it!" cried Frieda.

French stood over Blackwick, glaring down at him. "I am the master *here*. Call the woman. Call Beatrice Talbin."

Blackwick groaned but tossed his head in refusal.

Leslie averted his eyes.

Tondor tore off one of her boots and flung it at Leslie through the bars. "Do something, you dimwit."

French nodded from the captives to Blackwick. "Come, Davidson, you are a man of compassion. You come to me with pixies and little children. Do as I ask, and they will go free."

Leslie moved in front of Frieda and Peter. "Let them go. There's another way to summon Betty."

A werewolf sergeant shoved Leslie against the wall and slammed his fist across his jaw. Leslie slumped against Huck and crumpled to the ground.

Something metal clattered in front of Leslie. It was Huck's pocketknife. Leslie looked up at the lad.

Huck glanced down, winked, and shook his rope-bound wrists. Leslie nodded, grabbed the knife, and pushed himself to his feet.

Blackwick's body was bent over the stonework like a cornered animal. He heaved groans of excruciating pain.

Haydee blinked once and clutched her husband's hand. "He'll die before he betrays his love."

French motioned to Ilda. "We need him alive."

Ilda grumbled and, from the corner, she lifted a black amphora into her arms. She reached into the amphora and grasped at the chalky substance it held, muttering, "The crushed remnants of the Neverbush and the ground cinders of the golden scale snatched from the sacred table in Alsó-Világ." She held the amphora over Blackwick's head. "Stop squirming, shadow man." She tipped the amphora and dug out handfuls of the powder upon the burning wax of his frame. The powder absorbed the acidic reaction, suppressing the fire, and soothing the fissures. "Now, perhaps Monsieur French will concede to allowing me to try a different way. *My way.*"

French hesitated. He spat a curse, then nodded to Ilda.

Ilda cackled. She set down the amphora and waved her hand toward Avian. "Tell your brothers to fetch me the book."

Avian whispered to the ravens. "Marquis, Milverton, Moriarty, and Silver Boot, fetch the book for sister."

The ravens cawed and flapped up into the tower. They returned in moments, bearing the *Tome of the Netherdragons.* They dropped it in Ilda's outstretched arms.

Leslie was furtively cutting through the ropes that bound Huck's wrists. He had to work slowly, stopping whenever someone looked in his direction. He was on the last strand.

Ilda threw open the cover and read aloud from a page. "*Eenan inthum Margina gangen. Inthum Tramen onsem sangen.*"

A green mist broke out from the tome, like long, ghostly fingers, and whistled with a shrill, suctioning wind that dragged Blackwick toward it. He fought against it, but the force of the wind whipped around him and vacuumed him into the pages.

Skender sent out a distressed howl and looked to the lieutenant to help Blackwick. The lieutenant's mouth was firm. He looked away.

The ropes around Huck's wrists snapped, but before he could take a swing at his captors, the wind caught hold of him.

Skender disregarded the lieutenant and latched onto Huck's pant leg with his teeth, pulling him back with all his strength, but only succeeded in being dragged toward the book as well.

"Let go, Skender! Let go, you crazy dog!" shouted the lieutenant, but Skender refused to let go. The lieutenant threw himself at the hound and yanked him free of the boy's pant leg. The hound sent out a high-pitched whine as the lieutenant kept his arms firmly around the dog to hold him back.

Huck, Peter, Frieda, and the pixies all were pulled toward the book. Katrinka screamed. Frieda cried out, "Peter!" Peter reached toward Frieda. "Don't worry! We just need to — " But before he could finish, they had been pulled into the book, and the cover slammed shut.

Ilda laughed. "Now, we have even more leverage. Mr. Mallowan, if Blackwick will not summon Beatrice Talbin, perhaps you will oblige."

Leslie paled. "They aren't dead, though?" He cast a worried look at French. "You said you wouldn't hurt them."

French did not answer. His brooding frown was focused on the tome.

Upon not receiving an answer, Leslie looked from the werewolves to Avian. "They can't be dead. They're safe, right?"

"Dead?" repeated Avian as her ravens roosted once more upon her shoulders and arms. "No, no, not dead. But safe, no, not safe."

Ilda sneered. "Only Beatrice and her tin of ashes can help them now."

Leslie folded the Barlow knife and closed his eyes.

CHAPTER 30
PERLGATE (1930S

In the drawing room at Perlgate, Aunt Amelia sat Betty down on a chair and rang for tea.

"That will be all, Sarah," said Aunt Amelia after the girl had dropped off the tray on the tea caddy.

"Yes, mum." The girl heaved a tired sigh and left.

Aunt Amelia poured the tea and used the tongs to pinch a cube of sugar and plop it into the China cup.

Betty's head was swimming, and her chest ached. She had a vague memory of Hamberdeen hailing a cab and Aunt Amelia whisking her away. But it was all a haze overshadowed by the maddening roar of death at the bottom of Reichenbach falls.

"Tell me the truth, Betty." Aunt Amelia clanked her teaspoon on her saucer. "You've been off intercessing again, haven't you."

Betty nodded weakly. "He died. I can't believe he died."

Aunt Amelia choked. She set down her cup. "Leslie?"

"Oh, no," she quickly reassured her aunt. "Not Leslie. He's in Neverland."

"Oh. Good." Aunt Amelia stiffly resumed sipping her tea.

"I thought he would survive. Sherlock, I mean. In the stories, he survived."

"With all the risks that man takes, I'm surprised he didn't pack it in long before." Aunt Amelia lifted her pince-nez to her nose and examined the label on the tin of shortbread. "That girl. You'd think she'd enough sense to open a tin and place the biscuits on a platter like any civilized domestic."

Betty cringed for the poor girl, knowing too well what it was like to be an overworked piece of the furniture, invisible, that is, until something went wrong.

Aunt Amelia pressed her lips in a perturbed frown and watched the tea in her cup. "Mr. Holmes is not one to pop off without at least expressing his profound regrets." She offered the tin to Betty for her to help herself.

Shortbread was the last thing Betty wanted right now. "But he did," protested Betty, putting the shortbread tin out of her sight and into her bag without thinking. "I couldn't save him. Moriarty was supposed to go over, but, in the stories, we find out that at the last second, Sherlock managed to get loose and climb up the side of the mountain to hide, so that he could convince everyone he was dead. That way, he could avoid the vengeance of Moriarty's chums. But it didn't work like that. He really went over. My powers were too weak, and the corruption was too strong." She clutched her bag as her lower lip trembled. Finally, the tears pushed themselves over her lashes and down her cheeks.

Uncle Eric blustered into the drawing room, muttering past his moustache about someone throwing out his morning paper before he had a chance to read it.

Betty sobbed between short, sharp intakes of air. "It's probably still in the breakfast room."

Uncle Eric started as if Betty had appeared out of nowhere. "I say! It's young Beatrice! How are things these days? Off on holiday, they told me. A splendid time, I trust. Girls in your position don't get to travel much, more's the pity."

Aunt Amelia shot her husband a sour expression and shook her head. "Not now, Eric. Betty's had a disappointment. Can't you see she's crying? And what in Heaven's name is that!" Aunt Amelia extended her index finger toward the floor.

Betty lowered her hands from her face and looked where her aunt had pointed. When she realized what *that* was, her breathing began to regulate once more. "Portia."

The gray kitten rubbed against Betty's legs, back and forth, purring nonstop.

"Is that thing *yours*?" asked Aunt Amelia with a tight frown.

Betty gathered Portia into her arms and held the kitten's soft face close to her own. "Yes! She came to me, all the way from Vandor." She squeezed the kitten in a warm hug and cradled her like a doll. Portia did not even protest. She just gazed with awe and empathy into the tearful eyes of her human. "You knew I needed you."

Uncle Eric cleared his throat and pulled at his moustache. "There, there, Amelia. It's quite all right, I think. She can keep it as long as it does not get into my things. Now, wipe your tears, my girl, and stiff upper lip. Life is full of disappointments, and we can't always count on rich relatives to get us out of a scrape. Why, I remember my first excursion to Cairo, when the other chaps beat me to the tomb. Did I sit there and blubber like a baby? Not me. I just squared the old shoulders and determined my next move. Say, maybe what you need is a cruise. Meet a young man. Get married."

"That's an excellent idea," agreed Aunt Amelia. "And take that beast with you."

Portia and Betty exchanged looks that agreed no matter how much you thought your aunt understood, relatives would be relatives.

Uncle Eric reached into his desk and withdrew a travel pamphlet. "There you are." He tossed it on the table. "Up the Rhine? Down the Suez? A stopover at Monte. I hear that some girls would give their eyes to see Monte. You pick the place, save up your money, and before you know it . . ."

His voice faded into the background because as Betty gazed at the map on the open page of the pamphlet, the words "Cairo, Egypt 1890s" superimposed over Northern Africa, and she heard a voice – it was her cousin Leslie's voice – calling. "We need you, Betty! Hurry! Come to Cairo!"

Before Betty knew it, she felt herself and her kitten swept away in a sandstorm of map fragments.

Aunt Amelia was too busy muttering about what dirty, hairy, fur-ball spitting annoyances cats were to notice Betty had gone along with the tin of shortbread. And Uncle Eric simply wiped his monocle and muttered to himself, "Dash it all! She might have at least waited for me to book it with our travel agent."

PART FOUR

INTO
THE DESERT

CHAPTER 31
THE MENA HOUSE HOTEL (1890S)

Since the opening of the Suez Canal in the 1860s, Egypt had been a go-to vacation spot for fashionable Europeans, particularly after news of Sir William Petrie's reports on the pyramids of Giza. And with a view of the pyramids, where better for a European to set up lodgings than the Mena House Hotel, which, in addition to lawns for tennis and croquet, had recently announced its latest renovation, a swimming pool framed by swaying palms.

Betty arrived from Perlgate into the pool of the Mena House Hotel. The portal had given her the latest 1890s swimwear, bloomers and a sailor girl top. The waters of the pool were sparkling clear over the colorful brick-tiled floor.

Portia had materialized on a canvas patio chair, where she was guarding Betty's messenger bag and the tin of shortbread that had tumbled out. The kitten prrowed, clearly relieved she had not landed in the water.

A splash behind Betty drew her attention. She found Leslie swimming toward her from the deep end of the pool, wearing navy colored, knee length shorts and a matching short-sleeved top. "Well, there you are." Leslie spluttered on pool water. "Sorry to summon you so abruptly, but we can't get on very well without you."

Betty swam to the edge of the pool. "Did you make it to Neverland in time? Are Blackwick and Tondor all right? What about Frieda?"

Leslie avoided her desperate gaze as he treaded water near the side of the pool next to her. "About that. They're not *in* Neverland anymore. They're 'booked' . . . uh . . . somewhere close by."

Betty wondered why he was blushing. "Did you find the clue? Did you stop the corruption?"

"Oh, yes, that. I need to tell you all about that. But first, you won't believe who was here when I arrived." He pointed toward the patio entrance of the hotel where bamboo furniture and sun umbrellas were set up for the tourists in the shadows of palm trees.

Daniel Khumalo, the dark and handsome Intercessor of Zulu ancestry, emerged from the hotel, dressed in a white dinner jacket and loose slacks. Watching him carry himself with youthful confidence toward the pool, Betty couldn't help but recall that it had been only a year since she first collaborated with the twenty-something Intercessor. At the pool side, he smiled and extended his hand to Betty, and she accepted his help out of the pool.

"Betty. I did not expect to see you here. But it is a good thing you came." Khumalo snapped his fingers at the waiter with a word or two of Arabic and pointed toward a large, fluffy towel hung over the back of Portia's chair.

The waiter set down his tray and brought the towel to Betty. Betty dabbed her dripping hair as she smiled at Khumalo. His shining eyes were a welcome sight. "It's been a long time."

"Too long," he agreed.

Leslie hefted himself out of the pool and eyed Betty's towel with envy. "Never mind me, ol' girl." He raised a perturbed eyebrow. "I prefer to dry the old-fashioned way. I think it's called *sunburn*."

Both Betty and Khumalo glanced back at Leslie, annoyed by his disruption of their reunion.

"There are towels on the shelf there, Mr. Mallowan," Khumalo informed him curtly.

"*Inspector* Mallowan," Leslie corrected him as Betty handed him her towel. He ran it vigorously over his bare arms and legs.

Khumalo squinted at the sunlight. "The hotel lobby will be much more comfortable." He offered Betty his arm.

Betty hesitated. "Dressed like this?"

"This is a resort. Your attire is perfect." He smiled, and Betty linked her arm lightly with his. He guided her through the pointed archway entrance into the hotel. Leslie draped the towel around his shoulders and noticed the tin on the canvas chair. He checked to make sure the others were not watching and reached for the tin. Portia growled and flexed her claws.

Leslie glared at the kitten and withdrew his hand. Cursing to himself, he followed Betty and Khumalo. Portia emitted a loud meow. Betty stopped, looked back at the kitten, and shook her head. "What is it, you silly kitty?"

Portia nudged the messenger bag and shortbread tin and yowled as if telling her mommy cat that she had caught a prize mouse. Betty smiled. "Thank you, Portia." She threw the strap of the bag over her shoulder and picked up the tin. "We must not forget *that.*"

She hurried back to Khumalo, and the kitten stretched, plopped down from the chair, and paraded after Betty, with her tail and nose lifted at the precisely aristocratic angle to match the hauteur of the resort's clientele.

The lobby was deliciously cooled by a large wooden ceiling fan.

"I came to Cairo a few months ago," explained Khumalo. "*The Book of Ancestors* describes the Giza Plateau as a gateway to the Netherworld. The book predicts that a foolish mortal will arrive and open that gateway. All the signs point to a time close to this one." Khumalo gestured Betty and Leslie to the cushioned wicker sofas in a side nook of the lobby, ensconced between more ferns in clay pots. Betty sat back, the tin in hand and

Portia curled up on her lap. Leslie eyed the tin with interest and chewed on his lip.

Khumalo spoke in a hushed tone. "Isn't it rather curious that it is also at this time that a certain eccentric billionaire shows up with his Seven Wonders of the World Tour? Right here at the Mena House Hotel, in the very shadow of the pyramids."

"Yes, Thomson French is very rich and very powerful," announced Leslie, as if he hoped he was being overheard. "I was lucky enough to book us tickets for the tour. We've got rooms here at the hotel."

"Thomson French?" Betty recalled Blackwick mentioning that name in connection with the treasure chests he had discovered. "And what about Blackwick and the others?" She looked from Khumalo to Leslie for an answer.

Leslie ripped a frond off a fern. "I told you. They'll join us later. Oh, is that a tin of shortbread? If you're not going to eat it . . ." He reached for the tin.

"This? Oh, I better keep it. Portia would never forgive me if I didn't."

The steward showed Betty to the third floor of the hotel. The corridor was carpeted in gold with red fringe. Exotic stained-glass lanterns hung at intervals along the wall. At the far end of the corridor, Betty glimpsed a hunched figure peering out from a doorway, watching her. Betty stopped to see who or what that figure was, but whoever or whatever it was started, drew a black hood over its grizzled hair, and ducked into a room, slamming the door.

"Who was that?" Betty asked the steward, but he replied in Arabic, and she had not yet mastered the language enough to translate.

Betty found she and Portia were to share a room with a woman they had never met. The woman half sat, half lounged on one of the two beds, with a tour brochure in one hand and an unlit cigar in the other. She wore a belted khaki jacket and

197

Turkish trousers with the puffy legs stuffed into her boots. She introduced herself by striking a match on the side of her boot and lighting the cigar. "Tulliver's the name. Maggie Tulliver. And yes, darling," she said, noting Betty's surprise, "I'm one of those 'New Women' you read so much about. I'm not married, and I don't plan to be. I do hope you decide to wear *that* to the formal dinner tonight." She indicated Betty's bathing attire. "And the mule pack and kitty pitty are the perfect way to accessorize. What an absolute scream it will be." She poised her cigar's point toward the ceiling as she blew a whimsical wreath of smoke past her smirk.

Betty blushed as she let Portia climb down from her arms onto the other twin bed. "I – I lost most of my luggage, and I –" She set the messenger bag on the free bed and the tin on the bedside table.

"But you remembered the important things, I see. The wardrobe can tumble overboard, but God forbid you lose the shortbread!" She laughed. "No fretty fret, darling." She had a curious lisping accent that softened her manly façade. "I'm sure our stalwart crew of wayfarers will rise to the occasion." She pushed herself to her feet and glided with a weary resignation past Betty and out the door.

She was not gone long. "Here. This crepe number should look smashing on you. Courtesy of Madame French herself." The cream-colored dress had an asymmetrical cut, one side a toga style mantle, with a single strap over the opposite shoulder. The hem was lined with square-shaped symbols like those found on ancient Greek architecture.

Betty held it up to herself as she stood before the floor-length mirror. Portia prrowed in approval.

"It's beautiful! I wish Ed –" Betty glanced at the woman and blushed again.

Miss Tulliver ground her cigar butt in a marble ashtray. "Oh, so the little girl's got a beau. Don't bother me in the least, sweetie. We take what comes, don't we? Now, you go ahead and dress. I'll be downstairs. I hate not being punctual for dinner." Miss Tulliver paused at the door to their room, and Betty propped herself halfway on her elbow to show she was listening. "Wait until you meet the rest of the crew," added Miss Tulliver. "None of them's an actual pastry for the eyes, except maybe that Khumalo chap. He's got good shoulders. Monsieur French wouldn't be so bad if he was a bit taller and wasn't so distracted by his wife."

"Monsieur French? The billionaire?"

"Oh, yes, that does add heaps to his looks, don't it. See you downstairs, love."

CHAPTER 32
THE SUSPECTS (1890S)

The gentlemen of the tour relaxed in the lounge before dinner. They shook their heads, aghast at Miss Tulliver sitting by herself on the garden patio, sipping a whiskey on the rocks. Leslie, with his 1930s perspective, was not as shocked as the Edwardian gentlemen present. Where he was from, it was not unusual for a working-class woman to mooch a swig of the good stuff at the local, and, of course, there were the sirens of the silver screen with their lip rouge and cigarettes, setting a poor example for the giggling girls of Bedfordshire.

As for the male members of the tour, they consisted of the following: an American reporter with a loud tie and rumpled suit; a hedonistic lord with a face that hung in a constant poppy field of boredom; and a white-haired, bespectacled explorer, the stereotype of the European in exotic climes.

Leslie turned back to face the bar and said to Khumalo, who sat beside him, "Monsieur French certainly has gathered an odd assortment of loonies and louts." He tapped his cigarette into an ashtray. "I wonder why." He sincerely hoped Khumalo would not suggest that he, *Inspector* Mallowan, was one of the loonies and louts.

Khumalo leaned toward him. "One of them is a subdragon, a spy for Ordog."

Leslie coughed on his cigarette smoke. "Avian?"

Khumalo frowned. "No. Another subdragon. You see this ring?" He twisted the ring he wore to display the raised filigree of a gold serpent with a diamond eye. "An interesting feature of this ring is that the diamond eye turns a different color when a subdragon is nearby. Back in *King Solomon's Mines*, the eye turned red. That should have told me at once that Gogool was Avian in disguise."

Leslie studied the jeweled eye of the serpent. "But now it's yellow."

Khumalo nodded and turned the ring to hide the decoration. "So, Inspector, whom do you suspect?"

Leslie twisted his smirk to say something sarcastic, but he realized Khumalo was distracted, his eyes softening as he looked in the direction of the staircase.

Betty descended the stairs. Her Grecian dress was bordered with hand-blown mercury-lined beads that dazzled in the electric lights of the lobby. A woman adorned in a floral-embroidered gown of gold lamé met her at the foot of the stairs.

Betty recognized the jasmine-scented perfume as it brought back images of a leveled gun and the veiled woman the gentleman had called Haydee.

Haydee's mouth curved in a fraction of a smile as if she knew what Betty was thinking. "Good evening. You are new to our tour. The night has cooled comfortably. My husband assures me dinner will be excellent."

"Indeed, Haydee, my dearest." The voice was that of the gentleman who had called on Milverton back at Applegate Towers. Betty watched him approach from the other side of the lobby, dressed in chic eveningwear, draped with an extravagant velveteen cape fastened at the shoulder with a cameo brooch. "We at the Seven Wonders of the World Tours provide every luxury our distinguished guests could wish for. I am Thomson French, and this is my wife, Haydee." He smoked his cigarette at the end of a long holder and sported a signet ring.

Thomson French. Ah, yes, now she remembered where she had heard that name before. *The Count of Monte Cristo*, Alexander Dumas' novel about a young man wronged and imprisoned in Chateau d'If who returned as a wealthy count to inflict his revenge. And Haydee, the companion of the famous Byronic hero. Betty recalled that, in the book, the count sometimes used the incognito of a representative of the law firm Thomson and French as he spun his web around those who had wronged him.

French held his cigarette to the side as he appraised Betty. "I've seen you somewhere before. Or maybe," his green eyes made a quick tour of Betty's physique, "it's the dress."

"Yes, my darling." Haydee gently drew his chin back to her. "I lent Miss Talbin some of my clothes. I hope you don't mind."

"Mind?" He brushed the back of his wife's gloved hand with his lips. "Your charity is one of your most endearing traits. Now, come, my friends. Tonight, we feast, tomorrow, the pyramids!"

Khumalo met Betty as she crossed the lobby, and his admiring face glowed. Betty hadn't seen him smile so brightly since the time in Kukuanaland when she and her friend Foulata had giggled about him being a good catch. And now, he did look handsome and rather gallant in his evening attire. He offered her his elbow to accompany her to where the gentlemen and ladies of the tour were congregating around a long table set for a sumptuous dinner. Cards had been placed on each setting to indicate who was to sit where.

Betty nudged Khumalo and subtly signaled with her head toward French. She formed the name silently with her lips. "The Count of Monte Cristo." Khumalo frowned, nodded, and pondered French like a psychologist noticing the symptoms. Betty whispered, "We need to talk after dinner."

Leslie dropped a word in Betty's ear as he passed. "They're all suspects."

"Suspects?"

"One of them," replied Khumalo softly, "is a subdragon." Before Betty could ask any more questions, Miss Tulliver approached, and Betty sidestepped to allow room for her to pass.

"Evening, darling." Miss Tulliver squeezed past Betty and Khumalo. "I hope your cat isn't mussing my new stockings upstairs."

"Oh, no, Portia is careful not to . . ." Betty nearly tripped over a man's shoes. She looked to see the faded shoes belonged to the explorer with gray, bushy eyebrows and mustache. He was slouched against a pillar of the archway framing the dining area, smoking a pipe.

He dropped his pipe and muttered a curse as he bent to retrieve it. He peered over the rim of his thick spectacles at Betty. "Oh, madame, excuse such bad language," he said in a thick Norwegian accent. "I am not of usual like so bad manners. Forgive please. Herr Sigerson." He put his free hand over his heart. "Explorer."

Betty nodded a brief reassurance to the man and darted a questioning glance at Khumalo, wondering if the thick spectacles could be part of a disguise for a subdragon.

Khumalo pulled out Betty's chair for her. The Norwegian explorer was seated to her left and to her right was a middle-aged, well-dressed gentleman with a neatly trimmed moustache, who smelled of expensive pomatum and cologne. The place card before him simply read "Lord Henry." He bore the look of boredom so fashionable among the well-to-do at the turn of the century.

Miss Tulliver sat across from Betty. She shook her folded serviette out and dropped it neatly across her lap. To her left was a short American, who wore a wrinkled suit and crooked tie and punctuated his sentences with a half-smile and a wheezy sort of laugh. The American was next to a chipper, pointy-nosed woman with a plain but eager face. On Miss Tulliver's right sat Khumalo. On the other side of Khumalo was Leslie, who watched French as if awaiting a signal.

A gong sounded. The lights dimmed, and French positioned himself at the head of the table, his hands raised like a magician about to perform a miracle. His wife glided to his side like the magician's beautiful assistant.

"Ladies, gentlemen," announced French, "welcome to the inaugural feast of our Seven Wonders of the World Tour, the first phase of which will culminate with a visit to the famous Pyramids of Giza. Tonight, their silhouettes will delight you while you dine." He indicated the large rectangular window that afforded a spectacular evening view of the great pyramid guarded by the Sphinx with the lesser pyramids in attendance. "But for now, Mesdames and Messieurs, let me treat you to a taste of Egypt, no expenses spared."

He clapped his hands to summon the waiters. First, the waiters brought ewers of water to wash the guests' hands. Then, a low light gleamed from a hidden stage lamp and focused on the tray carried in by the next round of waiters. They removed the silver cloche, and steam carried the succulent aroma from the platter with flaming shish kebobs skewered through chunks of tender lamb upon a bed of couscous. As the waiters slid the pieces of meat onto the guests' plates, they stifled the flames with their utensils. The main course was served with brown-spotted flat bread the waiters called "Eish balady."

By the time the coffee and baklava were served, the guests were satisfied and comfortable enough to engage in casual conversation.

"Will they let us explore inside the pyramids, do you think?" Leslie shot a glance toward French, but the gentleman ignored him.

Miss Tulliver lit her cigar and leaned back in her chair. "I doubt it, darling. I've been here on this sort of tour before, and all they ever let me do is climb to the tippy top of the dear thing. If you ask prettily, I'm sure Mr. McFey there will prop up his cam and snap a posy of you and the Sphinx. No doubt Sphinxy will sit up and purr if you scratch the darling behind its ears. After all, he's just the great ancestor of that kitty pitty of Miss Talbin's."

Leslie scowled at her baby talk. "I've been on a few digs myself, you know. My father is a . . ."

"Coal-tar derivatives," interrupted Herr Sigerson in a loud voice. "Ja, *that* is the thing worth the exploring."

Betty tilted her head. Coal-tar derivatives? Why did that term sound familiar?

French smiled and set aside his demitasse. "But you have seen so many more interesting things in your travels, professor. Florence, Tibet, Persia . . ."

"Persia!" exclaimed the American, who was flushed with too much after-dinner wine. "Now, there's a place I'd like to see. Isn't that where they do that thing they call the hoochie coochie? Heh heh. Bet they have some terrific babes there. Oh, ladies, pardon moi, heh heh."

The woman beside him slapped his hand. "Frank, really! Don't mind my husband. He comes from a good family, but working as a reporter has taught him such bad manners."

"Darling," drawled Miss Tulliver, with a glare of contempt at the reporter, "if all you can do is stare at a woman's navel while she swings her bustle about, you've no more intellect than a baboon."

"That's me. Monkey McFey they call me, heh heh."

"Please, Frank!" pled his wife. "Personally, I want to see the ghosts." And she poked her nose forward, as if eager to catch the reaction she had sparked.

"Ghosts?" echoed Lord Henry through a yawn.

Mrs. McFey beamed as everyone turned their eyes to her at last. "Yes, it's delicious. They say a ghost of Pharaoh Whatchamacallit still haunts the great pyramid, guarding the passage to the underworld."

"It is the Sphinx," put in French. "The Sphinx comes to life and speaks to those who are worthy. So the legend says."

Betty chilled at those words and glanced again at Khumalo, but his expression only revealed disapproval of Miss Tulliver's cigar smoke. "I, too, have been researching the history of this land," he announced. "Another legend says that the Sphinx was built to seal in something much worse than a ghost." He stared conviction in the direction of French.

French remained aloof.

Miss Tulliver smashed her cigar. "So, is it true that the pyramids are cursed?"

"People are always curious about exotic things that are cursed," complained Lord Henry. He shined his monocle on his lapel and replaced it by widening his eye and scrunching his face into a grin. "Yet the real curse is either being too young to understand the pleasures life presents or being too old to enjoy them. Wouldn't you agree, Miss Talbin?" He surveyed Betty with a leer that made her uncomfortable. There was certainly something oily and sinister about Lord Henry.

"A lot of tosh," sniffed Miss Tulliver. "You're an intelligent man, professor. What do you say?"

The explorer watched the ceiling with interest. "The Khalifa of Khartoum once to me confided, 'Evil is unavoidable, but inevitably, the judgment, it catches up.'" He took a pipe from his pocket and filled it with tobacco from a small pull-string bag.

French motioned for the waiter near him to refill the American's glass. Mr. McFey's eyes shone at the generous portion poured from the bottle.

"But about your explorations," continued French. "What is it you seek?"

"Once," replied the Norwegian, "the High Lama in Tibet to me described a corruption."

Corruption. Betty turned her full attention to the old man beside her. The soft lighting of the dining area and the glow from the rising moon outside played upon his features, so it was difficult to read his thoughts.

The explorer continued. "Corruption, said the Lama, comes from the choices we make, to do the thing that is right or the thing that is wrong. When we see the thing wrong as if it were right, and the thing right as if it were wrong, ah, then, I think we die, little by little, and we are no longer able to notice. But," continued the Norwegian, "the High Lama saw the hope. He showed me a scroll written in ancient Tibetan calligraphy, and the writing described a conch shell from which was birthed the

206

conscience of humanity. If the one who is chosen will on that shell call, the guardian of the shell will return to reawaken our conscience. It is that same shell that I seek. I am told it is here I may find it. Until then," the old man lowered his eyes wearily to his pipe, "we see vice, slaughter, and . . . slavery, eh, Madame French?"

Haydee gasped and dropped her spoon. "How did you know?" She clutched the bracelet around her upper arm.

The explorer shook his head as he struck a match. "One would think they would outlaw slavery by now." He paused before setting the match to the bowl of his pipe and said to Betty, "Oh, do you object to pipe smoke, Miss Talbin?"

Haydee pushed herself from the table. French frowned darkly at the explorer. "How dare you say such things about my wife."

With an indignant glare, Haydee strode from the dining area. Her husband scowled as he surveyed the others at the table. "Please, enjoy your coffee. I will see you all at breakfast." He rose and marched after his wife.

Leslie wiped his mouth with the corner of his serviette and mumbled an apology. He also rose and traipsed after French.

Lord Henry leaned toward Betty with a suave uplift of his eyebrows and a subtle distend of his nostrils that made her stomach churn. "The moon is beautiful, Miss Talbin, and the night is cool. Would you join me on the veranda?"

Khumalo came to the rescue. "Miss Talbin promised me a turn in the gardens before retiring."

"Yes, you sillies toddle off," said Miss Tulliver through a yawn. "I want to read the racing column before beddy bed." She paused halfway as she rose, her body still bent. She put her hand to her forehead as if to ensure it was stable. "And you've had enough drinky!" she snapped at Mr. McFey.

The American smiled genially and hiccupped.

CHAPTER 33
THE MARGINALIA (THE BENT YEARS)

The whirlwind from the forbidden book had died away. The wire cage was gone. Tondor awoke on her back in a wasted landscape, alone. The skeletons of dead trees clawed at the sky. Green lightning ripped through the murk and sizzlcd the colorless stubble that once had been a meadow.

The pixie struggled to push upward, fearful of what may have become of Katrinka. She used her dagger like a climbing peg to drag herself across the wide, empty field.

She tried to move her tired wings, but they were wilted and dim. She looked at her hands, dismayed to find her pixie dust had turned to handfuls of dirt, which sifted through her fingers.

Poor little pixie. The voice rumbled like an invisible giant.

"Who are you?" She tried to pull herself to her feet, but she stumbled, and her face hit the mud. "Peter! Katrinka!" She waited, but the only response was the thunder and the lightning and the wide expanse of a dark, dying world.

You are all alone now.

She gulped, but the swallow stuck in her throat. No Peter? Poor Katrinka, out there somewhere, watching the world die, alone, without anyone to protect her.

No one believes in fairies anymore.

"That's a lie!" Tondor shook her fist at the lowering clouds.

No one believes in you, Tondor Char. Wars are fought by mighty heroes, not by the feeble, not by the worthless.

Pain was gripping her body. Her heart was too cold to sparkle any longer. She crawled under a cleft in the rock and hugged her knees close to her chest like an infant afraid to be born.

Peter Pan woke from a long neverness to find himself bound to a great, black mast. Pirates with greasy moustaches and blue chins crowded in with their cutlasses and blunderbusses. Peter gagged when one held a foul bottle marked with a skull and threatened to pour him "his medicine." He shook his head vigorously to focus.

"Avast, ye rum rats and barracuda bait!" announced a man's voice with the perfectly rolled r's of one educated at Eton. The crew parted like the sea by a divine hand to reveal a tall gentleman of high breeding and cruel eyes. Peter knew this man. The hook he wore, where his hand should have been, gave him away.

Peter flung a glare of bravado at the pirate. "Let me go, Hook, or I'll call your old friend to have a little talk with you. Make that a little *tick* and a *tock*."

Hook waggled his index finger. "None of that, none of that. Young man, you've eluded and outsmarted me since the first doodle doo doodled its doo in Neverland. But, bicarbonate of soda, you have crowed your last crow. Behold! I've got a bit of leverage to lend ballast to me threat."

He twirled in a tarantella quick-step to the side and revealed Frieda, balancing precariously on a wooden plank outstretched over the roiling, green-crested sea.

"What shall it be?" demanded Hook. "Give to me your eternal youth. If you don't, your little friend plunges to her death among the sharks, the krakens, the piranhas, and other equally nasty, bitey things."

Frieda tossed her head with defiance, her glasses balancing at the tip of her nose. "Don't mind me, Peter. Vorever will save us. You'll see."

Hook burst into laughter, dabbing his watering eyes. "Ah, how touching. But Vorever has nothing to do with Neverland. He never has. He never will."

Peter lowered his brows and frowned. His eternal youth. He sought inside for that soothing forgetfulness, that ignorance of danger and loss. But instead, he found fear, haunted memories, and panic for young Frieda.

"Give me your youth," pressed Hook. "That means, you will need to swear on all that is lovely and wonderful that you will grow to six foot two, wear uncomfortable shoes, shave every morning, and spend all day worrying about not enough time and not enough money. You'll have gobs of headaches and get all fat and hunched over, and one thing – the most important – you must never, ever have any fun at all."

Peter stared, too horrified to speak.

"Well?"

The boy lifted his chin, but he had no words.

Hook shrugged. "C'est la vie!" He waved his handkerchief. The pirates gave Frieda a shove.

Peter's heart beat like the desperate wings of a caged bird. Vorever would show up, or a regiment of pixies, or the mermaids!

They didn't.

Frieda screamed and was swept into the cold, endless deep. Peter's insides turned to ice, as if the waves had engulfed him, not her . . .

Huck woke to see a sky filled with green stars floating past above. The wash of rippling water near his ear startled him, and he realized it was he that was floating, not the sky. He lay on the wooden planks of a homemade raft, with a lantern bobbing from a makeshift tent.

He pulled up to a sitting position and rubbed his tired eyes, wondering where the werewolves and the shadow man had gone.

A boy sat at the other end of the raft, his knees hunched up and his hands folded atop his knees supporting his sharp chin. His mischievous eyes glowed green and his mouth spread into a grin across his freckled face.

Huck blinked and rubbed his nose. "Do I know you?"

"Sure ya do," answered the boy in a ragged voice. "It's me. Your ol' pal, Tom."

Huck felt the worry fall off his shoulders. "I sure am happy it's *you*, Tom."

"And well you should be. You sure are in a pickle. Yep. You've gotten yourself in a barrel full of trouble, and it takes someone like me to get you out of it."

"I'm stuck in this here book," said Huck. "How does a body get out of a magic book, Tom?"

"You don't," replied the boy with a shrug.

Huck's eyebrows raised, and his mouth hung open. "How come? Seems there's got to be something a man can do when he's up agin it."

"Can't ya see, Huck? Getting stuck in this here book is the greatest stroke of luck a feller could ask for." The boy lay back on the raft and folded his hands behind his head. "Nothin' to do but laze around on this here raft, look up at the sky, and dream of all the things you don't have to do. No fences to whitewash, no nagging grownups to run from, no school to play hooky from, and no stupid stories to bore you to tears. Just a long, long river."

"Yeah," sighed Huck with a smile. "You're right." Huck leaned his back against the mast and yawned. "A long, long river. But," he yawned again, "what about Blackwick? What about the pixies? Seems I should try to . . ."

"Shut up!" The boy flashed a glare of rage at Huck but let it soften back into a grin. "I mean, you've done your bit. Now, there's nothing more to do but relax and dream, dream and relax."

"Yep," sighed Huck, pushing his straw hat over his sleepy eyes. "Dream. Relax. The long, long river."

Blackwick jolted awake and scrambled into a sprinter's "set" position, darting a wary glance all around. The room was dark but familiar. That damp chill, that lichen-crawling wall, the hollow plunking of a rusted pipe. It was the cellar of the charity school, where the headmaster Bickerstaff had often locked him in to think better of his rebellious ways and repent.

The darkness gripped Blackwick's chest as the walls seemed to crash in on him. He pushed himself to his feet and rattled the door. It was securely bolted shut.

He turned at the clanking of chains. A dark figure, slumped on the discarded mattress in the corner, lit a lantern. The lantern glowed a cold, pale green, casting crescent-shaped gleams upon the chin and cheekbones of the figure.

"Good evening." It was a voice Blackwick never thought he would hear again.

"Count Tepov?"

The chains clattered as the man coughed. "Looks like we meet again after all." Tepov made a tired attempt to smile through his misery.

Blackwick knelt on one knee. "This can't be real."

"Yes, one of those hellish nightmares." Tepov sniffed a cynical laugh. "They come for us all sometime. Especially for soulless creatures such as you and me."

Blackwick stiffened. "I'm not soulless like you. Betty –"

"Ahh." Tepov leaned his head back against the rock wall and ran his tongue across his dry lips. "The delectable Beatrice Talbin."

The wolf within Blackwick growled and shot out a hand to squeeze Tepov by the throat, but the hand passed through the count's shimmering ectoplasm.

Tepov's shoulders shook with laughter, accompanied by the jingling of the chains that bound his wrists and ankles. "Please. Still as much a fool as ever. Don't you realize?" He tilted his head, his long, unkempt hair hanging to the side as he narrowed his green-tinted eyes at Blackwick. "There's no more you and Betty. Ever."

Blackwick stood and kneaded his palm with his fist. "You can't keep me here."

"It's not because of this place." Tepov fixed him with pitiless eyes. "It's because of who you are."

The light from the lantern grew stronger, casting a triad of shadows upon the cellar walls. The first was the shadow of a wolf, standing on its hind legs and sending up a mournful howl. The shadow in front of Blackwick was the spritely silhouette of a youth with a Robin Hood cap. The shadow on the other side was the outline of a man, shoulders set back, and head held high.

"A werewolf?" Tepov sneered. "What feelings can a beast have for someone like Betty? Nothing but the basest passions. What long claws you have. The better to crush her frail body with. And what sharp teeth you have. The better to rip apart her delicate flesh. Oh, yes, a fine companion you'd make for such a sweet, young girl."

Blackwick bowed his head under the count's relentless glare, weighed down by self-inflicted unworthiness.

Blackwick's reaction lent momentum to Tepov's energy. "And . . . a child. A poor, rejected child." He sighed in mock compassion. "Yes, I suppose Betty might tuck you into a drawer to keep you safe or let you listen in on the stories she tells the other children. No, of course not. No one has time for a wayward waif, do they?"

"That's enough."

"But now we come to the likeliest of the three. *Professor Edmond Davidson.* Handsome. Charming." The chains clanked as Tepov lifted himself to his feet. The shackles forced him to stand hunched over, but his eyes glazed with triumph. "Oh, but wait. Edmond Davidson didn't give poor little Betty the time of day. He was too busy making a name for himself and showing off for that society girl, that Daphne Graham."

Blackwick clenched his fists at his side. "You're wrong. I always looked after Betty."

"The only one you ever looked after was yourself." Tepov watched Blackwick with eager anticipation.

Blackwick stumbled backwards against the opposite wall. It was cold and damp, but he barely sensed it. "You win. I am a freak. A monster."

"At last. You come to the truth."

"Yes. Like Bickerstaff used to say, 'What makes you think you deserve anything, you little brat? Why not confess your sins and die?'" His hand reached instinctively for his dagger. It slid from its sheath, and he held the point towards his own chest. Tepov's grin widened.

But a peace permeated Blackwick's chest, like hot buttered rum on a brisk Yuletide evening. He lifted his head, puzzled by the peace, but into his ear softly rumbled the voice of Vorever, saying, "Put the dagger away. You are Blackwick. And your legend has just begun."

Startled at finding the dagger in his hand, Blackwick cast it aside. Instead, he reached inside his vest, where the peace seemed to originate. He drew from his vest his book that glowed as if infused with sunlight. Pages fluttered of their own accord to a specific selection. Words were etched into the page in a firm, golden calligraphy. He heard Betty's voice saying what the calligraphy had written. "Edmond. Wherever you are, don't give up hope."

The words were like a balm upon every cut, every scar, every fear he had ever borne. He replaced the book inside his vest, and his hand brushed against the tin of ashes he had slipped from Betty's bag. He closed his eyes and laughed past grateful tears of dripping wax. "Count Tepov." His voice was soft but firm. "You lose."

And the apparition of the count and the triad of shadows disappeared into the gentle folds of darkness.

CHAPTER 34
SPIES AND TRAITORS (1890S)

Betty lay awake, watching the sheers hover in the breeze whispering through the half-open balcony doors. There was too much to think about to sleep, what Khumalo had said about a subdragon spy and what the Norwegian explorer had said about the conch shell. Miss Tulliver snored in the opposite bed. She had dropped off as soon as her head reached her pillow.

After dinner, Betty and Khumalo had strolled in the Mena House gardens, their gazes drawn to the crescent of moonlight above the great pyramid. The sliver of light was echoed in the rectangular pools of the garden rills between the rows of flowers. The light scent of Khumalo's cologne comforted Betty as they paused beside the garden wall. "The moon looks so magical." She rested her arms on the wall's ledge. "Even on Vandor, the moon is often lost in the clouds. But here . . ."

He leaned against the wall next to her, his rich voice exuding a hint of his Zulu accent. "'Art thou pale for weariness. Of climbing heaven and gazing on the earth. Wandering companionless among the stars that have a different birth, — and ever changing, like a joyless eye that finds no object worth its constancy?'"

She blushed, both pleased and embarrassed. "So now you're quoting Shakespeare." She tried in vain to suppress her smile.

He wrinkled his brow. "No. Shelley."

"It can't be Shelley." She scrunched her nose playfully, though she realized she had not read as much poetry and classical drama as she should have. "You're trying to trap me. I know my Shakespeare."

He shrugged. "Very well. 'When my love swears that she is made of truth, I do believe her, though I know she lies.'" He bent closer to her and whispered, "*That* is Shakespeare."

His fingers, on the ledge of the wall, nearly touched the tips of hers. She felt a sort of electricity in her fingers, like a magnet drawing her hand to his. When she allowed herself to face him, it was as if she had never truly seen his eyes before, but she could read the poetry there more clearly than any spoken word. At last, she asked, "So, which one is it? The subdragon?"

Khumalo contemplated the pyramids. "I suspect Miss Tulliver."

"Because she's unconventional?"

He frowned. "What else would an unattached woman her age be doing so far from home?"

Betty heaved a sigh and shook her head.

"If not Miss Tulliver, who?" he asked.

"I don't know. It's a bit of a toss-up for me, between Mr. McFey and the English lord. McFey looks like he could be hiding something." She leaned her back against the garden wall. "Do you think the subdragon is working for Ordog or The Epilogues?"

He knitted his eyebrows. "Epilogues?"

"Oh, I forgot. They're a new faction out to free Zed-Cyphrr. We've been following clues on the chart to try to stop the corruption from spreading, at least until Vorever can return with reinforcements."

As she spoke, Khumalo had been drawing closer and closer to her. Now she was gazing directly into his eyes and finding it quite difficult to concentrate.

"What clues have you found?" he murmured as his gaze wandered, from her eyes, to her nose, to her lips.

"Three so far," she answered. "The heart double broken from Sydney Carton."

"And the other?" He barely touched a wisp of hair near her ear.

"'The words never spoken from Sherlock Holmes.'" At remembrance of Holmes falling to his death, she swerved her attention from Khumalo, to the faraway moon.

Khumalo sat on the wall and plucked a flower from a shrub. "And the third?"

"A clue for Neverland. Find the foe that is a friend."

"And did you find that?"

Betty blinked, startled and confused. "Actually, I don't know. Blackwick, Leslie, and Tondor went to Neverland. Did Leslie tell you anything?"

"No. He only said he was here on secret Intercessor business."

Betty tapped her finger on the wall and pressed her lips together in thought. "That's odd."

"He will tell us all about it tomorrow, no doubt."

They said goodnight at the foot of the stairs. Before she started up, he took something from his pocket, a gold necklace. He removed his serpent ring and strung it on the chain like a pendant. "A gift." He folded it into her hand. "For the Keeper of the Golden Vigil. The eye of the serpent will change color whenever a subdragon is near."

On her way to the room, Betty had caught another glimpse of the hunched figure watching her. The lighting was dim in the corridor, but she recognized the protruding eyes and wrinkled visage. The old woman from the Carpathian village, Ilda.

Now, unable to sleep, Betty propped herself on her elbow. "Portia?"

The kitten was perched on a cabinet table like a ceramic cat idol, ears tensed forward, tail twitching.

"Do you think Blackwick is all right?"

Portia prrowed.

Betty lowered her eyes with a shy smile. "Yes, I know. Daniel is quite nice. And maybe . . ." She gazed back at the ceiling, and, as she watched the shifting light and shadow of the fan, she became puzzled and sad. She picked up the necklace Khumalo had given her and sifted its golden links through her fingers. "You know, Daniel didn't even notice the rash on my hand. He didn't ask why the mention of Sherlock made me sad." She set the necklace down upon the table. "Blackwick noticed." Betty turned over on her stomach and hugged her pillow to her face. "I wish he was here right now. Edmond. Wherever you are, don't give up hope."

It was after eleven o'clock, but through the open door came the rattle of horse-drawn hantoors and a tide of voices speaking Arabic. The scent of jasmine was overpowered by strong cigar smoke. Two men were speaking a few feet away.

Betty climbed out of bed and drew on the hotel bathrobe. Behind the sheers were the shapes of three people on the balcony. Betty placed her hand on Portia's head to quiet her, but the kitten continued to complain in a low growl.

"You hear that? What if she's awake?" It was Leslie's voice.

French replied, "She must be asleep by now. I paid the waiters good money to drug the wine."

"But this one did not drink wine. I watched her." The third voice was Haydee's.

"Well, *Inspector* Mallowan, you said she had the tin. Do you want to help us or not?"

"I will, I will," protested Leslie. "But what should I say if she wakes up?"

"You are a clever fellow," said French. "You will think of something. Now, throw away that cigar and go. The door is open. See?"

Leslie, shirtsleeves rolled up to the elbows, parted the sheers, and slipped in. He was startled by the two cat eyes glaring at him.

Leslie fluttered his fingers in a nervous greeting to Portia and circled around the kitten. He surveyed the room, sweat shining on his forehead. He turned to find Betty, flattened against the wall, watching him.

He licked his lips the way he did whenever Aunt Amelia had caught him sneaking into Uncle Eric's whiskey or cashbox. He managed a forced laugh. "Ah, yes, I just . . . I saw someone, and I wanted to make sure you were safe. So many strange characters about."

"Yes. There are." Betty's eyes were steel.

"So, um, the ashes. You have them safe somewhere?"

"They are safe," replied Betty. "I think you should get some sleep."

"Yes, you too." He hesitated, running a glance over the room. His eyes lingered on the little table between the two twin beds. Betty followed his line of sight to the tin of shortbread. *He thinks that's the tin with the ashes.*

He caught her watching him, and he blushed and turned to exit. He hesitated and looked back at her. "Sure you're fine?"

"Yes."

"Very good. I'll, uh, toddle off to bed, then." Leslie granted her one last forced smile, and he backed out onto the balcony.

Betty released the breath she had been holding steady. She closed the door after him and drew the heavier drapes firmly across the two panels.

"Cousin Leslie, a traitor. Why am I not surprised?"

Portia offered no answer.

CHAPTER 35
MEANS AND MOTIVES (1890S)

Betty had difficulty waking Miss Tulliver the next morning. A pungent whiff of ammonia jolted the woman out of her drugged sleep.

"You don't have to get up. I could ring for room service," Betty offered as Miss Tulliver nursed her pounding head with a moist sponge.

Miss Tulliver groaned. "The Mena House is famous for its generous breakfast buffet, and today we visit Khufu and his chums. It'll take more than a knobby noggin to deter me."

Fortunately, Miss Tulliver had one or two backup outfits suited for an excursion. In fact, she had one that went perfectly with Betty's messenger bag. Once both women had pinned up their hair, buttoned and belted their khaki jackets, stuffed their wide-legged pantaloons into their boots, laced and tied their boots, and adjusted the pith helmets at a slant primed for adventure, they descended to the hotel gardens as the sun splayed its rays from behind the points of the pyramids.

Khumalo looked handsome in white trousers, matching belted jacket, and tan hat as he rose to greet them on the garden patio. He offered to fetch the ladies something from the breakfast buffet. Miss Tulliver shooed him away. "No, no. There was something odd about the wine last night. From now on, Maggie Tulliver serves her own food." She pushed past him toward the buffet.

Betty sat across from him at the bamboo table. The eager brightness of his smile echoed feelings from the previous evening. But Betty frowned to prove to him she was much older and wiser than she had been in the garden last night. She sat back in her chair and pushed her hat behind her head so that the strap at her throat held it in place. "Did you know about Leslie?" She shot him a glance to check for a flicker of untruth.

He laughed and poured her some tea. "I know about his promotion to inspector. He never stops reminding me. I sometimes . . ." His eyes met hers, and he abruptly righted the teapot in mid-pour. "What have you learned?"

His expression was honest, so she decided to take a chance. "Leslie was in my room last night. He was looking for the ashes. Whoever has those ashes can recreate the page that will release the power of Zed-Cyphrr. Do you see? Leslie has betrayed us."

"That is most unfortunate," said Khumalo, "for *him*."

"And if Leslie was lying, Blackwick and the others are not coming after all."

Khumalo held Betty's tense hand in his. "I think we should look at the chart."

She was about to produce the chart from her bag, but before she could, Mr. McFey, his wife, Lord Henry, and Miss Tulliver brought their breakfast plates out on the patio.

"What a morning, heh heh." Mr. McFey slid into a chair. "I didn't think I'd ever wake up in time for the old coffee and donuts."

"Really, Frank. People don't eat donuts in Egypt. Forgive him," his wife added to the others with a chirpy, nervous smile. "He's usually quite brilliant."

Lord Henry drew his chair close to Betty and dropped her a suave, tired glance. "Only dull people are brilliant at breakfast."

Before Lord Henry had a chance to barrage them with another epigram, Sigerson joined them on the patio and lit his pipe.

"No breakfast, Professor?" asked Mrs. McFey.

"You're missing out on a real treat," added Mr. McFey.

The explorer shook the match to extinguish its flame. "No. No breakfast for me. I don't have hunger much times."

Betty unpocketed the necklace and glanced at the serpent's eye. The eye was topaz. *But which one is it?* She surveyed the members of the tour with suspicion and leaned closer to Khumalo. "You find out what Leslie is up to. I'm going to examine the chart in my room while everyone's here at breakfast." When she rose to leave, the strap of her bag caught on the chair, yanking it off her shoulder. The Norwegian hurried to help her gather the items that had scattered across the patio. Some loose change. The rolled chart. The conch shell. She apologized for the mishap, thanked him, and proceeded into the lobby.

She was heading toward the stairs, when she saw, among the guests and native merchants, Ilda, wearing a tasseled shawl over her head and shoulders to blend in. In her cupped hands, she held a bowl filled with lotus blossoms floating in water and was purporting to sell them to tourists.

Now was the time to deal with the opposing side. Betty took a deep breath and marched up to Ilda. "It feels like a long time since the Carpathian inn."

Ilda tilted her head, and her mouth hung in a silent cackle. "And where are your friends today, beautiful young woman? You had many friends to stand with you against Ordog in the village. Will you fare so well against the mighty one of power?"

Betty's knees felt wobbly, but she breathed in deeply through her nose and straightened her spine to exude calm confidence the way Yamada had taught her. "An Inter-Story Intercessor has an army of friends," she quoted her Sensei. "Every library, every bookshop, every page, and every word are allies to those who know how to read." In all honesty, she did wish more of her Intercessor friends were here, especially now that Leslie had betrayed her and Blackwick was missing.

Ilda maintained her fake smile for the passing tourists to whom she offered the bowl of lotus blossoms. "But not all books are your friends, eh? *The Tome of the Netherdragons*. Safer in our hands than in yours, I think. Better if you join with us, eh?"

Betty spoke through clenched teeth. "Join with you? Not for all the jewels in the crown."

Ilda chuckled. "But to save your friends, eh? Perhaps then? Monsieur French wishes to talk with you. He knows where to find your friend Blackwick. He says . . ." She paused, offered a price to a native in Arabic, and continued. ". . . Meet him in the training room, on the other side of the stairs."

Not that I trust you for one minute. But let's just say I'm ready to do away with guesswork and get some frank answers for a change. Betty rounded the stairs to confront Monsieur French a.k.a Edmond Dantes a.k.a The Count of Monte Cristo.

CHAPTER 36
CROSSING SWORDS (1890S)

Betty entered the training room to find French alone in the center, wearing form-hugging white trousers and a padded white shirt. He stood with his heels together and his hand upon the pommel of a foil, with the point touching the floor.

"Beatrice Talbin." He acknowledged her with a nod of respect.

"Edmond Dantes." Her nod was a bit more reserved. She removed her pith helmet and held it in the crook of her arm.

"We've met before."

"At Milverton's Estate."

"Before Milverton. We called you the weeping lady. In the garden, by the old well. Do you remember?" He took a step toward her, still leaning a bit on the hilt as if it were a decorative walking stick, offering little support but serving as an excellent prop.

Betty frowned, wondering how much to concede. "I once had a pilgrimage to a well." She discreetly drew the necklace from her pocket and glanced at the eye. It was clear.

"More than once, I assure you." He raised the thin blade and examined it. "You regularly haunted that well. You see, I was a servant at Vlad Tepov's lodge. During my long exile from home, I endured the existence the Accusers forced upon me. I have a great hatred for the Accusers, and especially Ordog. He stole something of immense value from me."

Betty raised cynical eyebrows. "Your famous treasure?"

"No. My dignity. My life. My soul." He fixed her with fiery green eyes.

"What did he offer you for your soul?"

French granted her a small smile and stepped backwards to select another sword from the rack. "You mean as he lured your cousin, Edmond Davidson? You are like him, you know. He was kind to me. You, too, have eyes that are kind. But, I think," he added, studying her, "a little more intelligence and, yes, determination." He extended a foil, hilt toward her.

She looked at him and looked at the sword. She had limited practice with the foil. But she decided this was a challenge she would not shy away from. She set aside her hat and her messenger bag and accepted the foil, balancing the pommel in her palm and thumb as Tondor once had demonstrated.

He smiled sidelong at her and raised an eyebrow. "Perfect. Now a duel between gentlemen – or, that is, between two who honor loyalty and who never forget a wrong."

Betty extended into *en guard* position. "Do you really think Zed-Cyphrr will help you?"

"Ah. You know our purpose." He raised his sword before his face, then, swept it in a downward arc to accept her challenge.

"Yes, I know what you seek." She thrust her sword forward.

He parried and disengaged. "We searched your room." He circled around, still on guard. "Very clever to leave a decoy. That was a tin of cookies. Where is the tin with the ashes?"

A smile curled at the corner of Betty's mouth as she watched her opponent for his next move. "Ashes? I think shortbread would go much better with tea, don't you?"

"I am not the boy Hansel. I am not tempted by sweets. Something greater, something that we can restore and set free at last."

"Speaking of gingerbread houses, what did you promise Leslie? A place in your kingdom?"

He lunged. Betty blocked it with her blade. "Not bad, Miss Talbin. However, I must insist." He stomped forward, backing her toward the opposite wall. "Where is it?"

Betty managed to deflect his attack. "I used to sweep out ashes from the grate. But I'm not a housemaid anymore."

He tilted his head. "Come. Work with us, and we can stop the Accusers. Work against us, and you will be caught up in the retribution."

Betty's wrist ached as it strained and twisted to block each cross. "I told you. I don't have the ashes."

"Please don't lie to me. I have endured lie after lie all my life." Each stressed syllable was punctuated by a clang of the swords. "I thought I could rely on *you* to tell me the truth. *You.* The favored one of the Golden Dragon."

"I *am* telling the truth." Their swords X-ed between them. French gritted his teeth. Betty pressed her lips.

"I see. I must be brutal." He pushed against her sword with added force. "What if I told you your friends are in danger? The only way to free them is to give me the ashes." He disengaged and stepped backwards but kept his sword ready, like a rook facing a pawn in a game of chess.

Betty breathed in slowly. "In danger?"

He shrugged and circled the point of his sword toward her. "It is out of my hands. They are imprisoned in the *Tome of the Netherdragons*. Only the ashes can release your friends."

Betty's face drained of color. She backed away from the sword. Through unsteady lips, she whispered, "You have made a terrible error."

"Why? How? I have planned it all perfectly. I know you will do anything to help your friends."

Betty's sword dropped and clattered on the glossy wood floor. "I truly wish I had the ashes now. But when Avian followed me into the tea shop, Blackwick slipped the tin out of my bag. I didn't realize it was gone until later. He took it. To keep me safe." She cringed at the thought of him being so clever with his gallant sleight of hand.

French's eyes widened in alarm. "No. You must be lying." He raised his blade and charged toward her. Betty braced herself, no time to retrieve her weapon.

A foil blocked the attack.

Professor Sigerson, sword in hand, pushed back with the calm strength of one who had been well-trained. Maintaining the block, he tucked his chin and raised his eyes to French over the rim of his spectacles. "I think you will not kill her today, eh?"

French relented and threw down his sword. He glared from Sigerson to Betty. "You should never have let him take it. Now your friends are trapped inside the tome for all time. The page was the only key. And now there is no way to get it back. Ever."

The explorer gave a little shrug. "Losing is not such a bad thing. Even the greatest must sometimes fall."

French cursed. "There must be a way. There must be. I have come too far." He stormed out of the training room and slammed the door so hard the room rattled.

Sigerson shook his head and tsked. "Such much fuss. Fortunately, I've had a little practice with the dummies." He waved the sword for emphasis and put it away on the rack. He turned back to Betty with a smile that promised a witty remark at French's expense, but the smile faded to concern as Betty crumpled.

The explorer stretched forward and caught her. She leaned against his vest. The watch chain felt cool and comforting to her feverish cheek. She mumbled weakly, "There must be a way. If we find the right page of the right book . . ."

He pressed her forehead with his hand as if the touch could withdraw the fever and guided her to a sitting position on the floor. He knelt there beside her, monitoring her symptoms.

"What is going on?" She stared into her two empty hands, the palms clammy and shaky. "Sherlock dead and now Edmond and Frieda. Why?" Her hands clenched, and her eyes filled with tears.

Sigerson heaved a sigh. "Ja, ja. It is ever such. Friends will be here, and, poof, they are gone." He shook his head at the cruelty of the universe. "But we can trust in Vorever. He has purpose for it all."

"You know about Vorever?"

"Bosh, what kind of explorer would old Sigerson be if he did not study the deities of ancient times?"

"But where is Vorever now?" she asked. "He's so far away."

"Perhaps," said the explorer, pushing himself to his feet, "he is not here because he *knows* he can trust *you*."

Betty stared up at the tall man before her. "But my friends. They're trapped. Monsieur French says the ashes were the only key."

"Oh, this much, that much." He bent and picked up Betty's hat and her bag, then extended his arm to help her to her feet. "But one does not always need a key to open a door, does one? Hm?"

Betty sought his mysterious expression as she accepted his help up. "What do you mean?" She took the hat and bag he offered her.

"Sometimes it just takes the right combination or the right tools." He nodded an encouraging smile at Betty. He studied her features and glanced at her hands with concern. "You've had a rough time of it. I think a little tea, perhaps."

Betty walked with Sigerson into the lobby and allowed him to order her some tea and biscuits. The dining area was nearly empty, with only a few waiters cleaning the tables and clearing away the breakfast buffet. The explorer took his pipe from his pocket.

Betty was distracted by a middle-aged couple passing the table, the man, tall and stalky, with crinkled eyes and a neatly trimmed mustache. He glanced at Betty as if delighted to run into an old family friend. He gestured his wife's attention to her, and they approached the table. He drew a magazine from his coat pocket.

"Miss Talbin. Fancy meeting you here," he hailed in a brisk Edinburgh accent. "Have ye read the latest issue of the *Strand*?"

Betty blinked, confused. "Me? How do you know my name?" She looked at Sigerson, hoping he could provide a clue, but he was intent on unclogging his pipe.

"Why, everyone knows *you*," laughed the man. "I was telling the lads at the cricket club if it wasn't for you that old curmudgeon Holmes would still be dead. But thanks to you, the heaviness that bogged me down was lifted, and I decided why not. Let's give that old know-it-all another chance after all." He handed the magazine to Betty. "There's a bonny tale in this issue that will tell you all about it. Yes, Holmes is still alive. Though confidentially," the man leaned close to Betty and whispered, "I doubt his stupid friend Watson is aware of the fact." He glanced sideways at Sigerson and chuckled. "Oh-ho! And don't you try to ignore me. I know who *you* are – *Professor Sigerson*!" He winked and nudged him with his elbow.

The woman with the gentleman tugged on his arm. "Come along, Arthur. I don't want to miss our cruise down the Nile!"

"To think, my own character, real as life before me, and me on a schedule." The man she called Arthur shrugged and followed his wife.

Betty gulped as a startling realization struck her. It couldn't have been, could it? She wanted to catch up with the man, to beg him to explain, but he and his wife had already disappeared into a hantoor. She didn't remember meeting Sir Arthur Conan Doyle before.

He said the heaviness that bogged him down . . . The corruption? Perhaps when I placed the letter from Holmes on the chart?

Betty turned her scrutiny to the magazine. There was the date in a circle on the bottom right of the cover, Dec. 1893, the same issue in which "The Empty House" was first published.

"He's quite right, you know." The explorer's voice had lost its Norwegian accent, replaced by a rich and precise English diction.

She met his gaze. "Sherlock!"

He put his long finger to his lips. "Sh!"

She looked around cautiously and lowered her voice. "Sherlock. How can it be you? Moriarty killed you."

Holmes wriggled with silent laughter. "It worked beautifully. Poor Watson wrote a most tender and convincing account. But I thought you, of all people, would have figured it out by now."

Betty stiffened and raised an indignant chin. It stung the more because it was true. She *should* have remembered the alias Sigerson from the story "The Empty House." But she refused to admit it to him. "I did not figure it out because you, sir, died at Reichenbach Falls. I saw with my own eyes. Moriarty pulled you down into the chasm . . ."

He frowned. "Odd. I don't remember you there. Were you there really?"

"Yes, I was," she huffed. "Don't you remember? You looked me right in the eyes. I tried to help you. But there was no way you could have escaped."

Holmes leaned back with a satisfied smile and folded his arms at his chest. "Ah. But Moriarty did not count on my knowledge of baritsu. That's a Japanese form of wrestling, you know." He closed his eyes with the serene bliss of bestowing a nugget of rare knowledge.

Betty had always found that reference in the short story about "baritsu" a bit odd, and when she had asked Yamada about it, he had insisted there was no such thing as a Japanese form of wrestling called "baritsu." She could not resist the opportunity to address the issue. "I'm sure you mean jujitsu."

Holmes sniffed, his pride offended. "Well, *you* may have learned jujitsu, but, for myself, I studied *baritsu*. And it was quite handy. Poor Watson." His expression softened as he once again looked at the *Strand*. "He, too, was convinced I had gone over the falls." Betty noticed tears barely forming in his eyes. "I never did tell him, but he is quite a good writer. I was counting on that. He has a way of capturing the public's imagination with his turn for the sensational. And it had to be convincing."

Betty sat up straighter, and her eyes sparkled. "That's it! What I saw was 'The Final Problem.' It wasn't until later that

Doyle decided to bring you back. That's why you don't remember seeing me there. I was in the original version, and you were in the revised version, the one where Sir Arthur rewrote the encounter to explain how you survived. *Doyle had to rewrite your reality in 'The Empty House.'* Undo what had been done. Don't you see? Even when they say it's hopeless and there is no other way, we still have a chance to change things."

CHAPTER 37
THE EPILOGUES (1890S)

Khumalo ascended the grand staircase of the hotel, sliding his hand along the banister as he curved into the lantern-lit hall. His white suit and tan hat lent exotic contrast to the shadows. He made a sweep of the hallway in one glance, looking for Leslie's room.

That cousin of Betty's. Khumalo frowned his intolerance. Loyalty was important to him, loyalty to his ancestors and loyalty to his friends. For Leslie to have broken that trust with Betty was unforgivable. If it were up to him, Leslie would be shunned by the Intercessors, exiled into one of the contagion-ridden books he had helped to destroy.

Khumalo found the door to 205 ajar, so he nudged it open with the toe of his boot. He found Leslie lying on the bed, his shirt unbuttoned and untucked, his hair uncombed. On the table beside him was an expensive box of El Ray Havana cigars. "Oh, hallo, Khumalo old chap," slurred Leslie. This early, and he had already been drinking too much.

Khumalo yanked Leslie forward by the sides of his shirt. He wrinkled his nose in disgust. "You smell like a traitor."

Leslie pushed Khumalo away and fell back against the headboard. He hovered an unsteady hand over the cigars, let the hand drop to pick one up, frowned at it, and threw it like a dart against the wall.

Khumalo shook his head. "So, is that what Monsieur French promised you? A box of cigars?" He scooped a couple of half-unwrapped gourmet chocolate bars and waved them at Leslie. "Sweets?"

Leslie flinched as if Khumalo's glare had jabbed him in the gut. "Go ahead. Tell me what a disappointment I am. Tell me how I'm the scum of the earth and how poor little Betty had been counting on me." He ran a hand over his unshaven chin.

Khumalo clenched his teeth and could not speak. He tossed aside the chocolate.

Leslie pushed himself to his feet, poured water into the basin, and washed his hands.

Khumalo's convicting eyes followed him.

Leslie shifted his shoulders as if trying to relieve an itch in the middle of his back. "Well?"

Khumalo bent his head forward, his eyes raised, forcing Leslie to meet his unwavering gaze. "I don't understand you. You fought with us side by side against the titans. Mr. Hamberdeen treated you like a son. Edmond and Betty are your cousins. What in the name of Vorever made you do it?"

Leslie focused on scrubbing his hands together. "Yeah, you know."

Khumalo raised a knowing eyebrow at Leslie's hand washing. "I think you've washed them enough."

Leslie wrung the towel in his hands. "Now don't give me that holier-than-thou business. How do we know the Epilogues aren't right? Thomson French is the Count of Monte Cristo, for God's sake. We both know the Count of Monte Cristo isn't the bad guy, at least not in the comic book version, he wasn't."

"The Count of Monte Cristo was a man who was wronged. And when a man thinks the whole world is against him, it is easy for him to assume he has the right to destroy everyone else. But no one has the right to decide the destinies of others. That is why Vorever gave us a choice. But this new friend of yours wants to summon Zed-Cyphrr. Think, Leslie. *The Epilogues*. The end of the book. The end of everything we know and care about."

"Oh, please." Leslie's exasperated groan was not making points with Khumalo. He pushed past the Intercessor to throw himself back on the bed as if sinking into a resigned sleep would relieve him of any responsibility.

Khumalo slapped Leslie to wake him. Leslie's eyelids fluttered open, and his eyes wandered groggily about the room. Khumalo shifted as needed to keep Leslie's straying focus on him. "Betty says you went to Neverland to find the 'foe that is a friend.' Did you succeed? Leslie, look at me. *Did you succeed?*"

Leslie shrugged and reached for a cigar. "You're all against me. I guess you would say *I* was the foe."

Khumalo gave the idea consideration but shook his head. "No. *You* are a friend that became a foe. Not quite the same thing. Was there anyone or anything in Neverland that you first took as an enemy? Someone or something dangerous that surprised you by helping you or your friends? Think. Even if it seems like nothing to you, it may have more significance than you realize."

"Surprises?" Leslie's lips smirked around his cigar as he lit it and puffed smoke from the corner of his mouth. "Since I met you lot, I've had nothing but surprises." He pressed on the fingers of his left hand one at a time as if counting them would help recall all that had happened. "Katrinka the pixie surprised me, but not the way you mean. There was a crocodile pirate, but he didn't help us, far from it. And Huckleberry Finn. We thought he was working with the pirate, but he was under a spell. But foes? Friends? It's too confusing." Leslie threw his face into his hands.

Khumalo shook him by the shoulder. "What else do you remember? Think!"

"There was a dog. A hound." Leslie stood and paced the room, his voice becoming less slurred and more excited. "He belonged to one of the werewolves. Lieutenant Tynan was the werewolf's name, and Skender, yes, Skender was what he called the dog. A scary dog, too. But, when Huck was being pulled into the book, the dog surprised me by trying to save him." Leslie froze for a second staring in wonder into space as if replaying the scene on the plaster of the hotel wall.

Khumalo grabbed Leslie by the wrist. "That must be it. Do you know where this dog is now?"

Leslie pulled his arm free and moved to the window. He flicked back the blinds and checked the view below. Khumalo joined him in peering past the sun glare down to the hotel portico and circular driveway. There, a train of camels knelt in a queue outside the hotel, saddled and draped in expensive silks with golden tassels.

"A camel caravan? Really?" Khumalo shook his head. "The pyramids are less than half a mile that way."

"Didn't you read the brochure?" Leslie waved it with a world-weary laugh. "The Seven Wonders of the World Tour includes an exotic night under the stars among the splendor of the majestic monuments. It's part of their plan."

Khumalo noted one of the camels was harnessed to a cart packed with camping gear and crates, another to a large cart laden with black chests covered by a great, white canvas. While the camels grunted and hummed, their keepers calmed them by holding their reins firmly and speaking softly. The guide, a large man muffled in a white cloak and keffiyeh, seemed to be explaining something to the members of the tour. Resting on his haunches in the shade of the portico was a gaunt hound, his eyes steadied upon the broad-shouldered guide.

"That's the dog." Leslie pointed. "There."

Khumalo rubbed his chin. "Are you sure?"

"You can't miss him. He's not the sort of dog we see in England."

"You say it's the werewolf's dog." Khumalo's gaze drifted from the hound to the men handling the camels and equipment. "So, that guide, perhaps even the camel trainers, are werewolves."

Leslie met Khumalo's concerned expression. "Yes, and they say they can summon Zed-Cyphrr. They say he's bigger and more powerful than Ordog and Vorever put together."

235

"No dragon is as powerful as Vorever."

Leslie did not acknowledge Khumalo's last remark. "Look! Monsieur French. What is he doing?"

Khumalo pushed open the window, watching and listening to what commenced below.

French stormed past the caravan, yelling something about the day's plans being called off, and he slammed a bag that clanked like coins into the hand of the guide.

"I wonder what changed his mind," murmured Leslie.

Khumalo's face lifted, impressed, having no doubt it was Betty who had thwarted their plans.

"But wait," said Leslie. "He's talking to that woman."

"His wife?"

"No, I think – yes, that's Avian, disguised as Madame French's assistant. There with the bracelets and veils. Her eyes look like they could burn a hole through a wall."

"Avian! What is she saying to him?"

Whatever the female assistant said had the miraculous effect of clearing the storm clouds from the face of French. He strode with his usual confidence back to the camel caravan, tossed another bag to the guide, and the guide resumed preparing the tour members for the trip as planned.

French gestured for the lead guide and three of the camel trainers to follow him.

Khumalo hit the back of his hand on Leslie's chest. "Come. Betty needs our help."

"It is a dangerous habit, playing the hero. I advise against it, old man," said French.

The disguised Holmes had shifted his weight to spring from his chair, but his movements were arrested in mid-action when the nose of a pistol was pressed against his temple. The lieutenant and two of his men arced around Holmes' chair, and Betty's peripheral vision told her French and one of his men were behind her.

She met Holmes' eyes and accepted the message that they were outnumbered.

"Mr. Khumalo and Mr. Mallowan, where are they?" demanded French.

Betty and Holmes remained silent.

"Where are they?" The lieutenant tossed a pouch into the hands of a wide-eyed waiter in the lobby.

"They went upstairs," the waiter informed them after checking inside the clanking pouch.

"Then, let's wait for them. There. At the foot of the stairs." French shoved a pistol into Betty's ribs and nudged her into place before the stairway. The lieutenant prodded Holmes at gunpoint, and Holmes complied with his demand.

Betty breathed in sharply when she heard Khumalo's voice on the landing, worried what French and his ruffians might do. Leslie and Khumalo descended then froze in the middle of the staircase.

"That's right," said French. "Come down, slowly."

Betty fidgeted and frowned at the pistol. She felt her fingers tense around the strap of her messenger bag. She sent a sharp glare at Leslie.

Leslie slumped down two steps, paused, and glanced back at Khumalo.

Khumalo did not budge. "Lower the gun."

"Not until . . ." French indicated the remaining steps with his chin.

"Put the gun away, and we will talk."

"I'll drag him down for you," growled one of the lieutenant's men.

"No. He's a brave man. I respect that." Monsieur French inclined his head in a bow toward Khumalo and put the pistol back in his shoulder holster.

Khumalo continued with Leslie to the foot of the stairs.

Holmes, resuming the mannerisms of the Norwegian explorer, motioned toward the wicker furniture in the seating area of the lobby. "May have seat? Much better if like gentlemen we talk." He smiled easy politeness.

French relented, and once Betty and Holmes had seated themselves in the sofa and Leslie and Khumalo had drawn up the chairs on either side, French leaned against a column framing the seating area and kneaded his knuckles. The lieutenant and his men loitered nearby, watching, while the blades of the ceiling fan spun flickering shadows across the sun-misted scene.

Khumalo gave Betty the type of focus an administrator would give the CEO, his attitude suggesting all others present were extraneous. "What do you need me to do?"

Betty looked away from French and allowed the steady gaze of Khumalo to infuse her with confidence. "There may still be a way to save Neverland and rescue our friends."

"Right," inserted Leslie, leaning forward on his knees and twisting his hat in his hand as he darted a guilty glance toward his cousin, "just give them their blinking ashes."

Betty shot annoyance under her eyelids at Leslie. "Blackwick's got the ashes."

Leslie drew back. "And he's . . . What do we . . .?" He looked toward French for an answer.

French rubbed his signet ring. "We have the *Tome of the Netherdragons*. The book has revealed a secret to Avian. There is a ritual that will call forth the ashes and release those trapped within. The ritual will require us to work together. It makes sense, does it not?" French tilted his head back and closed his eyes. "I want revenge. You want your friends. If you follow our instructions, everyone is happy."

Holmes chuckled.

French's eyes snapped open. "You laugh, Professor?"

"No," Holmes assured him. "I would never laugh at *you*. I was merely thinking about oysters." French looked at Leslie as if the young man would know how to translate this odd phrasing, but Leslie sank further back into the chair and tore a leaf from the

238

potted fern beside him. Holmes prattled on. "Curious things, oysters, and so prolific."

Apparently giving up on Leslie, French turned to Betty.

Betty shrugged but had difficulty suppressing a knowing smile. The odd bit of dialogue reminded her of something Holmes had rambled about when pretending delirium in one of the stories, and she caught on to the idea that he was conveying a coded message. She played along. "So true, so true," she sighed with exaggerated solemnity. "One never knows with oysters. It's a wonder the whole bed of the ocean is not one solid mass of oyster."

Holmes fed off Betty's morsel of encouragement. He wrapped an arm over the back of the wicker sofa and crossed one leg over the other, like one about to plunge ahead full into conversation. "It's their *shells*, you see." He turned his hand over as if imagining the swirling shape of a shell in the air in front of him and examining it with interest. "The shell is a remarkable thing. The friction builds it up. Calcium carbonate and sediment from the sea. Building, building, all the time. Yes, Miss Talbin, I commend to you the shell." He tapped his finger on her messenger bag and lifted his eyebrows.

Betty followed the direction of his finger and returned a subtle nod. *The Mer-shaman's conch. Of course. Call the Mer-shaman. That's what Tondor had said.*

French was clearly not amused by the bivalve banter. "Bother your oysters and bother your shells. If you want to save your friends from certain death, you will cooperate."

Miss Tulliver stormed in from the front entrance, more than a little miffed. "All right, now, it's going to be a scorcher in a bit. If we don't get our camels lopping along soon, we'll all die of sunstroke or of boredom, whichever claims us first."

This was just the distraction Betty needed. While French reassured Miss Tulliver of their soon departure, Betty slipped the conch shell from her bag, set it to her lips, and blew, producing a resounding, haunting call.

"Stop her!" The shriek was from Ilda. She had followed Miss Tulliver in and now stared at Betty in horror.

The lieutenant yanked the shell from Betty. "I apologize, ma'am, but the lady says no." He handed the shell over to French.

Betty gave a little shrug and sent a small, mission-accomplished smile to Khumalo. He, in turn, folded his arms and gave her a congratulatory nod, and her heart warmed.

"Really, chaps!" Miss Tulliver rolled her eyes. "It's not exactly music hall stuff, but if it makes the silly girl happy, well, why not."

French and his men ushered the tour members out of the lobby and toward the waiting camel caravan.

"Don't worry, *Count*," said Betty as she passed him on her way out the hotel door. "You are right. There *is* a way to save my friends."

"By the way," put in Miss Tulliver, joining Betty on the front portico, "something odd turned up in my carry along case. I believe it's yours." She picked up a fluffy, gray kitten and plopped Portia into Betty's arms.

CHAPTER 38
THE PYRAMIDS OF GIZA (1890S)

Harangued by merchants from both sides of the street, the Seven Wonders of the World Tour paraded from the hotel toward the open desert area. The camel train plodded uphill for half a mile in the late morning sun, the great pyramid before them growing more enormous the nearer they drew to the Giza Plateau.

The Sphinx crouched at the gateway to the plateau, a towering monument of mystery. As they passed under its shadow, Portia clutched the horn of Betty's saddle with nervous, extended claws. Betty whispered to the kitten, "Don't worry. We've got this."

As if echoing her shaky voice, her camel emitted a nervous groan. She gripped the reins more securely. Miss Tulliver, who was an old hand at these adventures, had shown her how to hold the reins. "Firmly," she had said, "but no tugging." *That's the way to deal with these Epilogues . . . work with them for now but let them know who holds the reins.*

Khumalo drove his camel alongside hers. He appeared confident and relaxed, one leg crossed over the saddle in front of him, his shoulders and waist swaying in a natural motion with the camel. He nodded toward the hound sitting in the back of the cart. "Leslie suspects the dog is the foe that is a friend."

Betty was not convinced. "I wouldn't go by what Leslie says. Look at him, riding alongside Monsieur French as if he was his henchman. And speaking of people not to be trusted . . ." She craned her neck to look back at Lord Henry, dawdling along as if he was in no great hurry. His impudent eyes burned like shiny yellow pebbles at her back as he lifted a leather-gloved hand and traced a double curve downward in the idealized shape of a woman's figure.

Betty shuddered.

"He's a real beauty, isn't he." Holmes drew his camel on the other side of Betty. "I met him before in Selby. If ever I could land that one in the Old Bailey, I'd count it a good day's work."

The American couple brought up the rear. Mr. McFey was sneaking gulps from the flask he had filled at the hotel bar. Mrs. McFey looked a bit sick from the jostle and bumps of the camel.

"They seem all right," said Betty.

"Perhaps," said Holmes, "but I did notice Mr. McFey helping himself to a pocketful of Monsieur French's treasure. I wonder if our host will even miss it."

Miss Tulliver, riding with the guides, seemed born to sail the desert on camelback. She shouted gibes at the Americans for their lack of spirit. "Don't dawdle now! Embrace the adventure!"

"I like her," said Betty. "She's brassy and bold. A little like Miss Fernsby with none of the rough spots ironed out."

South of the Sphinx were the ruins of an old temple surrounded by a crumbling rock wall. Nearby, the camel trainers helped the tour members dismount and went about setting up the camp. French, confident in his close-fitting trousers, tall riding boots, and open-chested poet shirt, strode through the hubbub of disguised werewolves with orders to unload the gear, water the camels, and prepare refreshments for the guests. "And the large pavilion with the gold fringe, that belongs to Madame French and me. Set it up on the far side of the plateau, there in the shade. And see that Madame's things are handled with care."

He stopped where the lieutenant was helping Betty from her camel. French put one foot on the short rock wall and leaned against his knee toward Betty. "What do you think, Miss Talbin?" He gestured toward the Sphinx. "The guardian of the passage to the Netherworld. It has stood sentry for thousands of years, waiting for me to arrive at last."

Betty glanced at Portia, who was curled on her shoulder, agreeing with the kitten's expression that French was taking this "chosen one" role a bit too seriously.

"But for now," said French, "we must be patient a little longer. Settle in and wait for the moon to –" His eyes caught on the glint in the serpent suspended from Betty's necklace. He tensed. "What does that mean?"

"It means there's a spy in your tour group. One of them is a subdragon, and we suspect, in league with Ordog."

French whipped in a 360-degree arc, checking each point of the compass. He clutched her hand so tight it hurt. She winced. "Mingle. Look around. See if your talisman can uncover the spy. Then, report to me. Ordog's interference would be tragic for us both. Remember, he once enslaved Davidson the same as he did me."

Betty was glad when he released her hand. Still half facing her, he walked backwards toward the carts where he joined Khumalo and Sigerson. He directed their attention toward the sky, the point of the great pyramid, and the paws of the Sphinx as if explaining some impending alignment of all three.

Mingle. All right. I'll start with the least suspicious. Of course, one often finds that the least suspicious is the most likely to be the guilty party. That's how it is in those Agatha Christie novels anyway.

Betty found Miss Tulliver instructing the workers on the proper way to set up a tent. "Hallo, Betty. You look a bit all in. Try a slosh of this." She handed her canteen to Betty.

Betty swallowed the gritty water and pushed her knuckles across her mouth. She was not quite sure how to begin.

Miss Tulliver fanned herself with her helmet. "The sun's whooping it up like blazes, but a little roughing it never harmed anyone." She pulled back the flap of her tent. "Still, no sense in roasting like a pig. Pull up a cot and give your toesies a rest."

Betty ducked her head and followed her in. She let Portia down to explore the inside of the tent. It wasn't too much cooler inside, but at least they were out of the sun. Betty sat, trying to ignore how the metal frame of the cot dug into the back of her thighs. "Miss Tulliver . . ."

"Oh, bosh. Call me Maggie. If you can't call your own roomie by her first name, it's a washout from the start. Sure you won't smoke?" She offered a cigar to Betty.

"No, no." Betty waved it away. "But I am curious. What brought you to Cairo?"

"Ah, that. Well, you see, my dadsy, he's pretty well off, and he wants me to settle down and marry, but I won't have none of that, now, will I? No. I'll be drummed out of hell before I take the bands. So, I'm off to see the wonders of the world. And will you look at me." She laughed with a good-natured defiance. "Back home it's flood season, and here I'm in a roaring desert. What about you, Bets? You running from the bands too?"

Betty lowered her eyes with a shy smile, and, as she did, she checked the pendant on the necklace. It was clear. Miss Tulliver rang true. "Something a bit bigger than that. Frankly," she dropped her voice to a whisper, "I'm on a secret mission, and I don't trust anyone, especially Monsieur French and Lord Henry."

"They're fishy, all right. Well, if that hoity-toity Thomson French or that geezer of a lord gives you any strifey, you can count on Maggie Tully to give them a wallop where the bells ring."

Betty laughed. "Thanks, Maggie." She interrupted Portia's enjoyment of swatting at a loose string on the cot and reshouldered the kitten. "Off to question more suspects." She winked, and Miss Tulliver punched the air to cheer her on.

Betty found Mr. and Mrs. McFey sitting on crates, gazing at the pyramids.

"Oh, there you are. Have you heard anything?" asked Mrs. McFey. "Do you know if we get to see inside the pyramids?"

Mr. McFey shook his head and shared his weary, tolerant expression with Betty. "She's after spooks. She can't stop talking about it. Yackety yackety. Now me, I go more for the spirits that come in a long, cool bottle and make everything look peachy rosy. Speaking of which, do you think our host keeps the strong stuff in the big tent?"

Betty adjusted her necklace, pretending to move the pendant out of Portia's reach, but really using the gesture as an excuse to check the serpent's eye once more. Still clear. The McFeys were not subdragons. She assured them she would make inquiries and get back with them.

"So, who is it, Portia?" Betty wondered as she headed across the camp back to Holmes and Khumalo.

The kitten mewed.

Betty laughed. "Yes, what if it was Leslie all along." She stopped in her tracks near the rock wall and shielded her eyes from the sun as she scanned the plateau. "Speaking of Leslie, where has he got to?" She grew worried at finding no trace of her cousin anywhere in the camp.

"Beastly." The voice of Lord Henry behind her made Betty jump. Portia's fur rumpled.

Betty turned to find him leaning against the crumbling wall of the ruins, taking her measurements from under languid eyelids. "If I were a pharaoh, I'd insist on being buried someplace comfortable, where the music is soft, the water is cool, and luscious grapes are served by beautiful men and women."

Betty scrunched her nose. He smelled of sweat-drenched linen. He ran his thumb along the ends of his mustache and peered through his monocle at Betty with a lazy leer. "You wouldn't mind feeding me grapes, would you?"

Betty was relieved when Khumalo inserted himself between her and Lord Henry. He glared at the lord and shifted his glance to Betty to gauge her safety. She nodded and held his forearm, wanting to send Lord Henry the message that she was not available.

"You were asking about the location of the pyramids." Khumalo redirected the conversation. "It may interest you that long ago the Nile flowed freely, creating glorious waterways all around the Sphinx and the pyramids. They say the pyramids were pure white and glistened like diamonds above the clear waters of the inlets."

"Hmm," sniffed Lord Henry. "If I were pharaoh, I wouldn't be so careless as to misplace something so large as the Nile." He raised his droll eyebrows at Betty as if his wit had scored her eternal devotion. It nauseated her.

Khumalo ignored the lord's attitude and continued with his lecture. "They say the waters have been trapped in sub-terranean pools beneath the pyramids. *The Book of Ancestors* mentions a lever located somewhere in the complex. The lever is said to set in motion a great treadwheel that will open the floodgates and release the Nile once more."

While Khumalo spoke, Betty glanced at her pendant. The serpent's eye was glowing like goldenrods. She shot a glare at the Englishman. "So, *you* are the subdragon."

Lord Henry shrugged. "Why do clever girls always think themselves extraordinary? Youth is admirable. Beauty is admirable. But being clever takes too much work for someone who should simply be young and beautiful." The next second, his face distorted into a fiendish glare. He snarled as he grabbed Betty's pendant, yanked her closer to him, and hissed into her face, "Go back to your own story, Beatrice Talbin."

Khumalo struck Lord Henry's grasp free of the pendant. "Do not touch her, *umlungu*."

Lord Henry stepped back, his chest heaving. His disparaging glance drifted up and down Khumalo, landing on the dark contours of the Intercessor's face. "I should have known *you* would be the lady's lackey."

Khumalo grabbed Lord Henry by the collar and shoved his back against the rock wall. "Choose your words wisely, son of a fallen dragon."

Betty angled herself beside Khumalo and steadied her nerves enough to demand, "Where is Ordog?"

Lord Henry remained silent.

Khumalo gave him a warning shake.

Lord Henry turned away with a shrug. "So many ringleaders and nobody following. When Ordog comes, he will force these fools to their knees. And my brothers and I will watch and laugh."

"Brothers?" Betty forced Lord Henry's chin to face her. "How many other subdragons are here?"

"Speak up!" ordered Khumalo.

Lord Henry sneered. "We are *all* here."

Betty exchanged a glance with Khumalo, then returned her interrogation to Lord Henry. "What do you mean, all?"

Lord Henry raised a mysterious eyebrow but kept his lips sealed.

Khumalo grimaced and released his hold on Lord Henry. "Tell your master Ordog that if he doesn't want his other eye burnt out, he better stay clear."

"Oh, but that was done by — " Lord Henry stopped, stunned, and looked in surprise at Khumalo. "You?"

Khumalo directed his attention to Betty.

Lord Henry paled. "Her?"

It was Khumalo's turn to smile.

A golden thread of dragon power wound around Betty's forearms, a warmth surging in her veins. She raised her eyes, and they flickered blue.

Lord Henry shrank back. He mumbled something about them soon being sorry and sidled away.

CHAPTER 39
THE SPHINX (1890S)

L eslie wandered alone among the pyramids. He had much more weighing on his mind than people gave him credit for. What if the Epilogues were right? What if they could defeat Ordog once and for all? Lay siege to Alsó-Világ, all hail the two-headed dragon champion, and crowns and confetti all around. Cheers! But what if Betty and Khumalo were right? If the Epilogues were about to issue in another Great War to end all worlds, then one ought to do something about it.

Glancing eastward, he saw Cairo just down the hill. If only the pyramids provided phone boxes, he'd have the local authorities here in a jiffy. Perhaps if he commandeered a camel. They were right there at the edge of the plateau, tethered in the shade of the Sphinx, chewing and spitting, not overly impressed with their surroundings.

Right. Off I'll go, the charge of the Leslie Brigade, clopping downhill top speed to save the day.

But something in the back of his mind arrested his progress, that nagging "what if" dangling the prospect of the beneficent reign of King Leslie the First and a generous bestowal of knighthoods to all who pleased him.

Perplexed, Leslie leaned against a protruding composite of limestone near the pyramid wall. As his weight pressed against it, the hardened dust crumbled away and revealed, half-buried within the sands, a stone lever, crafted from the same limestone as the pyramid itself. Its worn surface bore etchings of hieroglyphs, hinting at some lost, secret purpose. He scratched his head.

A long shadow fell across Leslie, but he did not turn around. The snuffling of the hound and the drifting smoke of a hand-rolled cigarette told him it was the lieutenant with his dog. "What's that you found?" The older man's tone was like the headmaster coming upon a boy pinching a copy of tomorrow's exam.

"This?" Leslie shrugged. "One of those pull-here-sorry-you-triggered-the-trap-so-now-you're-dead sort of things."

The lieutenant offered Leslie an extra cigarette he had rolled. "You know a lot about pyramids, eh?"

Leslie accepted the cigarette and match. "I should. My father's a famous archaeologist, you know. He brought me here a few years back. I remember him telling me their names, Khufu, Khafre, Mykerinos." He tilted his cigarette at a rakish angle as he blew out a stream of smoke.

The lieutenant wrinkled his brow at Leslie. "Know what's inside?"

Leslie looked at him with a "Pfft, who cares" expression.

"Dead things." The lieutenant squinted at the setting sun. Then, widening one eye at Leslie, he added, "You and *me*, we're dead things."

Leslie laughed. "*You* may be one of them cursed werewolf sorts, but I'm well enough." He flicked his half-smoked cigarette away.

"We all make the best of our lot. I didn't ask for this curse." The lieutenant squatted and scratched his hound behind his ears. "I've seen things, and I've done things, and all that can be long forgotten if one day I can lift this curse, bring honor back to the name of Tynan."

"Will Zed-Cyphrr do that for you?"

"It's like this. If Vorever *is* all powerful, why'd he let them raze an entire village to the ground, people butchered, women, children, grandparents? My ancestor sold his soul to Ordog, so he and his brothers could avenge their people. The Crimson Dragon offered them strength, speed, power, but at a price. Wild things killing at the whim of their dragon lord, these men, once brave defenders of their people, were dragged down into a hell worse than anything your nightmares can imagine. But, thanks to your cousin, Ordog was defeated, and we had a chance. The old woman, Ilda, she gave us a shred of hope, and, Monsieur French, he was, for a time, one of us. He sees things the way I do, sort of. If we can't count on Vorever, and Ordog is washed up, the only thing for it is to see what this Zed-Cyphrr can do."

Skender sniffed toward the north, his ears upward. The lieutenant gave Leslie a glance, but Leslie remained silent, mulling over the soldier's words.

"All right, Skender. Let's go check the perimeter." The lieutenant whistled, and the hound followed him.

Leslie lowered his eyes, frowning at the uncomfortable pang of conscience the lieutenant had awakened. *Inspector Farnesworth would never sell his soul for power, not even for promises to be king.* He cringed. *Maybe if I do something quite brave and noble, I'll show Betty and them I'm not so bad.*

He imagined a scenario where, in defiance of the Epilogues, he confiscated the Tome of the Netherdragons and, though struck by countless arrows, he dragged himself to the top of the pyramid and, with his dying breath, called upon Vorever to release Blackwick, the pixies, and the rest. *Stout fellow*, they'd say as he recovered in hospital. *You're not a bad chap after all.*

Leslie blinked as a movement to the north pulled him back to reality. Was that old Khufu himself rising from the tombs? A cloaked figure lifted from the ground and hovered over the glinting sand toward the ruins of an old temple. The point of the hood and the width of the sleeves reminded Leslie of the depiction of the Grim Reaper he had seen in a Mickey Mouse cartoon. Seizing this as a chance to prove himself, he plunked his hat on his head and followed the figure. The figure paused, glanced over its shoulder, and the hollow within the hood fixed on Leslie.

Leslie thought about ducking behind the remnants of an old stone column, but he had already been spotted. He swallowed hard and followed as the cloaked figure disappeared behind a crumbling wall. Leslie rounded the wall, but the figure had vanished. Nothing but ruins and sand against a graying sky.

Leslie!

A whispery voice called from behind. Leslie scowled and looked around. "Who . . .?" He jumped, for he was face to face with the cloaked figure.

Leslie could hardly believe his eyes. "You?"

Sunset spread its orange veil across the darkening sands, and night swayed in by degrees. Troubled, Betty peered past the ruins, past the sloping dunes, out at the dusking horizon. Who would show up first? The Mer-shaman? Vorever? Ordog?

Portia mewed for her attention. Betty turned to find one of the guy lines on her tent was sagging, so she occupied herself by pulling it taut while Portia sat on her haunches like a lead-man inspecting her work. Betty felt Khumalo reach his arms around her to assist with the line. She yanked the line from his hands. "I can handle this." She was on edge. She had not meant to sound so sharp. She winced when his jaw dropped, and his brow furrowed as if she had hurt him. She crouched beside the tent stake and focused on attaching the looped end to the anchor. "Did you find Leslie?"

Khumalo frowned and swept the camp with one more searching glance. "No one seems to remember seeing him since late this afternoon." He lifted a roll of canvas onto his shoulder to move it out of her way.

A whisper of a breeze ruffled their clothing and rippled across the canvas of the tent, ushering in the longer shadows of night. With a touch of a worried smile, Betty pressed Khumalo's arm and moved past him to once more search the plateau. The looming frame of a werewolf imposed itself before the arch of the newborn moon.

"Monsieur French wants your report," growled the lieutenant. "I'm to accompany you to his pavilion."

Khumalo glared and threw down the roll of canvas. "She will not go without me."

The lieutenant shrugged and waved him to come along.

With the stalwart Intercessor at her side and Portia curled around her shoulders, Betty felt less shaky about the four large werewolves marching her in square formation across the plateau. They passed Miss Tulliver wandering near the pyramids. She peered around the side of the middle pyramid as if she had misplaced something. Betty had asked Holmes to keep an eye on Lord Henry, but Mrs. McFey kept the "explorer" distracted by chatting his ear off about some séance she attended last year. Betty sighed a bit of a laugh at Holmes' impatient weariness when Mrs. McFey repeated every other word with her stage voice as if that would ensure perfect translation into Norwegian. Mr. McFey had located a keg of lager. He pretended he wasn't filling his cask from the keg, making a not too funny American joke as they passed.

"Figured the keg would keep him amused," muttered the lieutenant after he was out of earshot. "Stolen lager, you know."

The pavilion rose from the desert landscape like a mirage. Its particolored canvas peaks and folds rippled in the scant breeze, half silhouetted in the rising moon.

Between the stretched canvas were brass-plated panels, embossed with the Monte Cristo coat of arms. The canopied entrance was flanked by two brass lantern posts, each guarded by a large, armed werewolf. Khumalo entered first, judged the interior relatively safe, and held back the canvas flap to allow Betty to enter. The werewolf guards fell in behind them.

Betty started as she was greeted by steam rising from concoctions in an array of bottles and tubes. Hanging from the center on a brass chain was an Edison bulb, its unsteady current flickering on and off with sparks on the filament inside the bulb. From somewhere in the back of the tent came the factory-like rumble of a generator.

In stark contrast to the ambience of 1890s industry, antique tapestries in deep jewel tones lined the walls. Upon a plush velvet cushion near the middle of the pavilion, sat Ilda, cross-legged. Propped against the shelves before her was a large book with a ragged, red cover engraved with twisted silver runes.

"That's it," whispered Khumalo. "*The Tome of the Netherdragons.*"

Betty nodded. She eyed the book with dread and could not suppress a shudder. A green threading writhed along the edges of the browning pages. She could smell the evil emanating from the book, and, as if in response to that evil, the scar on the back of Betty's hand throbbed.

Ilda muttered to herself as she poured an inky fluid into a vial. On the shelves were jars of herbs, extracts, powders, and loathsome, wriggling things. Betty's attention was drawn by a clicking, scraping sound coming from one of the medium-sized jars. Within the jar were trapped two cockroaches. The roaches scrambled around the edges, their muffled screams calling out in human voices. Betty scrunched her nose in disgust.

Haydee reclined on her hip in a curved crescent shape upon a silk-draped chaise lounge. "Please, make yourselves comfortable." She unfolded her hand toward some large, tasseled cushions to her right.

"In a few hours, the moon will be in alignment." French stepped out of the shadows bearing a cezve. "Sweet or unsweet?" He darted a polite smile at Betty before returning his attention to the cups upon a brass tray. "I remember Professor Davidson did not like his coffee very sweet."

"Just a little for me, please," said Betty.

"Medium sweet," said Khumalo.

"Ah, so moderate," sighed French as he poured the coffee. "For me, I like it sweet, yes, very, very sweet. I want everything the world owes me and more." After pouring the coffee and stirring in the sugar, he set a saucer upon a Persian carpet and filled the saucer with condensed milk for Portia. The kitten unwound herself from Betty's shoulders and slid to the floor. She sniffed the milk with suspicion and glanced a question at French. He, in turn, gently stroked the kitten along her back and across her tail, bestowing a beneficent smile upon the creature. Betty was hesitant to take his gesture as a good sign.

"Do not be afraid," Haydee reassured the kitten. "We are allies."

"For a time," Betty emphasized with a lift of her finger.

Portia lapped at the milk, but Khumalo set his coffee aside.

The lieutenant cleared his throat. "Avian is here."

French sat near his wife on the chaise lounge, balancing his coffee on his knee. "Let her in, lieutenant."

Avian swayed her hips as she glided in, her smoldering eyes registering each person in the room. Her veil-draped shoulders and arms invited her four ravens to perch as if she were a tree. There was something mesmerizing about the way she moved and the glow in her eyes. "The moon rises."

French turned to Ilda. "Is the ritual ready?"

"Just one more ingredient needed." She studied the contents of her vial with one open eye.

A not so beneficent smile crept across French's lips. "So, Miss Talbin, who turned out to be the spy?"

Betty set down her coffee. "Before I tell you the name of the spy, what guarantee do we have that you will do all in your power to free our friends?"

Haydee propped herself on her elbow and lifted her rounded shoulder in the merest shrug. "Our goal is to stop the Accusers. We wish no ill on your friends or on Neverland."

Betty was not convinced. Nonetheless, she released her breath. "It's Lord Henry."

"Ah, thank you." French granted her a gracious bow. "That is what I had hoped." He finished his coffee and handed the cup to Haydee. He turned to the werewolf guards. "Fyodr! Bram! Bring Lord Henry to me at once."

The werewolves snarled and withdrew. Betty and Khumalo waited, listening to the steady clock mechanisms turning on the shelf and the roaches clattering in their jar.

The curtains framing the entrance flew inward, and the werewolves burst in, pushing Lord Henry before them. They forced him on his knees.

French folded his hands behind his back and approached the spy. Betty tensed when she saw a dagger dangling from French's hand behind his back.

Lord Henry glared at French. "Ordog is no fool. You can't survive Zed-Cyphrr! By the time this night is over, you all will be nothing but dust and bones!"

French's fingers tightened on the hilt of his dagger. "The dust and bones will be your own, Lord Henry, and vengeance will be mine."

The English lord sneered at Betty. He sang in a sing-song baritone.

Tattletale, tattletale
Go and grab your mop and pail
Rag and brush, dust and bin
Can't undo the mess you're in

Without warning, he sprang at her, his rigid fingers reaching for her throat. French flicked ready his dagger, and Khumalo pushed himself between Betty and Lord Henry. The English lord gasped as his eyes met Khumalo's, and his face went rigid with stark terror. "It's you! I see it in your eyes! You're the one!"

The one? Betty stiffened and glanced from the back of Khumalo's head to the writhing face of Lord Henry.

"Yes!" declared Khumalo, his shoulders squared, his chin raised in defiance. "I am the descendent of Ignosi, he who vanquished the great serpent of old. The ring my friend wears was passed down to my fathers until it came to me. And by that ring, I swear you will release Lord Henry to return to his own pages. And you will once more be the cursed viper you are."

Betty was speechless with amazement. She looked once more at the one who called himself Lord Henry.

His face was strained and gray. His monocle slipped from between his brow and his cheekbone and cracked upon the floor. His eyes elongated into two narrow glints, his nose into two horizontal pits. His body took on the shades of the desert as he uncoiled himself, half human, half viper, ready to strike. "Now, my loves, you will all die the most painful death of the desert. Taste the venom of the Horned Viper! You first, Son of Ignosi!"

With a rasping hiss, the viper jerked forward, fangs spread wide.

The lieutenant fired his rifle.

The viper cringed, slumped forward, and squirmed on the ground.

Ilda grinned. "The dagger." French tossed the weapon to Ilda. She knelt with the dagger in one hand and her vial in the other and addressed the twitching viper. "Sit you still, my lord. Sit you still." After her dagger did its work, Ilda held the vial near his fangs. "I'll be taking a drop of that venom, my lord."

As Ilda bent over the lifeless scales, a raven squawked free of the coils and joined the others perched on Avian. "Aha, welcome, my brother!" Avian exclaimed, then turned her attention to French and his wife. "As for you, petty mortals, tremble and flee. For soon the mightiest one of all will be here, and none of you will survive his wrath." She morphed into the crimson, falcon-sized dragon and led the ravens out of the pavilion and into the night.

French paled. Haydee held his arm.

"Let's go, men! She can't get far!" The lieutenant lumbered toward the entrance.

"No." French stopped him. "Never mind her for now. She won't last long once Zed-Cyphrr is free."

The lieutenant heaved himself back and grumbled.

French gestured for Ilda to continue her task.

Ilda held up the vial containing a dark liquid, the heart of which pulsed with a green glow. "Behold the ink that will spell the doom of Ordog!"

"Then," French patted his wife's hand, "we are ready. Lieutenant! You and your men bring the crates with the weapons and the chests with my treasure to the eastern side of the Sphinx."

"Aye, sir!" The lieutenant hit his men to motion them to work.

"And now, to set the stage for the ritual. Ilda, the potion. Haydee, my cape." French paused before withdrawing and turned to Betty and Khumalo. "The performance begins at midnight. Don't be late." He swept back the curtains and guided the two women from the pavilion. He paused by the werewolf guarding the entrance. "Remain, Fyodr, my friend. When you receive my signal, you know what to do."

The werewolf grunted his acknowledgment, and French left with Ilda and Haydee.

Betty removed her helmet and wiped the side of her hand along her clammy forehead. She never wanted to go through that again.

Portia's ears twitched at the muffled screams from the jar with the roaches. Curious, Betty replaced her helmet on her head, sidestepped the dead viper, and knelt near the shelf, peering past the smudged glass of the jar.

"Let us out!" cried one roach.

"*Oui*," screeched the other. "We'll tell you everything! Just set us free!"

Betty, strangely touched by their plight, untwisted the lid to loosen it. Khumalo clutched her wrist to stop her. He frowned at the roaches. "Why should we? They are vermin. Omens of evil."

The first roach gave a hapless shrug of his appendage. "Such is life, Monsieur. We seek warmth and shelter, but we collide with the screams and the fury of the brooms. It is true your kind finds us most loathsome."

"There's no reason to leave them here," said Betty.

Khumalo held a hand for her to wait before releasing them. "What would roaches know?"

"We listen," explained the shrill-voiced roach, "and we hear their plans. They will not keep their word."

"Hist, Thérèse! Not until they let us go and swear to protect us from the foot-crush of our enemies."

Betty adjusted the strap of her bag on her shoulder and considered her options. "But can we trust you?"

Robert lifted one claw with due solemnity. "I swear by all that is filthy, by all that is diseased, that I will tell you everything I know . . . if you set us free."

"Very well. We'll chance it," decided Khumalo.

Betty unscrewed the lid. The roaches clattered up to the mouth of the jar, and Betty dropped it to avoid their twitching antennae and prickly claws. The jar landed on a cushion, and the roaches scuttled across the floor to make a getaway. Portia sprang into their path and hissed them back.

"Call off the monster, please," begged Thérèse, backing up and finding herself barricaded between Khumalo's boot and Portia's raised claw. "Please, mademoiselle."

Betty put a hand on her hip and tilted her head at the roaches. She wagged her finger at them. "You promised to tell us something important. Keep your promise, and I will tell Portia to let you go."

Robert cowered next to Thérèse, his black orbs watching the kitten's claws. He sagged and relented. "My name is Robert, of *Les Cafards*."

"And I am Thérèse."

"The one with the eyes like blood, and the ones with the snatching beaks, they work for the high priest of the Epilogues."

"Monsieur French?"

"No, another," said Thérèse. "The one who began the ending of all, the watcher of the two-headed dragon, he who has ushered in the corruption, who has sent his subdragon spies to possess the dark-souled ones of the story worlds. This high priest will not rest until he has what he seeks."

"Who is it?" demanded Betty.

"His name we do not know, alas," sighed Robert. "But he waits not far."

"In the Marginalia, your friends are trapped," said Thérèse. "To free them, do not use the ink they offer. Instead, write with your own pen the words of life, not death."

Robert raised his solemn orbs to Betty. "Mademoiselle, the ones who trapped us, they fear you, just as they fear us. You have power, yes? Do not let them crush you with their boots. Stand firm, look them in the eye, and tell them, 'I know you fear me more than I fear you!'"

As strange as it seemed, the words of the little roach encouraged Betty. She felt the warmth of Vorever settle over her arms and shoulders like a comforting caress.

Portia pawed the flap on the messenger bag, and the chart slipped out. Betty understood this as a sign and unfolded the chart on the floor to check it for any new clues. While she did, the roaches walked onto the parchment to the place where Neverland was circled. The area surrounding Neverland was burnt and wrinkled with decay. But as the roaches stepped on the landmark, the wrinkles smoothed, the charred areas restored, and the rips mended.

"*C'est impossible!*" Thérèse looked at her foreclaws in disbelief.

Khumalo frowned in thought. "Could it be? We have found the foe that is a friend?"

CHAPTER 40
THE RITUAL (1890S)

A sliver of moonlight hooked the pinnacle of the Great Pyramid and aligned with the forehead of the Sphinx. In the sprawling shadow of the Sphinx, the members of the tour gravitated to the crackling campfire.

The werewolves unloaded the crates and the black chests from the carts. They heaved them up on their shoulders and thumped them down. They stacked the chests in a pyramid shape before the stone tablet between the Sphinx's outstretched paws.

Mrs. McFey shivered and drew her cardigan close about her. "Is it time for the show?" She released a short, nervous laugh. "When does the Sphinx come to life?"

"Heh, heh," replied her husband. "Somehow it doesn't seem so far-fetched anymore. There's something in the air. Do you feel it? Do you feel it?" He prodded Khumalo with his elbow.

Khumalo's brow wrinkled with tension at the werewolves who climbed on the cart as they hauled the last chest to the top of the stack.

Miss Tulliver sat next to the disguised detective. "What do you say, Proffy? Is this a game of building bricks or some ancient Egyptian ritual?"

Holmes raised a finger with an impatient "tsch!" to signal for silence, as he remained on alert.

A burst of sparkling smoke erupted before the treasure chest pyramid. Betty jumped. Portia hissed.

French appeared amid the smoke. He raised his hands to acknowledge the hushed awe of his audience. "I promised you all an experience you will never forget. I will astound you with visions of wonder that would have pleased even the mightiest of pharaohs."

He reached toward the moon, and the nightglow converged upon his signet ring and shot out a blinding glare. When the glare subsided, the beat-up black chests transformed into golden caskets inlaid with sapphire, diamond, onyx, and emerald. Mrs. McFey clapped and cooed with delight. "Lovely, lovely!"

Mr. McFey grinned. "Well, whaddaya know!"

French continued without missing a beat. "You may be wondering what these chests are for." He posed like a winged Egyptian icon to the side of the golden caskets, one arm raised, the other lowered, while his wife joined him in a similar pose on the opposite side. "These chests, my friends, represent the long-lost treasure of Monte Cristo, willed to one Edmond Dantes years ago by a certain Abbé Faria, and this treasure has come to me, Thomson French. You, sir." He extended his hand toward Khumalo. "You have read of the prophecy in The Book of Ancestors. You know what the ancient writings say. The one who sacrifices his treasure to the Sphinx may unleash a power that will vanquish his foes. You, Miss Tulliver!" He aimed his finger at her like a master of ceremonies choosing a volunteer from the audience. "What would you give to get back at those who have wronged you?"

Miss Tulliver blew out a puff of cigar smoke before answering. "Half my kingdom? Isn't that the usual response in these cases?"

"Excellent answer," replied French. Haydee nodded to the lieutenant, and he cranked up an old gramophone. The needle dipped in and out of the grooves, exuding dramatic background music that resembled the drums and woodwinds of Cairo's past. "And this, my friends!" French flourished his cape, a flash of light glinted from his ring, and as he spun forward, he was wearing a high collared cape about his shoulders and a baldric across his chest. From the baldric gleamed a jewel-encrusted sheath. He flung a dramatic gesture toward the golden caskets. "This is not half but all that I own. And I am not Thomson French but the Count of Monte Cristo!"

Mrs. McFey gasped. Her husband laughed.

"Do not laugh, sir," warned French. "For tonight you will bear witness to the last stage of my plan. Tonight, you will meet Zed-Cyphrr, the mighty two-headed dragon that dwells in the subterranean passages below. This treasure, my friends, is the key to setting them free."

"Whoops," said Mr. McFey behind the back of his hand, as if pretending to tell a secret. "He's gone bonkers. How about if we just skip the show and tell ghost stories instead? My wife knows a real whiz-banger."

"Silence, you," snarled the lieutenant. He and his platoon threw off their cloaks and stood to their full werewolf height, their pointed ears upright, their teeth long and sharp. They wore bandoliers of ammunition across their broad, pelted chests. Cutlasses dangled from their belts, and rifles were balanced in their arms. Their eyes gleamed, and their muzzles firmed as they waited for French to give the order.

Mrs. McFey gasped a hiccup. "Why! They're –"

"Werewolves?" breathed Miss Tulliver, pushing back her helmet and staring with rounded eyes. "Well, I'll be dammed like a flood."

Betty clutched Khumalo's hand.

French faced the members of the tour, framed by his wolven troops, his legs apart, his arms akimbo. "Watch, and you will see what enchantments are in store to prove to you that there are mightier beings than barons and public prosecutors to decide the fate of mankind. Ilda!"

He made a sweeping bow toward the haggard woman, and she heaved herself out of the shadows into the glare of the fire. She bore the Tome of the Netherdragons before her like a shield as she chanted, her voice low but growing into a pitch of passion. "Portag vunen, hec tin sunen! Portag nimmen, eenan finnen! Portag vunen! Portag vunen! Avanti! Avanti!" Ilda's cry was punctuated by a low grinding of gears and hissing of breakers issuing from inside the Sphinx.

A stone portcullis lifted between the two stone paws, revealing a cave-like opening. Steps unfolded inward to create a descent into the darkness. Out from the opening extended tentacles of green mist that wrapped like a net of chains around the stack of chests and drew the treasure in. The edges of the chests scraped a trail in the sand as they were heaved into the mouth of the cave.

A loud groan collided with a sharp squeal. A voice boomed from the darkness, "It is good!"

A strident voice rejoined, "Yes! The armies of the fallen are ours! The war has begun!"

Mr. McFey pushed up his sleeves and jumped to his feet. "Wait a minute here. I signed up for a tour, not a revolution. If this is your idea of fun, count me out."

"Yes, Frank," whimpered his wife. "Let's get out of here right now."

Mr. McFey grabbed his wife by the hand, thumbed his nose at the Sphinx, and backstepped toward the tethered camels.

"Be still!" rumbled the voice. A green fireball cometed from the opening. The blinding glare zipped out like an abruptly ending reel in the cinema. Afterwards, all that remained of the McFeys was a heap of ashes.

Betty's stomach fell. She closed her eyes.

"The scales of justice demand a hefty price." French did not even blink. He stretched his arms toward the entrance. "I am honored you have accepted the gift, great one. What more can we do to aid your return?"

"Bring us the book!" The voice was like a multitude of witches chanting a curse. "The book is the portal through which we can break free of our long imprisonment."

French nodded to Ilda. Haydee helped Ilda place the book on the ground before the opening.

"I am Zed," came the deeper voice. "The final letter of the final word."

"And I," came the higher voice, "am Cyphrr, encrypting the words, twisting them to suit us, yes, to suit our special tastes."

The deep voice resumed, "Just one more step remains before we can reveal ourselves. Place the book upon the Altar of Eternal Death within the Hall of Records."

"Who shall do this, mighty Zed-Cyphrr?" asked Ilda.

The higher voice commenced. "Send forth the Keeper of the Golden Vigil, that we may grant her the deeper wisdom the tome will reveal. If she serves us, she will wield more power than she ever imagined! She will be like Vorever!"

There was a sneer underlying the grandiose promise. The energy of Vorever burned in Betty's palms, and she bit her lip to suppress her indignant retort.

The rumbling overlapped the higher voice. "And send with her he whom our servant slew at Reichenbach and yet lives, he who calls himself Sigerson. He knows much. Let these two bring the book." And the two voices collided and chortled, reminding Betty of when the knob of the wireless would stick between channels and static.

Werewolves grabbed her by her arms and yanked her to her feet. Portia slipped from her lap and mrrowed to attack mode, claws extended. The lieutenant's hound growled at the kitten. The werewolf dragged Betty toward the Sphinx.

Ilda forced open Betty's hands and thrust into one of them the vial of ink and into the other a black quill pen. "Do as the great one commands!" Her bloodshot eyes widened as she spoke and ended with a glare that conveyed an unholy threat.

Werewolves shoved Holmes onto the stage next to Betty. French smirked with contempt and ripped the spectacles and gray-haired disguise from the detective's face, revealing the sharp features of a man in his mid-thirties. "You didn't have me fooled for one minute, Mr. Sherlock Holmes."

Creviced in the nook between the Sphinx's nemes and ear, crouched Avian, watching all that transpired below. "As the mighty one foretold, they go to retrieve the ashes. They will not succeed," she hissed to her ravens, "but we will." Little red glints above their beaks reflected the gleam in Avian's eyes. She pointed her claw down toward a narrow hole in the Sphinx's left tear duct. The ravens flew in a Z-formation, zeroing in on the eye of the Sphinx, squawking and screaming their vicious intent.

PART FIVE

THE BATTLE

Chapter 41
INSIDE THE SPHINX (1890S)

Shoved down the steps into the Sphinx, Betty and Holmes collided with the dusty rock floor. Holmes pulled Betty to her feet. Portia whizzed through the entrance and looked up at her human with concern as the stone portcullis scraped down behind them and crashed shut in a billow of dust. The reverberations sent a shower of sand sifting through the cracks in the arched ceiling.

As the last rumble subsided, so did all light, and no matter how intensely Betty peered down the corridor, only darkness was visible. Portia's meow resounded like an eerie call for help from beyond the grave.

"Sherlock?" Betty pivoted clockwise, and her hands landed on the age-pocked walls.

"To your right." The detective's voice echoed, like a tour guide in an old cathedral.

She turned to his voice, and she caught the arm of the detective beside her.

"Still here," he said along with the sound of a match striking against the box. "That's better." The flame on the match quivered before him, and Betty was relieved to see the familiar brown hair, the sharp aquiline features, and the spark in his steady, gray eyes.

"I'll take the book," said Betty. "You light the way."

Holmes handed her the tome. "They said the Altar of Eternal Death. Well," he hovered the little flame over the crumbling walls and clicked his tongue, "no way but forward."

Betty's heart warmed as he took her by her free wrist, and, holding the match before them, guided her forward through the passage. Shortly, they came to a steep decline. The match died, so Holmes lit another and helped her edge down the sloping passage.

The deeper they descended, the more difficult it became to breathe. They came to a juncture that veered in two directions, one continuing forward, the other diverging to the left and downward. Betty stopped, pulled in a gasp of acrid air, and leaned the book against the wall to readjust its weight in her arm. As the book pressed against the wall, the square it touched pushed in with a hollow scrape, and the walls on either side of the passageway spread with veins of gold tracing the outlines of ancient hieroglyphics, which had before been invisible.

Holmes studied this anomaly with interest. He ventured to blow out the match. When he did, the gold tracing the hieroglyphics brightened enough to light the passageway.

"It's beautiful," breathed Betty in awe. She touched the gold running through the veins and was surprised how cool it felt. She recognized the symbols from the book Yamada had assigned her to study when she was bedridden. "I know these symbols," she said. "They are guides to the chambers within. One says 'writing' or 'library'. This other way points to 'death' or 'place of the dead.'"

"That must be the Altar of Eternal Death," said Holmes. "This way."

They followed the hieroglyphs down the passage to the left, but the way was blocked by double doors of stone.

"Let's try the other way," suggested Betty. "It may circle back around."

However, a few feet forward, they found their way once again blocked, this time by a great, round millstone, bolted in place by a crossbar.

Betty set the book on the ground and pushed against the crossbar to no avail. Portia's efforts to lend push power with her little paws were pointless. Betty moaned as she leaned against the millstone and crossed her arms. "We won't be able to move this in a thousand years."

Holmes studied the mechanism of the crossbar. Beneath the crossbar was a narrow opening, a foot wide and three inches high. "About the size of a letterbox," he noted.

"But what is it for? An offering to the gods?"

"Possibly." He ran his fingers over the frame surrounding the slot. "But it might equally be a trap of some kind. It could be a vent for a viper or even some noxious fumes."

Betty shivered, half expecting to hear a long, low whistle or the rustle of a gas jet releasing poisonous charcoal or sulphur fumes. "Perhaps if I reach in, I can find the mechanism to release the door."

Holmes caught her wrist to stop her. "The ancient Egyptian architects were fond of safeguards. Inserting your hand into this slot could trigger some kind of poison dart or axe. Fingers go in, fingers chopped off. That sort of thing."

Betty grimaced and backed away.

Holmes wiped his hands on his shirt. "I will be the first to try. Well," he managed a quick, little laugh, "goodbye, fingers." And he placed his hand into the slot, his jaw clenched, his eyes squeezed shut in anticipation of pain. Betty held her breath. A moment later, he released his own breath and withdrew his hand, all fingers intact.

"Thank goodness," sighed Betty. "Any luck?"

"Nothing."

"Now what are we going to do?"

"Well, it's a slot. Perhaps if we slipped something into the slot, say a piece of paper . . ."

"The hieroglyph did say something about writing," agreed Betty.

"Perhaps a book or a letter . . ."

"Or a magazine?" Betty slipped the rare edition of the *Strand* from her bag. She regretted sacrificing the copy of the magazine received from the hand of Sir Arthur himself. *But perhaps that's why he gave it to me. He somehow knew I'd need it.* She inserted the magazine into the slot.

A loud, low scraping accompanied the crossbar sliding out of the way from the millstone. Holmes drew Betty back a step as the millstone rumbled and rolled to the side into a crevice.

As it rolled away, it revealed a passage lit with a radiance that spread across Holmes and Betty. A voice from inside called to them. It was a kind, familiar voice.

"Come forth, Keeper of the Golden Vigil. I promised I would arrive. I have come, and I have brought friends."

"It is he," breathed Betty. "It is Vorever."

"Come," called the reassuring voice of the Golden Dragon. "I wish to have one of our talks. Mr. Holmes, stand guard at the entrance with the book, and do not let anyone or anything take that book from you."

Holmes accepted the tome from Betty and stepped to the side to allow her to move past him into the chamber.

She shielded her eyes as she entered a mist of gold. She and Portia stood before three colossal platforms of glossy wood, like the elevated podiums of judges in a royal courtroom.

"Welcome, Beatrice Talbin, Keeper of the Golden Vigil, to the Hall of Records, for even in the darkest places, Vorever's light still shines." A motherly voice embraced Betty with the warmth of Indian tea and honey. Betty craned her neck to gaze past the railing of the platform at the gorgeous, crested dragon with feathered wings the color of dancing flames. This dragon swooped down and gazed upon Betty with eyes soft as the dawn. "Vorever is wise to have chosen you."

"Thank you, Neverbird." Vorever presided from the largest platform in the middle. He guided a quill pen with the wave of his talon. It scratched across the parchment unrolled over the podium. "The commendation is duly noted."

"The child is ignorant. She is too young, as the wise Yamada has declared," came the echoey whisper of the dragon on the other side of Vorever. He resembled a minotaur with black horns and long curling beard. He blew a smoky snort past the gold ring in his nose. He studied Betty with eyes the color of verdant woods wrapped in moonglow.

Betty stepped backward to take in all three celestial beings. She felt like a lost bit of dandelion fluff in a forest, swept toward the roots of the mighty, patriarchal elms.

"Noted." Vorever once more guided the quill with a sparkling light. "And we will discuss this at length, Labyrinthius. For now, let us welcome Beatrice Talbin to the Council of Eternal Scribes." Vorever clapped down a golden gavel.

"But . . ." Betty waited for her voice to stop echoing. "We don't have time to discuss this at length."

Vorever folded his talons and hunched over to contemplate Betty. "Time does not control our fate. Have I not told you that before?"

"And," continued Betty, "why did Master Yamada never tell me about this Council?"

Vorever smiled gently. "And to think, only a year ago, you had never heard of Akira Yamada or any of the Inter-Story Intercessors. Every day our world gets a little bigger, and every day we realize how much we still do not know. Now, I regret, a war is coming to our world. It saddens me, but we must prepare for war."

Betty shuddered. She had heard rumors of war coming to England, and the thought of a long, cruel war encroaching upon all the story worlds frightened her. She hoped, she prayed there was something she could do to stop it before it began. "Is it true what Sir Arthur said? Can we really rewrite our story?"

"We are rewriting it even as we speak," said Vorever.

The phoenix dragon tapped her own gavel persistently. "We owe Betty an explanation. You see, child," she turned to Betty with a motherly smile angling up on her beak-like muzzle, "there are many good dragons in the universe, although they can be hard to find. When Vorever wishes to gain another perspective, he gathers the Council. We meet where stories reside, like here in the Hall of Records, where the memories of stories past are inscribed in all those scrolls and tablets on the wooden boxes behind you. I am Neverbird, dragon of the morning light, protector of children, and dreamer of tales!"

To express her exuberance, Neverbird undulated in a dance of flight in and out of the beams that crossed the vaulted ceiling. The flames that trailed from her wings scorched a map of Neverland across the ceiling. "Neverland is my favored realm, for that is where children escape and dream. Tales are born of dreamers, you know."

Betty smiled at the glorious display, but the smile waned as she remembered what Tondor had reported about Neverland. "Poor Neverbird. It must have been hard for you to see the corruption taking over your realm."

Neverbird plunged, as a bird stopped in flight, and returned to her platform, folding her wings like a blanket around herself. "Zed-Cyphrr seeks to break my will, and to do that, they attack the gem of my heart. But," she curved her long neck down to bring her eyes closer to Betty's, "thanks to you, the conch has been blown, the corruption is clearing, and Nothando is on her way, even as we speak."

A throaty rasp harrumphed from the minotaur-like dragon on Vorever's left.

"And this," Vorever gestured his talon, "is Labyrinthius, weaver of plots and subplots, forger of symbols and themes. He watches over the progression of characters, leaving a thread to guide them through a maze of decisions."

Labyrinthius folded his arms across his immense chest and frowned at the vaulted ceiling. "The Greeks of old knew how to forge a hero. Fire! Iron! Rock and sword! Through epic odysseys and woeful tragedies, crush and burn, melt and mold!" He inhaled as if breathing in the incense of the sparks flying from a

273

gargantuan forge, but as he released his breath his sigh settled into a groan of disappointment. He heaved his bowed head back and forth. "For this great undertaking, we need an Intercessor of age and experience."

Betty sagged as if the weight of the minotaur-like dragon had fallen upon her own small shoulders. "I may not be Ulysses, but I have traveled the pages of many books." She pushed back her helmet and dared a sideways peek at Labyrinthius. "And I did stand up to Ordog, you know." Although the battle seemed so momentous at the time, the memory felt strangely insignificant in the presence of these three colossal dragons.

Labyrinthius leaned his long, muscular torso over the stand and examined Betty. "How old are you?"

Betty's voice grew quieter. "I'm nineteen."

He grumbled a laugh. "Just a speck of pixie dust in the hourglass of eons gone by. You'll need to make decisions, little one, the really *hard* decisions." His brow lowered over his sunken eyes. "Are you ready for such a burden?"

Betty lifted her chin and held tight to the strap of her messenger bag. "I could have chosen any book on Vandor to make my home." This time, she did not shy away from the penetrating glare of Labyrinthius but met it with unwavering determination. "I chose this path. I chose this burden. I'm not turning back now."

"Easy at the start," said Labyrinthius, his voice drifting like a ponderous old man half-gazing at smoke rings that fade into memories. "But it's the last stretch that counts."

Neverbird cleared her throat. She reached down a corner of her wing and used it to nudge Betty's face toward her. "She is brave. She is willing. But would it be right for us to send one so young into such a test? The young should be free to laugh and to dream."

"That is why I have given her Blackwick," said Vorever. "From the legends of old, I have called him, the guardian of the lost and forsaken. He will be with her to bring hope when all seems lost."

Betty's heart lightened at the mention of Blackwick. "Then he's all right? He's safe?"

"Your friends are trapped in the Marginalia. There, they have had to confront their greatest fears."

"But how do I free them? Without releasing the tin of ashes, that is."

Labyrinthius stroked his beard and rumpled his brow. "What do you have with you?"

"My messenger bag, and . . ." She gathered Portia in her arms, and the kitten purred against her heart. "I have Portia. I have the chart. And, of course, I can always count on Sherlock."

"And you have me," replied Labyrinthius.

"And me," added Neverbird.

There was silence in the hall.

Vorever looked to the dragon to his left and to the dragon to his right. Labyrinthius snorted and nodded. Neverbird smiled upon Betty. Vorever once more clanged the gavel. "We are in agreement. You are ready. Go forth, Daughter of Vandor. Though you walk into the realm of the dead, you do not need to fear, for we will be with you to light the way."

CHAPTER 42
RELEASE THE NILE (1890S)

Khumalo, next to Miss Tulliver in the wavering glow from the campfire, watched French pace before the Sphinx. He spotted armed werewolves stationed as lookouts around the perimeter. To guard against Ordog, perhaps?

He whispered to Miss Tulliver, "This plateau is made up of intersections of causeways and channels where branches of the Nile once flowed. Somewhere in this complex, there's a lever that will flood the channels. Nothando, the wise shaman of the mermaids, might be able to reach us then. That's the one Betty was summoning with the shell back at the hotel."

Miss Tulliver raised her eyebrows and sniffed at the word "mermaids." "*That* should put a cramp in the old barmy brigade. But if it's a lever you're after, I might have seen it against the north wall of the great pyramid. I tripped on it when I was showing myself the sites. Shh! Big, strong, and brutish is here to check on us again." She played casual, patting the back of her hair, as the wolfish lieutenant and his hound made their rounds near the campfire.

He stopped near Khumalo and Miss Tulliver, squatted behind them, and used a twig from the fire to light his cigarette. "You're right, ma'am. There is a lever there. The one you call Leslie, he found it too."

"Oh, right, where *is* old sulky-face these days?" asked Miss Tulliver. "He's missing all the fireworks."

"Not sure where he's got to, but, if you need a way to reach the lever, Skender and I can devise a distraction for you." He rose and puffed on his cigarette as if nothing unusual had passed between himself and the prisoners.

Miss Tulliver's eyes met Khumalo's. "What do you say? Do we trust the big galoot?"

Khumalo looked from the werewolf to his hound. The hound gazed up at his master with undying devotion. "He'll keep his word," he decided.

"All right, Whiskers," Miss Tulliver addressed the werewolf without looking away from the fire, "at the count of ten, you throw a left hook at one of your chums, and Mr. Khumalo and I will scatter like billy-o, off toward Khufu's digs. Got it?"

Khumalo smiled, impressed.

"One . . . two . . . three . . ." the lieutenant counted gruffly under his breath.

Exiting the Hall of Records, Betty found Holmes seated on the floor, his back propped against the passage wall, the *Tome of the Netherdragons* nestled in his lap. His head was tilted gently back, his eyes serenely shut. She would have thought him asleep, except he was softly humming Offenbach's *Barcarolle* and tapping his fingers on the cover of the book as if on the strings of a violin. Holmes stopped singing as Betty's shadow fell across him. He smiled and sprang to his feet. "It's the bow control that's the main thing with *Barcarolle*," he mentioned as if continuing a conversation. "To move smoothly from the legato to the staccato without detracting from the seamless flow of the music." He lowered his forearm from the shoulder as his right wrist waved in and out to indicate the movement of the bow hand.

His casual tone comforted Betty, that Holmes could be here, trapped in a haunted passage, bearing a forbidden book, and still find pleasure in music.

Holmes stopped in his tracks and frowned.

"What's wrong?" she asked.

"This way won't do. That's a false door, remember."

"Not anymore. Look."

The double doors at the end of the passage rumbled, sand sifted from the cracks forming around its edges, and the two panels drew apart, revealing a dark corridor.

Together, they passed the threshold, and, as they did, a hot gust of wind blew through the tunnel, and flames sprang up on the torches that lined the walls.

The air thickened with foreboding. Past the archway waited a sinister chamber. Seven podiums of aged stone lined the far wall. Upon five of these podiums roosted Avian's brothers. The eyes of the ravens, with all the seeming of demons that were dreaming, burned like cinders.

Holmes' face was rigid as he stared past the feathered scavengers. For behind each bird loomed shadowy humanesque silhouettes, echoes of what they once were when inhabiting their human hosts. Betty shivered. In these silhouettes, she could make out the forms of the lizard-man Moriarty, the rat-man Milverton, and the horned viper that once had been Lord Henry. The other two were the outlines of a gorgon and a crocodile.

The ravens' eyes were fixed upon the center of the chamber, where stood an altar, hewn from obsidian. Its surface was polished to a ghostly sheen, reflecting the forms of Betty and Holmes as they approached.

"At last!" The female voice of Cyphrr soughed through the chamber in a green mist. "The tome has returned. Our corporeal form will soon be free!"

The ravens squawked and shook their wings. Betty glanced back, wishing Vorever, Neverbird, and Labyrinthius would come roaring in.

"Place it upon the altar." Thus commanded the voice of Zed.

Holmes bent his eyes upon Betty. "Shall I?"

"No," she said. "I can handle this."

Holmes held the book out of her reach. "These are deep waters, Betty, and I will not allow you to drown."

"It's all right." She tightened her jaw to keep her voice from quivering and rubbed the back of her scarred hand. "I have some immunity."

His eyebrow signaled disbelief, but he relented.

Portia prowled along beside Betty on their way to the altar. The kitten narrowed her eyes at the ravens as if to communicate what great lengths a kitten was willing to take to protect her human. The ravens stared at the book in Betty's arms, their eyes burning brighter and wider every step she took.

She placed the book upon the altar. It settled with a weighty, resounding clunk. The silver and green dragon runes illuminated the front cover.

"Open the book, and free your friends!" Zed-Cyphrr ordered, their two voices merging into one.

Betty hesitated.

The ravens cackled and exchanged disdainful smirks. The shadows behind them twisted and hovered to the tune of their amusement.

Betty took a deep breath and threw aside the cover, on guard for any ghosts or goblins that would scream out of the pages. The ravens' beaks were spread wide and eager for what fearsome thing would come. There was the rattle of old, browning pages, and nothing more.

"Write upon the pages," ordered the voice of Zed. "Use the ink the old hag gave you."

Betty took the ink and quill from her messenger bag. She set the vial upon the facing page and dipped the quill into the venom. The tip of the quill, stained with the ink, sizzled and smoked. The shadow of the horned viper hissed and swayed.

"Write as I dictate," said the voice of Cyphrr. "*Inthum arcanti gefulen maneth. Eenan forthum avanti shoalen.*"

Betty hovered the tip of the quill over the page, recalling what the roaches had said: "Write the words of life, not death." She thought and thought what those words of life could be.

Portia sprang upon the altar and stood with her front paws upon the facing page. She stared at the gutter, stared at Betty, and stared at the gutter again. Betty followed Portia's stare. "What is it? Ah, there's something in the margins." Betty leaned in closer and puzzled to interpret the black scribbles.

Holmes unfolded his magnifying glass from his pocket and held it over the scrawls. The lines on the bridge of his nose puckered grimly, and he handed the glass to Betty. She peered through the glass and read the words aloud. "*No one believes anymore.*"

She moved the glass to the scrawl a little lower. "*Just a little more sleep.*"

And another . . . "*Don't go, Frieda!*"

Betty gasped at the name of her friend. She and Holmes mirrored each other's realization. The words came from their friends trapped in the book.

"Look. Here's another one," noted Betty. "It says," she held the glass a bit closer to read, 'I will always love you, Betty, even if I do not live to see you again. Signed, Blackwick.'"

Betty let the magnifying glass drop onto the page as the last message sank in. She smiled. Blackwick loved her.

Holmes, too, smiled, a small, sad smile. He lowered his eyes, and when he raised them, they were just as energetic as ever. "And now," he spoke in barely a whisper, "you must follow the example of Sir Arthur himself. These are cries for help. *You* can rewrite them as declarations of triumph."

"Write as we dictate!" ordered the voices of Zed-Cyphrr.

Portia mrrowed in defiance and swatted the vial of ink. The vial rolled from the page and off the altar and smashed to pieces on the dusty floor. The ink spread, sizzled, and evaporated into the darkness.

The ravens croaked and puffed their wings like hunchbacked gargoyles. The mist whipped around the room in a frenzy, forming the shape of two dragon heads glaring down upon those near the altar. "The ink on the quill! Use it! Hurry! Your friends are at the breaking point!"

Betty remembered what the roaches had warned, that she was to use her own ink, not the ink given to her by Ilda. She snapped the quill in two. The act of defiance awakened the energy of Vorever in her veins, a thrill like waves of warmth buoying her above a storm. Letting the energy guide her, she drew a rapid half circle of golden light in the air, and the chart lifted out of the messenger bag. Betty caught the scroll between her hands. As she drew her hands apart, the energy sparked from her palms, burning the chart, transforming it into a golden candle.

"What is she doing?" The green mist dragon head with the female voice peered with angry suspicion upon Betty.

"Is it part of the ritual?" roared the green mist dragon head with the male voice.

Portia fft'd at the mist as if to silence them so her human could concentrate.

Betty tipped the candle toward the margin.

"No!" screeched the green mist dragons at once. "It's the candle of Vandor! Stop her!"

The ravens flustered their wings and screamed toward Betty. Holmes reached his forearm in front of her as a barrier to ward off their sharp beaks. But the ravens squalled past Holmes and bombarded Betty. She froze at the onslaught of ravens pushing off her hat, tearing at her hair, barely missing her eyes. She covered her head with her arms, the golden candle clutched in her hand. Portia's fur stood on end as she yowled and hissed.

"Ma'mselle, do not be afraid," called a tiny voice from the floor. It was the roach, Robert, squeezing into the chamber through a small crack in the corner of the room.

"By the Golden Dragon!" Thérèse followed Robert into the chamber. "The monsters with beaks. We will stop them."

The roaches looked to the bases of the two outer podiums. On one podium was a circle of gold in the shape of a scarab.

On the other was another circle of crimson, also in the shape of a scarab.

The roaches exchanged nods and marched up to the podiums. Thérèse crawled to the circle of gold, and Robert ensconced himself in the circle of red. The circles were dials, and the roaches found that their movement could turn the dials. They pushed around in a circle, and the dials turned, and as the dials turned, gears clanked, chains clattered, stone scraped against stone. The wall behind the podium rose, and a sandstorm gusted in, grabbed hold of the ravens, and suctioned them out of the chamber. Portia dug her claws into the page of the tome to keep from flying away with the wind. The winds overpowered the green mist and pulled it into the billowing sands beyond the wall. Once the last stream of mist had been vacuumed away, the roaches turned in the opposite direction, moving the dials back around the other way. The rapid click-clack of descending chains resounded, and the wall slammed shut.

The roaches, weary, collapsed to the dust, worn by their great effort, but something had happened. They had trans-formed. The two roaches, in their efforts, had adopted the color and shape of the dials, changing from dirt-colored roaches into shining gold and crimson scarabs. They looked at one another in wonder, joyous in their new garb.

"Now, ma'mselle, the words of life!" called the two scarabs.

Betty replaced her hat on her head and wiped stray strands of hair from her eyes. Holmes clamped a hand on her shoulder and nodded his solidarity. She set her candle over the open page and dripped the wax underneath each of the notes. The wax formed in gold the messages Betty spoke. "We do believe in you, Tondor Char. In you and all your fellow pixies." And beneath the next message, "Awake. Arise. Your time is now." In response to the message about Frieda, she said, "Frieda, don't leave us. You're my best friend." And finally, she whispered close to the words of Blackwick, "We will see each other again."

CHAPTER 43
THE MARGINALIA ONCE MORE (THE BENT YEARS)

Tondor crumpled in the cleft of the rock. Her face had dimmed to a bluish white, an alarming contrast to her dark red tresses. Her wings drooped like a white witch moth in the rain.

No one believes in fairies.

But a tiny flutter of life twittered in the distance. Another faint chirp responded. Then a trill like a chorus of piccolos defied the gloom, and a gleam of golden light ripped through the clouds. Through the parted billows, a stream of sunshine spread across the wasteland. Trilling and twittering, a flock of hummingbirds zipped across the stubble, and in their wake, a verdant field of grass, daisies, and violets unfolded as if their vibrant wings were conducting a symphony of life. The golden swirls that swept along with the hummingbirds sang out, "We do believe in you, Tondor Char!"

Tondor pulled out of her hiding place. She was not alone after all, for from behind another rock climbed Katrinka, who looked equally surprised to see Tondor. Katrinka staggered toward Tondor, and Tondor feebly lifted herself to her knees and crawled toward Katrinka. They fell into each other's arms, wept, and smiled. Each had nearly succumbed to the conviction she was the last fairy alive. But now the sunshine warmed them, the color returned to their smudged faces, and the golden spar-kle of magic spread once more through their wings.

"Isn't it wonderful, Tondor," cried Katrinka. "Humans still believe in us. There's still hope. Even for silly, little pixies like me."

The golden loop of hummingbirds spread across the sky and conjoined into the phoenix-like form of Neverbird. "You are not silly at all, little Katrinka," sang Neverbird's motherly voice. She spread her fire-feathered wings and swooped close to the pixies. "And we have work to do. I need someone to help me rescue our own Frieda and Peter Pan. Can I count on you?"

Tondor wiped her tears. "You can count on us, Neverbird."

A bit awkwardly, Katrinka tossed her hair, gave her friend a sheepish wink, and took Tondor by the hand. "We will both help."

Neverbird nudged them onto her neck. "Hop on board, my children. I see a light ahead, and I can hear the ocean. Neverland forever! Neverland mahai!"

Huck had drifted to sleep, but the flame in the lantern shot up. A loud voice like thunder shook the sky. "Awake. Arise. Your time is now!"

Huck stirred and realized the raft had been sinking and he was nearly submerged in the muddy waters. He started to his feet just in time to escape drowning. His companion on the raft was not Tom Sawyer at all, but a goblin squat and leering, with red, gleaming demon eyes. It hissed, "Go back to sleep, boy! There is no place for lost boys among the living."

From out of the lantern billowed Blackwick's shadowy form. From the lantern, he flitted to perch on top of the little tent at the far end of the sinking raft and glared past the wide brim of his hat down upon the goblin, like an avenging angel. "What is lost can be found."

"And what's alive can be drowned!" The goblin gargled with laughter and scooped water into its hands to splat upon Blackwick.

But a large foretalon interposed itself between the deluge and Blackwick. "Do not touch him!" a rumbling whisper warned. The dark clouds spread, and among the rays of moonlight, Labyrinthius emerged. The goblin squealed like a pig at the sight of the colossal dragon. The dragon brought his furrowed brow close to Huck, but there was a twinkle in his frosty eyes. "Fight on, brave warrior, champion of the river, and wielder of oars!" He gave Huck a grandfatherly wink.

"You got it, sir!" Huck turned on the goblin. "As for you, you no good varmint . . ." He raised his oar and bopped the goblin over the head. The goblin stared, stunned and dizzy, as Huck hollered, "I'm not lost. The Mississippi River is near to kin to me. You can't be lost so long as you follow the shore and watch the stars. And besides, ol' Gramps is here to watch over me now, so there."

The goblin shrank and squirmed at Huck's display of courage, its eyes darting from Huck to Blackwick and up at Labyrinthius in sheer panic. The goblin shrieked and dove into the water.

"Leave him," said Labyrinthius. "We've other business to see to." He breathed into the sail of the raft, and the raft sped forward into the starlight, Huck steering with his oar and Blackwick holding the lantern as a beacon to guide them in the right direction.

Huck steered the raft into a misty inlet where a creaking, ghostly ship was anchored. Its shrouds hung loose and ragged, like cobwebs on wet boughs after a whopper of a rainstorm.

A girl screamed, and the scream went from high to low, descending fast. Huck worked the oar as hard and fast as his lean muscle would allow toward the hull. He expected to hear a splash, but there was no splash, because a cloud of pixie dust swirled down from the sky and caught the girl just in time. A phoenix-like dragon swooped down, skimmed the surface of the water, and reappeared on the opposite side of the ship with the girl they called Frieda in her arms and Tondor and Katrinka topside on the dragon's back. Tondor fluttered down to replace the fallen spectacles on the girl's nose, and Katrinka blew some extra pixie dust around the girl to restore the rosy to her cheeks and the fluff to her blond hair.

Peering past the sparkles, Frieda caught sight of Huck and waved brightly. "Oh, hallo! So happy you're all right." Neverbird gently let her down on the raft.

"Welcome," said Huck as he helped her aboard. He removed his straw hat and placed it over his heart. "Glad to see you safe, ma'am."

Frieda blushed. "I'm grateful to you, sir, and to you, Neverbird! And you, too, Blackwick!"

Blackwick nodded once, but his attention was fixed on the ship.

Captain Hook thrust his long nose over the railing and gnashed his teeth as Neverbird dipped past the hull. "By Zed and by Cyphrr! Not the Neverbird!" He shook his fist at the phoenix-like dragon looping in graceful rings in and out of the mist, cheered on by the two pixies.

Hook and his crew writhed in their fury, and their eyes went all white, like the empty eyes of phantoms. They muttered inarticulate curses, and as they did, they morphed and glopped into the goblins they were.

Labyrinthius coasted close to the ship, peering past the tattered sails at the goblins. "Hallooo, little goblins," he sang in a deep, melodic voice.

The goblins gaped up at the ominous dragon overshadowing the ship.

Labyrinthius used one talon to draw aside the sails. He peered close at the goblins and gave them a little "Boo!"

The goblins, in a panic, scampered over the deck like a galvanized flea circus.

Blackwick sprang from the raft, caught a swaying rope ladder, and swung onto the deck of the ship.

"Shadow!" called Peter from where he was bound to the mast.

Blackwick shook his head at the lad's predicament. "Never could look after yourself without me." He set his hands upon the ropes that bound Peter, and the warmth from his palms burned through the fibers. Together, Peter and the shadow man turned upon the goblin crew, in an adjacent stance as if Blackwick were a taller, stronger reflection of the spry youth.

Blackwick drew his sword. "What do you say, Peter? Do we let them go? Or do we make them walk the plank?"

"No, worse!" Peter grinned as if a terribly delicious mischief had just inspired him. "We should make them all grow up." He retrieved a cutlass from the deck and waved it in tune with his words like a baton. "We'll make them all grow up. The lot of them! They'll wear stuffy clothes and shoes that squeak and grumble about taxes and match scores."

Labyrinthius nodded as he stroked his beard and contemplated the sky. "And their tea will be cold, their kippers burnt, and they'll never, ever get a holiday, not even when they're very, very good." He concluded with a "shame on you" glower directed at the goblins.

The goblins gasped and exchanged looks of horror. And in one accord, they scrambled over the railing of the ship and plunged into the misty waves of the sea.

"What ho, good sir dragon," exclaimed Peter. He slapped his knee and laughed. He leapt onto the railing with a rambunctious crow. "That'll teach that scurvy crew, eh, Mr. Dragon? Eh, Shadow?" He looked over his shoulder with a good-natured gloat.

Blackwick was about to congratulate the lad when a horrible crash and shriek exploded the deep.

Peter tumbled across the deck. Blackwick whisked himself to the rigging as water cascaded from the monstrous dragon head that burst out of the water and leered down upon the ship with eyes of ghostly green. This new creature was larger than any dragon Blackwick had seen. It was purple splotched with silver. Another angular dragon head rose aft, lifted by a long, eelish neck of silver mottled with purple. The *Jolly Roger* nearly capsized against the tidal wave rolling back from the mighty torso. The two dragon heads roared, like a landslide amid the wail of an untuned horn.

"It's Zed-Cyphrr!" Tondor peered past Neverbird's crest. Katrinka unsheathed one of her friend's swords. She twirled it on high, battle ready. "Come, Tondor! Come, Neverbird! We'll show this monster what Neverlanders are made of!"

"No!" called Neverbird, weaving her way back toward the ship. "Labyrinthius! Hold them off, while I take the pixies and children out of here. Come along, Frieda," she added, gliding next to the raft. Huck helped Frieda board the back of Neverbird. "You go along," he told her. "I'm gonna stay put and help Mr. Blackwick."

"No," cried Frieda as she reached back for him, but Huck's face was set in a stubborn scowl and his shoulders pushed back in resignation. "Get on, now, Miss Frieda. Ol' Gramps'll look out for me." He used his oar to shove the raft away from Neverbird and toward the hull of the ship.

"I'm not leaving *you*, Peter," called Frieda extending her hand to Peter Pan as Neverbird flew past the deck. "No excuses!"

"I can't leave my shadow!" Peter frowned and plopped himself down cross-legged on the upper deck.

The *Jolly Roger* was swallowed in darkness as the vastness of Zed-Cyphrr eclipsed the sky. Frieda's face paled in horror as the dragon coiled around the hull, the two heads weaving like twin cobras plotting to strike.

"You have to go, Peter," insisted Blackwick.

Peter shut his eyes, puffed out his cheeks, and hugged himself with his crossed arms. "If Blackwick stays, I stay!"

Blackwick heaved a sigh and looked to Neverbird for assistance. Neverbird gave Blackwick a knowing nod. She maneuvered between the two sets of snapping jaws, and with gently set teeth, she plucked Peter up by the back of his jerkin and bore him away from the ship. He waved his arms, kicked his feet, and shouted his protest all the way up through the opening in the clouds.

Huck climbed aboard the ship to join Blackwick. "I'm here for keeps," he insisted. "We're practically blood brothers, though, I reckon, a feller of shadow and cinder may not have blood, leastwise not the kind we're used to."

Zed-Cyphrr's heads dove toward the deck, but Labyrinthius, with a puff of smoke from his nostrils, interposed himself between the two-headed dragon and the ship.

Zed-Cyphrr fixed their eyes upon the hulking shape of the minotaur dragon. "Slave of Vorever," shrilled Cyphrr. "You are no match for us!"

Cyphrr emitted a harsh gargle as she avoided the dark dragon's grasp and dove beneath the waves. The dragon's tail swung up behind Labyrinthius and pounded him on the head. While Labyrinthius recovered from the blow, Zed stoked his green eyes, focusing on the rotting wood of the ship. The ship lurched upward as Cyphrr snaked underneath the hull, scraping her spine along its keel. She looped up from beneath the black waters. Together, Zed-Cyphrr's unified stare ignited the ship, and the decks combusted into flames.

Blackwick snatched Huck from the deck and whisked him up to the crow's nest. He had just dropped Huck off when a billow of flames swept Blackwick away.

"Blackwick!" Huck peered down from the crow's nest, his anxious face streaked with ash and sweat, gaping to see if Blackwick had survived the inferno. There was no sign of Blackwick.

Labyrinthius inhaled like a hurricane in reverse. He let the stream of air flow across the deck, pushing the flames back. Huck held his breath, hoping, fearing.

From out of the flames on deck, emerged a shadow. The shadow was Blackwick. The brim of his hat lifted, revealing eyes that blazed with a steadfast purpose. He funneled to the figurehead of the ship. There, he stretched out his hands on either side, drawing the flames to himself. As he did, the flames ceased devouring the charred remains of the ship and furled around Blackwick like a living cloak of burnt orange and blood red. He closed his eyes as the fire infused his form with even greater power. The flames smoldered into muscle and energy along his frame.

Zed-Cyphrr's attention was fixed on the shadow now, the shadow whose heart was beating against a tin of ash. The two gargantuan heads strained their open jaws toward Blackwick, one from stern and one from stem. "Give us the ashes!" the two heads chanted in unison.

Blackwick leapt to a swinging yardarm to avoid the twisting lurch of the dragon's heads. "Stay still, morsel," hissed Cyphrr. Her jaws snapped at Blackwick, but he whipped out of her way as the dragon's head crashed into the water, casting a mighty wave over Blackwick. Labyrinthius arched his wing over the shadow man, shielding him from the torrent.

The two dragon heads roared at one another, one rumbling like an earthquake and the other bellowing like a foghorn, as they coiled themselves around the ship to crush it.

"Get Huck out of here," Blackwick said to the minotaur dragon.

Labyrinthius' brow rumpled in concern, but the shadow man had set his gaze upon the two-headed dragon and was not to be argued with.

"Come, little Ulysses." Labyrinthius plucked Huck from the crow's nest and planted him on his back. "Your courage is needed elsewhere."

Huck stared back at Blackwick, shock mixed with disheartened betrayal straining his features. "I guess he just don't believe in me."

"He believes in you, young one," Labyrinthius reassured him as he worked his wings and pushed off the air currents with his back hooves, carrying the lad toward the opening in the clouds. "In fact, he trusts you with the most difficult quest of all."

"What quest?"

"To shine a light of hope in your own story world. To remind people about a thing called conscience. It's much needed."

Blackwick crouched on the beam, his arm hung over his raised knee. His grim amber slits assessed how long before the skeleton hull and beams would snap in the dragon's crushing embrace. He raised his eyes to the sky. The sparkle of Neverbird with the children and pixies and the silhouette of Labyrinthius with Huck were disappearing into the mist toward a golden speck of light.

Blackwick nodded, and his features relaxed. It would be all right.

He braced himself.

CHAPTER 44
NOTHANDO (1890S)

A vian waited in her hidden roost between the Sphinx's nemes and his ear, her eyes fixed upon the sealed passage into the Sphinx. Her brother subdragons were long overdue. An odd ruckus in the camp below distracted her vigil.

The werewolf platoon had fallen into a boisterous brawl. Fur flew. Fangs bared. It was a gnarly, snarling free-for-all. Avian stretched her neck for a closer look. *What mid-moon madness has struck this band of outcasts?*

The one formerly known as Miroslav shouted for that oaf of a lieutenant to call his men to order, but the lieutenant was up to his muzzle in the scuffle. He hurled a kicking, howling miscreant over one shoulder and slammed his free palm against the long nose of another brute.

What Avian did not notice was Khumalo and Miss Tulliver crouched in the shadows of the Great Pyramid. "There it is." Miss Tulliver clapped a hand on the lever against the pyramid wall. It was still half buried by mineral deposits and caked over by a layer of debris. It wouldn't budge.

"Look around for something we can use to free it," said Khumalo.

Miss Tulliver lit a match and used its light to search the ripples of sand. Khumalo spotted a sharp-edged corner of brick. "This will do. Keep watch."

He went to work scraping away the deposits while Miss Tulliver stationed herself on the opposite corner to serve as lookout.

"Hurry!" she urged Khumalo. "Ooh!" she added under her breath, standing on tiptoe and stretching to catch a distant view of the brawl. "That must have hurt the old bean. Oh, not the claws, sergeant! Oh, gosh, that's not playing by the rules." She glanced back at Khumalo. "They're running out of rage. Are you just about done?"

French strode from the base to subdue this roiling mass of werewolves. He held a grenade over his shoulder, his finger dangerously close to the pin. He had the look of a man who had no compunction about releasing that pin. "Lieutenant! Order your men to attention, or you all go back to Alsó-Világ in little pieces!"

The lieutenant shook himself and whistled for Skender. Skender reluctantly removed his teeth from the leg he had been worrying. The werewolves staggered apart like drunken men and wobbled back to a semblance of attention.

French lowered the grenade and scanned the uneven line of werewolves. "Now, gentlemen, you may not have noticed, but something seems to be missing. Get out there and find the prisoners. Bring them back."

The werewolves looked toward the lieutenant, who relented with an open-armed shrug and threw his muzzle forward to encourage the others to comply. The werewolves exchanged questioning growls then lunged into the moonlit ruins and scattered among the pyramids, in search of the two remaining members of the tour.

Before Khumalo could pry the lever loose enough to move, two werewolves pounced from the shadows and caught him back into the darkness.

Miss Tulliver leapt to the lever and pushed against it with all her might.

Something hummed and wound into motion beneath their feet. Stone scraped against stone, and a whirring crescendoed closer and closer.

The camels stirred in a panic. They sent up moans of impending disaster and broke free from their tethers, stampeding from the plateau in a cloud of dust.

They had fled just in time, for out from the pyramid poured a rushing flood, filling the channels that had long tasted nothing but sunbaked sand.

The werewolves howled at the torrents of waves. They straggled and clawed up the uneven blocks on the pyramids, swinging out of the path of the coursing water.

The surge of the Nile propelled Khumalo and Miss Tulliver away from their captors. The Intercessor wrapped an arm around Miss Tulliver, and with his free arm, reached in vain to catch hold of the walls of the pyramid as they were eddied past. Drifting toward them among the flotsam was one of the carts. Khumalo and Miss Tulliver dragged themselves up and balanced their weight on the boards to ensure the cart stayed afloat. As Khumalo shifted his weight to keep the cart from dipping, he caught sight of something approaching from the east. "There she is! Nothando!"

Skimming through the inlet, breakers crashing on either side of the wake, Nothando powered like a torpedo toward the Sphinx. At the base of the Sphinx, before French and his retinue, the Mer-shaman breached the surface, her muscular body glistening with the Nile, her fierce eyes fixed on Ilda.

"I have heard the call," announced Nothando. "I have come to take back the book and to bring my daughters home again."

She dove under the current, swished further out into the waterways, and emerged in the moonlight. She placed her hands on both sides of her mouth and sang.

Neverland Mahana
Neverland mahai
Mahano Mahano
Kalai! Kalai!

Bobbing up in a rainbow ballet of shimmering scales and billowing tresses were a score of mermaids. They dipped beneath the surface, their faces submerged except their haunting eyes.

Nothando spread out her hands on either side, catching moonbeams reflected from the water. "Fear not, my daughters. Neverland is healing, and the one who stole the book awaits judgment."

Ilda, like a balloon losing its helium, collapsed to her knees upon the stage. "Forgive me, all-powerful mother of the sea! The temptation was too great!" She raised her trembling, gnarled hands in supplication, but her lopsided smirk was not sorry at all.

"You." The Mer-shaman focused her finger at Ilda. "Your action devastated Neverland. You forced us from our home." Her eyes flashed retribution. "You put my daughters in danger."

Ilda's head sunk upon her chest, but amid the straggles of hair, her eyes darted about as if in search of a way to outsmart this foe.

French struck a defiant stance between Ilda and Nothando. "What will you have? Wealth? I have treasure enough for us all."

Nothando frowned upon the little man. "The book."

"You're too late, Madame," he said. "The book has been delivered to the altar."

She shook her head. "This will not go the way you think, Miroslav."

CHAPTER 45
THE BRINK (THE LIMINAL YEARS)

The charred bones of the Jolly Roger's beams and planks snapped in Zed-Cyphrr's crushing coils. Blackwick fixed his mind's compass on Betty. He had kept his promise. He had protected her and those she loved. The ashes would remain here, inside the book, where they belonged. And the story worlds would be the better for it.

The two heads of Zed-Cyphrr plunged in toward Blackwick.

The newly released branches of the Nile criss-crossed the limestone causeways. The waves swashed against the ancient Egyptian structures. On the high ground of the Sphinx's base, Ilda yanked French around to face her strained expression. "Nothando will ruin everything! The conch you took from that girl! Give it to me. We must destroy it and send her back to the sea!"

"Don't do it," interposed Haydee. "Once we have the book and the ashes, the conch could prove a powerful tool."

French lifted the shell from one of the crates of ammunition. He rotated the conch to examine its whorls, but his mind strayed elsewhere. "Miss Talbin should have returned by now."

He pivoted to face Khumalo and Miss Tulliver who had disembarked from their wave-tossed cart. "What is this plot of yours?"

Khumalo simply folded his arms and looked away.

French followed the impassive face of the Sphinx upward, searching. *A flicker of movement, there behind the Sphinx's earlobe. Avian!*

French handed the conch to his wife and whipped his binoculars from his belt to his eyes, focusing northward on the pavilion at the other end of the plateau. *Time to act. Avian senses the ashes, and I must obtain them before she does. And when the floods and furies rise, one must have wings.* He lowered the binoculars with a knowing smirk. *Fortunately, my pavilion is not just a pavilion.*

"Haydee," he said. "The flare."

The lieutenant, his olive trousers and tan shirt clinging to his wolfish frame, dragged himself and his hound up onto one of the causeways and out of the flood. His boots scraped against the worn stone as he clambered onto a firm footing. His first thought was for his platoon.

"Bram," he panted. "Bruner. Sergei." He scanned the flooded plateau. Dawn ignited the horizon behind the pyramids. The lieutenant squinted, shielding his eyes from the brilliance. He snarled and swiped at the shifting light as if to stave off its glare. Outlined in red were the wolven figures of his platoon, scrambling out of the water and up onto the sides of the pyramids.

The sunlight worked its reversal on the lieutenant, and he rolled his shoulders, readjusting to his human form, claws withdrawn, bones restructured, flesh replacing fur. His platoon, too, were caught in the wrack of the daylight metamorphosis. Their claws clung to the staggered stonework of the pyramid, but the sun stabbed their eyes, and they writhed as bones wrenched and reshaped. Momentarily sapped of strength, they dropped from the pyramid walls into the water and floundered in the rushing waves.

"*Mahana! Mahana!*" The Mer-shaman waved her daughters toward the pyramids, in the direction of the drowning men.

The mermaids buoyed the men to the surface and guided the soldiers across the flooded plateau to the causeway, where the lieutenant and his hound waited and pulled the men up to dry ground. "Well, strangle me with wolf's bane," declared the lieutenant as his eyes met the determined gaze of Nothando. "First time I've seen anyone give a spit about me and my kind. We may be on opposite sides, ma'am, but I promise I won't forget this."

The two heads of the dragon converged upon Blackwick. The humidity rolling off their tongues had the clammy, sick odor of disease.

A spear-shaped beam of light caught Zed in the throat, sending the two heads flailing back as a silver ooze burbled from the wound.

Blackwick clung to a shred of sail and leaned out to see whose hand had directed the spear. Vorever plowed from the sky toward the enemy, with Betty poised like a ship captain between the Golden Dragon's horns. Her hands shimmered with warm, golden light.

The two-headed dragon recovered quickly. They roared like a train squealing on the tracks and crashing into a chasm. Vorever hurled himself toward them. Betty clung to the Golden Dragon's spikes for stability as he charged the foe.

The eyes of Zed-Cyphrr, once dark, now pulsed with an eerie, sickly glow of nuclear fury. They aimed those eyes at Vorever.

Vorever whipped behind Zed-Cyphrr. He reached around a muscular arm on either side of the two-headed dragon, yanking back their necks. The radiating ray from their glare flew wild into the sky. As the two-headed dragon reeled in fury, one of their arms swiped across the ship, capsizing the remnants of the vessel into the sea. To prevent himself from plunging into the waves, Blackwick leapt from the yardarm toward Betty's outstretched hand.

But while Blackwick was in mid-leap, Zed-Cyphrr caught him between two talons to snuff him out like the flicker of a guttering candle. "We will take the tin of ashes, little shadow." Blackwick winced under the crushing pressure of the talons.

Betty pushed herself from Vorever and spread her arms on either side. Golden swirls of light braceleted her arms from her wrist to her shoulders. Superimposed over her shoulders, materialized two enormous golden wings. Working those wings and guided by the energy of Vorever, she rocketed between the purple talons tightening on Blackwick and pulled him free. She landed Blackwick safely upon the head of Vorever.

Vorever narrowed his eyes at Zed-Cyphrr.

"You do not frighten us!" cried Zed-Cyphrr.

Vorever's frown was set. His eyes were electric blue lava. "We are not here to frighten you. We are here to stop you."

Zed-Cyphrr puffed out their chest with a show of bravado. "How can you stop us? You are just one dragon, and two orphans nobody wanted."

"Hold on, my children," the Golden Dragon advised his passengers. "We are about to show this fearmonger what one dragon and two orphans can do."

Zed-Cyphrr drew their heads closer together to present a more unified front and restoked the radiation in their eyes. Blackwick folded himself over Betty to shield her from the intensity of the impending blast.

Zed-Cyphrr discharged the radiation at the Golden Dragon's head. The night flashed a neon green, but Vorever's wings arced before him, absorbing the ray. When Betty lifted her head to look past Blackwick's arm, she gasped at the smoke rising from Vorever's scorched wing.

Out of Vorever's maw came a golden blast that sent shock-waves across the sea, pushing back the scales of Zed-Cyphrr. The force threw Betty and Blackwick back into the clouds.

Betty's wings caught the air currents, and she soared up behind Blackwick and flung her arms around his chest.

Zed-Cyphrr set their glares upon Betty and Blackwick. But before the two-headed dragon could release the radiation, Vorever clamped his talons, one on each head of Zed-Cyphrr, and shoved them beneath the waves. Their radiation fizzled as they burbled in the depths.

Betty and Blackwick glided up through the clouds together, Betty's arms locked near his heart. Blackwick extended his arms on either side, guiding the wings for her as they soared past the mist.

"Now, Blackwick!" Vorever continued to press Zed-Cyphrr's heads beneath the waves. He called over his great shoulder, "Throw the ashes into the sea, and get out."

Blackwick nodded and reached for the tin of ashes.

Betty directed Blackwick's attention to a golden nebula spread across the sky beyond the clouds. "Do you see that? That's the signal. Sherlock is burning the ripped edges of the torn page. I told him as soon as the fire burns out, he is to close the book. That gives us just enough time to break through."

As Betty propelled her and Blackwick toward the nebula, she glanced back at Vorever, dread for his safety pulling at her heart. Assailed by the raging waves, Vorever continued to tax his strength to force Zed-Cyphrr beneath the surface. She could sense the strain in Vorever's muscles though the Golden Dragon's sapphire eyes were undimmed and his courage unbowed. Those eyes glanced up and met hers, and for a moment, her eyes reflected the blue light of his.

He sent her a smile of rugged reassurance, his eyes crinkling at the corners as he silently conveyed that he was a tough, old dragon, and she should not worry on his account.

Blackwick let the tin of ashes drop to the dark waves below.

Zed-Cyphrr crashed out of the sea. As they gasped for air, one claw ripped across the sky, leaving a black, jagged tear. "Ravens of the corruption!" they screeched. "Return!"

Through this tear, burst the ravens.

"Now! Now!" screamed Zed-Cyphrr to the ravens. "The ashes!"

The swarm of scavengers nosedived for the plummeting tin, and one raven grazed the peaks of the waves and caught the tin in his beak. The flock flew toward the nebula in a torrent of discordant squawks. "We have it! We have it!" And they disappeared into the burning folds of the sky.

Zed-Cyphrr roared their triumph, and Betty worked her wings in pursuit of the tin.

Both of Zed-Cyphrr's heads rotated toward Vorever. They aimed their eyes upon the Golden Dragon, stoking the blast of radiation. Vorever lowered his muzzle and rolled a weary expression up at the two-headed dragon. He huffed his vexation and lunged forward.

Betty focused on the nebula as if her will could wrench the tin from the ravens. As the dancing light of the nebula engulfed her and Blackwick, Betty glanced over her shoulder at Vorever. She saw the Golden Dragon hurl his body against the torso of the two-headed dragon, and Vorever received the full force of the radiation in the chest. Zed-Cyphrr dragged merciless talons across the scales of Vorever, but their roars faded into the distance, and the squawks of the ravens grew louder.

CHAPTER 46
THE FORBIDDEN TOME (1890S)

Holmes touched the flame of Betty's candle to the ripped edges in the gutter of the tome. As he watched the edges burn and blacken, his eyebrows bent into a frown. Betty had until the fire burned out to escape from the tome with Blackwick.

He shifted restlessly. He shouldn't have let her enter that dark world. He should have been the one. By the Lord Harry, if anything happened to Betty . . .

"Monsieur." Robert's voice interrupted his train of thought. "The edges are burned. The fire has died. It is time to close the book."

"We can spare one minute more." Holmes lifted his finger. "Betty will make it."

Thérèse's head sagged to the altar. "Close the book, monsieur. There is no more time. They will be trapped, but so will the ashes, and so will Zed-Cyphrr."

Holmes' eyelids dropped as he breathed out long and slow. He gave the front cover a resigned push. The pages fluttered in a fast descent to collide with the back. He pressed his lips, shoved his hands into his pockets, and stared straight ahead at the empty podiums where the ravens had been, envisioning the bleakest possible scenarios.

As the last leaf drifted toward a finale, the book quivered. The pages flew back, and out from the crease squalled a flock of ravens, their angular bodies growing larger as they flapped free of the binding.

Portia shot up on her back paws and swatted at the birds as they flew past. She claimed a few feathers, but the birds did not linger. They bolted from the chamber in arrow formation, their clatter echoing down the passage. "It's ours! It's ours!"

The detective swept aside the discarded feathers and felt along the silver book-edge finishing as if seeking a pulse.

A shadow whirled out from between the pages, like dried ink turned to powder. Mingling with the shadow were sparkles of golden light, like the stream of sun through a stained-glass window cascading upon the sacred text in a cathedral. The spirals intertwined in a love dance of shadow and light from the altar. The shadow reconstituted into Blackwick, and the light spun into the form of Betty.

Holmes pressed the cover closed and exclaimed, "The ravens!"

Desperate, Betty turned to Blackwick with a silent plea.

"I'll retrieve the tin," swore Blackwick as he slide-stepped toward the entrance. He skidded to a pause and glanced back at Holmes. "Make sure Betty gets to safety. I'll meet you outside." He gave Betty a reassuring nod, but not waiting for a response, he took off after the scavengers.

The empty podiums behind the altar rattled. Sand sifted in a steady stream from cracks in the ceiling. Holmes gave the ceiling a dubious glance as if judging the integrity of the structure unsound. He placed an arm around Betty's shoulders to draw her from the chamber. Before she left, however, she gathered the *Tome of the Netherdragons*, and, guarding it close, she accompanied Holmes back into the passage.

The ground beneath them shook. The scarabs scrambled from the altar and disappeared swiftly into the safety of a tiny hole in the corner of the floor.

Betty glanced at the tidal wave of sand surging behind them, squelching the torches lining the passage one by one. She quickened her pace toward the exit. Holmes struck his last match to reveal the stone portcullis still blocking the way out. Portia mewed her fear, but her mew was an echo suppressed by the sand crowding the passage.

"This way!" Holmes tugged Betty down the passage to the right. "The Hall of Records must lead to another exit."

The match flame died, but the hieroglyphs threading the walls still glowed. The millstone that had earlier rolled into the crevice now rumbled and heaved once more across their path. Holmes pushed Betty before him through the quickly closing space, and he slid past just as the millstone thudded against the wall beside him, blocking the flood of sand.

Betty and Holmes stood within the high-domed chamber, pausing to catch their breath. Betty looked up at the empty platforms where the Council of the Eternal Scribes had earlier presided.

"Will Vorever be all right?" she asked, her voice responding with a lonely echo.

"Vorever will do what must be done," replied Holmes, feeling along the opposite wall for any crack to signify a secret panel. "Just as you and I must." His fingers landed on a loose brick. He pressed the square inward, and a stone panel slid to the side. He bowed toward Betty. "After you, Miss Talbin."

Betty and Portia moved toward the opening.

A thunderous gavel clanged. Betty arrested her progress and turned to the platforms. Once more in his place, Labyrinthius lowered his heavy brow upon the two mortals and the kitten.

Holmes nudged Betty by the elbow toward the exit. "Time is of the essence."

"Hodge podge and double the dodge," grumbled Labyrinthius. He waved his foretalon, and the panel slid shut in Betty's face. "Do you know what will happen if you step out of this chamber with the forbidden tome?"

Betty blinked, puzzled. "Isn't that what we're supposed to do?"

"If you leave the Sphinx with that book, this is what will happen. There will be a great quake as Zed-Cyphrr pushes past the Earth's crust. The landslide that follows will bury Mr. Holmes alive. In shock, you will drop the tome, and the one called Ilda will retrieve it. She will open the book and unleash terrors the world has never before seen. It has always been the way with those who covet power."

"But . . ." The energy of Vorever warmed Betty's temples as she drew in an enlightened breath. ". . . We can rewrite that part."

"Exactly. You, child, will walk out of this Sphinx, but you will not have the tome. I have a plan." Labyrinthius gave them a knowing wink. "Mr. Holmes, where would you hide a book?"

Holmes needed only a second to decide. "In a library, among other books."

Labyrinthius nodded a grim smile of congratulations. "And if it's books you need, I have books." He pushed aside a pile of scrolls and from the wooden box retrieved a bundle of old tomes. "After all, this *is* the Hall of Records. We have books, books of old and ancient lands. Rare books. Books only one such as yourself could appreciate." He bent over the bundle, scanning the spines. "*The Origin of Tree Worship, Catallus*, and *The Holy Wars*. No one will notice a battered old tome among such priceless editions. And who would suspect a seedy, old book collector, stooped with the burdens of the ages?" He gathered a scoop of dust from the floor and sifted it over Holmes. When the dust cleared, the detective was disguised with white hair, wrinkled skin, a crushed top hat, dark glasses, and an old, frayed frock coat.

Betty recognized the disguise from the short story "The Empty House." It was the disguise he would cast aside when revealing to Watson that he was still alive after all. *What a shock it will be to poor Watson.* Betty sighed and added *The Tome of the Netherdragons* to the bundle of books he bore.

Holmes coughed a little, his eyes lowered as one all too aware he had been entrusted with a weighty responsibility. "I shall find a safe place, sir, somewhere no one will dream of looking."

"So it has been rewritten." Thus spoke Labyrinthius. He snuffed a burst of smoke from his nostrils. The shimmering haze formed a portal, and on the other side of that portal was a low hanging fog and the clattering of hooves and rattling of carriages over the uneven pavement of Park Lane.

Betty caught Holmes by the arm before he departed. He glanced back at her from over the rim of his dark glasses. "Yes, my dear?" he asked, using his wizened old man's voice.

"Watson will be terribly glad to see you again." But her smile was sad. She hated to see him leave, and she wished she could join him on his pursuit of the next adventure Sir Arthur had for him.

A smile played on his lips, but the dark glasses masked his eyes. She liked to think they were blurred by the merest beginning of a tear. He patted her hand. "You have Blackwick here to keep you safe now," he said. "But we may meet in another story at another time. In fact, it's highly probable."

Labyrinthius prodded Holmes through the portal, and the smoke cleared, closing the scene on London, and opening the way for Betty and Portia to escape the Sphinx.

Blackwick climbed the shadow-marbled passage that wound upward. He detected each scrape of a raven's claw along the wall, each brush of a feather past the cobwebs, and each shift in the air currents against which pressed the raven wings. Even in the dark, he could see their gaunt outlines several meters ahead, stretching for the source of fresh air beyond.

The passage curved and slanted upwards toward the opening. The burnt orange of dawn glared through the aperture. Eclipsing that light wafted the billowing particolored canvas of a giant hot air balloon bearing a wicker basket with brass plates on either side. These plates displayed the Monte Cristo crest. French and his wife stood near the railing of the basket.

"Avian!" called French. "I know you're here somewhere!"

The ravens burst out of the opening and veered to the left and right to avoid the balloon. Blackwick wisped into a cloud of smoke and pursued the scavengers. He emerged from the eye of the Sphinx and whisked upwards to reconstitute on top of the limestone head.

French grasped a line and leaned out past the balloon's railing toward Blackwick. "You, Davidson! Give me the tin, and Betty will go free."

Blackwick lifted the brim of his hat, and his amber slits met French's eager gaze. "Too late! They have it." He extended a finger toward the ravens escaping into the dawn.

"*Les diables!*" French spat as he used his binoculars to determine which raven carried the coveted tin. Spotting the glint of metal in the beak of the one-legged raven, he whipped out his pistol and took careful aim.

The pistol fired, and the bullet grazed the raven. With a fluster of feathers, the raven's beak parted, releasing an astonished croak, and the tin plummeted to the limestone at Blackwick's feet.

As the ravens squalled away, the shadow man quick-crouched to retrieve the tin, his eyes fixed on French's pistol. It was a one-shot pistol, so he turned and made for the opposite side of the Sphinx's head.

French threw down his spent pistol and sprang to the railing of the basket. His cape caught the rising wind as he stared with unremitting purpose after Blackwick. "Davidson, wait!"

Blackwick paused warily at the opposite edge as the balloon's shadow stretched across him. Standing with his back to French, he inclined the brim of his hat, waiting to catch the next words.

French's voice carried from the balloon across the wind-swept expanse of the Sphinx's head. "You're a good man, Davidson. Because of that, I spared you once, though it cost me more than you will ever know. For the sake of that memory, give me the tin."

Blackwick heaved a regretful sigh, squeezed his eye slits shut, and shook his head. "We've both been to the land of shadows and back. We both have a second chance. This is mine. So, I'll be on my way." He was about to whirl into his ashen form.

"Stay!" The balloon hove in closer, and French leapt the length between the basket and the Sphinx.

He landed behind Blackwick, his rapier drawn.

Blackwick curled slowly around to face him, sword ready.

Knees bent and shoulders rounded, French locked eyes with the shadow man. "If you will not give it to me, I will have to take it from you."

Blackwick's response was a barely audible whisper. "No." He was returning the tin to the inside of his vest behind his baldric when a sandbag hurtled at his wrist and knocked the tin from his grasp. The tin landed on the limestone stretch between Blackwick and French.

French raised his eyebrows and smirked. "My wife has very good aim."

Blackwick scooped toward the tin. French lunged, and Blackwick bent backward to avoid the blade and rapid-twisted to the side. Jumping to his feet, he drew his sword and deftly blocked the next attack.

French gritted his teeth and pressed to outmaneuver the block. "The book has been delivered. Zed-Cyphrr will soon be here. Only the ashes in that tin can control them." He reached for the tin, but Blackwick shoved him away.

"You're wrong about the book. And I've seen Zed-Cyphrr. Nothing in this world can control them." Blackwick parried a thrust and leapt clear. French dove for the tin, but the shadow man gripped hold of his wrist. French cried out. Blackwick's palm burned into the man's wrist like fire.

Haydee tugged on the vent line, and the balloon descended at a slant toward the head of the Sphinx.

French's face contorted into desperation. He wrenched his wrist free from the fiery grasp and rammed his sword full force into Blackwick's heart.

The blade sank into wax and cinder. Blackwick gasped, for he felt the pain, a freezing, numbing sort of pain, as the metal hissed through the fiery core of his heart. French yanked back the sword. Blackwick groaned and sank to his knees. His flickering eyes fell on French's burn-scarred wrist, and he cringed, for he remembered a time he had met a wolf in the snow and had unclamped the jaws of a trap from that creature's arm.

French followed Blackwick's gaze to his wrist, and he nodded, as if he, too, remembered. He dropped the sword and cradled his wrist against his ribs.

"Move to the side," called Haydee. "I've reloaded the pistol."

"No," said French. "Do not hurt Davidson." He grimaced from his own pain and slid closer to Blackwick. "What can I do?"

French's voice was a muffled whir in Blackwick's ears. Blackwick's breathing grew shallow, and his vision dipped into smoke and shadows.

A montage spiraled across his mind's eye. A leering Ilda bottling a werewolf's last hope. Peter Pan's bittersweet send-off to his shadow. The light of a candle awakening his senses. Betty reaching to him past the ripple of flames. *Edmond! Do not give up!* The steady gaze of Vorever burning into his soul.

A heartbeat thumped in his ears, growing louder and louder. He felt the heat surge through his arteries. He felt the molten core warm once more.

His eyes snapped open. He reached out his hand to French. "Help me stop Zed-Cyphrr."

French pulled Blackwick to his feet and allowed the injured man to make use of his shoulder. "Whether to stop them or unleash them upon Ordog, the only way to control them is through the ashes in this tin." He picked up the tin, but Avian plunged from the sky and snatched the tin from his fingers.

Haydee fired the pistol, but the subdragon spun clear of the bullet.

The Sphinx heaved. The plateau tilted left to right. Cracks zigzagged across the limestone, and chunks of the monument crumbled under their feet. Haydee tossed a rope from the basket to the two men.

Avian soared into the clouds that gathered into a writhing, black, ominous mass. "At last, my love, at last!" Her retinue of ravens trailed after her and were soon swallowed in the depths of the storm.

CHAPTER 47
THE DRAGON CITADEL (1890S)

Dodging debris, Betty dashed from the side passage, around to the front of the Sphinx. The ground shook. The waters rolled and crashed against the base. Betty navigated through the spray while clumps of rock toppled from both sides of the Sphinx's head.

She stabilized herself against the Sphinx's outstretched arm and held Portia firmly, pulling the sides of her khaki jacket securely around the kitten, who clung close to her racing heart. Betty surveyed the plateau. No sign of Blackwick. *Blackwick! Where are you?*

The plateau convulsed. The limestone crumbled beneath her feet. She looked up. Two stone eyes and a stone smile hurtled from above to crush her. She screamed.

Khumalo leapt across sliding chunks of stone toward her. His long legs spread wide as he cleared the heaps and used the full weight of his body to throw Betty out of the path of the landslide. Together, they rolled from the base to the causeway. He pulled her to him before she toppled off the edge.

Regaining her breath, Betty rolled to lie flat on her back and clutched Khumalo's arm for safety. Her entire body ached. She tilted her head to assess the situation. Up close, Portia was staring at her, fur on end. Beyond Portia, the world looked like a gloom-darkened seesaw, toppling back and forth in the quake. She saw Miss Tulliver zigzagging to them, trying to balance herself on the causeway as she ran, her lips moving, but her voice inaudible amid the rumbles of the earth. The lieutenant stood in the center of the causeway, his face grim and alert. His men were crouched, weapons battle-ready, from one end of the causeway to the other. Skender's ears were stiff, his nose pointed toward the three pyramids. Betty steadied herself against Khumalo as he helped her to her feet.

"That," he said, nodding at the sky behind the pyramids, "does not bode well for us."

Betty followed his gaze to the black clouds. They twisted and pulsed with unnatural lightning, casting an eerie green hue across the Giza Plateau.

"Blimey," muttered Miss Tulliver. "Werewolves, earthquakes, and now cyclones even."

Betty closed her eyes as she recognized a familiar heaviness pressurizing the air. "It's no cyclone. Zed-Cyphrr is coming."

"You civilians stay back," ordered the lieutenant. "Whatever it is, we're ready for it."

A shriek of laughter from the base of the Sphinx sent a wave of terror down Betty's spine. It was Ilda, her exultant finger extended with glee toward the pyramids. "No one can be ready for Zed-Cyphrr . . . and me!"

The bellow of a hundred storms funneled up to the sky, and from the great pyramid of Khufu, the neck of Zed lashed like the boom of a mechanical crane. Atop the neck, his triangular head exalted with blazing eyes against the gathering storm. He wailed like a train bursting top speed through a tunnel. In response to that wail, the silver head of Cyphrr rammed out of the further pyramid. Crumbling bricks skidded down her neck. The upheaved mountain of rubble formed a rugged rim around the partially emerged titan, a forbidding dragon citadel.

The two colossal heads weaved above the ruins, and their body heaved. Their eyes pulsed from green to white in time with the lightning that sizzled in the overhanging clouds.

Khumalo grabbed a submachine gun from the stockpile and made sure the cartridge was snapped into place. He set his eyes upon Zed-Cyphrr.

Betty slammed her knuckles into her palm, hoping to ignite the strength of the Golden Dragon, to feel the empowering spread of wings lifting her out of her fears. Nothing. Instead, the old throbbing, prickling sensation from the rash snaked up and around her arms like increasingly constricting chains. Why was this happening? Why couldn't she simply channel Vorever's energy at will?

Bracing herself on the causeway, she darted nervous, apologetic glances at her companions. "Vorever will be here." She hoped speaking the words would make them true.

"Goody." Miss Tulliver gaped at the monster overshadowing the plateau. "Just in case, though, hand me one of those, will you." She reached for the guns.

The dragon heads rotated like radars as Zed-Cyphrr sought a target to strike. They unfurled their jagged wings, spreading them from one edge of the plateau to the other.

At last, Betty felt a spark in the middle of her palms. She clenched her fists as if that could rev up the energy. Impatient, she thrust her palms outward at Zed-Cyphrr. A pathetic flicker of energy sputtered from her palms.

"Vorever can't help you anymore," cackled Ilda. "He's dead. Or else he would be here now, wouldn't he."

Betty glowered at Ilda.

The rapid stutter of machine gun fire from the other end of the causeway drew Betty's attention. The cluster of soldiers at that end barraged the beast with their bullets, to no avail. Devastating rays burst from Zed-Cyphrr's eyes. A pile of ashes remained where the men had been.

The lieutenant's shocked expletive needed no translation. "Fire! Blast that thing to the Devil's Cauldron! Werewolf or not, no one is safe from that two-headed devil!"

Khumalo and Miss Tulliver joined the soldiers in bombarding Zed-Cyphrr with grenades and machine gun fire. The two-headed dragon targeted and blasted without dropping a beat. One soldier turned to dust in the fury of that ray. And another.

"Fall back!" ordered the lieutenant.

Ilda harrumphed at the two-headed dragon and punched her fists at her hips. She heaved herself to the edge of the base. "You idiot!" she screamed at Zed-Cyphrr. "You're killing the wrong ones! These are my followers! We'll need them to stop Ordog!"

Zed-Cyphrr zeroed in on Ilda. Their eyes pulsed green, white, green, white. Ilda's face turned gray.

"Ordog we know," rumbled the two dragon heads. "Vorever we know. But who are you?"

"I opened the book," declared Ilda, her hands straining upward. "I set you free!"

A loud hum crescendoed up from Zed-Cyphrr's throats as they aimed their intensifying radiation upon Ilda.

Betty squeezed her eyes shut. Khumalo threw his arms over the shoulders of Betty and Miss Tulliver and pressed them to lower their heads. The causeway shook in the aftermath of the blast.

CHAPTER 48
NOTHANDO'S CONCH (1890S)

Betty clawed up from the waves. She swallowed a long gasp of air past stinging pangs in her throat and lungs. *That blast must have blown away the causeway. Where is everyone?*

She clambered onto the bright pebbled shore, slammed her battered hat on the ground, and collapsed forward on her face. Portia, soaked, shook herself in a rapid rotation. Her incensed eyes and deep frown expressed the indignation of having one's wet fur spiking out in all directions.

Betty blinked at her kitten. With a great effort, she pushed herself up to survey her surroundings. She was no longer on the surface. In fact, the sky was an overarching cavern of stalactites, and the waters a great aquifer that flowed through this subterranean cavity. A distant thunder rolled, and the uneven glare of a lightning storm pulsed through the uneven cracks in the cave ceiling.

A low, weary voice resounded in her mind. *Betty. I'm glad you came.*

She turned to behold Vorever, his body sprawled across the length of the rocky shore. His wings were tattered, like the sails of an abandoned ship. His shoulders rose and fell with labored groans. The light in his half-held eyes was fading.

Thank you for being here with me. His lips bent into a smile, but he flinched in pain, and the smile faded.

Betty's heart ached as she surveyed his majestic scales, streaked with radiation burns and claw marks along the flanks. She huddled close within the cup of his outstretched talon and leaned her head against his thumb. Almost too exhausted to breathe, she gazed past a blur of tears at the green haze bleared across the sky. "You'll be all right," she whispered, although her sobs betrayed her fears to the contrary. "You're just tired."

"I am the words," he sighed, "and the words are me. If the story worlds die, so do I."

"But we closed the book. And Blackwick got the tin of ashes away. I'm sure of it. We can still defeat Zed-Cyphrr."

"A story is an increment of time, a moment of decision," coughed Vorever. "If at the crisis, they choose death and destruction, then death will lead to death, and soon the story will wither and fade from memory. And," his eyes rolled to hers, "so will I."

His eyelids drooped, but Betty still felt a faint warmth from his nostrils, shallow but steady. In desperation, she pushed against his talon as hard as she could. "Vorever!"

His eyelids dragged upward just a little. "The shell. Three times. And then the way will be clear."

"The Mer-shaman's conch," Betty remembered. "I'll get it. I promise. I won't let you die." She scrambled to her feet. "But we need to hurry. Come on, Portia."

But the kitten remained next to Vorever.

Surprised, Betty raised her eyebrows and tilted her head. People were not always reliable, but she could always count on Portia to scamper after her human. "Aren't you coming?"

Portia watched Betty with unwavering devotion but planted herself in resting panther position, nestled against Vorever's chin, refusing to budge.

"I understand," Betty reassured the kitten.

"I'll make sure she gets back to Vandor," promised the Golden Dragon. "Akira will need her."

Betty dragged her feet and paused at the shoreline, puzzled. "But how do I find the conch?"

"You know the way, Betty Talbin. You always were good at finding things." His shoulders slumped forward. Betty moved toward him, but a bright, golden light glared all around her, and she found herself pushing upward in the waves once more. This time the waves were littered with ash and crumbled limestone. Betty flailed her arms, trying to stay above the restless tide. The undercurrent was pulling her into its depths.

But the mermaids arrived and buoyed her up to the surface. Betty coughed out a spew of horrid-tasting water and met the eyes of the mermaid beside her. She was alarmed by what she saw. The mermaid's face was pale and hollow with haunted eyes peering out in fear past deep, black rims. Betty realized, then, if Vorever died, everything died, everything lovely and good.

"The conch?" Betty asked. "Have you seen it?"

The red-haired mermaid shook her weak head and guided Betty to a heap of rubble where the rest of the survivors were gathered in a huddle of terror and despair. The Mer-shaman herded her daughters together on the far side of the rubble island and used her body to shield them from the storm.

Khumalo pulled Betty from the murky waters to the dry ground. As she steadied herself against him, his eyes conveyed his unspoken concern for her safety. She pushed past him and marched to the center of the mound where the lieutenant was hunched by his dog.

"There's nothing now," he muttered as he frowned at the ground. Skender settled his chin on his paws with a whimper and focused on his master. The lieutenant stood and fixed his weathered countenance of rage upon the two-headed dragon.

The dragon, still only partially emerged above the plateau, had suspended the attack. Their eyes had darkened. Their mouths rested in satisfied smirks. The two heads hovered in a sleepy gloat over the devastation. But a low hum reminded the survivors that the dragon, though dormant, was merely restoking their energy.

The lieutenant caught Betty watching him, and he shirked away. "This is my fault. I envisioned something quite different. Now, the curse has won."

"Not if we find the conch and sound the signal three times." Betty fulcrumed in a half circle as she took stock of the few who remained, the Mer-shaman and her daughters, Khumalo, Miss Tulliver, four shell-shocked werewolves, and the lieutenant and his dog. "Who has the conch?"

Miss Tulliver drooped down on a broken chunk of limestone. "You mean that shell thingabob?" She retrieved some wet crumbles of cigars from her pocket, and, with a disgusted pfft, she tossed them to the ground. "Didn't Count Divvy-the-Doom have it last?"

"So he did." Khumalo shouldered his submachine gun and shifted his weight. "But he and his wife left before Zed-Cyphrr arrived."

"Their pavilion," added the lieutenant, his eyes to the side as if searching his peripheral vision for a memory. "The count said he had it specially made. A brilliant inventor built it to transform into–" Here the lieutenant broke off. He narrowed his eyes at the storm writhing above the latent dragon menace. The werewolf gleam sharpened his eyes as he focused on something no one else could see. "The balloon. It's caught in the storm, behind those clouds. They can't make it."

Betty tried to share his view, to no avail. "Do you see Blackwick?"

The lieutenant scowled and squinted. "No."

Betty's heart sank.

"But," added the lieutenant, "I can sense him."

Betty breathed once more. "Perfect. If we can help them land the balloon, we'll have the conch and the ashes."

The Mer-shaman dove into the heart of a cresting wave. The water enveloped her ebony skin and gleaming tail as she wove through the wall of water and resurfaced on the other side of the mound in front of Betty. "No need for them to land. Hold fast, child, for we shall ride the storm together." She spread out her arms on both sides and the swash surrounding her rolled into a platform of foam.

Nothando reminded Betty of Shakespeare's Prospero with his "cloud-capped towers." The Mer-shaman's eyes danced with the fury of the storm. Betty stalled and glanced at Khumalo. Grateful that he had been here beside her through all this, she reached for his hand. "If Zed-Cyphrr wakes up, I'll need a diversion."

He nodded. "You shall have it, Sthandwa sam." Betty was not sure what he had called her, but the warmth in his gaze assured her he was sincere. She nodded her trust.

Betty stepped into the foam. The muscles in the Mer-shaman's arms shimmered as she held them out before her, wrists together, and bowed her head over her arms. With a voice like distant thunder, she called upon the waters.

Ino ava ino mooli
Ava mana ava
Kalai! Kalai!

She yanked her arms apart as if breaking free of whatever held them together, and the waves that surrounded Betty and the Mer-shaman spun into a powerful whirlpool, rapidly building momentum. The whirlpool towered higher and higher, an aquatic spire, lifting the mother of the sea and the daughter of Vandor into the sky. They surpassed the clouds, and the whipping winds caught their hair, billowing the strands all around, two banshees of the wind and sea.

Above them, a little further north, was the floundering balloon. Its tattered canvas strained against the gale. Lightning flashed and revealed the wicker basket tipping back and forth like a toy of the storm.

Past her lashing strands of hair and the black clouds, Betty could make out the three passengers. Blackwick held tight to the lines, working to keep the balloon from dragging toward the steaming jaws of the dragon. Monsieur French used his sword to cut loose the sandbags, and the balloon lurched upward. Haydee, poised impassively at the prow, clutched a bundle to her chest. Betty knew it was the conch.

The balloon hove in Betty's direction. Blackwick's eyes landed on her, and he tossed a frayed rope toward her outstretched hands. But as the rope flicked past her hands, a rumble like an awakening volcano tremored the sky, and a huge talon wrapped around the Mer-shaman and snatched her from the pillar of water.

"No!" Betty spun toward the Mer-shaman, but her arms were not fast enough to catch her. The whirlpool spiraled downward, and the wind whipped the balloon out of her reach. Betty's mind raced. She tore the strap of her messenger bag from her shoulder and swung it like a lasso toward the fleeing basket.

Blackwick pressed the lines controlling the balloon into French's hands and dove for the lasso. Just as the whirlpool dropped out from beneath Betty's feet, Blackwick caught the lifeline and pulled her upward while she clung tightly to the bag. Haydee leaned out and clutched Betty's forearm to help her. As Betty scrambled into the basket, her messenger bag flew away into the storm

Betty's first thought was for Nothando. She rushed to the railing and gaped at the colossal dragon leering at the Mer-shaman grasped within their talons.

"This one we hate," roared Zed-Cyphrr. "She kept us trapped in the Netherworld for ages. But now we are free!" The grasp tightened around her body as if they would squeeze the life out of her. The Mer-shaman lowered her chin and lifted her defiant eyes to challenge their glare.

Betty reached for the bundle in Haydee's arms. "Give it to me! It's the only way we can stop them."

Haydee held the bundle closer to herself, turning her shoulder on Betty. "We can't lose this too!" She glanced at French.

French firmed his mouth. "We no longer have the ashes. There's nothing else for us here. Let her have the conch." Haydee heaved a sigh and extended the conch toward Betty.

Zed-Cyphrr railed their fury and beat their wings. One powerful wing struck the balloon, throwing it deeper into the storm. The basket careened wildly. The conch jolted out of Haydee's hands and plummeted past the clouds.

Betty dove for the conch.

"Betty!" Blackwick wrapped his arms around her to anchor her before her lunge sent her hurtling after it.

The lieutenant's eyes followed the descending object from the clouds to the top of the steep cliff of rock and rubble surrounding the dragon. His tense shoulders suggested he feared the object might explode.

Khumalo studied the object through his binoculars. "It's the conch."

Miss Tulliver stood beside Khumalo, dragging her hand across her soot-smudged face. "And Bets says something about sounding it three times. How in the name of Khufu are we going to do that now?" She grimaced at the dragon lording over the titanic mound, the Mer-shaman still clutched in their claws.

The mermaids moaned in fear, their arms swaying upwards toward their Mer-shaman, like hapless reeds in a merciless gale.

Khumalo tore off his shirt and leaned into a dive toward the waves. "I'll get the conch."

The lieutenant yanked him back. "You will do no such thing. Miss Talbin ordered you to distract them. That's what you'll do." His fierceness was not to be argued with. He stepped into the swash.

Skender barked and sprang at his master.

"Stay, Skender!" ordered the lieutenant.

The dog whined and whimpered.

The lieutenant gave him a severe scowl and pointed to the ground.

The dog dropped to his haunches, but his head hung, and his shoulders shook.

The lieutenant strung his rifle and his cutlass on the baldric over his shoulders. He dove into the waters and scooped the waves with powerful strokes as he headed for the dragon citadel.

Khumalo snapped another cartridge onto his submachine gun and looked to the soldiers that remained. "You there! The last of the grenades. And you, those machine guns. Our friends need a diversion. And we're the diversion."

Khumalo sprayed the dragon's heaving shoulders with a rattling discharge of ammo. The others followed his example. Their bullets ricocheted off the dragon's scales. Grenades exploded, but the beast merely shook off the debris. Zed-Cyphrr turned their glare from the Mer-shaman to the little island of rubble.

"Behold the ants before the storm!" gloated the two-headed beast. But that gloat gave Nothando the chance she needed. The clutch of the talons had loosened enough for her to push past the hold and propel herself into a dive. She crashed into the waves and, a few moments later, bobbed to the surface. She caught sight of the lieutenant. He had reached the citadel and had begun the treacherous climb up the mound of rubble huddled against the two-headed dragon's torso.

Khumalo and the band of survivors continued to barrage the dragon. Zed-Cyphrr's shoulders heaved upward, pushing against the barrier of the earth, determined to lift the rest of their body above the surface, stop the tiny weapons, and recapture the Mer-shaman. They did not yet notice the lieutenant.

The lieutenant clambered up the steep slope. For a moment, he wished the darkness of the storm would morph him back into his werewolf form. Ah, that would be the easy way. He gritted his teeth and used his cutlass as leverage in the packed gravel to heave himself up to the top of the mound. The bulk of the dragon glistened like wet leather before him. He reached for the conch. The dragon's body twitched as if suddenly aware of the lieutenant's existence. Their two heads converged upon the lieutenant.

Betty peered over the railing of the basket, her heart barely beating, as she hoped, she prayed the lieutenant would have time to sound the signal.

The lieutenant set the shell to his lips and blew a haunting call.

The two-headed dragon raised their talons on both sides of the lieutenant, their eyes gleaming with sadistic intent. They harnessed the lightning to their will. The lightning caught the lieutenant in its convergence. He jolted and fell to his knees, but he heaved himself up to his feet and blew on the conch again. Furious, Zed-Cyphrr released another round of lightning.

Betty shouted, "Zed-Cyphrr!" Her eyes flashed blue, and golden waves of light exuded from her palms.

Blackwick stood by her side. With a twist of his wrists, he ignited a plume of flames in each of his hands.

The two heads rotated deliberately toward the balloon, toward the light and fire.

Desperate to draw Zed-Cyphrr's attention, Khumalo and the remaining members of the platoon increased the intensity of their attack against the monstrous beast. Khumalo gritted his teeth, and his submachine gun panned the breadth of the dragon with bullet spray while his weapon ripped through an entire cartridge of ammunition.

Blackwick directed the flames at the two-headed dragon and Betty pushed the golden stream of light from her palms to guide the flames at the two pulsing pairs of dragon eyes. The dragon raged in a screeching treble accompanied by a discordant bass.

The lieutenant angled the conch toward the sky and blew the third call. At the echo of that call, the two dragon heads refocused on the grizzled soldier, and their lightning caught him in its ruthless tendrils.

Horrified, Betty let her arms drop at her side, and the golden stream of energy wielding the flames faded. The lieutenant convulsed in the dragon's galvanizing grip. The conch dropped from his limp hand, and his charred body rolled down the slope to the base of the citadel.

The gunfire and grenade explosions ceased. Skender stared, his ears propped forward, his tail stiff, as if expecting his master to jump back into action any moment.

As the last echo of the call died away, a pulse like a muffled boom zipped through the clouds. The clouds rolled back, and the sun once more spread its golden aura across the plateau. Vorever crashed up past the ruins of the Sphinx, the waters rolling back as he plowed toward the pyramid complex.

Vorever, his chest heaving, set his fierce eyes upon his foe. "Zed-Cyphrr! The tome is safe. The missing page is beyond your reach. I order you back to the Netherworld where you belong!"

"Vorever!" Betty cheered in triumph and threw her arms around Blackwick in her excitement. Vorever was safe. He had made it after all.

She helped Blackwick work the lines on the balloon to steer closer to the Golden Dragon. Vorever smiled at them and gave them a nod. Betty drew in the energy of Vorever, and her wings expanded. She caught Blackwick in her arms, and, together, they skydived down and lit on Vorever's shoulder.

To Betty's dismay, the Golden Dragon's wings were still tattered, his body still scarred, and a low, heaving rattle sounded deep within his throat. "You're not ready for this!" she said. "We'll handle Zed-Cyphrr." She pressed Blackwick's hand and gave him a look to say it's up to you and me now.

Blackwick returned a ready nod.

"No, my children. Your friends need you." Vorever lifted Betty and Blackwick from his shoulder. The muscles in his talons trembled as he gently set them near Khumalo. "Be brave, Son of Shadow. Be brave, Daughter of Vandor."

Once he saw they were safe, Vorever turned his attention to the balloon. French and Haydee clutched the railing, their faces pale as they assessed the immensity of the Golden Dragon. Vorever drew in a powerful inhalation, and French and Haydee braced themselves for the worst. Vorever released a long stream of warm air that billowed the balloon safely away from Zed-Cyphrr and into the dusking skies.

Vorever turned upon Zed-Cyphrr. Zed-Cyphrr continued to beat their raging wings, and their eyes pulsed green, white, green, white, and a crescendoing whine bellowed up from their throats.

One of Vorever's talons clamped over the face of Zed. The other talon clamped over the face of Cyphrr. "Do not hurt my children anymore!"

Zed-Cyphrr screamed as Vorever, with a powerful last effort, pulled them down with him beneath the surface. A rumble heaved the earth as the ancient layers of limestone and sand, blanketed over by the floods of the Nile, buried the two mighty dragons, Vorever and Zed-Cyphrr, deeper than the oldest pharaohs.

CHAPTER 49
NOT THE END (1890S)

It was a time for silence. The sun paid its respects to the battleground. The mermaids glided up onto the partially submerged stones, grateful for the sunlight glistening along their scales and touching their soulful faces as the floods began to recede, called back to the arms of the Nile. They sang their sacred song of mourning for the soldiers who had perished . . . and for Vorever.

Skender dragged himself onto the heap of rubble where lay the charred body of his master. The hound pushed his nose against the lieutenant's lifeless form. The dog pulled back, brow furrowed, questioning the silence, the lack of movement. One more desperate prod against his master's hand confirmed the truth. His chin sank upon the tatters of his master's uniform. His shoulders shook with heart-breaking whimpers, and his flanks heaved with inconsolable groans.

The four remaining members of the 10th Werewolf Platoon clambered up the mound and fell on their knees beside the body of their lieutenant.

After a long silence, one of them placed his hand against his heart and spoke. "You chose the hard path, my lieutenant, my friend, the way of sacrifice, the way of courage. Because of you, we, your brothers, still live, and the world is, for a little while, at peace. The name of Tynan shall once more be written in the book of the brave. For you, the curse is gone."

Skender whined, nuzzled his master's hand, and released a long howl of grief.

Betty, Khumalo, and Miss Tulliver stood solemnly at the foot of the mound, heads bowed.

"Gosh," was all Miss Tulliver could say. She rested her hand in the crook of Khumalo's arm.

Heavy of heart, Betty stepped aside. The ebbing waters pushed something against her boot. She looked down to discover the conch, washed up onto the slope where she stood.

She bent to retrieve it and reverently brushed its pearlescent whorls and ridges. A long, jagged crack scarred its once-glossy surface. *It's broken*, she told herself, *but it has survived. Like all of us.* The hot tears welling up in her eyes blurred the reflection within the shell's gloss. It was the reflection of a dark-haired woman, older, stronger.

She pushed aside her tears and scanned the ruins for Blackwick. He was at the far end of the plateau, a solitary shadow man perched on the crumbling peak of a pyramid. His black cloak waved in the breeze like the wings of a lost angel. Their eyes met across the distance, and she read in his gaze a profound regret and a resolve to set things right.

A small deliberate cough from near her feet vied for her attention. Climbing onto a broken block of limestone, two scarabs gleamed — one in molten gold, the other cloaked in dazzling ruby-red armor

"Ma'mselle!" called up the red scarab. "*C'est moi!* Robert! The Mer-shaman found us. Now we are far from the screams and free as the butterflies." He gave his magic-sparkled wings a buzzing flutter.

"*Mais oui!*" added the golden scarab. "Madame the Mermaid is taking us back to Neverland. She says they will need brave ones like us to help restore what the corruption destroyed."

Their assurance was just the thing Betty needed right now. She gave them a faint smile. "Thank you, brave warriors, for everything you have done."

"And the conch you hold," added Robert. "Madame the Mermaid says she will need it to open a portal."

Betty turned at the splash of Nothando emerging part way from the retreating waters near the mound. The Mer-Shaman's gaze swept across the scene with urgency, seeking out each of her daughters.

"The sun sets, and the waters withdraw," she announced. "Now my daughters and I must return to our home."

Betty stepped forward, the conch cradled in both hands like an offering. It felt like the passing of a weapon, like an honor shared between warriors who had fought side by side.

"Thank you, Nothando," she said.

"Until the next battle, Daughter of Vandor," the Mer-Shaman replied, her fingers curling around the conch. She raised it high above the field where her daughters waited, its surface glinting in the fading sunlight.

"*Neverland Mahai!*" she called, her voice a rallying cry. As she turned to go, Nothando glanced back at Betty, smiling in that sad way the wise ones have of knowing the future but choosing to spare the young.

Deep in the inner sanctum of Alsó-Világ, the eye of Ordog opened. He groaned, rotated his stiff shoulders, and sleepily smacked his lips. The souls had been most delectable. He stretched his talons, splaying each claw, and flapped his wings to shake off the cobwebs and dust. He uncoiled his scales and raised his crested head until it brushed along the arch of his cavernous chamber.

He wanted to reassure himself his treasure was secure, but, too indolent to rise, he preferred to consult the fiery sphere hovering in the crease of his palm.

What is this?

It was not his treasure that appeared within the haze but the likeness of his old rival Zed-Cyphrr. A sneer curled up on Ordog's muzzle, and a gratified wisp of smoke rose from his nostrils. *Zed-Cyphrr chained once more in the Netherworld? How charming, but inevitable. And Vorever gone as well?* Ordog sniggered his delight. *Very promising.*

But what was that movement amid the sphere? A crimson dragon no bigger than a falcon. Neck crooked downward in a servile pose, the subdragon crept into the darkness of an eerie chamber, a chamber with strange symbols and numbers scratched in chalk across the wall.

Avian. Ah, yes, now the name of the little dragon was remembered. But he shrugged and yawned and dismissed the remembrance as insignificant, not worthy of his lofty thoughts.

He saw her stagger into the chamber. A wintry blast tore open the shutters, and five puny scavenger birds flustered in through the window and perched upon five of seven busts that overhung the lintel of the door.

Ordog cursed that the chamber was so dark. His curiosity had been aroused, but the only light flickered from the dying embers of a massive fireplace that wrought their ghosts upon the floor. The ravens' eyes glowed like cinders as they stared with beaks agape upon a cloaked figure slumped in a ragged chair. To the left of the figure, a young man stood with a blank expression as one under a spell. *Leslie.* This name, too, Ordog recalled. He seemed to remember a crossbow, and that memory shot pain through his talons. But this cloaked figure. Who was this man?

"O High Priest of the Netherworld," Avian was speaking. "I bring you the ashes." She opened the tin, bowed low, and spread her talons toward the mysterious figure in a ceremonious presentation.

The cloaked figure spoke in a deep, whispery voice. "You have proven yourself worthy. You and I will be the rulers of the Epilogues. Zed-Cyphrr will be our slave. The chains that bind them are of no matter. When I call, they will come, and with greater power than before."

"What of Monsieur French?"

"He will join us. I am sure. And there is one more. One more I must persuade to join our ranks. The one the angels call . . . Lenore."

"But who is this, my master?"

"That is my wisdom, your mystery."

"What of Blackwick?" clattered the ravens. "What of the shadow man? Aww! Aww!"

"Silence! His legend will be forgotten, lost in oblivion." The man spread the ashes before the hearth and waved his hand over them in complex circular patterns. "His name will be remembered . . . *Nevermore*!"

LITERATURE REFERENCED

Intercessor Challenge: Are you an Inter-Story Intercessor? Can you locate all the literary references throughout Legend of Blackwick. If you are unfamiliar with any of the titles listed here, look them up online or check them out at your library to learn more about these magical portals.

Barrie, James
Peter Pan

Carroll, Lewis
Alice in Wonderland

Dickens, Charles
A Tale of Two Cities
The Pickwick Papers

Doyle, Sir Arthur Conan
Adventures of Sherlock Holmes
Memoirs of Sherlock Holmes
Return of Sherlock Holmes
The Casebook of Sherlock Holmes

Dumas, Alexandre
The Count of Monte Cristo
The Three Musketeers

Eliot, George
The Mill on the Floss

Grimm, Jacob and Wilhelm
Hansel and Gretel
The Seven Ravens

Haggard, H. Rider
King Solomon's Mines

Homer
The Iliad
The Odyssey

Irving, Washington
"The Headless Horseman of Sleepy Hollow"

Japanese Folktales
Tawara Tōda Monogatari

Kafka, Franz
Metamorphosis

Orczy, Baroness
The Scarlet Pimpernel

Poe, Edgar Allan
"The Raven"

Shakespeare, William
"Sonnet 138"
The Tempest

Shelley, Percy Bysshe
"To the Moon"

Spyri, Johanna
Heidi

Stevenson, Robert Louis
Children's Garden of Verses: "My Shadow"
Treasure Island

Stoker, Bram
Dracula

Twain, Mark
The Adventures of Huckleberry Finn
The Adventures of Tom Sawyer

Wells, H. G.
War of the Worlds

Wilde, Oscar
The Picture of Dorian Gray

Acknowledgements

Thank you for joining me on this adventure. You, dear reader, are the reason this series exists.

As Betty needs her fellow Intercessors, I have needed my beta readers: Dr. Victoria Ramirez Gentry, Nicholas Gentry, Vivyana, Jolene Scheepers, Mel Finefrock, Bethany Camille James, and Rebekah Cuyler.

As the candle on Vandor ever shines, so do those who have generously shared their love of this series: Aislynn Walsh, Kearstin Ellis, and Keri Marino.

We can, indeed, rewrite our own stories, but it takes a dedicated editor to ensure the revisions are correct. Thank you, Vivyana and Julie Burris, for helping me with developmental edits and proofreading.

Where would Neverland be without the stalwart Tondor Char? And where would I be without Tirzah Darnell? She sacrificed her own writing time to cheer me on through every phase of this book.

All it takes is faith and trust, and to those who have had faith and trust in me, thank you! Terry and Crystal, and my band of Star Wars friends: Sarah, Lydia, Shane, and Vlad.

A salute of respect belongs to Lieutenant Michael and Ericka Tynan, for not only inspiring the character of the Lieutenant, but also for their strong support of the.

Finally, to those Keepers of the Golden Vigil who have hosted author events for The Blackwick Series, thank you: Sylvia Garcia-Smith; Tammy Rand and Haylee Dobbs of the Coastal Bend College library; and Criste Bleibdrey of CC's Coffee Shop.

About the Author

Kathleen R. Cuyler graduated with her Master of Arts in English from the University of North Texas. She currently lives in Beeville, Texas, where she teaches English at the local community college. She has authored the textbook *Diving into the World of Literature* through Kona Publishing and Media Group. Forever Is Eternity is her debut fantasy novel and the first of a series of five books. When Kathleen is not teaching or writing, she loves reading, drinking coffee, and spending time with her pets.

Visit www.mochawavepublishing.com to visit the bookshop, follow her blog, and sign up for her newsletter.

About the Blackwick Series

The Blackwick Series follows Beatrice Talbin, a teenaged girl in 1930s England, who discovers her love of reading is more than an escape from the drudgery of her daily life. It's a gift that gains her admittance to the Society of the Inter-Story Intercessors. Traveling into the books she loves, Betty and her fellow Intercessors are caught up in a war between the Golden Dragon Vorever and the sinister dragon lords Ordog and Zed-Cyphrr.

🐉 Dragon Lineage 🐉

From the cosmos came the celestial dragons

Vorever   Zed-Cyphrr   Abyssmalith

Neverbird   Labyrinthius

From Vorever came the dragon titans

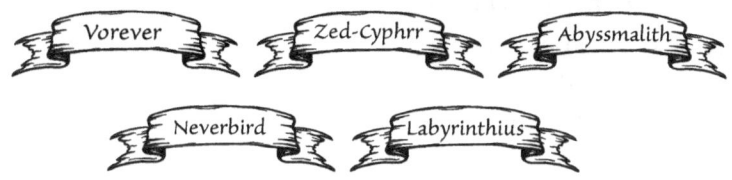

Ordog   Water-Ghoul   Serpentine

Death-Guardian   Diamond-Hoarder

From Ordog came the subdragons

Avian   Moriarty   Milverton   Esmé

The Marquis   Silver Boot   Lord Henry

Dragon Language Glossary:

Arunt: Are
Athana: Beginning
Avadni: Reward
Avanti: Go, Away
Aventiss: Come
Aya: Yes
Ba: Sing
Beethen: To exist, to be
Celvarin: Celestial Dragon
Corseesh: Beautiful
Deveethan: Defy, eliminate
Dirthic: North
Dothan: Does (used as a verb for questions)
Dom: Doom
Een, Eenan, Eenam: One (used for all personal pronouns)
Ēge: Fear (noun), Egen To fear (verb)
Eraath: Epoch
Fa: Find
Feelan: Forward
Feggintar: War
Feggin: Fire
Finetae: Epilogues or an epilogue of a book
Finnen: Find
Fithu: To breathe
Fortunan: Sold one's soul
Furnathar: Leader, master
Gaivarin: Entire universe
Gangen: Go
Gefulen: To feel or to fulfill
Gevehthen: Sacrifice (verb)
Grufen: Command (verb of command)
Ghulantan: East
Gudhan: Good

Hathan: Has

Hordin: West

Hunathane: Henchman

Infantis: Human

Inthum: Into; Inthem: Within

Ishata: Term of endearment; "my beauty"

Konnen: Can do something

Lathan: Let

Loklok: Slave

Malvaren: Corruption

Malwissan: Lie

Margina: Marginalia (like in a book)

Mithem: With

Modor: Mother

Mussen: Must

Nae: No one

Naewissen: Impossible

Nimmen: Take

Norsish: Deed

Nuthan: Now

Onsem: One / All of them

Pfash: Where (question word)

Portag: Portal

Portag nimmen: Take what is in the portal

Portag vunen: Open the portal

Rinthem: Beyond

Sangen: Endure

Saa: Lives

Scriffan: Book

Scriffvarin: A world within worlds

Shlekt: Bad

Sovool: Blood

Sovoolan: Tasted blood

Sullen: Dragon scale

Subvarin: Subdragon

Suthen: South

Thaa: There; over there
Thonen: Those / An article of some kind
Titanvarin: Dragon Titan
Tramen: Nightmare
Varin: Dragon
Verwand: Transformation
Vereeth: True; Vereethan: Truth
Vishin: Potion
Voreev: Time
Vorever: To live all for all time
Vunen: Open
Wissan: To know
Wollen: Will (verb)
Wyrmkin: Child of a subdragon

The adventure continues!
Read the next book in the Blackwick Series!

Follow Kathleen R. Cuyler at
www.mochawavepublishing.com
TikTok @mochawavepub
Instagram @kathycuyler
Facebook Mocha Wave Publishing.

For more information reach out to Kathleen on
info@mochawavepublishing.com

Scan the code and join the "Let's Talk"
newsletter to stay up to date on series news!